THE PEACOCK'S LEGACY

A Victorian Saga of Triumph Over Adversity

Sasha M Stevens

2/2/25

COPYRIGHT

Reader's Note: *The Peacock's Legacy* is a unique British English adaptation of the novel The Peacock's Heritage, initially written by the same author, Sasha M Stevens, in Americanised English.

TABLE OF CONTENTS

DEDICATION

I dedicate this book to my paternal great-grandfather, Edward George Harrison, and my maternal great-grandmother, Mary Hayes, both deceased. A search for their provenances inspired this saga.

ACKNOWLEDGEMENTS

I thank Kate Horsley, my tutor at Hull University; David Restaino from Reeds Book Editors, who helped me develop the novel; Arif Khan, who assisted with the synopsis; and Sarah and Sam, who helped me publish the book.

I couldn't have authored this novel without the support of my colleagues, especially Cheryl, Dorinda, Michelle, Rachel, Stella, and Sue. These students provided helpful critiques of my work and support for my efforts on my writing journey. I also thank Tabitha, Melissa, and Andrea for their encouragement.

Jeremy Ratcliffe is an excellent proofreader who polished the narrative, and Nick Castle is a fantastic book cover designer.

In absentia, I thank my paternal great-grandfather, Edward George Harrison, and my maternal great-grandmother, Mary Hayes, whose provenances inspired the story.

I give special thanks to my husband, Michael, who endured many days fending for himself and making me cups of coffee when I was squirrelled away with my writing. He is a gem.

DRAMATIS PERSONAE

- Brigid: The saga's protagonist
- Brigid's siblings: Padraig, Dermot, Angela,
- Michael and Joseph
- Brigid's husbands: Niall, Finnbar, and John
- Brigid's children: Dermot, Aisne, and Daniel
- Saor-Éire members: Stephen, Ezra, Caitlin,
- Amy, Alexander, and Robert
- Maura: Da's woman friend
- Saoirse: Brigid's boss
- Liam: The child informant
- Erin: Finnbar's daughter
- Seamus: Brigid's loathed suitor
- Mrs Klocke and Mrs Frankel: Brigid's servants
- Richard d'Estaing: Brigid's banker
- Vincenzo: Aisne's husband
- Candace: Daniel's wife
- Mr Spendlove: English solicitor
- George Garland: Candace's father
- James Lansdowne: John's brother
- Catherine Lansdowne: John's sister-in-law
- Ambrose and Wilhelmina: John's servants
- Brad: A young gardener

PART ONE: FAMINE TO FLEDGLING FENIAN

CHAPTER 1: FAITH & FAMINE 1836-1846

A crackling peat fire's flames created an alluring red and gold scene within the vast fireplace of the isolated cottage at the north end of the County Wicklow village. The cracked window frames and deteriorating mossy thatch let in the blood-freezing wind. Smoke from the fire deposited a rim of grime over every surface, including the ceiling and a scrubbed wooden table surrounded by six rickety chairs. Brigid Power, the Irish tenant farmer's seven-year-old daughter, dusted and polished the furniture with beeswax daily.

Throughout each winter, moisture cloaked the foetid atmosphere, and a musty odour permeated the cottage. It encouraged mould growth around the edges of the interior walls, providing a breeding ground for chest infecting diseases. In summer, the green field and trees on the property's garden and surrounding land provided a welcome respite from the cold and damp for winter-weary souls. A river teeming with salmon and trout flowed through the village. While its upper reaches belonged to the Manor House's estate, the lower reaches supplied plentiful fish to fill the bellies of a tenant farmer's family.

The imposing Manor House stood on a promontory overlooking the entire village. It boasted extensive grounds with wildlife, including squawking birds and honking geese. Deer stalked the far parkland, and chickens clucked in their pen beneath a gnarled apple tree. The gravelled drive was framed by majestic trees where scampered, red-coated animals with busy tails scampered among the branches. A gravelled path led from ornate flower and leaf-moulded iron gates to a sturdy double-fronted door with a brass deer's head knocker.

Village children dared each other to peer through the fence knothole, hoping to spy a screeching bird fan his colourful tail. When Brigid's Da learned his children played this game, his fury matched an angry donkey. He forbade them to go near the house under the threat of a thwacking with Da's brass buckled leather belt.

In fine weather, the distant hills veiled in a blue haze rose west of the village. Below the mountains lay a grey forbidding lough surrounded by hazel trees, blackberry bushes, and a boggy moor. Like many Irish villages, Ballyconstór's main street was lined by a granite Catholic church, the village pub with its illegal shebeen, a grocery store, a bakery, and a butcher's shop.

In stormy weather, the river rushed through the village with excessive speed, its grey waters spilling onto its green grassy banks. The distant hills then resembled tombs rising above the desolate moor and hidden behind a long grey veil of stair-rod-like rain. The village's mossy boreens flooded with brownish peat bog water when storm-driven winds bent the branches of exposed trees, cracking the weakest ones. Sensible villagers understood the dangers of venturing outside in such conditions.

The month of October often brought in storms rushing across the island with relentless fury. One night, Brigid and her sister Angela sat at their mother's long, slim feet as usual. Their innocent faces were filled with the wide-eyed anticipation of a happy fairy tale, not one of the evil eyes or dreaded wolves that scared them. Ma put baby Michael to her breast and gazed into the gleaming embers. The child's chubby hand tugged at tendrils of blonde hair escaping his mother's mob cap. The storm-driven wind howled, and Angela shrank back, her mouth quivering. Brigid, conscious of her status as the older girl, hugged her sister close.

Ma turned and regarded her elder daughter with soft eyes.

'Seven years ago, when you came into the world, your loud cries vied with a fierce spring gale, so we named you Brigid, meaning strength. You displayed that strength today.'

She reached out a slender, work-roughened hand to pat the girl on her head.

Unaccustomed to praise, Brigid preened like a peacock. As the wind's howling faded, Angela received a pat, too. Brigid released her hold on her sister's shoulders and bent her head to her bony knees. The evening's story was about a fairy who changed a girl's dull dark hair to gleaming golden locks.

'Kissed by a handsome prince, she became the most beautiful girl imaginable,' said Ma, who smiled and handed baby Michael to Brigid, enabling her to pile peat on the fire in a shower of sparks.

Brigid, holding, squirming Michael, could not believe the story. She handed him back to her mother.

'In Sunday School, Sister Philomena said fairies and goblins do not exist.' Brigid lifted her face and gazed at her mother, waiting for her reply.

Ma smiled and said, 'Mo stór, God created our imagination. Hence, people invent things like fairies to entertain and share stories.'

Brigid scrunched her face. 'I want God to give me golden hair like you and Angela. Did the devil make my hair red? I dislike it so much.'

She thrust her hand through the springy mop and pulled up her bony knees, lowering her face to hide the sadness that sparkled on her lashes. Brigid lifted her head to gaze at her mother and voiced a thought.

'Ma, why isn't Da here to protect us on a stormy night?'

Padraig, seated nearby playing checkers with Dermot, turned his head to catch his sister's gaze. He lifted his brows and swayed his head. So, Brigid did not press her question.

Instead, she dropped her head down to her knees and reflected on the events that prompted Ma's remarks about her strength.

Da had sent the boys and Brigid to cut peat from the boggy moor after their noon-time dinner. As they worked, the sky darkened, and a flash of lightning streaked across it, accompanied by a loud boom. Bloated ochre-coloured clouds spattered the children with fat raindrops.

With his croaky voice disappearing like a plover's feather on the wind, Padraig said, 'Dermot, take Brigid's hand. We must outrun the storm.' The two boys ran across the boggy ground like racehorses, with their sister between them.

Arriving home, the children's feet, shod in unmended boots, squelched on the flagstone kitchen floor, with Brigid's hair plastered to her head and her clothes drenched.

Ma clicked her tongue. 'The storm caught you, but I am pleased you reached the cottage without mishap in a bog,' she said sarcastically. She tugged off Brigid's wet clothing, wrapped the girl in a towel, and dried her hair with quick, deft movements that made her daughter squirm.

Ma's sons stood by the lintel, shivering, with faces downcast as water puddled on the surrounding flagstones. They ran their grimy, wet caps through their fingers in nervous anticipation.

Their Da, seated by the fire with a jar of Guinness in his hand, regarded them with contempt. 'You shameful weaklings. A bit of rain hurt nobody. Where is the peat I ordered you to cut? You must bring it home tomorrow, along with the shovels. Do you hear?'

He stood, took off his leather belt, flexed it, and, to Brigid's dismay at the injustice, gave each boy a resounding thwack.

Later, after supper, as the rain eased, Da pulled on his threadbare coat and stomped out of the cottage into the teeth of the wind. When Da had not returned by eight, Ma, having told her tale, sent her daughters to their shared bed without his goodnight kiss.

In bed, Brigid reflected on what had happened that morning before the storm, a promise-filled time. The girls picked luscious blackberries on bushes near the lough with purple juice staining their fingers. They then played with the family's dog, Scamp. At home, Brigid helped Ma cook the blackberries with apples from their gnarled tree in a pie for dinner, a task she loved.

Brigid thought about the thwacking given to her brothers. Padraig once explained Da did not thwack when he and Dermot were younger. 'It began after Da lost his job as a gardener at the Manor House. It is the drink that turns his temper evil. With a clear head, Da is a grand man for playing games. He taught Dermot and me to swim, fish, and steer a curragh.'

But while he also thwacked her, Brigid noticed Da spared Angela and asked Padraig why.

'Angela is Da's favourite child. She reminds him of Ma when they first met.'

'A father should not have a favourite. God loves everyone, so an earthly father should as well.'

Padraig shook his head. 'Do not speak about Da like that. If he were here, he would get angry and might thwack you.'

Brigid scowled at him. 'It's not fair. He thwacks for no good reason.'

She did not like Padraig's words because they suggested Da did not love her as much as Angela.

That night, lying in bed, Brigid thought *Da would send me with Padraig and Dermot to collect the peat unless Ma could stop him. I am sure he would not send Angela if she were my age.* Yawning, she observed the Man in the Moon, peeking through the clouds and pondering on her father. *I expect he's in the shebeen with his cronies.*

The moon's benign presence comforted the naive girl who could not understand her father's need for poteen. She snuggled up to her sleeping sister for warmth and closed her eyes.

Brigid's dislike for her Da was rooted deep in her mind that night when he should have been with his family. It overtook the dislike for her hair and grew thorny like a thistle, fertilised by his continued absence from the cottage while imbibing alcohol in the shebeen.

Catholic children prepared for their First Holy Communion when they were eight. Nobody asked Brigid if she wished to attend, and she wanted to hide from Da. Padraig found his sister a hiding place in the cowshed. But he cautioned Brigid, saying, 'You will be made to attend the classes. It would be easier to be meek than to be thwacked.'

Brigid said, 'Da has not stopped his drinking despite my prayers. So, God does not exist.'

On Saturday, Da, his fury causing him to overturn furniture and break the mirror on Ma's press, found Brigid hiding under straw in the cowshed.

'You wicked child, how dare you turn your back on God's holy words like a protestant.' Da took off his belt, his face red with fury, and gave Brigid two thwacks.

He grabbed her and frogmarched his daughter to the church, where he dumped her with a noisy thump in the nearest vacant pew. Brigid's rear stung as if she had been in a bed of nettles, but she folded her arms and gave the priest a sullen glare from her almond-shaped green eyes. Her stare, which had the potential to freeze boiling water, caused the other children to gaze at her with bewildered awe.

The priest lifted his head from his Bible, raised his upper body, puffed out his chest, and fixed a fierce gaze on Brigid, who did not flinch. He pushed his wrinkled face towards her; his teeth bared like an angry cur.

'Ye devilish girl. The evil eye must be on ye. How dare you defy your father and be late for God's Word? God demands obedience, and so do I.'

Father Byrne, oblivious to their lack of understanding,

burned the catechism into the children's immature minds each week. Brigid's sullen stare became legendary when he glared at her with malice.

'Are you listening, Brigid? God expects you to listen to me as I am here in His place.' His thick brows moved like two caterpillars crawling across his head. Brigid glared at him with a smouldering look, thinking brows resembling caterpillars turned into ugly moths to be killed with a fly swat. She grew to hate Father Byrne more than Da.

Brigid's questions about the Catholic faith grew with each week of catechism instruction. One question stuck in her mind, pricking like a thorn in a finger. While helping Ma, she plucked up her courage. 'Ma, is your Protestant God different from our Catholic one?'

. 'He is the same God, but people's faiths have different rituals and rules. You follow your father's Catholic faith.'

'But I want to follow you, not Da.' Brigid's brow puckered. She peeled her last potato, appraising it like a priest's head, thinking, *I will boil this potato as though it were Father Byrne's head.*

'I promised to obey your father when we married. Da wants his children baptised as Catholics.'

Brigid's eyebrows rose upwards. 'I loathe Father Byrne. He has yellow teeth and red veins on his cheeks. He brays at us, using words we do not understand. He did not baptise me, did he, Ma? Dermot said it was a priest called Father O'Malley.'

Ma put her peeled potatoes in the heating broth and nodded but did not speak. Brigid dropped in her potatoes and watched the water bubble over them. She wondered why God allowed horrible men like Father Byrne to instruct children.

He must stick to preaching to adults because his catechism lessons and Sunday sermons bore me. Sister Philomena is unpleasant because she drones on about sin and hellfire. She never answers questions.

Dermot, the most religious of the children, served Mass

for Father Byrne. Brigid loved her brother but not his religious fervour, which she did not share. 'Father Byrne is mean,' she told him after one catechism class. 'Niamh, her mother, is sick, and he got angry with her for being late.

Unlike their friends, Ma instructed her children to read, write, and calculate. Da, who could not read, made them read the Bible in Gaelic to him. But one day, for no reason, Brigid could fathom it. Da's face turned red with anger.

'Why waste time instructing the girls with gentlefolk skills? Teach them to cook, sew, and milk a cow.' He shook his fist at his wife.

Ma spoke calmly in English, 'They are not gentle born, but knowledge is a powerful tool.'

Her use of English infuriated Da, who spat and swore in Gaelic.

'You feckin' bint. Your gentlefolk skills never helped us any.' He swivelled to look at Ma's treasured brass clock. 'Girls do not need a clock, either. The moon and stars do for me and will do for them.'

Donning his jacket, he stormed off to the shebeen, slamming the door and rattling the crockery on the press.

Disgusted by his swearing, her stomach churning, Brigid wondered what Da had against learning and clocks. She stared at her mother's slender back, hunched against his insults. *I will find the answer to Da's objection one day.*

Ma taught the girls housewifery. Angela milked the family's cow, her sensitive fingers the right size to pull teats. She had deft fingers and soon became an expert at sewing and knitting. Brigid's powerful arms churned milk into butter, and she cared for the family's five hens, reared from chicks. Both girls learned to cook when Brigid made her first apple pie without Ma's help in the autumn of 1839.

Finishing his slice of pie, Da smacked his lips. 'Who made this pie, Susannah?'

'I did, Da.' Brigid glanced at Ma for confirmation but saw her eyes glisten, and Brigid's heart missed a beat.

'Well, you must cook pies now. Your pastry tastes better than yer Ma's. You will make someone a fine wife one day.' He smirked at his wife.

Brigid blushed and curtsied. But although Da's words praised her, they crushed her mother, and Ma's distress tempered Brigid's sense of achievement. She hated how Da had humiliated her gentle mother.

Ma owned the village's sole splendid copper boiler with immense pride. It helped Ma make extra income. She charged three pennies for a basket full of washing, which she washed when Da was absent. Brigid knew Ma had put her income in a box, hidden under a tablecloth in her press.

On a bright spring day when Brigid had turned eleven, Da brought home one solitary shilling from his wages of seven shillings. He left the shilling on the kitchen table.

'I am off to Paddy's wake and will not return until tomorrow.' He spun around and left for the shebeen.

Brigid woke when he rolled into the cottage as the church clock struck three. She heard him burp twice, then drop to the kitchen sofa and snore. Three hours later, she found him sprawled out with vomit staining his waistcoat and had to clean up his disgusting mess. *I hate you, Da. You are an appalling drunk, and I wish you had choked on your vomit.* But Da snored on, oblivious to her hate-filled thoughts.

The next day, a new rent collector stood at the cottage's door under Ma's bower of red roses, grinning and exposing rotten tobacco-stained teeth. Ma's cheeks flushed, and her eyes moistened as she opened her purse and rifled through it for the two-shilling coins she lacked. Brigid gave her a hell-freezing glare to the rent collector.

'I must evict you if you cannot pay, Missus. You know the landlord will not accept any excuses from you.' He smirked at Ma, making Brigid's blood run cold. His tone suggested Ma was a problematic tenant, which set Brigid's teeth on edge.

Ma retrieved two coins from a small box in her press and paid the obsequious *eejit*. He walked on whistling. Ma closed the door behind him and leaned against it.

'Keep what you saw Today from your father. It is our secret.'

She showed her daughters where she had hidden a spare key to her press and another for the box behind a loose brick above the fireplace.

'If I'm not here when the rent collector comes, you may need them.' After locking the press, she put her key in an apron pocket as a lone tear dropped her pale cheek.

Brigid's heart clenched as she witnessed her mother's distress. *What other secrets does Ma's press hold, I wonder?* But even with a spare key, Brigid dared not open it without her mother's permission.

For the rest of the summer, Da, who worked part-time as a groundsman and grave digger, drowned his wages in poteen. Washing hung daily on the line behind the kitchen using pegs bought from travellers in their red and yellow-painted caravans. Brigid noted how often Ma used her earnings to cover the rent. Her intense dislike of Da grew when autumn arrived, and he spent more time at the shebeen, not less.

During the warm months of 1840, Ma made it evident she must save income for the coming winter. Her downcast look melted Brigid's heart, and she embraced her mother. Despite the challenge, the strong girls coped with extra washing. However, Ma grew weaker, diminishing before her daughters' eyes. With hearts filled with dread at her frailty, the girls became indispensable to running the household.

Da became belligerent. 'I cannot abide pestering women,' he said when Ma wanted him to wear a clean shirt to church one Sunday.

'Leave me be.' He pulled on his soiled shirt and called to the children. 'Hurry, you idle *eejits.* Father Byrne expects us to be seated when Mass begins.'

His drink-depleted income caused the family serious financial worries, but he was unsympathetic. His sons grumbled and cursed while Ma struggled. For Brigid, cleaning up Da's vomit caused her sheer mortification.

In that rain-lashed autumn, Padraig and Dermot cut peat to pile in the garden shed. Brigid and Michael filled buckets of peat for the kitchen each day. Despite his tender years, Michael had a firm body and a determined mindset. Brigid found him a kindred spirit. Padraig and Dermot did the heavy outside work while Angela helped their mother with less arduous tasks.

This division of labour continued through the long, dark winter. Life was dull, like Da's unpolished pewter mug. Arduous work kept Brigid warm in the daytime, and she rose at dawn to light the fire. At night, the girls cuddled in their beds to stay warm as the frosts descended, and the bedroom window filled with diamond-like ice crystals. Those crystals gave Brigid shimmering delight among the dullness of the winter sky. She studied their beauty every morning, and the crystals lifted her spirits.

Winter turned to spring, and Da's absence grew more frequent with the lighter evenings, and he sometimes did not come home for two days and nights. He seldom tended the cottage's land. A talented gardener, Dermot tended the vegetable plot, adding horse manure before planting his seeds and tubers.

One hot morning, he came in for a drink of water, wiped the sweat from his brow, and sat in Da's chair. 'If we owned our land, I would not have to grow crops for our greedy English landlord.'

Brigid's brow furrowed. 'Who is this greedy landlord? His agent makes me grind my teeth so much I will wear them away.'

'The lord who owns the Manor House, of course. He holds most of the tenancies in Ballyconstór. Villagers say he has a colossal estate somewhere in England. He has not visited our village since his children grew up, but I heard he has a son who will inherit the title and assets.' Dermot's calm tone, which had the power to soothe his volatile sister, did not this time. It invited another question.

'His title? What is that?' Brigid said, jumping in with it before anyone else spoke.

'Lord is a name like sir, but grander.' The fire crackled as Dermot added some peat.

Intending to get outside the stuffy cottage, Brigid spotted raindrops on the window. She sighed at the sight of another wet morning and pricked her finger with the needle, a drop of blood dripping on the vest she had mended, which caused her to swear under her breath. She looked at Dermot.

'Does this Lord's property include his livestock, like the horses, chickens, and geese?'

'Yes, it also includes the tenancies and a stretch of the river. The Lord is a wealthy man.'

'When he inherits his title, the son must be kinder than the pitiless old man who shows no mercy to Ma.' Startled by an unexpected sound, Brigid put down her sewing. 'Ma is weeping. I must comfort her.'

But Dermot told her to leave their Ma alone. He would not elaborate, making Brigid anxious about yet another secret. She sat down, recalling the enjoyable experience she and Angela had four weeks before when Ma had taken them to visit Aunt Bessie in the seaside town of Bray. Ma, her face animated, had spoken of her fondly, and the women conversed while the girls played on the beach.

Brigid turned to Angela, who was knitting a shawl. 'What a carefree day we spent at Aunt Bessie's last month. Ma did not weep then, did she?'

Angela counted the rows of knitting she had done that morning.

'Aunt Bessie is a kind old lady. She gave me this ball of soft blue wool. I wonder if she is Ma's actual aunt.'

Brigid had forgotten to ask Ma. The day had been magical. The sun shone, tiny waves tickled her feet, and seabirds swooped to catch fish. Later, in Aunt Bessie's parlour, Brigid had looked wide-eyed at the shelves of books with leather bindings lining an entire wall. Bessie asked if she enjoyed reading. The girl nodded in reply, her mouth full of delicious fruitcake.

'Then choose two to read, and I will send others for Christmas and your birthday,' said Aunt Bessie with a warm smile.

The memory of that day caused Brigid to muse. *What a generous lady she is.* But Ma returned from the bedroom and broke Brigid's reverie. 'Girls, it's stopped raining, so pick some peas to go with the fish Padraig caught this morning.'

Eager to continue reading Austen's *Pride and Prejudice,* Brigid rushed out to pick the peas. When she had finished popping the pods, she collected her precious book. But dark clouds had rolled back and threatened more rain. Gone was the opportunity to read in her beloved spot beneath the apple tree with Scamp at her side. Brigid expressed her disappointment with a sigh.

Brigid's birthday coincided with the growth of the apple blossom. By her thirteenth birthday, a young woman replaced the child. The shape of Brigid's body changed, and her menstrual courses began. The menfolk, including Da, teased her about the village boys, saying they would want to steal a kiss from her soon. Embarrassed by her body's changes, Brigid hated their attention, making her want to curl up like a ball and hide them.

Ma gave her a leather-covered account book as a present. 'I need you to take charge of our family accounts since you have excellent writing and reckoning skills. Ensure you have enough money to cover the rent of two weekly shillings.' She smiled, took the wooden money box from her press, and passed it to Brigid. 'Remember, behind the loose brick, I hide a little golden key. Take the box and hide it from Da.'

I must have a decent brain when Ma gives the accounts to me. At first, Ma supervised her daughter, but Brigid, a competent bookkeeper, continued without help after a week's tuition.

During the summer, Ma developed an irritating and debilitating cough that reverberated around the cottage. Brigid checked her accounts, and her jaw dropped in disbelief. They revealed not a penny could be spared for a doctor's visit.

Musing on the issue, Brigid recalled the village herbalist, mistrusted by villagers who thought she cast spells, who lived in a cottage near the river. *Does she have a mixture to treat coughs?*

Brigid ran down the pebbled boreen to the river's edge. She knocked on the herbalist's door, and an elderly lady dressed in a bombazine frock answered. She wore round spectacles on a chain around her slender neck, and a beaky nose protruded from her wrinkled face.

'Morning, Ma'am. My Mammy is sick with a cough. If I help you pick herbs, would you give me a bottle or two of your mixture for coughs in return?'

To her delight, the woman said, 'I could manage more easily with someone to pick the herbs because my fingers are slow now.'

Brigid wanted to dance with joy. 'Oh, thank you,' she said, curtsying. As the girl worked, a hitherto unknown side to her personality blossomed. She found the task invigorating after being tied to her family's damp, musty home, and her eyes shone. The work so enthralled Brigid she asked to help again.

'Of course, my dear. You will make an excellent herbalist.' The woman gave Brigid three bottles of her cough mixture. Brigid preened like a bird fluffing its feathers with bliss. However, matters far more pressing than plans to become an herbalist soon took over her life.

With the help of the syrupy cough mixture, Ma's thin

body filled out, and the coughing lessened. However, the improvement was temporary, and the cough worsened as the seasons changed.

To Brigid's horror, Ma's belly grew, and the girl knew her mother expected a child. So, as Ma struggled to cope, her daughters' anxiety over their mother's health increased. Their Da, unconcerned, continued to spend his time in the shebeen.

Two months before the baby's due date, Brigid found her mother crouched over the kitchen table. The boys were cutting peat on the moor, and Angela had taken a new knitted shawl to a friend. Ma groaned in pain between coughs, scaring Brigid, who got her mother to bed.

In much pain and distress, Ma gave birth to a stillborn daughter. Brigid cut the cord on Ma's instructions with the kitchen shears and wrapped the dead child in a clean washcloth. After what she had witnessed, Brigid thought *it's no wonder why so many mothers die giving birth*. Brigid cleaned the bed and bedroom but found her mother's anguished keening challenging to witness.

'My child, my child,' Ma wailed, holding the lifeless body to her breast while rocking back and forth, tears streaming down her face.

Drained by the experience, Brigid left the bedroom for fresh air and found Da, Padraig, and Dermot waiting, their faces grim. 'One less belly to fill,' said Da, with a smirk that turned Brigid's stomach.

'You fecking louse. I will never treat my Moira with such contempt. Ma has lost your child. Have you no compassion?' His face was like a thundercloud, and Padraig stormed from the cottage. Brigid sensed his angry steps reverberate through the flagstones.

Tears brimmed in her eyes when Da followed him. *There is so much anger while Ma grieves,* she thought, when Dermot left to tend their land.

Angela came home within a few minutes, her face bearing

the tear-streaked marks of her distress. 'I met Padraig on the boreen. In God's name, however, did you manage alone? I should have been here to help, not gossiping.' Angela's voice quivered.

Angela's absence during the birth relieved Brigid because witnessing the event would cause Angela sensitive distress. So, Brigid chose not to scare her with details but busied heating broth. Angela took some potatoes and peeled them to put in the soup. Both girls' dismay increased with their mother's continued keening.

'When will this torment cease? It is destroying Ma's spirit.' Brigid said.

Angela nodded her head in agreement, her eyes shining with tears.

Brigid did not disclose to her mother the information she had gathered from gossipers about what Da had done with the baby's remains. He dug a grave in non-consecrated soil behind the churchyard, placed the child in it, and then vanished to the shebeen.

Brigid suspected Ma knew because she never enquired about the body. It saddened her, for the girl child had had no apparent imperfections.

Brigid was crushed, too, because nobody had thought to baptise the child in the frenzy of birth and clearing up. *Eejit Da should have done it, she* thought, a fire pit of anger burning at this neglect.

Ma's health did not improve, and her children feared some dreadful disease had taken firm hold. Brigid implored her father's help, begging him for his drink funds to summon the doctor. But Da refused. 'There is no pampering for soft women here, my girl.' He got up and left for the shebeen, coins clinking in his pocket.

Brigid reacted with disbelief as his steps died away, *you heartless eejit. Why did Ma marry you? You are of no use to anyone.* She shook her fist at his receding steps.

The life of relentless struggle continued, and the happy days when Ma played games with them took flight. Life took on a dismal hue that reminded Brigid of the hills and lough in winter. Brigid considered using rent money to send for the doctor, but Ma forbade her. 'You need those funds to pay the rent collector.'

Brigid's mood darkened without the means to ease Ma's suffering, a distressing fact plain to the whole family. Despite her failing health, Ma became pregnant again and gave birth in February 1844 to Joseph, but Ma's breasts did not swell. 'I'm sorry, but I can't produce enough milk for the babby.' Tears filled her sunken eyes as she gazed up at her husband.

'Is that so? Then I must find a wet nurse for you.' Da took the brass clock from its place on the kitchen mantle and, to Brigid's wide-eyed astonishment, said he would pawn it.

'I got eight pounds for it and can put the money to good use,' he said, smirking at his daughter when he returned.

Brigid, speechless at his smug tone, thought, *Filling the coffers at the shebeen is not helping Ma.*

Angela was out running errands. When she returned and learned what Da had done, her eyes filled, and her face reddened. 'Da is so cruel. Ma treasures that clock. Why can't he stop drinking instead?' She ran to the bedroom, sobbing.

Padraig's harsh and accusing voice followed her. 'Da is an *eejit.* He knows Ma is sick. He needs to keep his fecking langer in his breeches.'

Brigid did not understand what he meant, but when he repeated it to Da's face, it was clear Da did. His lip curled; his face reddened while a hand strayed to his belt. But Padraig was taller and broader than his father, and Da's hand fisted, resisting temptation.

'Ye girls tend to your mother and the babby,' he said, turning on his heel, the clock money clinking in his pocket. His face was thundercloud dark. Padraig left the cottage, too, for his nightly visit to his sweetheart, Moira.

Angela returned, and the girls stared at each other with open mouths. 'Da knew Padraig was ready to strike a blow,' said Angela, sniffling into her handkerchief.

'I am glad he did not. It would have been a dreadful sight. Ma has troubles enough without her son and his father fighting.'

Later, Brigid asked Dermot what Padraig's words meant. Dermot blushed, his neck reddening, and refused to explain. Desperate for understanding, Brigid spoke later that week to her catechism class friend Niamh, who had three older sisters. As she walked home afterwards, Brigid's mind filled with imagined sexual and authentic birthing images.

After Joseph's baptism, Ma was so weakened she remained in bed for weeks. When the wet nurse was absent, the girls cared for the child and scrubbed their mother's now bloodstained lace handkerchiefs with lye soap, which cracked the delicate skin on their fingertips. Afterwards, the clothes disappeared with Ma's sweat-soaked bedsheets into the boiler; Angela stirred them with a poss stick.

As she wrung the wet sheets through the mangle, Brigid reflected, 'Men have lives of ease, drinking in a shebeen while their wives toil and bear the babies. I find marriage to be a trial for women, and I'm unsure if I'll ever marry.'

'You don't want to become an old maid, do you?' Angela said, shaking her head.

'Being an old maid may be preferable to marriage, which brings nothing but sickness, babies, and relentless struggle.'

Winter came upon them, and snow fell in thick flakes a week before Christmas 1844. Da left the bedroom following a long, heart-rending coughing spell that had everyone stop up their ears. 'Brigid, for the love of Mary, will ye fetch the doctor, please? Ma coughed up lots of blood. Here is some money to pay him.' He handed her a half-crown coin from his drink jar.

Fifteen-year-old Brigid's eyes opened wide with

amazement. *He gives me his drink money.* The seriousness of Ma's condition sank into Brigid's marrow, and she ran the entire way to find the doctor leaving his house.

'Please, sir,' she huffed, out of breath, 'My Mammy coughs blood. Da gave me his drink money to pay you.' She did not understand the slur her words implied.

'She must be sick then.' The doctor's mocking tone betrayed his contempt for Da as he took the coin, climbed into his trap, and asked Brigid to join him. They found Da and Angela waiting at the cottage by the door, their bodies shivering and teeth chattering.

Angela's red-rimmed, fear-filled eyes beseeched her sister's. 'I would prefer to hear honking geese or some other screeching bird than Ma's cough.'

Brigid sensed a shiver run down her spine. The doctor examined his patient and, exiting the bedroom said, 'Mr Power, your wife has advanced tuberculosis or consumption.'

Brigid had heard how people who had caught the disease suffered. She quailed and sat on a nearby chair before her legs gave way.

The doctor rummaged in his bag and brought out a purple-coloured bottle of medicine. 'Give your wife two or three spoonsful per day of this physic, laudanum. Send Brigid or Angela to get the bottle refilled at my dispensary.' He glared at Da with menacing eyes. 'For heaven's sake, man, give up the drink. Your wife and children need your help. Keep the baby away; otherwise, he will catch the disease.'

The girls ran to his dispensary in any weather, fearing their mother's demise.

Ma's strength had dwindled to where consumption confined her to bed, and running the household became Brigid and Angela's full responsibility. 'I do not mind; work keeps me from going mad,' said Angela, chopping vegetables.

'Angela, my gut tells me Ma will die soon. How will we get Da to give us money to live on after she passes away? I fear he will drink more, not less.' Brigid's voice broke.

Angela's forget-me-not blue eyes glistened. 'You are right. He refused to give us money for a doctor but continued to drink. Will he give us money for the rent? I doubt it.'

Brigid did not think so either, or her heart was as heavy as a stone within her chest as she continued the day's work.

One spring morning, after Ma's coughing had prevented the family from sleeping, Da said, 'Ma has asked to speak to yous children, with Brigid last.'

Brigid trembled. *Has the end come? Oh, God, please, no.* She gulped on entering the stale, airless bedroom. Ma's face had deep hollows, and her smile was a bony grimace. Shocked, Brigid could not move until a rush of love filled her heart. Then she clasped her mother's frail body to her breast.

Ma's faint voice said, 'I love you, my brave daughter. Please care for our family. Your Da's not a wicked man. He is weak, but I have loved him since girlhood. Oh, he looked so handsome then.' Ma coughed, and grandfather. Be strong for me and...' She coughed, her voice fading.

'Yes, Mammy, I promise.' Brigid's voice strangled as tears trickled down her cheeks.

Ma touched the tears with her fingertips and smiled.
The family gathered at her bedside, reciting rosary prayers. Brigid kneeled beside Dermot, who led the prayer, and Ma passed away as the sun slipped behind the hills.

'Quick, Brigid, open a window to let Ma's soul leave her body,' said Dermot, his anxiety palpable.

Then Dal said, 'I'm off to the village.' Brigid's heart plummeted at such evil behaviour because she guessed the word village to be a code word for shebeen. The physical pain of loss gnawed at her guts.

Joseph cried, wanting his food, and she left the room a heartbroken girl to tend to him. She hugged the child, whispering into his downy head, 'I am your mother now.' She broke into heart-rending sobs.

That night, Brigid could not rest. Tormented by visions of Ma's last moments, she feared she might not have the strength to fulfil the deathbed promise. It sat on her sixteen-year-old shoulders like a sack of potatoes, and she cried into her pillow, praying to God for the ability to do Ma's bidding.

CHAPTER 2: A MATTER OF FAITH

Following tradition, women from the village sit beside the body of the deceased for three days to permit mourners to pay their respects. Ma died on a Saturday, and the family attended Mass the following day.

Father Byrne preached a damning sermon, his bulging eyes glaring at Brigid's family as he spoke. 'Any Catholic who attends a Protestant service without permission from the bishop commits a grave sin.'

He glowered at the Power family, his hooded eyes alighting on Brigid. 'The bishop is on his annual retreat. In his absence, I warn you to avoid Protestant services, such as weddings or funerals.'

Brigid started glaring back at him, her eyes wide in a blood-freezing gaze. Da squirmed beside her, and Angela, eyes lowered, fiddled with her blue shawl. The boys sat immobile with their eyes on their boots. The congregation ogled the family, shuffling their feet or dabbing eyes.

Their fawning nauseated Brigid. *Cowards, the lot of you. Someone must bury our beloved mother, grave sin or not. How dare Father Byrne forbid us to bury her until the bishop returns? That can't be a loving God's wish.* Love for her beloved mother surpassed that of a braying donkey in a bog.

She visited the Protestant Church of Ireland's Minister and asked him to perform the burial. The minister agreed to a simple service for which he didn't charge. Before she closed the casket, Brigid removed her mother's wedding ring. *As a last resort, I'll pawn it to cover the funeral expenses because Da won't contribute much money. I'll hide the rest to help pay for food or rent.*

The next day, Padraig and Dermot helped carry the casket to the church. They briefly lingered by the church entrance but refused to enter for the ceremony. Brigid beseeched Padraig to join her, but he said Moira's family would disapprove. Both boys left Brigid alone with the casket as their mother's sole mourner. Since Da, conspicuous by his absence too, worked as a grave digger, Brigid thought, *who dug the grave? Not Da, I pray.*

Da brought home a woven casket the day following his wife's death and put her inside but made no arrangements for the funeral. Mourners complained of a cloying odour. Brigid smelled it, too.

'Da, you must sacrifice some cash for embalming. We can't leave Ma to rot in her casket. Where will we put her for a month while she rots? In the cowshed?' Brigid focused her stubborn gaze on Da's face and yearned to hit him.

Da gave his daughter a haughty look of contempt, pivoted on his foot, and stormed out of the house. Brigid's anger towards this disdain caused her body to shudder.

The following Sunday, Father Byrne preached on obedience to the congregation. 'Repentant sinners wait for the Lord's second coming in purgatory. Unrepentant sinners who have disobeyed the church burn in hell forever.'

His contemptuous, sneering gaze at Brigid and roiled her blood. She got up, pulled her shawl tight to her shoulders, and walked out, keeping her eyes on the church door's latch. Father Byrne condemned her, his shouts of damnation reverberating across the church walls.

Outside, Brigid filled her lungs with fresh air. *I'm finished with the Church's rules. If God condemns me for my devotion to my mother, I'm done with Him, too.*

Soon, the villagers shunned Brigid, but she did not yield and walked with her head held high. No amount of coaxing by Angela to confess her sin caused Brigid to change. So, Angela said she would pray for her sister's soul instead and began attending daily Mass.

Da's visits to home became sporadic; although he left the rent money, he left no extra cash for food. Financial worries nagged at Brigid like Scamp on a bone, and she grew disconsolate with the anxiety. Angela urged her to stop worrying, but Brigid knew it to be a forlorn wish. When Da stopped paying the rent, Brigid had to use her mother's ring money.

Peggy, the wife of Keiron Devlin, owner of the *shebeen*, became the first villager to speak outright to Brigid after she left the Catholic church. With her distinctive inky ringlets bobbing and dark eyes glittering, the woman stopped Brigid on the cobbled boreen one morning.

Brigid licked her lips. 'What do you want, Peggy?'

'You know your Da has taken up with that Maura Flanagan woman who smokes a pipe and puts red-raddle paint on her cheeks, don't you? Well, Father Byrne says he lives in sin with her.' Her firefly-like eyes danced with mischief.

Brigid's temper rose. *Does Peggy get a thrill from watching my discomfort?* She tossed her head and said, 'Da gives you an income? You don't refuse his money, do you, you hypocrite.'

She pushed past Peggy, her back ramrod straight, but her stomach churning. *Why does our eejit Da consort with some evil woman instead of caring about his children?*

But the news revealed their father's whereabouts, and inside, Brigid's anger boiled like water in the kettle over the fire. Angela added fuel to it the following Sunday.

'After Mass, in front of other villagers, Father Byrne told me Maura has a husband in Waterford.' Angela burst into tears.

Brigid consoled her, hugging her tightly, her thoughts dwelling on Father Byrne's insensitivity. *If hell exists, I wish him to suffer eternal damnation.*

During the following weeks, without money from Da, the family lived in danger of eviction. Reluctantly, Brigid used the ring money to pay the rent collector. After she mentioned eviction meant the workhouse, Padraig turned pale and vanished for two days. He returned as Brigid lay awake, worrying. In the morning, he summoned a family council.

'You know Da has stopped leaving any money. Well, village gossipers claim Maura's caravan has left, and Da has left with her. I searched the entire area, and they were right. We can't expect any help again.'

'The fecker,' said Michael, a sturdy eight-year-old, interrupting.

'Brigid needs our help to pay the bills. I have a permanent job herding and milking cows, so my wages will cover much of the rent. Dermot, will you tend our land with Michael's help, please?'

Dermot nodded, his eyes glistening.

Brigid said, 'Angela and I'll take full responsibility for the household tasks. I'll take in additional washing, and Angela can knit woollens to sell while people still have money.'

But despite their efforts, the family struggled, and Brigid knew her carefree childhood had flown out of the window with Ma's soul. In July, Dermot, who had become a clever gardener, turned twenty. Angela and Brigid had watched him dig the potato crop into the soil earlier that summer with admiration in their eyes. He had planted other vegetables, too, in neat rows and the soil weed-free.

'Begorrah, he makes things grow with a commanding look.' Angela's eyes sparkled as she observed the green carrot tops and runner beans covered with bright red flowers.

'He talks to the potatoes and cabbages, and they spring up.' He ran off to play with Scamp, who barked exuberantly, and Brigid smiled at her young brother's cheeky innocence.

The warm summer, but with some days when Brigid could not dry the laundry.

'Vegetables will thrive,' Dermot grinned, responding to Brigid's complaints.

Then, as the apple tree's leaves changed to yellow, Dermot dug up his lumper potato crop. Brigid stood stirring chicken broth in a pot over the kitchen fire when she heard Dermot's anguished call. She wiped her hands with a rag and shaded her eyes from the low sun.

'What's the matter, Dermot? I'm in the middle of cooking dinner.'

Dermot beckoned her, his hand waving with agitation. Brigid ran up the path, and her body tensed when she saw Dermot's weathered face had turned pale.

'It's my potatoes, sister. The tubers are grey and mushy. We can't sell or eat them.' Dermot, losing his usual quiet self-control, buried his head in his hands and wept. 'God didn't hear my prayers.'

'I think it's because of worms. Dig up the crop in the other bed,' Brigid said, her mind on dinner preparations. 'Maybe those potatoes are healthy.'

When Dermot turned his gaze towards his sister, she gave him an encouraging smile. But Dermot did not return it. Instead, he shook his head. Then fear licked at Brigid's toes like flames of burning peat.

'How can we survive without potatoes? We will starve.'

Brigid did not reply. Her mind had turned mushy, like the potatoes. She forgot dinner and left Dermot to sit under the apple tree, thinking about their survival. Later, after hearing the news, Angela wept, and with no coherent plan, Brigid called a family conference that evening. The boys and Angela sat around the kitchen table, with Padraig in Da's armchair, their faces dark and fearful.

Brigid settled Joseph on her lap and gave him his evening milk bottle. 'We must make a winter survival plan. How can you help?'

'I'll try to take on another paid job from a well-off farmer,' Padraig said.

Dermot beamed at his young brother. 'Micky, I'll teach you how to fish and catch rabbits. We can dry the fish for winter storage.'

Michael's eyes shone with eagerness. 'I'll steal food from the Manor: eggs or chickens.'

Brigid gulped. 'Don't steal the chickens. The landlord will evict us, and you'll get transported to Australia.' An image of the local workhouse flooded her mind. 'Feckin' hell, I can't let us stoop so low that we steal,' she whispered into Joseph's downy head.

The girls bottled fruit, stored apples, and pears, and picked mushrooms to dry for soup. With Daisy's milk, eggs, and Dermot's vegetables, Brigid thought she would cope.

One morning in late October, Brigid turned over Daisy's straw, and she discovered a sack filled with flour. She gasped as her eyes lit up with joy. *I can bake bread and make pastry now.*

The boys piled peat in the garden shed; by the end of October, it couldn't hold more; Brigid crossed her fingers, and Angela prayed for their survival as winter blew in with gales and freezing temperatures so cold that the ice-laden branches on the forlorn apple tree cracked. Snow piled high outside the cottage, covering their half-acre plot. The imprints of birds' feet were visible on its diamond-like frozen surface.

Confined to her shed, Daisy produced less milk, and the chickens laid fewer eggs. By December, the thatched roof, already rotted, let in rain and snow. The boys plugged the gaps with Daisy's straw and old rags. The window frames deteriorated, and Brigid packed the cracks with straw.

Joseph's cot stood at the foot of Brigid and Angela's bed. As a tiny baby, he had slept in a kitchen drawer lined with straw and sacking. Brigid placed a cot on their bed because the drawer had become too small. Sometimes, fearful he would catch a chill, she took Joseph between them. She worried about disease, refused to go out, and begged Padraig not to visit Moira. He took no heed of her pleas.

Dermot sculpted a stick toy for Joseph and said Padraig was in love.

Brigid harrumphed. 'This is not a time for that nonsense.'

As the girls cooked turnip soup one night, Angela moistened her dry lips and, with her voice cracking, said, 'Today, I heard some people in the village starve to death. Visions of potatoes boiling and roasting fill my mind. I taste and smell them.'

Brigid, chastened by the news, killed two of their hens for Christmas, so the family ate their fill. Her famine-tormented mind eased for a few hours.

As they boiled the chicken bones for soup several days later, Angela's eyes sparkling with unshed tears said, 'Have you looked at Joseph's tummy? He resembles a pregnant woman. Begorrah, where is Da when we need him?'

Brigid needed to find out, but nobody knew, and without Da's help, she struggled. With the chickens consumed by the end of February, Brigid reached her lowest point. She cared not whether she lived or died.

Brigid sighed and, turning to Angela, said, 'I can't go on. If I throw myself into the lough, you'll have one less mouth to feed.'

Overwhelmed, she cried and held her aching head in her hands, clumps of hair ing out as she tugged it in her desperate state of mind.

'The Church considers suicide a serious sin, so please don't speak that way,' said gentle Angela, hugging her sister. 'We need your brains and strength to continue. I'm here to support you.'

With her heart heavy and her body growing weaker, Brigid continued to struggle. As the apple tree's foliage budded and hazel tree catkins waved in the wind, Scamp, Brigid's last connection to her childhood, passed away. When she and her siblings laid him to rest underneath the apple tree, Brigid sobbed so hard that she feared her heart would burst from her chest. But this outpouring of grief released Brigid's mind from the pit of sorrow that it had occupied since her mother's death.

CHAPTER 3: THE SECOND YEAR OF THE BLIGHT

Brigid watched Dermot and Michael plant their remaining seed potatoes on a sunny day in the late spring of 1846. Dermot muttered to himself as he dug the rich earth.

'Dermot prays over the potatoes again. He asks God to make them grow strong and disease-free, but my gut says God has abandoned Ireland, and they won't grow healthy,' said Michael, his boyish face unsmiling and eyes dulled.

Brigid ruffled his hair. Facing starvation had changed him from the carefree boy of a year ago. Brigid returned to the kitchen and used flour from a depleted bag in the cowshed to bake a turnip pie. The spring sun illuminated the surroundings, bringing peace to her tormented soul as she prepared pastry and reflected on what they had endured.

Padraig worked long hours tending sheep. However, Brigid became concerned about the tenancy.

'Angela, it ought to be in Padraig's name, as he is over twenty-one. But we need Da's and the landlord's agreement to change it.'

Brigid sought information on her father's whereabouts again. But nobody knew a thing, and disapproving village matrons clicked their tongues as the girl passed by.

Word of her quest soon spread, and after Mass the following Sunday, Angela reported that the village matrons had cackled, 'We don't give a toss where they went. They are a mortification to the God-fearing souls of this village.' Angela's face, pale and drawn, had tears trickling down her cheeks.

Throughout the summer, Brigid ensured the family ate well, feasting on fresh vegetables, rabbits, and fish. Joseph grew more robust, his famine-swollen tummy shrinking as he drank Daisy's now creamy milk, which pleased Brigid.

She walked along the riverbank with the toddler to watch Michael cast his rod. 'You have the makings of an angler, Micky. But watch out for the ghillie.'

'I've mastered the art of tickling trout. Watch.' He put down his rod, removed his boots, and waded into a still pool, where he tickled a fat trout into his net. 'We'll eat it for tea tonight.'

His youthful face split into a wide grin, and Brigid's heart lightened. Joseph clapped his hands, and Brigid smiled, patting the child's head. Brigid's pride in the child touched her core. Yet she recognised the possibility of a more challenging winter if the blight returned.

Brigid and Angela stored anything edible that would not spoil, such as turnips, beets, and mushrooms, above the cowshed, along with bottled apples, pears, and other fruits. The family held its breath when the apple tree's leaves turned brown.

Dermot dug up his potato crop. But the blight had ruined it again. He shed the sorrowful tears of defeat on his sister's shoulder, saying, 'Why God, oh why? Do not let us starve, please.' He tumbled to his knees on the freshly dug earth in fervent prayer.

Two nights later, seated before the fire, a much-chastened Dermot gazed at his sister.

'Brigid, I have sad news about our food supplies. The landlord must have learned we poached fish from his river last year because he sacked his ghillie and appointed a younger man to guard his stretch of the river. If no fish are in the lower reaches, I may have to tramp the lough instead. Every man in the village will be fishing.' His body folded upon itself and spoke to utter resignation.

Brigid hugged him. 'Michael will help you. He's transformed into a mean fisherman this summer after your tutoring.'

With his broad shoulders drooping, Padraig, sitting in Da's armchair, added to the unwelcome news.

'My employer had a letter yesterday from his daughter who had married a distant cousin from Mayo. She wrote they agreed to emigrate to America before the landlord evicted them. Many people in Mayo suffered from starvation and skin-darkening relapsing fever. Stranded by the roadside, those unable to board a boat fought for entry into workhouses. Men had to work on road gangs, breaking rocks to earn meals.'

Padraig paused for breath, his eyes haunted, and continued in a trembling voice. 'But my employer hasn't heard from them since and fears the ship might have foundered in a storm. He has begged me to stay working for him and increased my wages.'

Brigid's mouth opened with shock at the word "workhouse," and she gazed at Padraig with fear-filled eyes, saying,

'Young children die in workhouses. Dermot is too weak to break rocks and could die, too.' She pressed a finger to her lips. 'If your wages cover the rent and we store food like last year, we can survive without workhouses or rock breaking.'

The family prepared for winter but with less success than the previous year. Fighting broke out among villagers over what resources were available. Decimated, even rabbits failed to breed. Bushes got stripped before their berries had been ripe for a day, and mushrooms vanished as fast as they appeared.

Brigid baked turnip pies using her remaining flour. But one day, to her horror, she found the flour contaminated. She darted to the kitchen, where Angela sat by the fire, stirring the broth.

'Angela, I found weevils have spoiled the flour. Where is Da when we need him?'

Recalling her promise to Ma, Brigid broke into heaving sobs, wiping her wet face with a white cotton and lace handkerchief she had found in Ma's press.

Angela got up and embraced her sister. 'Brigid, our survival depends not on Da but on your resourcefulness. Ma knew that when she put you in charge of the accounts.' Angela's eyes glistened with unshed tears. 'Once, I was so close to Da. Now, I hate him for his neglect.'

'It grieves me that Da's neglect has soured your love. We know you're his favourite child,' commented Dermot.

Angela lowered her eyes. 'Da used to be so kind to me. I didn't understand why he singled me out.'

'It's your resemblance to Ma. He saw the girl he married in you.' Dermot resumed whittling, and Angela blushed.

Scrubbing the kitchen table, Michael said, 'Da is a disgrace. We should cut him off.' He took out his anger on the table.

Brigid took the rent book from the kitchen drawer. 'We can't, Micky. The tenancy is in his name. I imagine Da spends hours in some *shebeen* with his woman. The number of times I had to clear up after him is beyond my recollection. He can stay away forever if he keeps the tenancy.'

Michael looked up and shrugged his shoulders. 'He is no father to us.' He continued the vigorous scrubbing, venting his rage on the wood.

For weeks, the icy weather and aching hunger made Brigid's fertile imagination observe Dr Death lingering by the lintel. His lurking presence in her famine-tortured, distorted mind tormented her soul. He grins ghoulishly whenever I step outdoors. But aching hunger soon grew so intense it drove out other sensations, real or imagined.

The British government attempted to help the people of Ireland and struck a deal to ship Indian corn from America. The corn supplemented their paltry diet, although nobody knew how to cook it. Through trial and error, women learned, and the message passed through the villages by word of mouth.

'Boil it in salted water or fry it with lard if you have some,' advised a neighbour.

The family found the kernels challenging to eat from the cob because starvation loosened their teeth. Brigid mashed the grains after boiling the cobs and fried them with the eggs Michael stole from the Big House. She also made corn and nettle soup. But this stretched her cooking skills and inventiveness to their limits. Her last recourse became the weevil-filled flour, and after sieving out the weevils, which she threw on the fire, she found it made tolerable bread to eat with the soup.

But as winter turned to spring, their resources vanished, and Brigid caught Michael digging up and eating earthworms. He stared at his sister with haunted, sunken eyes and swallowed.

'The landlord must help us instead of sitting on his throne in some damnable castle in England.'

Brigid hugged her brother's thin and muscle-wasted body as he wept in her arms and regretted burning the weevils because they would have provided some nourishment.

In late March, Daisy died from hunger; her straw was used for filling holes in the thatch.

Brigid wept, saying, 'I ought to have taken better care of such a gentle cow. She had a sweet temperament, and I loved her.'

Angela smoothed her sister's head. 'You did the best you could, Brigid. It is a wonder she lasted so long with so little food.'

Padraig and Dermot dismembered Daisy to use any meat left on her bones, which the girls boiled for nettle and bone marrow soup.

A few weeks later, Padraig returned home with the terrifying news of relapsing fever in the village. Brigid knew from gossip that starving infants and older people died quickest, so she refused to go out lest she gave the disease to Joseph. Instead, Angela did any necessary shopping, and Brigid kept Joseph away from his siblings. Dermot had no land to tend to in the depths of winter, so to Brigid's horror, he resorted to working on a road gang for little pay, risking his health.

Michael now stole eggs from the Manor, but Brigid didn't enquire how. But she held her breath, her heart thumping each time she heard the door creak, wondering if he had been caught.

'You'll be transported if the landlord's caretaker catches you,' Brigid said one day, weeping.

Brigid persuaded Angela to stop visiting the village lest she catch the disease. 'We have no money for shopping.' She omitted any mention of her mother's ring money.

But Angela resisted her sister, reporting villagers with little strength to fight succumbing to the fever. Brigid grew more fearful, her eyes watching the faces of her siblings for signs. To her horror, Joseph caught it first. Brigid couldn't think how unless he had met someone at the garden gate.

The child's fever became so high he had convulsions. He surrendered within a day despite Brigid's attempts to cool his body. Her efforts to keep Ma's youngest son alive had come to nought.

Brigid blamed herself, and the defeated look made Angela comment, 'Which of us will be next?'

Padraig had not seen his sweetheart for several weeks. But against Brigid's advice, with fear licking his toes, he left to visit her. When he returned, his face awash with tears, he said, 'She is gone, Brigid, gone. My lovely Moira caught the fever and has died.' He sniffed and wiped his eyes on his sleeve. 'How will I live without her? We planned to be married next year.' His voice caught on his words.

Brigid's eyes searched his. 'Padraig, I know your heart is breaking. But we can't cope if you die. Please avoid anyone who will give you a fever. Can you live with the farmer and not come here? I fear Dermot will catch it breaking rocks.'

Padraig arranged with the farmer to live in the loft above his cowshed for a few weeks. 'I'll be safe; my absence will mean one less mouth for you to feed. It will also give me time to grieve. I'll leave the rent under the loose stone near the gate.'

Two weeks after Padraig left, Dermot returned from work, shivering, and went straight to bed. Soon, he became delirious. Michael followed him within a day. They both lay shivering, sweat beading their brows, raving about dancing devils, and Michael screaming in pain as his skin darkened. Brigid and Angela tended to their needs until exhaustion overtook them, and they, too, fell sick.

The fever-ridden Brigid lay on the kitchen sofa to keep the fire alight. But as her fever grew, profuse sweat poured from her tormented body. She hallucinated, glimpsing haunted, staring-eyed spectres pass by the window: the living dead on a slow march. Her hair fell out, and Brigid dwelt in fever hell.

As the fever subsided, her hallucinations vanished, and her befuddled mind cleared. Not a sound could be heard in the cottage. No screams, no anguished prayers, and the fear of solitude almost overwhelmed Brigid. She had to find out if her siblings had perished. Filled with terror, she crawled up the stairs to Da's room. It shocked her to see her brothers' bodies like peat bog soil, their eyes wide open, staring, with Michael's mouth stretched as if he screamed. She came close to howling as she gazed at them., She placed a hand over her mouth., her heart thumping in her ears. *Is Angela alive or dead? If she has passed, I shall scream to the rafters and throw myself into the river.*

Brigid crept into their shared bedroom and, to her profound relief, found her sister sleeping, her fever gone. The relief washed over her like water on the seashore at Bessie's as she crawled back to the kitchen sofa, where she collapsed.

Raising her eyes heavenwards, tears pouring, she thought, *I'm sorry, Ma. I have failed you. Your sons lay the heart of our family and, except for Padraig, have died. They will never give you the grandchildren you deserve. It is my fault.* Tears fell as she stared unseeing out of the kitchen window. *How will we tend our land in the future?* Sobs racked her body, and she dwelt in Irish hell.

Angela arranged for the three boys to be buried in the Catholic churchyard. 'You knew Dermot had dreams of entering the priesthood, didn't you?' she said.

Brigid sighed, her brow furrowing, and said, 'Dermot would have been a kindlier priest than Father Byrne.' Her tone was laced with sadness.

Brigid contacted Padraig to give him the news and ask him to attend the funeral. But to his children's astonishment, Da turned up, too. He looked grand in a fancy frock coat.

'Surviving on land's resources, we have been isolated from people here. Maura is a clever cook.' He smirked at Brigid, taunting her. 'We learned about the deaths of a passing traveller. You did a poor job keeping your brothers alive, Brigid.'

Too shocked to speak, Brigid turned her head, tears shimmering on her lashes. She was disgusted, her emotion evident in the set of her mouth, and Angela refused to converse with him, either.

The three siblings stepped in front of their father at the graves; Padraig's height prevented their father from throwing dirt on the coffins. Brigid would throw her father alive into a grave had one been vacant. No one inquired about how she financed the funeral and wake, including Da, who did not contribute a farthing.

After the funeral, however, Brigid went to bed and refused to eat. Her feelings of failure overwhelmed her, and weeping left her drained and weak. Angela visited the herbalist, who gave her St John's wort medicine, which the woman recommended for melancholy.

Because Brigid clamped her jaws, Angela had trouble administering the medication. After much pleading, Angela succeeded. In time, Brigid's dark mood lifted. But the impact of the deaths had been so profound the guilt lay like two sacks of potatoes on her eighteen-year-old shoulders.

In the spring of 1847, the fresh-smelling air enveloped the girls with a gentle warmth as they scoured the land for extra sustenance, such as wild leeks amongst the budding growth. Brigid learned Da and his hussy had taken residence by the village pond, so she persuaded Padraig to visit their father and demand he provide capital for urgent repairs to the cottage, lest eviction follow. 'Please tell him it is the workhouse for his beloved Angela if he doesn't help us. She will die in such a place.'

Padraig returned, saying, 'Da squirmed but gave me this silver. But visiting him mortified me.' He refused to say why, his face pale and hollow as he placed the coins in Brigid's slender hand, and she trembled.

Brigid answered a knock at the door on Monday morning to find the landlord's agent grinning. 'I heard about your brothers and persuaded the landlord to allow you to remain in the cottage while the fever raged.' He gave Brigid an obsequious smile that left her stomach churning as he grabbed the rent money. 'The landlord expects your father to repair the cottage by the winter. It needs thatching. Good day, Missy. I'll call again next week.' He walked on whistling, the silver clinking in his pocket.

Brigid shook her fist at his back and shut the door with a resounding bang.

'Angela, Da doesn't care about us, so he won't help with repairs. Padraig will have to manage with our help.'

'We're on our own for everything,' said Angela, her voice catching on her words.

The siblings picked up some threads of pre-famine life. However, the village matrons shunned them because of Da's behaviour. Angela left to pray at their brothers' graves each day, regardless of the weather. Brigid said, 'I fear you'll catch a fever again.'

But Angela took no heed, and a soft bloom appeared in her cheeks while her demeanour grew jauntier to Brigid's profound relief. However, she disregarded her health and caught a heavy cold that went to her chest. Like Ma had done, she coughed and coughed.

Angela saw the herbalist and brought Brigid a bottle of her cough mixture. She also brought bowls of steaming water to help her breathe, and within a few weeks, she recovered.

But the illness had taken its toll on Brigid's general health, so the girl returned to bed. 'I'll not catch another cold if I stay here, Angela,' she said, her mind muddled.

Angela encouraged her sister to retake the herbal remedy for depression, and Brigid's mood recovered by her April birthday. The warm weather helped her health improve, too, and she read beside the apple tree next to Scamp's grave most days as she healed. By June, she had regained enough strength to do laundry and earn some pennies.

Padraig and Angela tended the land throughout the summer, working late into the night to plant the vegetables. Padraig kept working for the farmer. But working two jobs became exhausting. He caught a summer cold that went to his chest.

Padraig's weakened body found it too challenging to cope despite Angela's herbal medicine, and the cottage remained unrepaired. He regained no weight and sometimes had trouble catching his breath. This worried Brigid as, in late September, the agent gave them one more month before eviction.

His evil grin tempted Brigid to send him to Da. 'But I fear it will do more harm than good,' she said to Angela, who nodded in agreement.

Two weeks later, with some improvement in his condition, Padraig helped Father Byrne clear the churchyard path of leaves and found a man sleeping on a bench beneath the church porch roof.

'Brigid, his name is Luke Duffy, and he's homeless. I hope

you don't mind, but I have invited him for supper.'

Brigid put in extra effort to make the meagre rabbit stew appetising.

When they had finished eating, Luke said, 'I'm a thatcher by trade, but when the landlord evicted my family, we planned to emigrate.' Tears trickled from his red-rimmed grey eyes. 'The fever so weakened my wife and daughters that they died in a ditch. I can't leave Ireland with my family forever in its soil.'

Brigid, moved by his plight, offered permanent shelter to tend their plot of land. As Padraig now slept in Da's room, not the loft above the cowshed, Brigid cleaned it for Luke.

He gave Brigid a faint smile. 'Thank you, Missy. I'll fix the thatch and crack windows in return for your kindness. If I board the loft room, it will make it warmer for sleeping. May I do so?'

'Of course. Do whatever you think will make the cottage more comfortable and mollify the landlord.'

Luke got to work and made a small bedroom for himself. He repaired the thatch and cracked window frames, removed mould, and whitewashed the walls. Soon, the dilapidated cottage appeared more inviting, and the landlord's smarmy, cravat-wearing agent arrived, gazed at the repairs, and grinned.

'The landlord sent me to evict you today. But someone has done an outstanding job.'

He grabbed his money from Brigid's unwilling hand. Then, giving her his evil, nauseating grin, he whistled as he strode down the garden path.

Brigid shook her fist at his back. *Why didn't you get the landlord to fix the thatch? But for sure, the eejit lives in that detestable, Irish-controlling country, England. The fecker, I hate him, for he shows no compassion.*

A spiky thistle took root in Brigid's death-clouded mind, and she concluded that keeping busy would deal with the depression afflicting her.

Luke proved an able gardener, and their plot produced edible vegetables and fruit that summer. To everyone's relief, starvation receded, and the fever did not return. Brigid took Michael's rod and went fishing. It provided food and gave Brigid a relaxing way of calming her mind. Padraig's farmer gave them a heifer, which grew into a sleek cow.

Brigid named her Buttercup for her beautiful golden colour. Many villagers sought Luke's help, providing him with an income and, thus, stability. About three years older than Padraig, he became like a brother to him, which pleased Brigid.

Throughout this time, Da's continued relationship with Maura remained a thorn in Brigid's side. She avoided the pond where villagers said Maura parked her caravan. Gossipers reported the pair smoked pipes from the caravan that blew an awful smell of opium around the place.

'The evil stuff even makes the ducks that come for the summer sleepy, and they stop quacking,' said Angela, with a shimmering gaze, after a shopping trip. Brigid shopped a few days later, and Peggy stood ahead in the line. Brigid pulled her shawl over her head to avoid Peggy spotting her, but she did.

'Ah, 'tis yourself, Brigid. My Keiron has employed Maura as a bartender. The hussy flaunts her curves, and men like to stare as she puts their tips in her corset. She brings in customers even if she smokes an evil pipe.' The woman's ringlets bobbed, and her eyes gleamed with malice when she left the shop.

Brigid's cheeks blazed; if the ground had split open, she would have liked to sink into the hole. However, Luke, who frequented the pub, reported that Peggy was correct. Brigid opined that Da and his mistress ought to go where their relationship did not cause disgrace to his children.

'He no longer pays a farthing in rent. He's more trouble than he is worth. With the coming of summer, Brigid's body filled out, her hair grew back, and she believed the worst of the famine lay behind them. However, the fever had caused such a devastating outcome that finding a fresh path to keep the remaining family intact consumed Brigid's mind for months.

CHAPTER 4: MOVING ON

In the 1850s, Home Rule became the topic for gossiping matrons. After Mass one spring morning, Brigid overheard two widows talking in the village shop.

'Jaysus, Connor Kelly has joined the Irish Comrades in America. It will break his mother's heart.'

'Aye, no young'uns in the village to continue our family names. We'll forget who we are at the pearly gates.' The woman cackled at her joke, revealing stumps like dead crows for teeth. 'You know Angela Power? A friend spotted the woman holding hands with a stranger by the riverbank.' The woman cackled again. 'She better wed before the babbies come. Her family has a reputation for sinful behaviour.'

Quailing at the dreadful slur, Brigid hid her face under her shawl and slipped from the shop. At home, she confronted Angela. 'What were you thinking to walk with a strange man in public? I felt mortified.'

Angela lowered her face, her eyes brimming with tears, and said, 'I'm courting someone. He is a widowed farmer from Carrick Magna.' She looked up to meet Brigid's accusing eyes. 'His wife died early in the famine, and she lies close to our brothers in her family's grave.'

Inside, Brigid fumed that her sister had said nothing about this relationship. She swallowed her anger, although her voice sounded harsh. 'How did you make his acquaintance?'

'I slipped on wet grass tending our brothers' graves a year ago.' Angela's eyes glistened. 'Cathal helped me up, and we began talking. Now, we meet twice a week, and if it's raining, we sit on the church porch bench where Father Byrne found us. He knows Cathal.' A tear dropped on Angela's cheek. 'Brigid, we have done nothing but fall in love. I kept it from you because of your melancholy. I thought knowing could make it worse.'

Brigid regarded her sister with suspicion. She doubted whether Angela told the whole truth. 'Does Padraig know?'

Angela shook her head. 'Few people know. Father Byrne approves, though, and gives us his blessing. He suggested we walk along the riverbank.'

Her temper rising, Brigid took a deep breath. 'Father Byrne sent you to walk in public, so villagers would shun us. Those village matrons are waiting to tar us with the same brush as they tarred Da. You must tell Padraig tonight.'

But Angela's voice cracked as she said she had no intention of speaking with Padraig. She went to bed early, citing a headache. Brigid couldn't force her sister to speak, so she explained the situation to Padraig herself.

His brow became deeply furrowed. 'Why did Angela keep it secret? Deceptive behaviour isn't in her bones.'

Brigid, reluctant to bring Father Byrne into the conversation, blamed her battle with depression.

This explanation failed to convince Padraig. 'There must be more to it. I'll enquire about the man. If his wife's family is local, someone will know him.'

A couple of days later, he had news. 'Cathal O'Leary is a farmer from a large, prosperous family in Carrick Magna. He owns over ten acres of land. His wife had a child during the famine but didn't survive, so Cathal raises the boy alone.'

'Aha,' said Brigid. 'The child needs a mother. Angela kept that from us. Did you find out Cathal's age?'

'Yes, and he is ten years older than Angela.'

'Another reason not to tell us. Do you think Cathal is a suitable match for Angela?'

'Based on what I have heard, yes, he's suitable.' Padraig stared into the middle distance, his eyes sad.

Remembering Moira, I expect, thought Brigid.

Padraig allowed Cathal to court Angela, and the girl glowed. Brigid invited him to Sunday dinner with his son, and the family found him a calm, cheerful man who clearly loved Angela. Brigid felt envy, despite her wishes for her sister's happiness, and observing her sister's joy filled, smooth-skinned face, she remembered her own face freckling in the sun as a child. She now avoided freckles by wearing a straw hat with a large brim. Her hair had re-grown a much darker red. She brushed it with Ma's silver-backed hairbrush and washed it more often.

At Christmas 1852, after several months of official courtship, Cathal asked Padraig for Angela's hand in marriage. A radiant smile spread across Brigid's face, grateful that Cathal possessed the manners to ask. The couple married in late August 1853. Angela made her wedding dress from a bolt of cream silk Brigid found at the bottom of Ma's press. Preparing to dress as her sister's bridesmaid, Brigid pondered if this would be her closest experience to being a bride. Filled with a yearning for her mother, she picked one of the remaining roses to adorn her hair. Then, at least, she had something of Ma supporting her.

Angela had forbidden their father from coming near the wedding. Luke supervised, promising to remove Da if he showed his face. After the service, a pony and trap waited to transport the newlyweds to their reception in Cathal's barn. Beer flowed from three enormous barrels for the men. Angela ordered elderflower, blackcurrant wine, and apple juice for the ladies. Cathal had hired a fiddler and a bodhran drummer to entertain guests.

After the speeches, Angela blushed when Cathal's older brother reminded him to do his duty. 'If you've forgotten the duties of a bridegroom on his wedding night, seek me out,' he said in a sardonic tone. Everyone laughed, and Angela's blush deepened.

But contentment filled Brigid's heart as the couple glided across the barn floor in a waltz, their love apparent to onlookers. Brigid whispered to herself, *what a happy family*

Angela has joined. I'll miss her tranquil manner and the comforting warmth she brought to our shared bed.

A tear of loneliness slipped down her cheek, dispelled when Martin, the village blacksmith, asked her to dance. A tall man with bushy eyebrows and twinkling blue-green eyes. Brigid enjoyed his company. Over the next few months, the couple attended several village events together. One spring day, he proposed marriage. But Brigid refused him. She watched with a constriction in her throat as his smile receded. 'I value your friendship, Martin, but I ought not to have given you the impression that we would wed. I apologise if I have hurt you.'

Martin assured Brigid he would care for her and understood her lack of deep affection for him, but she remained steadfast. They never met again, and Brigid heard he emigrated.

During the warm months of 1854, the villagers enjoyed a festive period. Luke courted Brigid, taking her to village events as Martin had done. Brigid sensed Luke's attention, which felt more like friendship than romance, so she asked Padraig if Luke had sought a deeper relationship.

'Luke cares for you, but it isn't a grand passion. If you have no wish to marry him, I'll explain. But please continue being our housekeeper.'

'Of course I will.' Brigid had caught a gleam in the new rent collector's eye. *Is he after courting me? No chance, the eejit. Rent collectors do not get a toe over my threshold.* She took in washing, and on winter evenings, they sat around the kitchen fire, the two men playing checkers while Brigid read or sewed. Brigid used her washing income to buy books and clothing from a catalogue, including an atlas. She studied it and mused on Ireland being a small place compared to America or Australia. She kept meticulous accounts, and the seasons rolled by in a tranquil rhythm until Da interfered.

On Brigid's twenty-sixth birthday, a thrush sang in the

apple tree, blossoming in full flush, which cheered her as she set off for the village store, thinking, *I'll make a birthday cake.* But Peggy Devlin, lurking on the boreen, stepped into her path, her inky ringlets wobbling.

Brigid stopped walking, her mouth turning dry. 'What do you want from me, Peggy?' She kept her voice level, thinking, *not another opportunity to humiliate me?*

'You know Seamus wants an heir, don't you?'

'Seamus, who? What does he have to do with me?' Peggy, known for her slander, made Brigid's heart pound.

'Seamus O'Hara, the wealthy farmer I heard you'll wed.' Peggy's ebony eyes danced a jig.

'What did you say?' The witch enjoyed playing with people's minds, and Brigid's spun.

'Your Da and Seamus met in Keiron's bar last week. Seamus agreed to pay ten years' rent on the cottage for your hand in marriage. His wife, a timid, barren creature, died of fever.'

By now, Brigid's heart thumped like a drum, trapped by Peggy's words, and she couldn't speak. Peggy giggled at her discomfort. 'Seamus is fifty if he's a day, with a porter belly and boasts about his thirty-acre farm. Your status will improve by marrying him.'

Brigid's hands itched to smash Peggy's face, like flattening a frying potato cake. She licked her dry lips and found her voice. 'The match would raise my status above yours.' Brigid gritted her teeth to stop herself from giving the witch more to gossip about, and, stomach-churning she glared at the woman before, shopping forgotten, she strode on to find her father.'

Da squatted his bony rump on the step of Maura's red and yellow caravan. His eyes glazed and unfathomable, he puffed evil-smelling smoke from a long-stemmed pipe. Brigid shouted his name to get his attention.

His gaze shifted. 'What do ye want?' he said, slurring.

'Peggy Devlin says you have sold me to a beast in marriage. She must be mistaken. Would you sell your daughter like a cow in a market, Da?'

Da removed his pipe and focused on his daughter, whose cheeks burned with fury. 'You're past the usual marrying age. I hear you have turned down two suitors. Since I can't finance a spinster, I have arranged your marriage. I got an outstanding deal, too.' He grinned, showing his tobacco-stained broken teeth. But his eyes gleamed like two polished brass farthings.

Brigid's temper grew worse than a donkey in a bog. 'You bastard, how dare you treat me like an animal for sale in a market?' She guessed he planned to transfer Maura into the cottage after she had wed Seamus. Brigid wanted to claw his bloodshot, evil eyes out.

Da surveyed his daughter with contempt before speaking. 'We meet Seamus tomorrow, so we do. Cover your hair and wear a clean apron. I'll fetch you after breakfast.' He replaced his pipe and puffed, dismissing Brigid with a stern but mocking look.

Brigid's hand itched to punch her Da in the teeth and knock them out along with his vile pipe. But she clenched her fists and, remembering Dermot's warning about donkeys in bogs, stomped away before she landed in one. Throughout the day, Da's words reverberated in her mind where prickly briars grew.

By nightfall, the terrors her father's plan had wrought so tormented Brigid's mind that she didn't sleep. Her nerves screamed while Peggy's description of Seamus consumed her thoughts like a determined mole digging his way across a meadow. *Is he as horrible as Peggy implied? I must see for myself before the whole county knows my plight.*

CHAPTER 5: BREAKING FREE

Seamus's farm lay two miles west of Ballyconstór in a tiny hamlet. The walk through the spring fields filled with bright yellow buttercups would have been pleasant if disturbing thoughts had not filled Brigid's mind.

The nostril-attacking odour of pig manure hit her before she saw the farmyard. Nobody had cleaned up the farm animal ordure, which lay in clumps. Brigid heard chickens clucking somewhere nearby and a cow lowing, both sounds that cheered her.

At the farmhouse door, Brigid shuddered. *The step needs a vigorous scrub, and I bet that dog's head brass knocker has not seen polish for years.*

Da lifted the knocker off the cracked brown paint and rapped three times. The door opened, revealing an unshaven, rotund, balding man who wore a stained shirt and breeches. Brigid wrinkled her nose. *When did he last wash?* The man led them into his parlour, and Brigid examined it with a critical eye. The dust lay inches thick on every surface, with papers strewn everywhere. Brigid's senses became engulfed by grime and disorder.

'Yon colleen is bonny and has the hips for childbearing,' said Seamus. 'Sit, girl, and look at me.' The farmer leered at Brigid, his pockmarked face glittering with beads of sweat, and Brigid's stomach lurched. She held her tongue as he cast his piggy eyes upon her and said, 'I want a pure bride who cooks and cleans, so I do,' his sneering tone mocking her.

Da nodded his agreement to the deal, and anguished, Brigid's fingernails dug into her palms. Seamus gave Da the money to finance the wedding, and Brigid wanted to say, *don't take it because I'll not wed him. Lying in a bog is preferable to sleeping with this ugly specimen of humanity.*

To her horror, Seamus demanded she work for him unpaid for two months before calling the marriage banns, starting the following Monday. Da agreed, and a grin split across his face as they walked out of the farmyard.

Brigid wanted to put the *eejit* to shame for his duplicity. 'Da, I loathe him. Anyway, I have lost my faith.'

'Find your faith then and do as Seamus asks.'

Brigid stilled her tongue until they reached the cottage. On arrival, she said, 'You live in sin with that woman, Maura, whom I know has a husband. I'm over twenty-one, so what right have you to sell me into marriage with a beast?' Brigid's shouts of anger hit the rafters.

Da pulled a bottle of whisky from his pocket and took a swig, taunting her with an evil gleam in his eyes.

'You fecking beast. By your behaviour with that hussy, you have tarnished the reputation of our whole family, including Ma. I bet you want to move Maura into the cottage after you get rid of me. That's the truth.' Brigid's body bristled with rage.

Da glared at her, his face grim. 'You'll pay for your slurs on my woman friend, you insolent girl.'

He undid his belt and ran Brigid for the door, but in her haste, she fumbled with the catch, and Da caught her wrist, twisting an arm behind her back. He threw her over a chair and gave her three thwacks, the most she had ever had.

Afterwards, Da opened his press, removed his old drink jar, and put Seamus's money in it, tightening the lid.

'You better work hard, my girl, because this cash will pay for your wedding.' Da stuffed the jar in his frayed jacket pocket. He left the cottage, glaring at Brigid, his eyes gleaming with malice, as he closed the door.

'You'll drink that money before the wedding, so you will.'

The words slipped out unbidden, but luckily, Da did not hear her. Brigid ran to the calm of Ma's grave, her behind stinging like a swarm of bees had taken up residence. Kneeling beside the grave, Brigid experienced a sense of being caught like a mouse in a trap with no means of escape.

The next day, resigned, Brigid set about cleaning the family's cottage and stocking up on provisions. With his brow puckering, Padraig arrived home for dinner and asked why Brigid had become so agitated.

Outraged, he said, 'I'll speak with Da. He can't do this to you.'

'Da wants to move in here with his hussy. I bet she refuses to share the kitchen with another woman, so he wants to marry me off to Seamus.'

Padraig's eyes opened wide. 'If you're right, Luke and I won't be welcome either. If she lives here, the bint must also keep house for us.'

'Villagers will shun you if you stay.'

'I'll get the truth out of Da, so I will.'

He left Brigid to find their father, his face like a thundercloud. But when he returned, he said he had made no progress with Da and had received the sharp edge of Maura's tongue into the bargain.

So, the following Monday, a forlorn Brigid reported for work. She beat the rugs, and the shower of dust choked her, got into her eyes, and made her sneeze. Thick cobwebs hung in the corners of the parlour, and it needed a stiff broom to remove them. Brigid tackled the dirt-encrusted windows with vinegar and old newspapers until they shone. But her arms ached from the effort.

She collected the water from the yard pump and heated it on the fire. She poured it into a tin bath to wash Seamus's bedding and clothing. Repulsed by the man's smell, shudders ran down her back. If possible, *I would put Seamus in Ma's boiler along with his body odour-smelling washing.* Brigid knew her thoughts were mere imaginings, but they pricked her conscience.

The kitchen proved challenging to clean. The range hung thick with lumps of grease, and soiled pots, pans, and dishes lay on every surface. Brigid spent an entire day cleaning and blackening the range and washing plates. Scouring and polishing pots and pans took another day. Then she scrubbed the surfaces and the flagstone floor. The next day, Brigid discovered Seamus had delivered a supply of peat and an ill-spelt message. *Peat fer the fire. Bake meet pasties. I like 'em fer dinner at noon.*

By then, Brigid knew Da had sold her as an unpaid cleaner, cook, and child bearer. She walked the two miles home each night, but Seamus never offered her a lift in his buggy as he drove to the village *shebeen*. Instead, he waved his whip at her, and since darkness descended late in the July evenings, she even saw his evil smirk.

Each day, Seamus came for his meal at noon and gobbled up everything, wiping his mouth on his sleeve. Brigid's stomach churned.

After a few weeks, Seamus said, 'Ye cook well. I'll give ye that. Your pastry is lighter than Roisin's.' He did not praise her for anything else or comment on her cleaning.

But one morning, the farmer cornered Brigid as she kneaded dough. He grabbed her shoulders and swung her around, so his hot breath fell on her face. Seamus pushed her against the table and forced his tongue into her mouth. His breath tasted like rotten food, and his body smelt of cow dung and sweat.

An icy shiver ran through Brigid's body when his hands roamed her flesh, and his member grew firm, pressing against her belly. Her stomach lurched when he pulled his tongue out, leered at her, his teeth like a line of dead crows, and shoved a hand in her blouse. Her eyes bored into his piggy ones as she jammed her knee into his privates, the place where it hurt her older brothers.

Seamus let go, yelping. 'Yer bint. I'll bet you as soon as

we wed.' He put one hand in his pocket and pulled out a blue stoned ring, which he shoved over her dough-covered finger. 'Ye resisted me, so I know ye is pure. This ring belonged to Roisin. Now it is yours. I shall call the banns on Sunday. I want an heir come the spring.' Seamus glared at her, his piggy eyes dark with pain. 'I'll give ye next Sunday off to spend with yer Da. Make sure he recovers from the betrothal celebrations in the shebeen. He drinks me under the table, so he does.' Seamus smirked, making Brigid's stomach churn again.

I bet he does. Brigid reflected. *He is a committed drinker, honed by years of practice.* But terrified by his dreadful marriage prospect, she wondered how to escape. *I'm a rat in the proverbial barrel.* Then, knowing that after visiting the shebeen, Da would go to Maura's caravan, not the cottage, she called on her friend Niamh for advice.

'I thought of stealing Seamus's money and running away. But Da took it with him after beating me. What can I do now?'

'Visit the palm reader. It worked for me.' Niamh blushed, twisting her gold wedding ring.

The soothsayer lived in a tiny cottage that smelled of mothballs. The woman ran her fingers over the creases in Brigid's palm.

'You'll meet a tall, dark-haired stranger who will change your fortunes.' Her brow pleated. 'You face many challenges in your life. I see babies. Yes, and a journey over water. Your life has a strange destiny, but it is misty.' She looked up at her client, her violet eyes narrowed and held out her palm. 'Threepence, please, Missy. Come again, and I'll use the tarot cards on the mist.'

Brigid gazed at her blowzy face and then paid her with a coin from her washing income, the bells of balderdash ringing in her ears. She would not revisit even if someone paid her. *A misty future? Ugh.*

As the sky filled with dark, scudding clouds, she ran home. To her dismay, Brigid found Da and Maura sitting by the fire, its flames flickering shadows on the walls, newly whitewashed by Luke.

Maura held his drink money jar and shook it in Brigid's face. 'I'll accompany you to Bray tomorrow, where I know a seamstress.'

Da glared at his daughter 'Your fecking bint of a sister ain't making no dress for you from your Ma's stuff.'

Speechless, Brigid watched Da unlock his press. Maura put the jar in it and held her hand for the key, giving Da an icy stare. Brigid enjoyed knowing that he must spend money at the *shebeen* and incurred Maura's vexation.

'This is a fine cottage,' said Maura, her voice tinged with envy. 'We are off to my caravan, but I'll return in the morning.

After they left, banging the door shut, Brigid thought she had the means to escape if she stole the money. But she must leave that night. Finding a kitchen knife, Brigid prised open Da's press. *The money is my payment for working as a domestic servant.*

She counted three ten-shilling coins and some lesser silver, and her heart leapt. The amount exceeded her expectations. Brigid had often heard the first train to Dublin whistle its departure at sunrise, and the plan came together.

The desperate woman searched through the papers in the press for her baptismal certificate, the only document that attested to her provenance. Her eyes blurred when she saw them filed by age, with Joseph's on top. Memories of her brothers, their lives cut short, filled her mind. Brigid found her document under Dermot's. She folded the certificate and put it in the pocket of her best apron. She wiped her wet eyes with a lace-edged handkerchief and prepared supper for Padraig and Luke, to whom she said nothing,

Brigid lay alone and watched the sparkling sky as night fell. The proverbial Man in the Moon looked so benevolent that he soothed her tensed muscles. Brigid's thoughts turned to Padraig. *I can't tell him about my plans, so I hope he understands what I will do.* She sobbed into her pillow, cursing Da for his cruelty.

When the clock in the church struck two, she dressed, tied her apron strings, and put on her boots. She studied Seamus's ring, and the sight sent shudders down her spine. *I do not know its value, but Seamus said it belonged to me, so I'll pawn it.* She wrapped a shawl over her head and shoulders and tramped the four miles to the railway station by the moon's light, arriving as the sun rose in a pink and gold glow over the horizon.

'Be Jaysus, what is a maid doing travelling unchaperoned at this hour?' The stationmaster stared at her face over his half-spectacles.

'I'm travelling to Dublin to meet my aunt, who will help me buy my wedding dress. My mother is dead, you see.'

The lies slipped from her tongue like melting butter. She held out the money for the ticket and flashed her ring in his eyes. The man gave her the ticket, sucking his yellow, crooked teeth. Brigid turned, ran to the waiting train, found an empty carriage, and sat by the window.

The whistling monster clattered from the platform in a cloud of steam. Brigid removed the ring and tied it to her handkerchief. Free from being a chattel for sale, her mind found some peace. However, a knot of anxiety remained in her stomach over her uncertain future until the swaying carriage caused her to fall asleep.

CHAPTER 6: DUBLIN

Brigid awoke when the train jolted to a stop in the station, and she saw some astonishing sights as she glanced through the carriage window. She gazed with gaping mouth at men in long tailcoats with tall hats and silver-tipped canes and women in crinoline dresses with heeled boots standing on the station platform.

Brigid felt inferior in her peasant dress. She wobbled, legs still half asleep, to the carriage door. Whistling and hissing noises assailed her ears, and the clouds of steam and soot trapped by the glass roof attacked her lungs. She coughed while her heart pounded, fearing the unknown until her bladder protested it needed relief.

Next, her stomach grumbled. *I wish I had brought a hunk of bread, as it's been hours since I ate supper.* Wandering the unfamiliar streets, she found a bakery and timorously opened the door.

The female assistant said in English, 'May I help you?'

Brigid swallowed her anxiety and asked for a currant bun, the English language springing from her core. After leaving the shop, Brigid spotted a small park where she sat on a bench to eat the bun. A blackbird hopped towards her, and Brigid rewarded him with a few crumbs. Then he flew off, and Brigid watched him, surveying the rows of houses around the park's streets as she did so.

The air did not smell fresh, like the air in Ballyconstór. Brigid, overcome by homesickness, bit her lip, gulping down the lump that threatened to choke her. and searched for lodgings.

She passed immense houses with mews for their horses

and unaffordable grand hotels, but nowhere did she see a sign for modest lodgings. She slowed and ambled when she reached Grafton Street, reading the shop door signs and peering in windows.

Brigid saw various shops: saddlers, bootmakers, and hatters mingled with sweet shops, jewellers, and tailors. Street hawkers displayed wares like vegetables and clothing while enormous cabs waited in the streets. Fear of the unknown licked at the edges of her mind, and Brigid felt overwhelmed.

After wandering for an hour, Brigid spied a shop with a sign above the door bearing the sign: Ezra A. Balcerzak, Pawnbroker. With careful consideration, Brigid removed Seamus's ring from her finger. Mustering her courage, she pushed the door open. A bell tinkled as she walked into the dingy establishment, filled with objects and trinkets like pictures, pottery, and even a piano.

The man behind the counter had a pointed grey beard and pale blue eyes. Leather braces held up his striped trousers, and a pair of half-spectacles perched on his nose.

In a strange accent, the man enquired, 'Missy, how can I help you?'

Brigid pondered the man's origins. *Has he fled somewhere, too?* She showed him her ring and asked what he would loan her for the jewel.

The man extracted a small eyeglass from his worn waistcoat pocket and examined it. 'This ring is made of pure gold with a well-cut sapphire stone. It must have cost someone a significant amount of money. Did you steal it from somewhere? I am a pawnbroker, not a fence.'

His hazel eyes stared into Brigid's, unsettling her. 'My fiancée ran off with another girl whom he got pregnant. I don't want the ring now.'

Brigid's stomach churned at the lie, yet the words slipped out like honey from a jar.

While stroking his beard, the pawnbroker said, 'Ah, then

you'll want a fair price. I'll lend you eight pounds.'

In a firm voice, Brigid said, 'Ten,' thinking, *Da got eight for Ma's clock, and I got six for her ring.*

'Oi, a barterer, so you are. Nine guineas?'

Brigid nodded, more money than she had ever encountered. The pawnbroker asked Brigid to sign a paper stating the loan, plus ten per cent needed to redeem the ring within thirty days.

'There are many pickpockets in Dublin. Watch out for small boys whose fingers are deft. I recommend you go to the bank around the corner and open a savings account. It is the safest way to protect yourself from thieves.'

Brigid thanked the pawnbroker, who, in English, said, 'You sure have much chutzpah, Missy.'

Brigid stepped over the doorway and set off for the bank, wondering what the strange word 'chutzpah' meant while the money burned a hole in her apron pocket. She hurried away from the pawnbroker's shop, her boots tapping a staccato beat on the cobbles. The bank, an imposing building, stood a short distance away. It had a bubble-glass window and a sturdy oak door with a bright brass knocker.

Brigid opened the creaky door and entered a beeswax-scented room where two dark green high-back chairs graced an empty grate. Opposite the chairs lay a polished wooden counter. The woman suddenly felt faint in this unfamiliar environment and sat on a chair, her heart thumping. Recovering her equilibrium, she calculated how much money to save.

An assistant in his mid-twenties with chestnut eyes and dark, lustrous hair came to the counter. He beamed at Brigid, and her heart fluttered violently. 'My name is McGrath. How can I assist you?' he spoke in lilted Irish English.

'I want to open a bank account, please,' she said, her stomach lurching as she crossed to the counter. 'I have money that I don't want pickpockets to steal.'

'A wise decision. How much money do you intend to deposit?'

Brigid's lower limbs trembled at his melodic tones, and she clung to the counter, her knuckles turning ivory.

'Are you unwell, Miss?' The gentleman lifted a hinged counter-piece 'I'll get you a drink of water.' He helped Brigid sit, rested the glass on a small table beside her, and sat on the other chair.

Brigid watched, awed, as he crossed one elegant leg over the other. She stilled her nerves by sipping the water, her eyes unwilling to meet his, and swallowed, her heart beating like the wings of a trapped bird.

'Sir, I wish to bank nine pounds and keep some money to spend as cash.'

'Please allow me to take your money and place it in our safe. I'll bring documents to sign and give you a receipt. I recommend you find a secure location to hide any cash you carry.' He smoothed his dark beard and gazed at Brigid with eyes so penetrating that she felt convinced she could see her bosom and cheeks burned.

Unbidden, a vision of Maura came to Brigid's mind. *Luke said Maura puts tips down her bosom, but that's not for me.* Brigid resolved to purchase a reticule resembling the ones she had noticed in the streets, carried by "ladies of quality." *Is it safe to trust him with my money?*

McGrath disappeared, his elegant strides making Brigid's heart flutter. Their meeting made Brigid's hands shake. The man brought a document and gave Brigid a copy. It stated how much money she had deposited and gave an account number. As Brigid signed her name as Brigid Murphy,' her head spun like a child's top. With an effort of will, she steadied her nerves, handing him the signed document with the warmest smile she could muster.

'You can take cash from your account anytime, Miss Murphy. Please keep this copy of our transaction and accept my card. Contact me if you need any further help.'

Brigid read his name, 'Niall McGrath, Bank of Ireland.' She stored the card and her cash in the handkerchief and put it back in her apron. McGrath escorted her to the door, and a tingle rushed up Brigid's arm as he held her hand to his lips. She left the bank with her heart racing, and she walked onwards as ethereal visions of McGrath's face flashed before her eyes. He had taken up residence in her mind like a cuckoo invading another bird's nest.

Brigid returned to Grafton Street and spied a cartographer's shop. She concluded walking further in this unfamiliar city without a map was unsafe, even if purchasing one cost precious money. Brigid needed to locate the dock area and learn about the regulations and costs of emigrating to England or America. After buying the map, she set off at a brisk pace until she reached a location where the odour of decaying fish assailed her nostrils, along with tangy air. It reminded her of the sea at Bessie's home.

She surveyed her surroundings and noticed sailors dressed in wide trousers and stained shirts ships unloading a ship. Beside the dock stood tall buildings of four or five floors with iron posts on the front. Brigid looked at the map and saw the word *warehouses* printed in the dock area at the River Liffey's entrance. She guessed they stored goods. Brigid noticed signs bearing business names, such as Cunliffe, Arbuthnot, and Company, printed on them too.

One ship, her sails rolled up, unloaded sacks with the words 'Produce of Barbados' stamped on the sacks. The sailors had dark skin and tight-curled hair, and they wore trousers but no shirts. After watching for a few minutes, curiosity overcame Brigid's strumming nerves, and she plucked up the courage to approach a sailor.

'What is in the sacks you carry?' said Brigid.

'Oh, Missy, you shouldna' speak to me. I jus' a cargo hand.' His deep, dark eyes darted around as his head swivelled, seeking, Brigid knew not what. ''Tis sugar from an isle in the Carib Sea.'

His rough accent differed from any she had heard before. Brigid had forgotten the location of the Carib Sea and wished she had her atlas. The man hefted a sack onto his head, his skin gleaming and muscles rippling as he moved to the warehouse, carrying the load. Brigid gazed at him, wondering how he carried such a load.

While the foreign sailor showed Brigid respect, other dock workers leered at her and shouted rudely. 'Pretty maids from the countryside like you are ripe plums.'

Brigid's mouth dried, and her poise disappeared at using such words. She quickly stepped along the dockside while her gut demanded they treat her kindly. Brigid's instinct urged thinking of emigrating, and she wondered where the passenger ships moored. The map showed them anchored far from the warehouses.

When Brigid reached the correct part of the docks, she found the ticket office, but the door did not open. A notice announced: *Ferryboats to Liverpool every day except Sunday from Dock 15 – third-class deck fare, three shillings. Enquire within for cabin fares.*

Brigid did not want her pockets picked and wondered what a cabin cost. The grimy window allowed her to see notices pinned to notice boards on the interior. However, they were too far to read, frustrating the girl.

A shaft of sunlight glinted on the water, a golden streak across the murky estuary, and she lifted her eyes to watch the dark clouds roll away. Soon, an intense sun shone above the murk, and Brigid's stomach groaned.

A hawker sold mutton pies from a stall on the quayside, and she bought one to eat in the shelter of a doorway, listening to the sea birds whirling overhead. Chains rattled in the distance, which, together with the dockworkers' shouts, created a hypnotic rhythm.

However, everything around her looked so different from Ballyconstór that she became homesick for green fields and even bogs. Brigid thought of Angela and Padraig. *Will I ever see them again*? Her eyes misted, for she had torched her bridges when she escaped Seamus. She could not go back.

After eating the pie, she wandered into a tenement area close to the docks. She had seen nowhere this dirty before. Claustrophobia enveloped her in the tightly packed streets, where decaying foodstuffs and other ordure lay on the cobbles.

Women wearing ragged and soiled shawls over dishevelled hair scurried around, their skirts' hems smeared with dirt. Children with runny noses and bare feet ran everywhere, yelling. Shocked to her core, Brigid hurried away. She had heard of similar places in Limerick and Cork. But tenements filled with destitute people in Dublin were unexpected. Brigid assumed the city's inhabitants would be affluent tradespeople and their like. She shuddered.

With the position of the sun well past its zenith, Brigid's feet protested they needed to rest. She spied a small grassy place with a bench and sat down, her eyelids drooping. The next thing she knew, a yapping dog snapped at her ankles. The animal's whiskered owner called the dog, bowed, and raised his hat.

Brigid's boots groaned at the mere idea of more steps as she got up to walk, but she needed lodgings for the night. She spoke to a cabby, who directed her to a street about fifteen minutes away. Exhausted, a headache developed while walking. She found the house with a 'Lodgings for Women' sign. At the green-painted door, a gleaming brass cat's face door knocker invited Brigid to knock.

A young woman wearing a starched apron over a dark-coloured dress answered. 'May I be of help?'

'I seek lodgings, and a cab driver sent me to this address.'

'Please wait here while I fetch Mrs O'Keefe.' The girl led Brigid into a narrow hallway, which smelled of a strange combination of fried food and beeswax-polished furniture.

The Landlady, who wore a high-necked dress and had a beaked nose, gave Brigid's appearance a candid appraisal with her eyebrows arched.

'I have one vacant room on the top floor of the house. Would you like to view it?' The woman sniffed with disdain.

Brigid nodded, perplexed by the woman's unwavering assessment. They climbed two sets of narrow stairs to the room, which contained a bed with an iron bedstead and patchwork coverlet, a press, and a high-backed chair with a side table. The room included a fireplace.

'I charge three shillings per week. The price includes a full breakfast and peat for your fire. I like my ladies to have a nourishing breakfast before they go to their workplace. We have a zinc bath and a privy in the yard. Next to godliness comes cleanliness; my ladies are quality, so they are.'

Her eyes roamed Brigid's face, descending upon the hair eluding her mob cap. Brigid grew uncomfortable with the woman's continued gimlet-eyed evaluation.

But despite the appraisal, Brigid saw she would be safe in the room. 'I'll take it, thank you.' She held out three shillings.

The woman snatched the money. 'I'll send Betsy to you with hot water and a towel.' She paused. 'Your pinched face suggests exhaustion. I will provide bread, cheese, and a glass of buttermilk for an extra three pence tonight.'

Brigid gave her the change from her dinnertime pie.

'We serve breakfast from six forty-five, following the gong that sounds at six-thirty.' Mrs O'Keefe turned on her heel and shut the door.

Brigid surveyed the room and opened the press drawers. They contained nothing but a 'penny dreadful' book. Then, a knock on the door announced the maid's arrival with water, soap, a towel, and a worn hairbrush. The latter sent Brigid's eyebrows up her forehead. *She thinks I need to brush my hair. The cheek. She must believe from my appearance I'm not a lady of quality.*

'I'll bring your food next. Mrs O'Keefe gave me this key for you,' said the housemaid, 'It unlocks the front entrance. However, she bolts the door at ten on weekdays and eleven on weekends.' The girl curtsied and left, returning with the food a few minutes later.

Brigid locked the door following the housemaid's exit and washed her hands and face. She felt embarrassed by her work-roughened hands and her scuffed old boots, which Mrs O'Keefe must have seen. While eating her meal, Brigid heard boots on the stairs. The ladies of quality had returned for the evening. Still, Brigid felt too exhausted to greet them. So, undressing, she climbed under the crisp sheets with the penny dreadful book, but it slipped from her hand, and she fell fast asleep.

CHAPTER 7: EMPLOYMENT

Brigid awoke to the sound of the gong, sunlight streaming through the window and lighting up dust motes in the air. She climbed out of bed and dressed as quickly as possible, brushing her hair, and replacing the mob cap, which, to her annoyance, bore specks of soot. Brigid hurried down the stairs behind an older woman. She entered a spacious dining room with a mahogany table set for five people. The older woman sat at the head of the table. Three more girls arrived, and one with blonde hair, a rosebud mouth, and a snub nose sat opposite Brigid.

'Hello, I'm Amy; you must be the new girl. My friends are Irene, Aoife, and Jenny, and I presume you have met Saoirse.' She inclined her head to the older woman.

Brigid nodded as Betsy entered the room and said, 'Oatmeal is heating in the range, and Mrs O'Keefe can cook a full Irish fry-up if you prefer. The eggs are fresh this morning.' She placed a jug of buttermilk on the table.

Amy said, 'Have the full Irish. Mrs O'Keefe is a grand cook.'

Brigid nodded her agreement to the housemaid as the odour of frying eggs and bacon sent a shiver down her back.

'Where do you work? We work at Clery's store on Grafton Street,' said Amy.

Brigid did not intend to disclose her emigration plans. 'I don't have a job yet. I used to be a housekeeper for a farmer, but he died. I thought I would try a city job for a change.' Brigid wanted the explanation to cover her work-roughened hands.

'Are you able to read and write?' asked Saoirse.

'Yes, in both English and Gaelic. I'm used to writing letters to shopkeepers and animal feed merchants and keeping accounts.'

Brigid's face reddened as she recalled Seamus's lack of literacy, and she bowed her head.

'Well, if you come with us this morning, I'll assess you for our unexpected vacancy.'

'It is office work. You don't meet the customers to chat with like us.' Amy pursed her mouth.

Breakfast arrived, and Brigid hid her unease at such questions by spreading her starched linen napkin across her knees, ready to eat as Ma had taught her.

Amy leaned forward and whispered in Gaelic, 'Clery's dismissed Finola in disgrace, and we heard her family disowned her. Her lover is married, so her family sends her to a Magdalene laundry. They are terrible places run by nuns who take the babies and hand them over to wealthy people.'

Brigid recalled a girl in Ballyconstór. Father Byrne arranged for the child to be placed with a wealthy couple. *The child's mother hung herself,* she recollected as her shoulder muscles tensed.

At Clery's store, Saoirse asked Brigid to read correspondence aloud and write responses in her handwriting, one in English and one in Gaelic. Saoirse then asked Brigid to calculate columns of figures. She scored full marks on everything.

'Whoever taught you did an excellent job,' Saoirse said. 'The post is yours, and you can start tomorrow if you wish. But you need some new clothes, my dear. Let me take you to the ladies' clothing department; they will help you choose suitable attire. Your wages are ten shillings a week, and Clery's also provides staff discounts on many products. We'll deduct the clothing costs from this week's wages if you wish. Is that satisfactory?'

Brigid's eyes shone. 'Yes, thank you.' She paused for a moment. 'My mother taught me the basics of reading, writing, and arithmetic. She said they would be useful skills one day.' Tears clouded her eyes.

Saoirse took her arm and introduced her to the two other staff members in the office. She showed Brigid an empty desk with a large blotter, two pens, and an inkwell.

'You'll work from here, Miss Murphy, and please remember to call me Miss O'Leary in the office. We allow two ten-minute comfort breaks in the day and an hour for your dinner at noon. The other girls in our lodgings go to a public house, where they use the snug. Shall we go down and get your clothes now?'

Brigid nodded and bought two plain day dresses, one dark blue and the other grey, a set of corsets, and two pairs of stockings. On impulse, she added a nightdress and a flower-sprigged muslin dress. Brigid then remembered her scuffed and worn-at-the-heel boots. So, leaving her packages with the shop assistant, she counted how much money she had left. The girl considered purchasing a small alarm clock she had spotted on the pawnbroker's display. *I'd rather not depend on a brass going to wake me up in the morning.*

Despite her breakfast, Brigid felt hungry, so she bought a pie from a street hawker and found a bench under the shade of a leafy sycamore tree in a small grassy park. Munching, she pondered what to do next and decided she would explore Dublin Castle.

Brigid toured the place and afterwards sat on a bench beside the walls. Turning her gaze to the sky, she saw the sun sink towards the horizon.

She retraced her steps to the pawnbroker's and opened the door to find McGrath talking to the owner. She stood back, her heart hammering when McGrath turned round.

'Why, it is Miss Murphy. How nice to see you. I trust you have recovered from yesterday's indisposition.'

'What can I help you with today?' said the pawnbroker.

'I saw a small clock yesterday. What do you want for it?'

The pawnbroker pointed to a display cabinet. 'Show me the one you like.' Brigid pointed. 'Four shillings,' the pawnbroker said.

'Half a crown, sir. Look, it has a cracked face.'

He grinned, 'You win, Missy,' and he opened the cabinet and took out the clock. Turning to McGrath with a sardonic grin, he said, 'She is a barterer, so she is. She won't tolerate any wrongdoing.'

McGrath gazed at Brigid, who handed over her half-crown, thinking the two men did not know her dealings with rent collectors. She had spent most of the cash she carried on her person with the remaining amount hidden under her mattress. *Time to return to my lodgings.* Brigid picked up the clock and curtsied, ready to leave the shop.

McGrath said, 'I can tell you are a resourceful young woman. Please let me escort you home.'

Brigid felt bewildered by such directness. 'I, er, have parcels to collect from Clery's, sir.'

'More reason to escort you, as I can carry your parcels. I assure you my intentions are honourable.'

Brigid agreed with some trepidation. But after collecting the cumbersome parcels, she felt relieved that she would not struggle to carry them alone.

As they walked, McGrath enquired again about her health after her indisposition the previous morning. Brigid assured him tiredness had afflicted her and did not elaborate. She smelled some unusual and pleasant odour in him but dared not ask about it. Instead, Brigid enquired about his job at the bank. She learned he had worked there since finishing his Trinity College studies. He had become the branch's Assistant Manager six months ago. Brigid related the abridged story and her fortune in getting a new post.

Brigid felt relieved on arrival at her lodgings, as the conversation had become too intimate. Having forgotten her key. She rapped the brass knocker, and the housemaid answered.

'Please hand the parcels to Betsy, Mr McGrath, and thank you for your help.' Brigid curtsied to him.

'Thanks for the pleasure of your company, Miss Murphy. We'll meet again, I'm sure.'

He bowed and kissed her hand, sending tingles up Brigid's arm. As he walked on to his lodgings, his steps on the cobbles rang a melody in Brigid's ears.

'He is a bit of all-right, Miss,' said Betsy. 'By the look on his face as he kissed your hand, you have caught his fancy.'

'Mind your own business, Betsy,' Brigid said, flustered, and turned, ready to ascend the staircase.

'Oh, it is you, Miss Murphy.' Mrs O'Keefe came out from her parlour before Brigid had climbed one step. 'I'm not used to my ladies coming home this early.' She paused, beckoning the hovering housemaid. 'Betsy, please take Miss Murphy's parcels to her room.'

Mrs O'Keefe regarded Brigid, placing a monocle on her gimlet eye. 'Have you obtained the job I heard Saoirse mention to you?'

Brigid nodded, thinking Mrs O'Keefe to be nosy. *Will she put up the rent?* After climbing the stairs, the woman closed the door and checked her room for signs of intrusion. She resolved not to leave anything in view that might identify her.

She opened the press drawers and put away her new clothes. After washing her hands and face, Brigid read the penny dreadful and became engrossed in a ghost story. Time passed until the stomp of feet and the chatter of voices disturbed Brigid's concentration and prevented her mind from entering a spooky castle. One voice shouted outside her room, jolting her.

'Please join us for supper, Brigid. We have fresh bread.'

'I had a mutton pie for dinner, but I ate it some hours ago. Your meal sounds appetising.'

'Ah, for sure, 'tis no bother, Brigid.' Amy ran down the stairs, her blonde hair escaping its pins and her skirts flying. Shaking her head at the sight, Brigid thought about how young and innocent Amy appeared. *She runs, but not from a disgusting, smelly beast.*

The tasty and filling meal of fresh bread with Kerry butter and scrumptious Irish cheddar cheese. A jar of pickled onions stood on the table beside some tomato chutney. Brigid thought the food an extravagance.

Saoirse made a pot of Indian tea. 'I get tea at cost as an employee benefit.'

Brigid had never tasted the drink and felt wary of its strange colour, which reminded her of peat water from the bog. But it tasted pleasant and smooth with milk and sugar added, and she drank a second cup. Judging by the other girls' youthful appearance, Brigid speculated they were around eighteen. Her eyes misted with memories.

Saoirse broke her reverie. 'You have come from the countryside, I believe.' Her gaze penetrated Brigid's core, and the girl's hands shook as she set her cup on the table.

Perhaps sensing her new friend's discomfort, Amy replied for her, outlining Brigid's words at breakfast. Saoirse nodded, but her intense gaze caused Brigid to blush. *Saoirse suspects there is more to my story than I'm prepared to reveal.* But when Saoirse's gaze softened, and she asked no further questions, Brigid's anxious spirit calmed.

The girls chatted about their families, and Brigid responded with care. 'I have a married sister and an older brother.' She did not mention the brothers she had lost, but Saoirse's eyebrows rose, and her lips pursed. *I am right. She knows I'm holding something back,* thought Brigid, who escaped to her as soon as possible.

She found the flower-speckled curtains drawn, and the coverlet turned back. Betsy had been in the room. But Brigid had the foresight to put her cash in her skirt pocket. She thought Betsy to be very nosy and said she would turn down her bedcovers at night.

Exhausted by the day's experiences, she undressed. Then she remembered her baptismal certificate still in her apron pocket. Removing and unfolding it, Brigid gasped at the name Brigid Pope on the document. *Feck, who is she? Did Father O'Malley give Da the wrong certificate?*

Brigid's eyes scanned the room, wary of any potential threat, but knowing her father's inability to read offered a sense of security. *But Ma must have read it.* Puzzled, Brigid studied the faded scrawl and concluded she could alter it at work. The certificate proved her identity. *I'll need it when I emigrate, even if I use the name of Murphy in Dublin.*

Sighing at the incompetence of drunken priests, Brigid put the certificate under her corset in the press. She sat reading the ghost story until the light faded, then closed her book and pulled back the curtains to let in the moonlight. The moon's waxing presence comforted her as it had in Ballyconstór. She nestled into the feather mattress and did not wake until the front door slammed in the morning.

Brigid woke from a dream about Da and Seamus. She carried such damning secrets she feared. *Something or someone will catch me out,* she thought. Brigid lacked a feeling of security while alone in the house.

Brigid fetched the tin bath, filled the tub with hot water from the stove, and washed her body and hair with lavender soap. Unlike the rough shards Brigid had been used to, the soap created bubbles. In the sensual, warm water, Brigid glimpsed Mr McGrath's face with his haunting chestnut eyes and shivered despite the warmth.

Brigid had reached her room wrapped in a new towel just as the front door swung open, and the chatter of girlish voices travelled up the stairs. She checked the clock and noted the girls had been out for forty-five minutes. *Services at Ballyconstór took an hour or more if Father Byrne's sermon droned on.*

Amy rapped on her door. 'You missed a grand sermon, all about the sins of the flesh.' She spoke through the keyhole. 'Father Joyce goes on about it, but people sin anyway. He has long lines at the confessional.' She bounded along the corridor to her room.

Amy's loud footsteps caused Brigid to think. *Bounding away like that, your hair will escape its pins, so it will,*

After a light breakfast of toast and jam and a brief rest in Mrs O'Keefe's parlour, the girls prepared the food for dinner.

'Why didn't you attend Mass with us?' Amy's brow wrinkled.

Brigid had expected this question and gave the close-to-the-truth answer. she had rehearsed while bathing. 'I have lost my faith, and attending Church will make me a hypocrite.'

The girls exchanged glances so full of Catholic guilt that Brigid felt their censure. But it did not disrupt her composure. However, she chafed on Monday when a warm sun shone all day.

The atmosphere in Clery's office felt stuffy for a girl used to sweet-smelling meadow grass. She yearned for the fields around Ballyconstór.

After the girls reached their lodgings that evening, Brigid said to Amy, 'The weather is perfect for a walk to the River Liffey after a sweaty day in the office. I like fresh air.'

Amy's face clouded. 'It isn't recommended for a woman to venture to the dock area alone. Shall I come with you?'

From her voice, Brigid deduced Amy had no wish to walk there, so she declined her offer. 'I'll keep to the busy paths. But I intend to walk whenever the weather is fine.'

Brigid preferred Amy to remain unaware of her intention to visit the ticket offices. Brigid slipped out of the front door when the girl went to the privy. A sea breeze had blown up and gusted around Brigid's skirt, with the walk refreshing her office-jaded senses and salty air tingling in her nostrils. But a shuttered ticket office left Brigid frustrated again.

She spotted a woman wearing tatters of clothing and her four ill-clad children waiting nearby. Something about the woman brought memories of Ma. *Is it the way she holds a baby to her breast?* Brigid blinked back tears and addressed the woman in Gaelic.

'Excuse me. Is a boat due soon? You look ready to sail.'

'We're waitin' to catch the midnight ferry to Liverpool.' The woman cradled her youngest child at her breast and gestured her disapproval to her young son. 'Feckin' hell, Jimmy, will you stop scratchin'.' She faced Brigid again. 'To be sure, we slept in a boarding 'ouse last night, but the mattress had fleas. We ain't spending another night there.'

Brigid spotted the telltale red welts on her neck as the woman shifted the baby to her other breast. 'Jenny, stop scratchin' your head too.'

Her daughter's tousled red hair had white flecks that moved, and Brigid would bet sixpence the child had not caught them in the boarding house. Thin and pale, the children looked hungry. Touched by their evident plight, Brigid's heart melted.

'Missus, you can't leave without feeding the children. Please buy them a pie for their supper. A woman sells them at her stall less than a quarter of a mile from here.' Brigid gave her a shilling, thinking *how virtuous it feels to help someone less fortunate than me.*

The woman smiled, showing several broken teeth. 'That is right, kind of you. We have not eaten since yesterday. We are joining my husband, who is working down a pit in Lancashire. Got us brick-built row house, not a sod 'ouse like we had in Limerick.'

The woman's dark eyes glittered in the evening sunlight as she fixed Brigid with a piercing gaze. 'You going to England too?'

'Not tonight, but in a few weeks. Can I ask where you'll sleep on the boat?'

'On the deck. The cabins are scarce and kept for the gentry. The man in the office claims they are dreadful pricey.'

The woman coughed and spat on the ground. Her sputum

had flecks of red in it, and Brigid's blood ran cold.

After wishing the woman luck, Brigid walked onwards until she had turned a corner. Then Brigid ran the remaining distance home and hurried to her room. In its safety, she splashed water on her arms and cheeks. She sat in her fireside chair until tranquillity restored her equilibrium.

Later, under the bedclothes, with her mother's dying face before her, Brigid sobbed into the pillow. She turned and stared at the moon, seeking his benevolent comfort. But the man remained hidden behind clouds. Brigid lay back on her pillow as grief overwhelmed her, and she wept again.

CHAPTER 8: SAOR-ÉIRE (FREE IRELAND)

Brigid found her new job and friends' company fulfilling. Opting not to emigrate, she stayed in Dublin for a few months because of her comfortable lodgings and income. *The stationmaster would tell Da and Seamus that I took the train to Dublin if they were looking for me. But I hope Padraig will tell Da he has had word of my emigration.*

The girls attended Irish dancing in Sweeney's each Saturday night and invited Brigid to join them. After much persuasion from Amy and Irene, Amy bought a green skirt and cream blouse and accompanied the girls. After a couple of weeks, her clumsy steps, which had amused Martin, improved under Amy's tutelage. One sultry night in late August, she sat alone at the table while studying unfamiliar dance steps.

'Miss Murphy, how delightful to see you. I note you sit alone. Will you permit me to join you?' From a position behind her, a male voice spoke in Gaelic, expressing delight.

Brigid recognised the voice. 'Hello, Mr McGrath. I apologise, but I'm not a skilled dancer, so I prefer to watch and imitate the steps in private. But please sit down.'

'I'm sure a pretty girl like you can dance with an experienced partner.' His dark eyes searched her face. 'May I buy you another drink?' His voice sounded soft.

Brigid trembled. 'A glass of water, please.'

'The warm weather brings many people out.' McGrath left her to collect the drink. He returned, saying, 'I have seen you here before. Amy's brother is a friend.'

Brigid's throat constricted as he spoke. She sipped the water to ease it while she studied his appearance. He wore more casual clothing than in their first meeting. But his eyes, face, and athletic body had Brigid's senses reeling. When he spoke next, a flutter of butterflies assailed her stomach.

'Your gorgeous green eyes enchant me,' he said as his chestnut eyes burned with passion.

Amy left the dance floor and spoke. 'Hello, Niall. I did not know you two had met. Come and dance with us.'

Brigid, her cheeks hot, resisted. Her upside-down emotions disturbed her equilibrium. *Such feelings will affect my concentration on the dance steps,* she thought as her confidence faded.

'Amy, I'm too tired. I'll leave while it is light enough to walk home,' Brigid said, her spirit suddenly uncomfortable in the hot room.

'Let me escort you,' McGrath picked up her shawl from the floor.

This request sent Brigid's emotions whirling to the heavens, and she experienced dizziness. But despite her spinning emotions, Brigid knew walking home alone would be challenging. So, with reluctance, she thanked McGrath and let him escort her.

The sky sparkled with starlight, and a full moon brightened the night. They walked in spellbound silence, with Brigid enveloped in warm summer air until McGrath broke the spell. 'Miss Murphy, may I call you by your Christian name, please? The charming name makes me think of bridges over the river.'

Brigid said he could use it, providing he allowed her to reciprocate. Niall then grabbed her hand and tucked it into the crook of his arm.

'Brigid, what is your opinion of Home Rule for Ireland?'

The question took Brigid aback as her heart fluttered at his touch. She pondered her response. 'I never gave it much thought before. Why do you ask?'

'A small group in Dublin has started a local home rule movement called Saor-Éire, Free Ireland. It aims to free our land from English control. I'm a member, and so are Amy and her brother.'

The news of Amy's involvement left Brigid astonished and gasping. 'Amy is a member?' Her tone sounded dubious.

When they reached her lodgings, Brigid removed her arm from Niall's and rubbed her palms together. 'Thank you for walking me home, er, Niall.'

Brigid's heart began thumping as Niall took her right hand, his dark eyes gleaming in the moonlight, and kissed it.

'May I escort you for a stroll in the park tomorrow? I'll collect you at three o'clock.'

Brigid nodded spellbound, her tongue tied in knots like used string.

'Thank you. I'll look forward to more conversation. Goodnight, extraordinary girl.' He raised his tall hat and walked away, whistling.

Brigid stared after him, mesmerised. She stood before the door, thinking of those eyes until a gust of wind blew. Then, coming to her senses as the door knocker gleamed in the moonlight, she fumbled for her key.

The house hallway contained two candles on a small table. Their flickering flames mimicked her pulse. In a stupor, Brigid carried one candle to her room. *I'm an eejit agreeing to go for a walk with an unfamiliar man. It isn't done.* She shook her bemused head. Yet his eyes continued to bewitch her, and her dreams became populated by strange men who danced jigs.

The next day, over breakfast, Brigid asked Amy to explain more about Saor-Éire. 'Mr McGrath mentioned you belong to it.'

Amy touched her finger to her lips and then mouthed, 'In my room.' There, she outlined the movement's purpose, leaving Brigid thinking about English landlords and their goals. *Amy, a city girl, can't comprehend the obligations of an*

English lord on tenant farmers.

At three o'clock, Brigid, dressed in her sprigged muslin dress and a bonnet, waited for the housemaid to answer the door. After exchanging pleasantries about the fine weather and other inconsequential subjects, Niall took her arm. Brigid spoke little, awed by the fine ladies wearing big-brimmed hats and carrying parasols.

The sultry air caused Brigid's corset to stick to her sweating back. She smiled with relief when Niall suggested they rest on a bench under an oak tree. Brigid placed both hands in her lap.

'Tell me about Saor-Éire, please. Amy has told me something about it, but I'm interested in learning more.'

Niall wiped his perspiring brow with a white handkerchief. 'I joined three years ago, a year after Stephen, who learned about it from his father, Robert, its security officer, whose day job is a police inspector.'

Brigid's body trembled. *Has Amy been spying on me,* she thought. *There must be far more information of which I'm unaware. Can I trust this strange man?*

Niall continued speaking. 'Unhappy at college, Amy's brother Stephen dropped out after a year to work in a solicitor's office and spend more time with Saor-Éire. However, we both got to know the organisation's leader, Finnbar Hayes, whose charisma awed Stephen.' Niall paused, his eyes flirting with Brigid's, who lowered hers. 'Amy recommends you join us and oversee our accounts.'

Astonished, Brigid fiddled with her reticule. 'Since Amy is a friend, I'll attend a meeting to see if it is a suitable organisation to join.'

Brigid dropped her head, not wanting Niall to hold her eyes longer. *I would walk barefoot on burning peat embers for a man whose dark eyes gleam with such evident passion.*

'Brigid, our movement is so secret that we can't allow people.to observe full meetings. Come with Amy to the coffee house tomorrow evening for an informal meeting. I'll ask our leader to join us.' He paused and touched the sweat on his brow. 'I forget my manners. The sun is so scorching; I'll buy us each an ice cream to eat.'

Brigid nodded her assent, wondering what ice cream tasted like. Niall vanished for some minutes, and Brigid untangled her confused feelings for the man. She had acknowledged Martin and Luke's attentiveness, but neither made her senses reel like Niall. He returned with two tubs of ice cream. The smooth taste soothed the fluttering in Brigid's stomach, leaving a new flavour lingering on her tongue.

Afterwards, they took another turn around the park. Stopping near the gates, Niall said, 'It's too hot to walk further, so I'll pay for a cab to take you back to your lodgings.' Before Brigid could protest, he had hailed one. 'Twenty-six Belmont Street, please, cabby.'

He helped Brigid into the dark interior, which smelt of tanned leather. As they sat down, Niall gazed at her again. Embarrassed by his directness, Brigid blushed, staring at her fingers intertwined in her lap, her body tingling. Brigid thanked him for his company when the cab stopped and prepared to climb out. Niall offered his hand to help her, and her arm tingled at his touch. He asked permission to take her to the park again the following Sunday, and Brigid agreed. She crossed the cobbled path, her stomach performing cartwheels.

'Please join Amy at the coffee house tomorrow evening,' Niall said as the cab drew away.

Coffee house. Where is that? From nowhere, Brigid had strange tugging sensations in her lower regions. She had never experienced such intense feelings before. *Whatever causes them? They embarrass me.*

On their way to work the next day, Brigid asked Amy about the coffee house. Amy explained she met Stephen there on a Monday, sometimes with other Saor-Éire members. Tomorrow, she would meet Stephen, Niall, and the movement's leader, Finnbar. 'They are dying to meet you, so please come,' said Amy.

Brigid rode with Amy to the coffee house in a cab that hot evening. Outside, three men waited, chatting. After alighting from the cab, Brigid scrutinised the two men beside Niall. Amy's brother looked like his sister. The older man had dark, untidy hair, a beard, and a brooding look. Brigid guessed the man to be Finnbar.

As Amy introduced him, he stared unsmiling at Brigid, ignored social etiquette, and did not speak. Stephen, a perfect gentleman, asked about Brigid's health and thanked her for coming. Finnbar still didn't say a word.

He is the most pompous, rude man I have ever met. It's worse even than the rent collector. Brigid's stomach clenched at the thought.

Once seated in a booth with their coffee, Finnbar explained the movement's aims and asked Brigid where she had learned her accounting skills. She told the lie she had told before about the farmer's accounts, which caused her heart to beat like a caged canary.

However, to Brigid's astonishment, Niall took her hand as if he sensed her discomfort, and shivers went through her arm. Amy praised Brigid's accounting skills, and in no time, she agreed to join the organisation at its meeting at Sweeney's in ten days.

On Sunday, Niall took Brigid back to the park, where they listened to a band playing popular music and ate ice cream again. Brigid felt absolute bliss in his company, as if no one else existed but him.

Many people gathered in Sweeney's on the appointed day, where Stephen welcomed Brigid. Niall appeared and took her hand, leading her to a vacant seat at the front of the gathering. Tingling passed through her fingers at his touch, and she couldn't focus on her surroundings until Finnbar spoke, his mesmerising eyes and penetrating stare silencing the chattering audience.

Brigid listened spellbound as he chatted about his recent travels to County Mayo and how people with low or no incomes experienced oppression. His words resonated as Brigid recalled Luke's experiences. She lowered her head lest Niall saw the blush of secrets creep up her cheeks.

Finnbar's deep voice attracted his audience's attention. 'Friends, we must recruit more members for our cause.' His eyes raked his audience. Then, turning to a broody-looking, spotty youth, Finnbar bade him stand. 'Do you wish to join Connor?'

Frog-like, the boy croaked, 'Yes, sir.' Finbarr swore him into Saor-Éire as the organisation's messenger.

Next, he turned to Brigid, who repeated her oath in a trance. Afterwards, Niall clasped her arm and helped her sit. The audience applauded as Finnbar welcomed the new members. Brigid had joined a Fenian organisation, which she had not known existed until a few days ago. The entire experience seemed unreal. *I must accept the discomfort of membership in a Fenian organisation.* Her heart fluttered at the thought. *What would Padraig say?*

In her heart, Brigid knew the answer.

CHAPTER 9: COURTSHIP

Niall escorted Brigid to the park most Sundays that autumn and met with her, Amy, and Stephen at the coffee house. Brigid grew to like her appearance since Niall praised her so much, telling her that her green eyes were the most beautiful he had ever seen.

They found a mutual appreciation of novels and poetry. Niall enjoyed the works of Charles Dickens and Edgar Allen Poe. They shared an interest in geography, too. Brigid mentioned her childhood atlas and described the ship she saw unloading on the docks. Their conversations stimulated her awakening mind.

At Sweeney's, Niall encouraged her to dance, and when the fiddler played soft music, Niall placed his arm around her waist. As they danced, Brigid had a sudden surge of inspiration.

'Is the fiddler also the pawnbroker I saw you with when I bought a clock?'

'Yes, he belongs to Saor-Éire.' I needed to speak with him, so I visited his shop.'

'His accent is strange. Where is he from?'

'Ezra comes from Poland. Where Jewish people like him experience oppression. He fled after being involved in an insurrection against population cleansing pogroms and is helpful to Saor-Éire because he can enter areas of Dublin in which native Irish can't for fear of arrest by the British.'

Brigid's whirling emotions refused to be still, and soon, she lived for Niall's touch and the passion in his eyes. She wanted him to kiss her lips and caress her body and found the emotions and sensations he provoked in her disturbing.

One sunny Sunday, Niall took her for a picnic by the sea. They enjoyed walking along the shore, at ease in each other's company. He brought oysters and a bottle of elderflower wine, and her taste buds tingled with the delightful new flavours. She longed for his lips that day, but though he came close, he did not kiss her: a perfect gentleman. He grasped her hand in the cab back to Belmont Street and kissed it as she left the vehicle. Brigid knew then she was in love like Elizabeth in Austin's *Pride and Prejudice*.

On Monday, Brigid struggled to concentrate on her work. In her mind, she traced the outline of Niall's lips, the dimple in his chin, those dark eyes and whiskers that had brushed her face in the swaying cab. Brigid knew she blushed, remembering his firm body's outline against hers while dancing, causing those strange sensations in her nether regions.

To her annoyance, Brigid had difficulty concentrating on the ledgers and had to recalculate the figures. But dinner time came, and she found Amy waiting for her at the store's staff entrance, and the two women walked arm in arm to Sweeney's.

Amy had become a firm friend and had explained her job at Clery's as a ploy to draw spies' attention from her father's role with Saor-Éire.

'I enjoy the freedom from parental control and the opportunity to earn my money.' To Brigid's surprise, she gave her age as twenty-two. 'Stephen is my big brother, and we're close. Niall is his best friend.'

Something in her tone caused Brigid to question whether she concealed a critical fact:

'My mother wants me to get married, but I have not found the right man yet, and I'm enjoying my freedom too much to settle down. A husband would not let me dance at Sweeney's and would forbid my membership of Saor-Éire unless he became a member, too. Can you see me married to gloomy Finnbar or spotty Connor?'

Brigid stifled her giggles lest Saoirse, walking behind them, heard.

'Stephen believes Niall is smitten with you. He speaks of little else, praising your skills, eyes, and glorious hair.'

'Don't be silly. We are friends, which is all.' Brigid cast her gaze downward.

Amy challenged Brigid to say it to her face, and Brigid blushed. But upon reaching their lodgings, to Brigid's relief, Betsy opened the door. Brigid rushed to her room, bolted the door, and flung herself on her bed. *Is Amy, right?*

Trying not to think about it, Brigid developed a raging headache while trying to calculate the ledger columns and hold back visions of Niall simultaneously. So, at Mrs O'Keefe's, she lay down to rest at seven o'clock with a vinegar cloth on her forehead instead of visiting the coffee house.

On Tuesday, Brigid intently recalculated Monday's errors and did not hear Amy's whispered call from the office doorway.

Brigid's colleague tapped her on the shoulder. 'Miss Murphy, a girl at the door is trying to attract your attention.'

Brigid turned, astonished. 'Oh, it's Amy from Haberdashery. I wonder what she wants. Please watch for Miss O'Leary while I speak with her.'

Amy said, 'I have a note for you. Niall came in and gave it to me this morning. Last night, his eyes looked so sad without you beside him. He wishes you better health today.'

Brigid took the note, and a blush suffused her face. 'Niall has invited me to dine with him at The Three Peacocks restaurant next Saturday.' She paused and studied Amy's expectant expression. 'I can't go somewhere the gentry frequent. I have nothing suitable to wear.'

'Don't worry, my friend Irene will help you find something. But I need your answer. I'm supposed to be on a comfort break. Stephen is meeting me at dinner time for your reply.'

Brigid hesitated, then heard the unmistakable click of Miss

O'Leary's heels in the outer office. 'I'll accept the invitation if you promise to find me a dress.'

Amy nodded and dashed off. Brigid sat at her desk just before her superior entered the room, her blood pounding in her ears. She wondered why Niall had invited her to such a classy establishment. But under Miss O'Leary's eagle eyes, Brigid concentrated on the ledger. She tried her hardest to banish thoughts of Niall, hoping she would not develop another headache.

The week passed with agonising slowness. On Thursday, Amy came home in a cab. She had two gorgeous dresses in her arms. Brigid gasped, and her stomach tightened.

'Amy, I don't have the money to buy one of those dresses. They must cost the earth.'

'Shush, the frocks cost nothing. I have them on approval. My being a policeman's daughter has its advantages. I told the supervisor I must attend an important dinner with my father on Saturday and needed to choose between the dresses at home. Luckily, we are about the same size. Let us try them on later. Irene has brought some fresh bread, and I'm famished.'

'You sure are a practised liar,' Brigid said as Amy laid the dresses on the bed. 'You'll go to confession on Sunday, won't you?'

Amy blushed, batting her eyelids at Brigid.

After supper, Brigid tried on both dresses. A red frock with a low-cut bodice fitted to the waist and a broad, hooped skirt fitted her, but she preferred the other. Sewed from emerald velvet fabric, it had a neckline adorned by lace and stylish puffed sleeves. Though the first dress fitted well, it showed too much cleavage.

'I must lace my corset tight to fit in the green dress,' she said, gasping.

'I'll loan you my finest corset, which laces up extra tight.

You can borrow my best accessories, too.'

Brigid slipped on Amy's pumps, but the shoes squashed

the big toes. Her brow puckered with disappointment.

'You'll be fine; you don't have to walk far. Niall has arranged a cab to collect you at seven-thirty. I'll style your hair into a bun and fasten it with a green ribbon. You look beautiful, Brigid. The green colour sets off your rich auburn hair. It is so lovely and thick, not pump water like mine.' Amy pulled a mock grimace, and Brigid blushed.

On Friday, Brigid bathed, rinsing her hair with beer, as Angela used to do. The girls practised tying Brigid's hair, with Amy pulling out a few curly tendrils to frame her face. 'Wonderful. Where did you learn to use beer?

'My sister used to do it sometimes, making her hair shine. She married years ago and moved. It has been a while since I last saw her.' Brigid felt the conversation about her background had become too close for comfort. 'I'm tired, Amy. It's time I went to bed. Thank you for everything. You are a treasured friend.' Brigid kissed her friend's cheek.

On Saturday, the customers clamoured into the store, and Amy missed her lunch break. Brigid took Amy's and her wage envelopes and put them in her reticule when she had filled them out. She hailed a cab when the whistle sounded at the end of the workday and gave Amy her wage packet.

At home, Brigid had sixty minutes to get ready. Amy laced her corset until the dress fitted, though Brigid could barely breathe. 'I have some lavender water you can wear.' Amy took a glass bottle, tipped it up, and put some of the water behind Brigid's ears and on her wrists.

Then she appraised her friend. 'Hmm, don't turn around yet. I'll lend you my twenty-first birthday pearl necklace with the ivory centrepiece of the Queen's head.' She removed a box from her press and placed the necklace around Brigid's throat. 'There, now look in the mirror.'

Brigid gasped at her image. 'That isn't me. It is some fashionable gentlewoman.'

'Yes, it is, and you look like a gentlewoman. You have a

natural regal bearing, and it will bowl Niall over.' She paused, tucked a stray hair into the bun, and handed Brigid an ivory shawl. 'Don't hurry downstairs when he knocks. Let Betsy call you. A gentlewoman mustn't appear too eager.'

Brigid smiled, recalling Ma teaching her the same thing, making her walk tall and balancing a book on her head. She gazed at her image again, remembering when she had wished for a fairy to change her locks and her eyes had misted. Brigid's heart rate leapt when the door knocker banged thrice, and red suffused her cheeks.

Betsy's awed voice called out, 'A gentleman caller is waiting for Miss Murphy.'

'I've put your door key in your reticule. Slow steps are best in tight pumps. Then they don't hurt, trust me.' Amy smiled, pinching Brigid's cheeks to brighten them again.

Amy guided her friend out of her room, and Brigid descended gracefully. Niall stood in the hallway holding an enormous bouquet of red roses; the sight of them took from her squeezed lungs what little breath the corset allowed. Brigid curtsied and accepted the flowers. She buried her nose in the fragrance, remembering Ma's bower and her eyes grew misty.

Amy stood behind Brigid, whispering, 'Say thank you.'

'Thank you, Niall, the roses are beautiful. I'll give them to Amy to arrange.'

Amy guided her friend out of the door with a gentle nudge from her elbow. Niall's appearance set Brigid's pulse racing, and her tongue felt like shoe leather. Fresh shaven, with his hair trimmed, he wore an elegant dark evening suit and a cream waistcoat with shiny buttons. Guiding Brigid down the steps and along the short path, he helped her into the waiting cab. In the dark interior, an invisible thread pulled their gazes together.

When the cabby pulled up his horse, Niall helped Brigid get out as another cab drew up. Brigid gasped when an elegant woman in her mid-thirties wearing a midnight blue dress with her smooth dark hair parted in the middle climbed out, followed by a man donning a top hat and holding a silver cane. Despite Amy's efforts, Brigid felt like a fish fresh caught from the lough.

Niall held her arm in his, patted her hand, and escorted her into a busy restaurant decorated with green and gold wallpaper and matching curtains; a soft, deep-pile dark green carpet on the floor cushioned her toes.

A waiter welcomed them, led the pair to a white cloth-covered candlelit table, and handed them menu cards.

'I'll give you time to read the menu before taking your orders. The restaurant is busy tonight.' The waiter had a strange, nasal accent.

Brigid observed the other customers, and the highbrow English spoken in the general hubbub alarmed her. The woman thanked her Ma for insisting on teaching English and social etiquette. She gathered her senses, waiting for her pulse to slow and enable her to read the menu, but she didn't understand the words.

'You choose for me, please, Niall.'

Niall's face clouded. 'The menu is in French. My apologies. I ought to have requested one in English.'

When the waiter returned, Niall chose leek soup, liver terrine, and chicken breast in a cream sauce with Duchesse potatoes for them both. The meal tasted delicious, and Brigid's eyes misted as she recalled the chickens she had cooked in the famine.

During the meal, they discussed city life.

'Please permit me to take you to the opera one evening. There is a Farinelli production coming to Dublin soon. I'm positive it will be a splendid production.' Niall smiled a winning smile.

'Thank you, Niall. I would love to go. I like the Irish folk music that Ezra plays, too. He is a superb violinist. Where did he learn to play the instrument?'

'In Poland, I expect. His father was a Polish Count.'

Brigid's heart rate quickened as she dreaded Niall referring to her past. But he did not. He complimented Brigid on her appearance.

'You are the most beautiful woman in the restaurant.'

Brigid blushed and commented all the ladies looked stunning. She wondered about Niall's family because he had never spoken of them. She gathered up her courage. 'Where does your family live?'

His face clouded. 'My parents have passed. Mother lost her life to a fever during the famine, which brought my father much pain. He didn't recover from her death. My older brother, Sean, found him hanging from the rafters a year later. Sean then emigrated. I have heard nothing from him since 1848. Stephen's family took me in as a son. Robert and Diedre have been so compassionate and generous.' His eyes became moist with tears.

Brigid reached out a hand to touch him. 'I extend my heartfelt sympathy to you for your loss. It must have been heartbreaking for you to lose your family.' But she thought. *If only you knew my background.* Her thoughts stopped when the waiter arrived. Niall whispered something in his ear, puzzling Brigid when she caught words sounding like 'crapes suzzy.'

The waiter smiled and nodded. He removed the dishes and advised that there was a delay in serving dessert. He winked at Niall, who reached into his jacket, extracted a small box from his pocket, and put it in front of Brigid. He got down from his seat and kneeled on one knee.

'Brigid, I love you with all my heart. I invited you to dine with me tonight to ask you something.' His eyes implored hers, and Brigid shivered. 'Please do me the honour of becoming my wife.' He opened the box, and within sat a gold ring with a trio of green and white stones, winking at her in the candlelight.

Speechless, Brigid sat like a statue, her eyes wide, and mouth open. Utterly unprepared for the proposal, Brigid's heart leapt with joy. 'Yes, I will.' No suitor had made her soul sing like Niall. She longed for the fairy tale to go on.

Niall slid the ring onto her finger, and it was a flawless fit. 'We are engaged.' He kissed her hand gleefully.

Brigid blushed as people nearby clapped.

'You may kiss her on the lips now, son,' joked one elderly gentleman.

Niall obliged and kissed his bride-to-be as the waiter placed two glasses of champagne and their desserts on the table. His face bore a smug grin, and Brigid guessed he knew about the proposal.

Niall lifted his glass. 'A toast to our future together.'

The champagne bubbles tickled Brigid's mouth, causing a giddy sensation after a few sips. The crepe Suzette tasted unlike anything she had eaten before.

'We meet Father Joyce at St Catherine's church on Sunday at four o'clock to discuss the wedding.' Niall's face beamed, and the older man chuckled.

Brigid gulped, for it dawned Niall had expected her to accept his marriage proposal. The pace suddenly felt too fast, and Brigid felt like a fish reeling on a line.

The engaged couple left the restaurant at ten o'clock, and Niall had a cab waiting. Brigid's world faded as Niall kissed her trembling lips in the cab. Then, on arrival at Mrs O'Keefe's, he helped Brigid to the front door with a big grin, white teeth gleaming in the moonlight.

'I'll collect you at three tomorrow. Please bring your baptismal certificate with you. Father Joyce will need to see it.'

He whistled a jaunty tune as he departed, and Brigid wondered how he knew she had a baptismal certificate.

Her feet appeared to float above the ground until she bolted the door in the safety of her room. Her senses returned as the fragrance of roses filled the air. She inspected her body with the light from her bedside candle. Her alabaster skin resembled a statue, and she had firm breasts. She cupped each one. Feeling embarrassed by her sexual thoughts, Brigid settled into bed and wished Ma were alive to explain things she did not fully understand,

Then, with a sudden burst of insight, she sat bolt upright. *Niall is introducing me to a priest without knowing my vow not to have a church wedding. He knows so few things about me, including my real name. Oh feck, how do I tell him?* Brigid's mind whirled over her true provenance, sleep eluding her. She had the uncomfortable sensation of needing to bolt like a frightened horse. When she drifted off, her dreams filled with visions of her drunken father, steam trains, and emigration ships.

After the girls left for church in the morning, Brigid folded Amy's dress and bathed. The soft water made her skin smooth and soothed her nerves. She wore a new brown tweed autumn gown for breakfast but not her ring, and she was not ready to reveal her engagement. Over dinner, Amy gave her a pointed look.

'I had a lovely evening, thank you. I have folded the dress for you to return.' She pondered if her words highlighted her deceitful eyes.

After helping wash the dishes, Brigid returned to her room. She locked her door and put on the ring, examining its glints as it caught beams of autumn sunlight. But the temperature had dropped, and a brisk wind blew dead leaves along the cobbled yard. Brigid donned a new cloak and covered the ring with gloves. Amy had planned to visit her parents for Sunday dinner so Brigid could leave the house without her friend noticing.

When Niall rapped the knocker, her mind filled with foreboding. She had less confidence than a small child meeting a stern priest and thought, *I'm caught in a spider's web of deceit but must now confess the truth.* She gazed at her image in the mirror. *I ought to have thought twice about my answer to Niall's proposal. Everyone was watching in the restaurant, so I said yes under pressure. Once he knows the truth, he may call off the engagement.* The reflection stared back. She added an extra shilling to her reticule for a cab home if necessary.

After closing the front door, her legs felt like jelly, but Niall took her arm, and they strolled to the deserted park. Brigid braced to tell Niall the truth and thought, *would bite my nails to the quick without these gloves.* As she opened her mouth to speak, Niall surprised her with a kiss.

'Brigid, I know your real name and story. You grew up in Ballyconstór, in County Wicklow, and your name is Brigid Power.'

Brigid gasped, and her gut twisted. Tendrils of fear slithered up her toes, snaking up her trembling legs as she wondered what more he knew about her.

'Before we admitted you to Saor-Éire, we did our standard background checks.' Niall patted her hand clenched to his arm like a limpet. 'The stationmaster at Bray remembered you, and his description matched Ezra's. Other discrete enquiries by Robert Gallagher, Amy's father, revealed the rest of your background.'

'I had to escape Niall. Seamus's hold over me left no other option.'

'I'm so in love with you, mo stór, that I proposed marriage early in our courtship because I can protect you from your Seamus's and your father's wrath if you take my name.'

Brigid stared into his eyes. 'You want to marry me despite my background? I'm far beneath your social status.'

Niall opened the park gates. 'Your background does not matter to me. I would love you if your mother were a woman of the streets and your father a convicted felon, which he deserves to be. Do you know the shebeen in Ballyconstór sells illegal poteen brewed by Seamus with your father's help? They also sell unlawful opium. Robert plans to raid them when the men are brewing. With luck, the judge will send them to Australia.'

Brigid gasped and said, 'So Da got the money for fancy clothes and opium by illegal means? I have hated my father since I turned eleven. He is a drunk who tormented us, especially our beloved mother. I wish they would hang him for his cruelty.' Brigid couldn't hold back the tears which rolled down her cheeks. 'We starved while he drank.'

Niall directed Brigid to a bench, clearing the seat of leaves with his left hand. 'Brigid, there is more. Since he once worked for the owner, Robert believes your father stole the sapphire you pawned from a collection in Ballyconstór's Manor House. It sounds like a ring that belonged to the lord's late wife, and the thief remains at large. Police found nothing missing in the house except jewels from her ladyship's jewellery box, which the thief The owner ordered his ghillie sacked despite the man protesting he had never been inside the house except after the break-in.'

Brigid's eyes grew wider. 'Da forbade us to go near the house, and he thwacked us for spying on quacking ducks, honking geese, and other creatures when he found out.' Brigid's toes curled. 'Was Da the thief? He lost his job as their gardener when my brothers were young, and Padraig said he changed afterwards.'

'There is insufficient evidence to convict anyone. However, since the ring belonged to the English gentry, Finnbar asked Ezra to hide it. Saor-Éire will use it to buy guns and ammunition to fight against British rule.'

Brigid sat open-mouthed and speechless with shock. *Guns, what have I joined?* Once she found her voice, she confessed to Niall that she had not slept the previous night.

'I feared you would break off our engagement when I told you about my background.' She paused and fiddled with the reticule, taking out a handkerchief. 'Even after my lies and pawning a stolen ring, you are still willing to marry me?' Brigid blew her nose, wondering about Seamus's deceit. 'I put you in danger by accepting your proposal.'

Niall answered by kissing her lips, not caring who saw. 'You stole my heart when I saw you looking beautiful but vulnerable in the bank. I wanted to take you in my arms and tell you so. Now I love you even more for your bravery.' He looked at his pocket watch. 'We must hurry if we are to keep our appointment at four. Father Joyce belongs to Saor-Éire. He accepts the reason behind our haste to wed.'

Her lips parted in surprise, and her eyes widened. 'A Fenian movement includes a priest? It can't be true.'

'I assure you it is true. Some members want their identities hidden, and we respect their wishes. But we aim for freedom for Ireland, and Father Joyce is a trusted confidant.'

On arrival at St Catherine's, the priest welcomed them and asked his housekeeper to bring some tea. 'My cousin in India ships it to me,' he grinned.

'Thank you for seeing us at short notice, Bernard. Allow me to introduce my fiancée, Brigid Murphy.'

The priest nodded as Brigid curtsied. 'Please sit.' He gestured to the chairs beside his desk. 'Niall tells me you are baptised but don't attend church. He also says you have been living in Dublin with an assumed identity.' He paused, watching Brigid's expression. 'Something terrible must have made you reject your faith. But I believe you have a baptismal certificate?' His smile reached his eyes, which sparkled with empathy.

Brigid cast her eyes downward and twiddled with her reticule's strings. She had forgotten the document. 'I left my baptismal certificate at my lodgings. I'll pass it on to Niall.'

'Thank you. I can't perform the ceremony without proof of your baptism.' Father Joyce steepled his fingers. 'There is another matter. You must permit Niall to bring your children up in the faith if you are to marry in the Catholic church.'

The priest watched Brigid's face. His gaze made the woman's palms damp.

'Yes, Father. But once children reach adulthood, they can

make up their own minds.'

The priest gave a sad smile. 'The Lord welcomes back his lost sheep, my dear, and I shall pray you'll return to the fold.'

Niall took Brigid's trembling hand in his. 'We desire a modest ceremony to honour our love and commitment to each other.'

'I'll arrange that, but Brigid, you must sign the register in your real name. You must inform the witness too, Niall.'

'I'll take care of it, Bernard.'

The pair settled on a date in early December. Brigid felt ecstatic as the priest treated her respectfully, unlike Father Byrne, who treated her like a donkey. The following day, she took her baptismal certificate to work. Brigid removed Father O'Malley's faded ink with ease. Her name read Brigid Eleanor Power when she used fresh ink, and the elegant handwriting Ma taught her. She also wrote over Father O'Malley's faded signature.

Then Brigid heard noises in the outer office. She blotted the ink and folded the certificate, slipping it into her reticule and focusing on the ledger. But the numbers swirled, and Brigid couldn't concentrate. She kept thinking, *who is Brigid Pope?* Brigid had never met the girl whose last name did not sound Irish. *What were my siblings' last names? I never looked.*

Staring across the room, Brigid recalled tears had blinded her eyes when she took her certificate from Da's press. She had read none except Joseph's. The puzzle unnerved her.

That evening, she took the document to the coffee house. She waited until Stephen and Amy talked about a family matter and slipped it under the table to Niall's hand. Niall took it and put the document in his pocket.

'I'll show it to Father Joyce after Mass on Sunday,' he whispered. Brigid crossed her fingers, hoping her deception would not be spotted.

CHAPTER 10: MARRIAGE

On her return to Belmont Street, Brigid knocked on Amy's door and told her about the wedding plans. 'You knew Niall would propose, didn't you? It is why you took so much trouble to get me ready.' Brigid stared at her friend with mock sternness, which made Amy giggle.

'Yes, I did. My father told Stephen and me about how you ran away from the farmer, so Stephen suggested Niall's proposal sooner than planned, and he needed little persuasion.' She examined Brigid's engagement ring.

'While searching for your new home, Stephen has found an apartment you'll like. It is on the ground floor of a corner house on North Reading Street and comes with a garden and an apple tree. I recall you once saying you loved cooking apple pies.'

Brigid failed to recall it, but she felt pleased someone had remembered. Stephen received the keys from the agent and took Brigid and Niall to view the property. 'Oh, Niall, I love this apartment. The garden feels like a countryside haven even though it is a short walk to your bank and Clery's store.'

A sturdy cast iron range, in need of blacking, with a baking oven and a hot plate, graced the kitchen. A small scullery led off the room, and Brigid wished she had Ma's boiler. But it contained a large sink with a pump. A tin bath hung from a nail.

The bedroom and parlour needed cleaning, but the dirt looked nothing like Seamus's grime. *The second bedroom can become a nursery.* A deep sense of peace settled within her spirit.

Niall regarded the place with a critical eye. 'Well, it needs cleaning, and we need furniture.'

'Oh, don't worry about that.' Stephen glanced at Brigid. 'We have it in hand.'

Niall's brow furrowed. 'What is the rent?'

'Seven shillings per week and Finnbar will pay the deposit as a wedding present.'

'Will the landlord accept six shillings and sixpence? The place needs whitewashing and cleaning before it is habitable.'

'I think so. The landlord is a Saor-Éire sympathiser.'

Stephen enlisted a pair of Saor-Éire members to do the cleaning and whitewashing. Somebody sanded the wooden floors and gave them a coat of varnish. Brigid cleaned the range and found the pots and pans she needed in Ezra's shop. She stood in line for seventh heaven when she noticed a brass bed with a feather mattress, a rocking chair, and a wing-backed chair for the kitchen. Smiling at Brigid's animated face, Ezra opened a drawer full of wedding rings.

'Choose the one you like best. It is my wedding present. I'm keeping an engagement ring someone pawned as surety.' He tugged his beard and winked at Niall.

Brigid blushed but, rummaging, found the right ring to fit behind her engagement ring. 'I'll take this one.'

'Hmm. I must increase the price to redeem that other ring.' Ezra grinned at Brigid.

Niall's countenance reflected his solemn demeanour at their joshing. Ezra dropped his chin, glancing at Brigid under his bushy eyebrows as she giggled.

'It's a joke about how I pawned Seamus's ring,' Brigid said to soothe her annoyed husband-to-be.

Niall, distracted, wandered to an oak table in the shop and did not hear her. 'If we add chairs, the lot will fit in the kitchen. Reserve it, please, Ezra,' his annoyance at the joking evident in his tone.

Ezra smiled at Brigid. 'I'll find some chairs, too.' She thanked him.

The week of the wedding had freezing weather with hoar frosts and stinging sleet. Friday's day off allowed her to move her belongings to the apartment. The room at Mrs O'Keefe's, which had been her sanctuary for several months, looked bare, and Brigid felt sad at leaving behind her friends. *You sustained me in some dark hours, and I'll be forever grateful.* She placed a box of candied fruits on the dining table with a note expressing her gratitude.

On Saturday, after Brigid had visited the hairdresser, Amy helped her step into her ivory satin wedding gown. She found a pair of long ivory gloves with a cape lined and edged with green fabric in Clery's wedding department. Then Amy donned her gown of green satin, matching Brigid's cape.

Prompted by a tap on the front door, a trembling Brigid and confident Amy set off to the church in a cab driven by a Saor-Éire member. Brigid had a tremendous surprise at the church. Padraig and Angela stood waiting by the church door.

Stunned, Brigid turned to Amy. 'How on earth did you find my family?'

'My father found your sister. I wrote to her, and we agreed to meet at my parents' house to have identical dresses. Your sister made them. She made her wedding dress, too; she showed me. I thought it was beautiful. She is a brilliant dressmaker.'

Overcome with memories, a tear dropped on Brigid's cheek, but Amy was ready with a handkerchief. 'Don't you dare ruin your face for Niall,' she said, shaking her finger at her friend.

Angela hugged her sister and beamed with delight that she had finally found happiness. 'As you guessed, Da evicted Padraig and Luke and moved his woman into the cottage, but a police officer arrested him and Seamus a week ago. They are in prison, and the authorities will send them for trial in the New Year,' she said.

Padraig, who preferred to speak in Gaelic, said, 'Da's anger could have set a house on fire, and he glared at me like he used to when he thwacked us. He wondered if you had any part in their arrest.' He grinned at Brigid and Stephen. 'I'll give my sister in marriage, so I will.'

Tears clouded Brigid's eyes again, but Amy gave her a stern look. 'No tears, not until Niall has seen your beauty.' She re-arranged Brigid's veil.

Padraig then took his sister's arm, and they proceeded down the aisle with the two girls holding Brigid's train off the flagstone floor. Amy's family occupied the front left row, and Niall's face broke into a broad smile. As he joined his bride at the altar, Brigid's nerves settled. They exchanged vows, and soon Father Joyce pronounced their legal union. The bliss-filled couple exited the church into the bright sunshine and the joyful sound of ringing church bells.

z

A carriage drawn by a gorgeous chestnut horse, wearing a red rosette and white plumes, awaited to escort the newlyweds to their reception at Sweeney's. The wooden floor looked swept and polished. White tablecloths covered the stained tables where porter jugs and chrysanthemums in vases stood like sentinels. An enormous, decorated cake stood to one side on a plinth. Brigid's eyes misted, and she shivered. 'Who arranged all this, Niall?' Her shaky voice revealed her anxiety at the cost.

'Amy and your sister, with help from Saor-Éire members.' Niall clutched his bride's hand to steady her nerves as they greeted their guests.

After a sumptuous meal of turkey and roasted vegetables, Stephen gave a heartwarming speech how about their behaviour as young boys, tripping up police officers with twine at dusk and tying door knockers together for fun. He spoke about fishing off the pier at Dún Laoghaire and Niall falling in the water while trying to reel in a fish. Niall grinned at the memories as people laughed.

A photographer captured the moment the newlyweds cut

their iced wedding cake. Afterwards, everyone received g a piece of the cake, and Ezra entertained the guests with his violin.

'He plays Beethoven, Chopin, and Mozart,' said Niall, still holding his bride's hand. 'He also informed me he had a surprise.'

Later, after the celebrations, which included speeches and the cutting of an enormous cake, Ezra struck up the tune *Mrs McGrath*. Niall said, 'Ah, that is the surprise. I wonder where he found the music?' He clasped Brigid's hand. 'It signals time for us to leave.'

The newlyweds left Sweeney's as people cheered and threw dried flower petals over them. In the carriage, Niall kissed his bride until she had no breath left. The cabby drew up outside the apartment, and when Brigid climbed out into the chilly air, she shivered, pulling the cape tight.

Niall opened the door, 'Welcome to our new home, mo stór.'

He bowed, and Brigid giggled at his antics, which ended when he swung her into his arms and carried her over the threshold and into the parlour.

Astonished to see it now furnished with a blue velvet sofa and matching chairs, Brigid stroked the material and spotted matching curtains at the window.

'This furniture is our wedding present from Amy, and 'Oh, someone has lit the fire. How kind.' Brigid sat on the sofa and held her hands out to warm them. The fire sparked and then glowed as Niall piled on more peat.

'I must check the range, which burns coal.'

He disappeared, leaving Brigid on the sofa quivering with anticipation, her senses alert. Niall returned, carrying glasses and a champagne bottle. He uncorked the bottle, and the cork shot up to the ceiling, making Brigid laugh. Once the champagne had pervaded her body, the shaking subsided. Then, despite being a little light-headed and filled with expectation, Brigid relaxed. As the daylight faded, Niall lit some candles and took one into the bedroom. He disappeared for several minutes. *What is he doing while my body aches for his touch?*

When he came back, Niall extended his hand. 'I set up a warming pan in our bed this morning. I have removed it.'

Brigid opened her mouth, but Niall silenced it with his lips pressed in a tender kiss and led her to the bedroom. Brigid gasped. Red rose petals littered the bed's coverlet.

'The petals are roses from your mother's bower Angela picked for her wedding and pressed. She scattered them early this morning.' Niall removed them into a small box and turned down the bedding.

He focused his tender eyes on his bride, 'Come to bed, mavourneen,'

Bewitched by his eyes, Brigid murmured, 'Undo the buttons on my back,' and spun around.

Niall then pulled off her corset and released her breasts, turning her to face him. Brigid's pulse rate increased. She crossed her arms over her breasts, but Niall kissed each and then tugged off her undergarments. She stood naked with goose pimples on her arms as her husband pulled off his clothing, leaving them on the floor and exposing pale flesh, long limbs, and firm muscles.

Niall laid Brigid on the bed, kissing every inch of her body as passion consumed them. Brigid pulled Niall towards her, his member firm, and as he entered her secret place, Brigid felt a sharp pain. Then they moved in unison, and exquisite sensations coursed through Brigid's body until she cried out. Niall cried out, too, and shuddered. He withdrew, and the pair lay in the moonlight, passion spent.

'We are one,' Niall's voice choked with emotion.

Brigid stroked his face. 'I love you to the ends of the earth, my husband.' Then, recalling he had no family, she clasped his right hand in hers, kissing each of his knuckles. 'Mo stór, you have someone who loves you by your side for the rest of your life.'

CHAPTER 11: MARRIED LIFE

Brigid drifted from a dream of a glittering castle and a handsome prince. She lay in that twilight zone between sleep and full waking when Niall's head appeared from the bedclothes entangled around them. He got up to light the range while Brigid lingered in bed for a few minutes.

She was close to drifting back to sleep when she heard Niall call. 'Brigid, hurry, or the toast will burn. The eggs are ready.'

Brigid rose shivering in the cold room and donned her new dark green robe. They ate breakfast, watching a robin on the windowsill. Brigid saved him some toast crumbs, thinking about Saoirse's wedding gift, an extra day off.

'To give you time to settle into your new home,' she had said with a twinkle in her eye.

Brigid had not told Niall; she wanted to surprise him with her cooking skills. The food left by Saor-Éire ladies had saved her from cooking over the weekend. She kissed Niall goodbye and waited until he turned the corner opposite the nearby grocery and butcher shops.

Brigid donned her coat, then closed and locked the front door. She spotted a street urchin of about ten years old lurking on the corner. Brigid found his presence on the street strange and wondered what he wanted. She double-checked that she had locked the door securely. The street was empty when Brigid returned, but she felt uneasy and had no desire to see the boy again.

Brigid had found apples stored in the scullery and had purchased pastry ingredients. So, with a delicious menu in mind, including her legendary apple pie, she set to work. She heaped more peat on the kitchen range, thanking Padraig for cutting an enormous pile. She peeled the apples, reserving the skins to make the delicious apple tea Angela used to make. Soon, her hands were covered in flour as she rolled pastry and filled the baking dish with pie crust and apples. Then she prepared dough to bake fresh bread, peeled potatoes, cut cabbage to make colcannon, and put two pork chops in a dish to cook in apple juice.

After cleaning the kitchen, Brigid ate fresh bread covered with redcurrant jelly and relaxed in her rocking chair. It startled her when someone knocked on the door with a letter for Niall. She did not recognise the spidery but elegant handwriting. *I wonder who it is from?* She thought, turning it over before placing it on the mantlepiece.

At five thirty, Brigid changed into a clean dress and apron. She tucked her hair into a pure mob cap when she heard the front door open and then shut with a bang. She hurried from the bedroom to kiss her husband.

He gazed at her with a pleated brow and glistening eyes. 'Where have you been? I met Amy on my way home, and she said you had not been at Clery's today, and I was worried sick.'

Brigid kissed his lips. 'Saoirse gave me the day off at our wedding reception, and I kept it as a surprise for tonight. I'm sorry you ran into Amy.'

His brow smoothed, and Niall sniffed. 'What have you cooked?'

'It's a surprise, mo stór, and I must see to it.'

Brigid turned into the kitchen and heated some apple tea while Niall disappeared into the bedroom. The pork chops she had bought that morning had been slow cooking, so Brigid fried the colcannon and put the apple pie back in the oven to warm.

She prepared the table with two sparkling glasses filled with leftover wedding wine. They dined while gazing at each other, entranced and awed. Niall praised Brigid's skills. 'You are some cooks. I wish I had wed you sooner.'

'A letter came for you today.' Brigid smiled, rose, and took it from the mantlepiece to give to her husband. She sat down and picked up her glass while he opened the seal. 'Who is it from? The handwriting has kept me intrigued the entire day.'

Niall's brow furrowed. 'It's from Finnbar and concerns some work Saor-Éire intends to do.'

'What work?' Brigid guessed from Niall's expression it must involve something dangerous. She recalled the street urchin, and an icy shiver crossed her body.

Niall re-read the letter, crumpled it, and threw it in the fire. He stood up, took Brigid's hand, and led her to their bedroom. He silenced her protestations about washing the dishes with kisses as he undressed her. Soon, she lost all sense of time in his arms, letters, and street urchins forgotten.

The newlyweds developed a pleasing daily rhythm and conversed in Gaelic at home. One evening, Brigid took home a pamphlet on a bookkeeping course, which she had kept on her desk at work for some time.

The booklet arrived while she considered emigrating, but she had forgotten all about it. Brigid read the course details, which stated it ran for three hours every Tuesday evening in a workers' education venue near their apartment. She knew many men did not permit their wives to study, but she thought, *I'm sure Niall will allow it when I explain how it will help Saor-Éire,*

Niall said, 'After qualifying, you could work from home. I know small businesses will pay for help with their accounts.' He put a hand on his wife's stomach, his chestnut eyes soft and inviting, and her senses reeled.

Brigid signed up for the course, starting in January 1856, during her dinner break the next day. Niall arranged for someone to escort her to and from classes for safety reasons. 'As the wife of a Saor-Éire senior officer, you must be watchful. Our organisation is at risk of being spied upon.'

By now, Brigid had seen the street urchin on the corner six times and told Niall of her concerns. 'He's never spoken to me, so I'm unsure if he's watching someone or lurking like boys do.'

Niall's brow furrowed. 'We must take no chances. I need a detailed description of Robert. He will have someone tail you.' He took Brigid's hand, sat her on his knees, and kissed her.

Brigid had not drawn pictures since childhood, but Niall liked them, and the boy vanished. Their daily activities soon had a fixed pattern. Still, Brigid became watchful, respecting that marriage to Niall exposed her to risks not envisaged in her unmarried status.

Their passion continued to delight, and they made love every night. They laughed at the same things, took walks in the crisp air, their boots crunching on frozen ground, and read to each other on dark evenings in January and February by the fire. Sometimes, they played checkers and card games, which Brigid often won, much to Niall's annoyance.

'It comes from having older brothers who were excellent players,' Brigid said, laughing at Niall's expression.

However, despite her blissful new life, it lacked something more fulfilling. Brigid wanted a child.

CHAPTER 12: THE STREET URCHIN

Niall invited Finnbar to visit to discuss the letter Brigid lit the parlour fire to avoid disturbing the men's conversation with kitchen noises. When he arrived taciturn Finnbar showed little interest in Brigid, which annoyed her. The man lacked manners, but Brigid offered him some apple tea.

Afterwards, she retreated to the kitchen, leaving the men to talk. Seated by the fireplace, she picked up the embroidered tablecloth and thought Finnbar's arrogance reminded her of Father Byrne. A frosty shudder went down her spine.

When the front door slammed shut, Brigid glanced at the clock, which showed ten in the evening. Finnbar had stayed for two hours. Niall entered the kitchen, looking tired and dishevelled.

'Will you have some warm milk before bed?' Brigid said, her brow furrowed with concern.

Niall nodded and left for their bedroom. Brigid took the milk through but found Niall fast asleep in his combinations, shirt and trousers scattered. Brigid set the milk aside, folded his clothes and pulled the covers over him. While undressing, she wondered what the meeting could have been about as it had exhausted Niall.

Brigid questioned her husband as they ate their breakfast porridge in the morning. Yet he supplied no details beyond that Saor-Éire had action plans and resumed eating his meal. Then he looked up.

Brigid, have you seen the street urchin again?'

'No, not since the police have patrolled the streets. Why do you ask?'

'Finnbar wants a small top team to meet each week, but the coffee house is too public. I have offered our home the night you are at your bookkeeping course. I proposed we make it plain that we are card players. Poker games are played in many houses, so they'll be accepted as familiar to nosy neighbours.'

Brigid felt uneasy about the plan. 'Our home may become a target for spying, or worse.'

'It's the price we must pay to begin our work. Robert Gallagher's police officers watch senior Saor-Éire officers' homes, so don't worry. We'll be safe.'

Brigid forced a smile and pretended to be satisfied with the plan. But deep down, she longed for the carefree life she had imagined when she married Niall. Each morning, when Brigid left for work, she double-checked the front door's security.

She felt unseen eyes on her back, her gut twisting, telling her to be careful. But spotting no suspicious people, Brigid wondered if her imagination had become overstimulated. When she returned home each evening, relief washed over her when she spotted the police officer on the corner. The officer would incline his head in greeting.

One evening in March, Brigid returned from work with a sore throat and headache. After supper, of which she ate little, she retired to bed. Niall felt her forehead and declared she had a fever. He fetched a vinegar cloth and placed it on her sweating brow.

'You must stay in bed and take sick leave tomorrow. I'll send a note to Saoirse.'

Brigid remained in bed with a heavy cold for two days, fighting against it going to her chest. A loud pounding at the door on the third day startled her awake mid-morning. Thinking it would be the mail, she threw on her robe and shuffled to the door. On the doorstep stood the street urchin, thin-clad, without shoes and shivering. Brigid gasped. 'What is your business with me, child?'

'I have been waiting to catch you at home. I know your

husband is in some Freedom for Ireland group. I warn ye, the military is itching for trouble.'

His warning stunned Brigid, causing her legs to tremble as she looked for the absent police officer. But the alert child said, 'I'm well-informed about your police officer but quicker than him. Tell your husband to be careful.' The boy turned and ran like a hare, his bare feet flapping on the cobbles, leaving Brigid stunned.

When Niall returned home that evening, an anxious

Brigid was stirred a meaty broth, and he lifted her chin to kiss her.

'You must be feeling better, mo stór,' he said as Brigid ladled the thick broth into bowls and added some crusty bread.

Niall tasted the soup, smiled and said, 'This broth is delicious.'

'My mother used to make it.' Brigid blushed and, composing herself, relayed the boy's message. 'It has troubled me all day. I'm afraid for our safety.'

Niall reached to touch her hand, 'I'll ask Robert to step up the patrols. There is nothing more we can do except maintain careful secrecy.' He supped his soup. 'I wonder who this boy is? Ask for his name if you see him again.'

Brigid returned to work the following day but saw no trace of the boy. The police officer stood on the corner and followed Brigid to Clery's. He stood outside the store to escort her home in the same way. Brigid felt safer with his presence.

However, she thought about the courageous child who had warned Niall. *Who is he, and why did he warn us?* Brigid's mind spun with various possibilities. It upset her equilibrium, although she did not let Niall know. *Is he affiliated with the military in any way? Who else could want to harm Niall?*

Worry started affecting her work, and Brigid knew she had to take control. So, she sought help from Amy, who, from Brigid's description, thought that the boy must live in the tenements. 'I'll talk with my father for you and ask him to place an officer permanently on your street. Will that help?'

Brigid nodded, but her heart sensed something dreadful would happen. April brought rainstorms and unseasonably low temperatures, but Brigid discovered no sign of the street urchin. Her tense shoulder muscles relaxed as she and Niall resumed their evening walks in May.

As Brigid prepared vegetables for a roast dinner one Sunday, Niall praised Brigid's housekeeping skills. 'You budget so well and supply such tasty, nourishing food.'

Brigid bobbed a curtsy. 'Thank you, sir. I might have opened a boarding house and taken you as a tenant.'

Chuckling, Niall chased her to the bedroom, where he caught her in a kiss. Soon, in one other's arms, with passions aroused, they lost any sense of time or location.

Later, after eating their roast dinner, Brigid put down her knife and fork and gazed at her husband with shining eyes.

'I fell in love with you that first Sunday in the park. But your elegant appearance left me uncertain of how to behave. Your impeccable manners were unlike any man had shown me before.'

'Your behaviour challenged my prejudice about how girls from the countryside behaved.' Niall said, chuckling as he picked up his glass of water.

'My mother drummed manners into us. She made me walk with a book balanced on my head for deportment.'

'She taught you well because you've got a ramrod straight back. Discovering your background fascinated me, and I wanted to know more about such a courageous woman. Now I do. Come, forget the dishes, and let us make love once more.'

Brigid blushed at his boldness but complied, her body shaking with anticipation of exquisite sensations.

CHAPTER 13: ACTION

Brigid completed her accountancy course with distinction by the end of the month. Her tutor urged her to study for a higher qualification. 'You have a natural talent for figures. Your existing knowledge of the course content put you at a distinct advantage, and your contributions benefitted my other students.'

When Niall heard, joy suffused his face, and his eyes gleamed.

'What a clever wife I have. Enrol in the next course.' He paused, stroking his chin. 'The bank will be closed on Saturday because of additional back-office work before Easter. I'll be back for supper about an hour later than usual.'

Brigid used the extra hour to prepare a special meal, but Niall failed to return home by seven o'clock. *I'm glad I made a stew I can reheat. I wonder what is keeping him.*

After another hour without seeing her husband, Brigid paced the kitchen floor, her nerves frayed like a worn rope. Someone rapped at the door at about nine o'clock. Brigid rushed to unlock it and met a dishevelled and groaning Niall.

A cabby pushed him over the lintel and winked at Brigid before shutting the door with a loud click. Niall slumped to the hall floor and mumbled something unintelligible. The almond biscuit smell of whiskey overpowered her and left her thinking Niall was drunk. Taking a step back, she quailed, thinking, *I've had my fill of drunkenness for a lifetime.* She felt tempted to leave her husband where he lay, but as she surveyed his dishevelled state, he groaned.

Brigid gasped when she saw blood on his shirt, one eye bruised and swollen closed, and blood from his nose dribbling down over a split lip. She kneeled and moved his torn shirt, and he groaned, clasping his arm to his chest. Brigid had witnessed firsthand the effects of fights on her brothers and concluded that he had been in a dreadful skirmish.

Her mouth dried up, and she croaked 'Niall, can you stand? I need to get you to bed.'

His left eye opened, and he nodded. With Brigid's aid, he stood up despite his obvious pain, and she guided him to the bedroom. Niall had borne a brutal attack. The flesh over his ribs had the unmistakable imprints of boots, and Brigid's stomach contracted with fear. With a flash of insight, Brigid understood the cabby's wink. The attack Finnbar had planned must have taken place.

'Where the feck have you been, Niall? Someone has beaten you without mercy.'

Niall gritted his teeth with pain, 'Doing a warehouse raid. It turned nasty. Feckers waiting and jumped us.' He coughed and winced. 'Somebody tipped the feckin' army off. Knifed Stephen.'

Knifed Stephen? Brigid found herself consumed by the all too familiar spectre of death, 'Is ... is Stephen still alive?'

'Yes ... gone to his parents.' Niall lost consciousness, laying back on his pillow with his head lolling to one side.

Brigid remembered, as a small girl, Ma binding Padraig's ribs. She left Niall to fetch water, cloth, and soap to clean his face and found a bedsheet, which she tore into strips to bind his ribs. She set to work, her fingers wiping the blood from his face, revealing more bruising. Niall stirred, opening his unfocused and unbruised eye.

'Where am I?' he closed it again.

'At home, mo stór.' Brigid tore open his shirt and gasped. One boot had thumped him near his heart, the imprint unmistakable. *How do I treat such wounds?*

Niall stirred. 'Can you move a little so I can put bandages around your ribs? I'm overcome with fear. They may be cracked.'

Niall groaned, and Brigid feared he had a cracked head like Michael had when he fell from the cowshed rafters. Securing a strip of binding in the most damaged area, she tied a knot with trembling fingers.

Niall had fainted from pain, and Brigid tended to the other bandages until he regained consciousness. She had completed the third strip when he stirred and grabbed her hand.

'Feckers. Could have killed us.' Niall ground his teeth and mumbled something about the 'Feckin' knife.'

Brigid then inspected her husband for any knife wound but found none, for which she felt relieved. She soothed Niall, who continued to groan and thrash.

'It is me, Brigid, not the fecker that hurt you. Lie still. I have bandaged your ribs.'

Cautiously, she used the cloth to remove more blood from his face, fearful of hurting his swollen eye.

'Aargh, pain, much pain...' Niall touched his head, and his eyes closed.

Brigid's heart banged like a drum as she completed her tasks.

Once she had removed his boots and breeches, Brigid administered a measure of the laudanum physic to ease his pain. He soon slept. She undressed and climbed in beside him, staring into the darkness until her eyes closed. She gave him another measure of laudanum when she heard his groans in the middle of the night.

In daylight, Brigid could see the full extent of Niall's bruising. Neither of them could go to work. Niall needed to visit a doctor. Brigid dressed and wrote two notes, one to Amy and another to the bank manager, explaining that ruffians had attacked and stolen Niall's money while he walked home from a game of cards. Brigid knew Amy would guess the lie. Brigid opened the front door, her legs unsteady, intending to walk to the post-box on the opposite corner. When she spotted the street urchin hovering nearby, she had to hold on to the gate.

The boy ran across the street. 'I warned you to tell your husband to watch his step. The military intends to catch them.'

'Son, what's your name?' Brigid gasped, remembering Niall's request.

But the boy gave no answer and dashed away faster than a hunted fox, leaving Brigid bewildered and scared. At home, she lit the fire, heated the kettle for hot apple tea, boiled an egg, and forced herself to eat it with some soda bread. Despite the imminent arrival of April, the air felt chilly, and Brigid shivered.

She washed her dishes and sat in her rocking chair beside the range, pondering whether to call a physician. *I'll use the ruffians' attack story as cover.*

However, food and a glowing fire made her drowsy, and the sun had risen high in the sky when a loud knock at the door woke her. A postal worker had a letter from Amy. She explained the attackers had knifed Stephen in the chest. She wrote: *Doctors say he will recover under our parent's care, and mother has engaged a nurse. Saoirse has accepted your excuse for absence.*

Niall's voice called out from the bedroom, asking who knocked on the door. Brigid ran to him as he groaned, sitting up.

'Mo stór lie still. I must send for a doctor.'

'No doctors, please.' He eased himself upright. 'I'm hungry, mo stór.'

Brigid kissed his lips joyfully as relief swept through her. She said,

'Food is coming soon, my dear husband.'

She brought Niall some bread spread with jelly. Brigid asked where he might have pain.

'My ribs give me excruciating pain if I move, but not so much my head.'

Brigid administered another measurement of laudanum, and he slept. While she got on with household tasks, she worried about Stephen's fate. After pegging her washing out to dry in the wind, she prepared some bread and put the stew to reheat. Brigid then took a seat in her chair, exhausted by the ordeal.

She had drifted into sleep, and the room had grown dark when Niall roused her gently with a kiss. 'I'm sorry for the trouble I've caused you, mavourneen.' He eased himself into his armchair, wincing.

Brigid stared at her husband. 'Niall, your bruises, and wounds tell me you were in a bare-knuckle brawl. You stank of whisky, too.' Tears glistened as she recalled how tempted she had been to leave him where he lay.

'The cabby is a member of Saor-Éire. He waited with a bottle of whisky as a ruse in case we got stopped.'

'I grew terrified when you didn't come home at suppertime. I didn't think of Finnbar's planned action. Is that what happened last night?'

'Yes, and despite our meticulous planning, it turned nasty. The British military was waiting in ambush. There must be a traitor in the membership.'

Brigid's heart raced, thinking of the boy's warning. 'Do you know who the traitor is? The street urchin warned me, you won't be so lucky next time.'

'Next time? We'll discover the fecking spy by then. We have several new members, and although checks are necessary, a clever spy can forge a background.'

Brigid's eyes clouded, and she gazed out the window as night fell, her heart heavy. Brigid lit an oil lamp Ezra had found, giving the room a soft glow.

She stroked Niall's head with a caressing hand. 'I made a pot of your favourite stew last night. It is reheating, and we can have it with some crusty bread I baked this morning.'

She poured a glass of ruby wine into the stew pot. She stirred it through, a trick learned from Mrs O'Keefe, who had given Brigid two bottles of wine and two glasses as another wedding present. She tasted the stew; as expected, the wine gave it extra flavour. Brigid fetched two bowls from the press and ladled out the meal. She slathered butter on some bread, poured two glasses of wine and put Niall's meal on a tray. She seated herself at the table.

After eating, Niall had a healthier hue on the unbruised areas of his face. Since he refused to see a doctor, Brigid shooed him back to bed and gave him another measure of laudanum. She washed and dried the dishes and sat down to read while Niall slept.

At eleven, Brigid dispensed another dose of medicine, then undressed and got into bed, wondering what would happen to her if someone killed Niall. Brigid turned her face to the pillow and wept silent tears. She lay awake for some time before the mists of sleep obliterated her macabre imaginings of Niall's death in another raid.

Niall's condition had improved in the morning, allowing Brigid to go to work. When she arrived, Saoirse greeted her with extra warmth. 'Amy told me ruffians attacked your husband. What a dreadful experience.'

Brigid nodded and walked to her desk, where, to her surprise, she found an envelope addressed to her. It contained a letter from the store's directors congratulating her on their promotion to First Assistant Bookkeeper, with a two per cent salary raise, effective from the first day of the month. *April Fool's Day* mused Brigid with a rueful smile. But it soon changed to glee as Saoirse congratulated her.

At home, Niall said, 'You are such a clever woman: a wife, a nurse, and an accountant concurrently.' He kissed Brigid's hand and sent tingles along her arm.

Amy spoke with Brigid in Sweeney's four weeks after the attack. 'My parents wish to invite you to Sunday dinner in two weeks. Father wishes to discuss the matter of a spy in the organisation and will invite Finnbar, too. My mother suggests that women take a cliff walk while the men talk, and the cook prepares our meal. In fine weather, the view is captivating.'

Brigid's mind whirled. *A cook? One half of Ireland does not know how the other half lives.* But she accepted the invitation with grace.

Against Brigid's wishes, Niall had returned to work within a few days of the attack. Upon seeing his face, his boss laughed. 'Next time you play cards, make sure you don't win, then you won't get robbed.'

Brigid thought, 'Your boss didn't see the bruises around your ribs. He wouldn't have laughed then.'

CHAPTER14: DUN LAOGHAIRE

On the morning of the dinner, Niall washed, shaved, and wore a clean shirt without wincing. Brigid wore a simple dark red velvet dress with a matching cape. Robert's plush cab with black leather upholstery drawn by a grey horse pulled up outside their apartment and took them to Dún Laoghaire.

On arrival at the Gallaghers' home, Stephen thanked the driver. Brigid thought his manner too bright and his pupils too wide. The hand he proffered shook, and Brigid thought, *Has Stephen taken to drink after his injuries? After such a narrow escape from death, he'll have mental scars, which he could be drowning in whisky.* She frowned; her mouth pursed.

Stephen's mother must have noticed Brigid's concerned look because she said,

'The doctor assures us Stephen will recover his former strength. However, inactivity doesn't suit him, so at my urging, he has been reading the books on philosophy that he ought to have read at Trinity College. My concern is that he has been drinking whiskey while experiencing pain despite being still full of youth.'

She misses nothing, thought Brigid, impressed.

A housemaid took Niall's coat, and as Amy rushed downstairs, a knock on the door disturbed them. The housemaid opened it to reveal Finnbar on the doorstep. He stepped in and gave the women a piercing stare.

Nodding to Niall and Robert, he shrugged off his coat and turned to face Stephen. 'You look healthy enough, considering the life you lead.'

Brigid's stomach churned at such an impertinent greeting, which displayed no consideration for the host's or Stephen's emotions. She spotted a shadow across Stephen's brow, and her hand itched to slap Finnbar's face for his rudeness. But Stephen gathered his composure and said in English, 'Yes, I'm doing much better, Finn. Ready to catch the devils who attacked us.'

Robert ushered the men into his library. The door clicked as he closed it. With the manners of high breeding, Diedre took Amy and Brigid through the house grounds and onto the sea path. Brigid gasped; the view was awe-inspiring, with the sunlight glistening like glycerine on the dancing waves. The air had that salty tang Brigid appreciated, and the walk energised Brigid. The women discussed their work and interests, and Diedre revealed her source of income.

She said she financed Stephen's political activities and his participation with Saor-Éire. 'I run a soup kitchen in the tenement area for charity, too.'

'I enjoy working to earn my money,' Amy said,

'Amy, you need to settle down. It is time you got married.'

Brigid thought Diedre to be correct. *Someone must wed Amy soon to protect her from harm, given her relationship with Stephen and Robert as leaders in Saor-Éire.*

When the women returned to the house at twelve forty-five, Robert opened the library door. He invited them to join the men in a pre-dinner sherry. The book-lined shelves and Robert's ornate, polished mahogany desk amazed Brigid; the elaborate furniture was grander than the things at Aunt Bessie's.

The guests had finished their sherry when the housemaid announced dinner.

'Her name is Cecilia,' whispered Amy as they made their way to the dining room. 'Mother found her working in a rough school as a pupil teacher and rescued her. She is not Irish born. Her parents emigrated to Lancashire as skilled silk weavers. Cecilia was about twelve when they both died. She returned to Ireland to stay with her mother's family. Because of a strained relationship with her grandmother, she left and became a pupil teacher. She has had a tough life, poor girl.'

Brigid's gaze wandered around an ornate dining room, where the shining mahogany table met with silver cutlery and dazzling crystal wine glasses. Brigid was awestruck by the room's astounding opulence: ornate cornices, a crystal chandelier, delicate gold wallpaper, and thick piled pale green carpet.

Cecilia brought in a tureen of soup, and Diedre dismissed her with a nod and a wave of her hand, then ladled leek soup with the other.

'So, have you men hatched a plan to catch the spy?'

'Someone from an opposition movement in Ulster may have infiltrated us. We must scrutinise every member's background,' Robert said.

Brigid felt unsure how Finnbar viewed comments from women, given his penchant for ignoring them. Finnbar opined the spy could come from the North of Ireland, from an Orange Order Lodge.

'All backgrounds need to be rechecked, and members' accents noted.'

Brigid observed Stephen didn't speak but concentrated on sipping his soup with the elegant movement she recalled Ma teaching, and she copied him.

'Can you spare any men to carry out surveillance, Robert?' asked Diedre, her brow furrowed.

'I'll pass the task to two trusted members. Finnbar has agreed to our plan.'

Well, that's something positive, thought Brigid, watching Finnbar slurp his soup.

'I have faith in Robert's plan. We'll find the person.'

Brigid thought he could be polite when it suits him. I wonder what his background is like. Then, using her best English accent, said,

'How long will it take?' She avoided Finnbar's pointed gaze when she spotted a slight gap between his top front teeth that unnerved her.

'Nobody is sure. Such work is dangerous since the traitor's associates have shown they use weapons.' Robert sipped his soup.

The conversation continued with discussions ranging from the weather and the price of meat to the lack of hygiene in Dublin's tenements.

Diedre recounted her philanthropic work, commenting that nobody had closed the soup kitchen despite the Poor Law that had stopped such ventures in England.

'Because of the famine, many people flocked to the ports, hoping to emigrate, she added sagely.'

Brigid thought. *Diedre, you can't comprehend a peasant's experience during the famine because your wealth closes your eyes to it. You won't understand what it feels like to starve unless you have experienced it.*

Over a dessert of stewed apples sprinkled with cinnamon and covered with cream, the guests discussed whether married women should be permitted to take employment.

Deidre declared a strong passion for it: 'Men underestimate women's resilience and intelligence. There will be no need to question the matter in the future. Women will demand their rights.'

Brigid noticed Finnbar's eyebrows shooting towards his hairline and his eyes closing in disagreement. It surprised Brigid he tolerated women anywhere, even at an elegant dining table.

Cecilia arrived with the coffee. 'Will that be all, Madam?'

'Yes, thank you, Cecilia.'

After a brief curtsy, the girl's gaze lingered on Finnbar before she closed the door.

Robert said, 'Cecilia is a covert member who can recognize the writer of a document by their handwriting, even without a signature, after seeing it once before. She is an expert who writes in copperplate and makes excellent copies that fool most scrutineers.'

'Our system allows Father to receive originals of any message from which he redacts names,' Stephen said. 'We photograph the documents, give them a code, and store them. Cecilia can match any document to a coded example. We have trialled the method, and it works.'

Brigid recalled Finnbar's spidery writing, which she would spot anywhere, and pondered on her non-covert role. 'The girl sounds like an ingenious asset. Finnbar, do you keep members like Cecilia hidden for security reasons?'

'Yes; Cecilia's capabilities are singular.' He glared at Brigid, and her cheeks burned.

And Mine are not? Brigid thought, biting back a stinging retort.

After dinner, the men retired to the library for port and cigars, and the women chattered and drank coffee in the parlour. Brigid and Niall left at four o'clock, travelling in Robert's cab.

Brigid kicked off her heeled shoes at home, dropped into her rocking chair, and said, 'I'm tired, Niall. I enjoyed the occasion, but it has been an exhausting experience.'

Niall kissed her and added peat to the range of the fire. They spent the evening in mutual reflection on the day's conversations.

'I thought Finnbar's arrival remark to Stephen to be inappropriate and unkind.' Brigid pursed her lips with disgust.

'Stephen has had a rough time. He was lucky the knife missed his heart. Robert called in a doctor who stitched the wound and prescribed a diet rich in liver and spinach,' Niall said, smiling at his wife.

Brigid considered Stephen's mental health. Since she knew the signs of someone who drank too much alcohol, she told Niall of her fears.

He stared at his wife for a few seconds. 'You are observant. This is confidential information known only by a few individuals outside the family.' Niall leaned forward with his elbows on his knees. 'Stephen prefers men if you understand me. Finnbar's insensitive remark stemmed from that reason. I wanted to punch his nose for it.'

Brigid sat open-mouthed. 'Oh, feck. Does this explain why we never hear about girlfriends and why his mother suggests he is still a youth?'

Niall said, 'Diedre has accepted it, but Robert thinks Stephen can resist the behaviour, and they have intense arguments. I have known Stephen since my youth, and his sexual orientation has never affected our friendship. I love him like a brother. Amy, unable to tolerate the arguments, left with Robert's consent and started work at Clery's. It distanced her from Stephen and their father's work with Saor-Éire.'

'I see,' said Brigid. Oh, poor Stephen. Is there no way to help him?'

'None that we know of. Robert insists he remains celibate and lives at home until Amy weds. He won't have Amy's reputation and prospects damaged.'

Brigid thought of the conversation on the sea path. 'Well, the sooner Amy finds a husband, the better.'

Niall got up and held out his hand, 'It's bedtime for us, mavourneen.'

Brigid fell asleep the minute her head hit the pillow.

CHAPTER 15: PREGNANCY

At breakfast on Monday morning, Brigid got a letter from Angela, who apologised for not writing sooner because she had been unwell and expected her second child that summer. She wrote: *The police sent Da and Seamus for trial towards the end of March. The judge sentenced them to ten years of hard labour Padraig went to the trial and reported that Da had changed. The fire has gone out of him. But Padraig and I have no interest in seeing him. We think the sentence is too lenient.*

As Brigid read the letter to Niall, she said, 'He deserves life for what he did to us and Ma, who loved him.'

'You can stop glancing over your shoulder now, mavourneen. Your father and Seamus are no longer part of your life.'

'I must write to Angela tonight and congratulate her on her pregnancy.' Brigid folded the letter and collected her coat, thinking, *I wish the judge had sentenced Seamus and Da to transportation or even hanging.*

After work, Brigid deals with mundane matters like cleaning the apartment and preparing supper. But one night, Niall returned home to find Brigid asleep in her chair with no food prepared.

He touched her temple, and she opened her eyes to see his creased brow. 'Are you not feeling well, mavourneen?' he said.

Brigid gazed at his face. 'My body ached more than usual after I washed the bed sheets and cleaned the apartment. I'm unsure of the reason.'

'I smell the beeswax, and you must have cleaned with extra vigour.'

Brigid got up, her spirit contrite. She prepared a cold supper of cheese, ham, and bread, followed by a slice of apple pie, wondering why she was fatigued despite sleeping.

While Niall went to church the following Sunday, Brigid ironed her washing and noticed no monthly rags among the items. *When did I last use them? In March?*

A moment of insight led her to make a doctor's appointment. She asked to finish work early, sending Saoirse's delicate arched eyebrows towards her hairline.

The doctor examined Brigid and said, 'Mrs McGrath, you are carrying a child who is due to be born in mid-December. I'll refer you to an eminent gynaecologist if you wish.'

Brigid, understanding she couldn't financially handle the fee, said, 'I'll manage with yourself and a competent midwife.'

'Please see me in a month, Mrs McGrath. I must check on your progress.' The doctor beamed at Brigid, his grey eyes twinkling with fatherly benevolence. 'It is your first child, I think. Give my congratulations to your husband.'

Brigid thanked him and walked home on a cushion of air. Her excitement grew as she prepared a special meal and waited for Niall to return.

Niall threw off his jacket. 'At five minutes to three, a woman wanted to withdraw funds to hire a private investigator. She thinks her husband is seeing another woman. I couldn't stand her chatter. If you had seen her, you would sympathise with her husband. She must be hell to live with. She made me late starting my back-office work.'

Brigid handed Niall a glass of champagne from the last bottle saved from their wedding.

'Why have you opened the champagne? We were saving it…' Niall's eyes dropped to her stomach.

'Yes, mo stór. You'll be a father by Christmas.'

'You are expecting a child?' Niall sat down, his face pale. 'I'll be its Da by Christmas?'

'Yes, I saw the doctor today. He sends his congratulations.'

Niall collected himself. 'You must sit down, mo stór. No wonder cleaning the apartment tired you.'

'I'm expecting a child, not sick. I have supper prepared, your favourite, fresh mackerel from the market.'

Niall's eyes lit up, and when served the food, he ate with gusto. With a slight sensation of nausea niggling at her stomach Brigid ate a smaller portion. They retired early, meaning to sleep, but lost themselves in each other's arms.

Afterwards, Brigid prepared mugs of steaming cocoa but found Niall fast asleep. So, she set down the cocoa and examined her stomach by the candle's light. Brigid could see a small mound.

My beautiful child, are you a boy or a girl? Whichever you are, I hope you grow up healthy and happy and never suffer from starvation or mistreatment. I'll protect you with my life, I promise.

The days passed, and the pair continued their evening walks, the fresh air helping Brigid's nausea. In late June, Brigid experienced a fluttering in her stomach. 'It's the quickening.'

Niall touched her growing belly but couldn't detect any movement.

'You'll feel it soon, the doctor told me,' Brigid grinned.

By July, her bump became hard to disguise. One dinner time at Sweeney's, Amy asked the question on everybody's lips. 'Are you expecting Brigid, or have you been overeating?'

Brigid's cheeks burned. 'The child is due in December.'

'I guessed it; congratulations,' said Irene. 'You look like my sister did when she expected a baby.'

When Brigid told Saoirse the next day, tears glistened in the woman's eyes, and she pushed her spectacles up her nose. She left the office and returned a half-hour later.

'My apologies, Brigid, but I congratulate you. Clery's will keep your position open for six months after you give birth. I'm sure you'll find someone to care for the child by then. I told the manager the store can't afford to lose an employee as diligent as you.'

Brigid's mouth fell open in surprise. The offer was most generous, for employers seldom kept positions open for women with children, and Brigid thanked her.

Saoirse said, 'Please supervise Fergal's training to take over in an acting position starting in November.' She sniffed and wiped her nose.

Brigid's contentment continued until Finnbar, visiting relatives in Waterford, returned. She hoped he would not organise any raids. The street urchin returned at the same time.

He said, 'Somebody in your group is a snitch. Tell your husband to find out who.'

Brigid's heart raced as she thought the movement had re-vetted members. Upon hearing the boy's warning, Niall sent for Finnbar, who ordered scrutiny of new members' backgrounds. At the next official meeting, Robert set officers to watch their movements.

Niall came home two days after the meeting to say, 'We identified two new members whose backgrounds looked suspicious, and police monitored their movements. One went straight from the meeting to a lawyer's office in St. Anne's Square. The tailing police officer reported a middle-aged man in a frock coat admitted the suspect. Upon the men's departure, the officer uncovered a telegraph machine and a letter in the wastepaper bin, describing possible armed action.'

Brigid's heart quailed. *Armed action? Oh, no.*

Niall continued. 'Finnbar thinks the man is an Ulster spy, but Robert is unsure because the man's background checks passed scrutiny. However, Finnbar thinks he may use an assumed identity. He has ordered a closer watch on his movements.'

'Is he in league with someone from Ulster, then?' said Brigid, her heart thumping.

'That's possible. But Finnbar plans to attack the lawyer's office on the next cloudy night and give the feckers a scare. Ezra has built an incendiary device in the room behind his shop.'

Brigid's mind spun. 'A bomb?' she quavered.

'Don't worry, mavourneen, I'm not involved in the action.'

Fatigue overtook her Brigid. Yawning, she said, 'Let's go to bed, mo stór. I must get up at six-thirty.'

The married retired to the bedroom, and when in bed, Niall turned to kiss his wife goodnight, but she had been fast asleep. Niall stroked her face and blew out the candle.

Finnbar, Ezra and one of Robert's men who functioned as a lookout led an attack on the lawyer's deserted premises a few nights later.

'The bomb caused a lot of damage,' said Niall in a smug tone. 'Ezra is an excellent bomb maker.'

The next day, newspapers covered the raid, reporting that looters had stripped the building. The lawyer, his face contorted with anger, journalists reported, had no clues on who had done it. They portrayed his rage in a caricature sketch alongside newspaper reports. The caricature reminded her of Seamus, and Brigid shuddered.

At dinner time the next day, Amy had news. 'The raid let Saor-Éire obtain specific legal documents, prompting Stephen to enquire about his employer's backing towards becoming an apprentice solicitor. Father said a proper qualification will prepare him for his future and work with Saor-Éire.'

'That's wonderful news,' said Brigid. 'How long is the training?'

'Three or four years. Stephen's clerking position exempts him from some basic training. But father must pay the solicitor a fee.'

After learning the news from Brigid, Niall acknowledged awareness of Stephen's decision.

'Finnbar demanded it as we need a competent legal person in the leadership.' Niall then divulged more about the raid on the lawyer's office.

'Saor-Éire members looted the place, and Cecilia

received several documents to decipher. Stephen checks the correspondence for spying clues and checks those in Gaelic, which Cecilia can't read. So far, none of them relate to Ulster, so we think the infiltrator is a military spy. In the future, Cecilia will require a bilingual assistant proficient in English and Gaelic, as Stephen will be too busy. We are searching for someone suitable.'

The solution soon fell into Brigid's lap.

CHAPTER 16: BIRTH

The doctor saw Brigid each month and pronounced that the pregnancy had progressed satisfactorily. A colleague at Clery's found a low stool and placed it under her desk. Brigid's skin glowed as her pregnant state became more apparent. Her hair had a lustre that shone like russet apples.

Over the summer, they searched for baby goods. Brigid decorated the nursery walls with pictures of animals. She joined the local library to borrow nature books and buy sketchbooks, pencils, and watercolour paints.

The eager mother-to-be began drawing sheep, cows, and exotic animals like parrots, lizards, and monkeys. Then she cut out the pictures and pasted them to the nursery walls. A carpenter by trade, one of the movement's members made a rocking crib. His wife made coverlets and curtains. Brigid sewed an extra quilt with leftover fabric and stored it with cloth nappies in a small press Ezra found. He also discovered an old rocking chair, which he repaired and varnished.

In September, Niall planned a delayed honeymoon to Amy's parents' country cottage. Brigid enjoyed walking in green fields again, watching cows brought home for milking and farmers harvesting their crops.

A harvest party at a farm involved excessive drinking and dancing, but Brigid's belly was too large for her to join in. Instead, she enjoyed watching Niall attempt to dance with the buxom barmaid, who got her feet muddled just as Brigid once had, and she giggled. The break was just what Brigid needed to be contented in her last months of pregnancy.

At home, as the October nights drew in, Brigid began knitting a newborn infant's layette of bootees, a jacket with mittens and a cap in yellow wool. The nursery faced north, and Brigid knew from her experiences with Joseph that the child would need extra warm clothing. *I'll burn a peat fire on the coldest nights to prevent my* precious child from catching a chill.

At Clery's, she organised the handover of work to Fergal, a diligent young man with the makings of an excellent accountant. He admitted to courting a young housekeeper, and Brigid explained he would have better prospects if he had the proper qualifications. Eager to advance, Fergal signed up for the next available course. *He will soon overtake me and gain a promotion or change positions to another employer*. Brigid thought

In mid-November, Brigid finished work. The month brought in a lot of yellowish, smoke-filled fog. Brigid sat by the kitchen stove rather than venturing into the smog and risking a chest infection. She had her groceries delivered by a boy on a bicycle.

To keep busy, Brigid knitted or read books about the world beyond Ireland, such as the West Indies, which sounded like idyllic islands. The book on animals introduced her to creatures in far-off lands, like a parrot she stuck on the nursery wall whose habitat was in Australia.

She often fell asleep by the warm fire, forgetting to prepare a meal. It made Niall laugh when he found her waddling around, harried, preparing a meal. Her forgetfulness had become more pronounced in the last weeks, which worried her.

In a letter, Angela explained the problem had been resolved after childbirth. With relief, Brigid sighed, fearing her mind would become muddled like a person of mature age. The McGraths spent several evenings discussing names for their child and wrote lists, ranking them until two words came out on top: Dermot for a boy and Aisne for a girl.

Ezra had become a frequent visitor and firm friend whom Brigid loved and respected for his wisdom and sense of fun. Chuckling one evening when he arrived for supper, he said, 'You won't have enough free time to play cards once you are a father,

Niall.'

Brigid glanced at her husband's face, which had turned red, and giggled. Knowing she would have her hands complete by Christmas, with the baby's due date around the sixteenth, Brigid began preparations for the season in early December. But she became irritable as she found sleeping difficult and complained to Ezra over supper. 'I can't get comfortable. Niall needs to sleep on the sofa.'

'Arú, it will come in time for Hanukkah, so it will,' said Ezra, grinning.

While they waited, Niall prepared for the child's baptizm by asking friends to be godparents. Brigid wanted Ezra to be a godfather, and to her surprise, he explained that his Polish family had baptised him as a Catholic.

'After my father's sudden death in a fall from a horse, my mother returned to Germany. She was the daughter of a wealthy Jewish jeweller who met my father while he was a student in Germany. She raised me as a Jew, and I had my bar mitzvah at age thirteen. Later, I attended Heidelberg University and planned to be a lawyer, specialising in land purchase. When I turned twenty-one and applied for my adult papers, German authorities discovered I was born in Poland and sent me back.'

Ezra sipped his cooling coffee and continued. 'My Jewish roots are deep, and I became involved in agitation against pogroms and learned to make bombs. I had to escape with a price on my head, leaving my intended wife, Kalina, behind. Nobody has replaced her in my heart. Well, not until I met a girl with a ring who married someone else.'

He grinned, his eyes glinting in the table's candlelight, and Niall raised his eyebrows.

December 16th came and went, with Brigid cleaning the apartment like a fiend.

'The birth won't happen until Christmas at this rate,'

she said to Niall in frustration.

Then, early in the morning of the eighteenth, Brigid woke with an excruciating backache. She brewed herbal tea after getting up. The pain eased when moving around, so she said nothing to Niall and made him breakfast. The pain moved to the front after he departed for work. After a few hours, it became frequent and agonising. Brigid shuffled to the front door and called to the young police officer who patrolled the street, asking him to fetch the midwife.

'Ye have the pains on ye, Missus, so you do. My Mammy has ten of us, and I know the signs.'

Brigid nodded, groaning, as he dashed down the street. She closed the door, leaning against it in pain. The midwife soon arrived, placed a mat atop the bed, and filled the kettle over the fire. As another pain gripped her, the woman got Brigid onto the bed. The fresh-faced police officer fetched Niall, who came into the bedroom, his face chalk white with fear, and held his wife's hand.

But the midwife soon sent him away. 'Off to the pub with ye, mister. Your wife will give birth to the baby before closing time.'

Brigid heard her mutter something else about men, yet another pain attacked her. 'Ye can push now, Missus.'

The midwife cut the umbilical cord with Brigid's knife. She wiped the child with a clean cloth, swaddled him, and handed him to his mother.

'Ye have a healthy son, Missus.'

Brigid cuddled her son and offered him her breast to suckle. Tears shimmered as she thought of her deceased brothers, especially Dermot, *who will never know his namesake nephew*.

Niall returned as the midwife finished cleaning up. 'Ye have a grandson, Mister, so ye do. Make your wife a cup of apple tea and toast while I finish tending to her. Then ye can see the babby.'

Once the midwife had left, Niall brought the crib from the nursery and placed it next to the bed. 'His room is uncomfortably cold for such a little boy. I'm his Da, so I must care for him and his beautiful mother.'

The pair lay awake in the moonlight, watching their son.

But around four in the morning, Niall fell asleep while Brigid held Dermot at her breast, contentment filling her. She inhaled the scent of a newborn child and understood her true calling in life – motherhood. The knowledge filled her with joy. But she felt sadness, too. *How Ma would have loved a grandson.*

As dawn light filtered through the curtains, Brigid placed the baby in his crib and lay her tired head on her pillow. An insistent knocking at the door startled her awake.

The midwife called through the letterbox. 'Is there anything I can help you with, Missus?'

Niall stumbled out of bed to let her in, and she started doing the housework. Dermot fed while the midwife complimented Brigid's motherhood coping skills.

'Yer proper milk will come in soon, Missus,' she said, checking Brigid's postpartum state. Brigid nodded, her eyes half closed.

Niall peered inside to say goodbye before he left for work. He looked dishevelled and bug-eyed, so unlike her well-groomed husband that Brigid laughed. The midwife left around eleven, saying she would return tomorrow, and Brigid should sleep.

'I left ye a stew for your husband to heat for yer tea.'

Niall returned about two hours later, looking contrite. 'The manager found me asleep at my desk, so he sent me home to sleep in a bed. He has given me two days off.'

The news made Brigid smile. She sent Niall to the kitchen to heat some mutton broth and cut some crusty bread. They ate the meal, gazing at their son, amazed by their creation. Soon, life became dominated by feeding and nappy-changing rounds, and Brigid felt fatigued feeding Dermot herself.

Despite Brigid expressing her misgivings about attending a church service, Niall arranged Dermot's baptism for the end of January with Amy and Ezra as godparents. Neither Padraig nor Angela could attend, but Robert and his family came.

Dermot did not cry when the priest poured holy water on his head. He bawled in Amy's arms afterwards.

'He needs to feed,' said Brigid, her cheeks burning with embarrassment, wanting to leave.

After the final blessing, it took them ten minutes to walk to the apartment with Niall pushing the new perambulator. Brigid left Niall to entertain their guests and disappeared to the nursery. Nursing a hungry baby had become a valuable bonding experience for Brigid and Dermot. Later, Amy held Dermot again, and Brigid caught a dreamy look in her friend's eyes.

After the guests departed, Brigid informed Niall that Amy looked ready to settle down.

'She has a broody demeanour about her.'

'But she must meet the right man. One of whom Robert and Diedre approve,' Niall said.

Dermot thrived during Brigid's maternity leave. As the weather grew warmer, she walked him in his perambulator in the local park, where she met other new mothers and exchanged tips on childcare. Brigid visited the library to find books on the subject but found none. Instead, she kept a diary of Dermot's developments: his first smile, crawl, and weaning date.

Dermot was a sturdy child with dark red hair that grew straight. He resembled his namesake, except for his nose, which had his father's aquiline shape.

A proud mother, Brigid was ready to show her son to anyone who wished to see him. The boy began crawling at five months, and his parents had to keep his fingers from low cupboards lest he extract the contents. Ezra found him a wooden train set, and Niall put the train on the tracks. Then, his son giggled with glee by making the train. As a mother, Brigid found it gratifying to see such a bond between father and son develop.

In April, the empty apartment above the family got a tenant, Caitlin O'Grady, a widow in her early fifties. The two women became friends when Brigid invited her to drink apple tea on a sunny afternoon in May. Caitlin took to Dermot, and he to her, holding out his chubby arms and smiling.

'Oh, 'tis good to hold a baby.' Caitlin's eyes glistened. 'I became a widow not long after my daughter Jenny's birth, and I brought her up alone. I was a schoolteacher, and my position included a small cottage. But my daughter and her family perished from the fever in the famine.' Catlin took a handkerchief from her pocket and wiped her eyes. 'Bereft, I left Donegal and came to Dublin as a nanny. My charge, David, is now at school in England, so I'm no longer needed. I miss him so much, Brigid. When he writes to me, I can tell he isn't happy. The other boys bully him.'

'What about the boy's mother? Does she not visit her son?'

'We saw little of her, as she spent most of her time in London. David's father is the wealthy Conservative Member of Parliament for Donegal. He has rented the apartment above yours for a year. I have a small income from the money my farmer husband left me. Still, it won't cover the rent, so I must seek more affordable accommodation next year.'

Her eyes glistened, and Brigid placed Dermot in her arms.

Brigid's six-month maternity expired in June, and seeing how well Caitlin cared for Dermot, she asked Niall whether to employ her as their nanny, and he agreed. Brigid asked if her friend would take the job in return for a salary to help pay the rent.

Caitlin's deep blue eyes lit up. 'What a perfect solution for your son and me. He is a darling little boy.'

Brigid then visited Saoirse, asking permission to work

from home one day per week.

'If it were anyone else, the manager would disagree. He will agree to your request because he knows I value your skills.'

Saoirse blushed, leaving Brigid to ponder if there was more to the relationship than manager and employee.

In no time, Dermot crawled to Caitlin's stairs, his tiny face screwed up. 'He wants to walk,' said Caitlin, coming down to collect him. 'I bet he walks before he is a year old.'

She was right, and he took his first steps at ten months. Soon, he said his first obvious word, 'bird,' and pointed to a robin.

'My clever son,' said Niall, swinging him around so the child squealed with glee.

Caitlin began singing Gaelic nursery rhymes to him, and Brigid asked her if she was fluent in Gaelic.

'Of course. My pupils in Donegal expressed themselves in Gaelic. Many children spoke only that tongue. Why are you enquiring?'

Taken aback by this unexpected response, Brigid said, 'I do hope Dermot becomes bilingual because, although people speak English in Dublin, I want my son to be fluent in Gaelic too. Niall and I speak it in private.'

She refrained from discussing Saor-Éire, but Brigid thought she might have found the helper for Cecilia.

'Please tell Finnbar about her, she said to Niall.'

'He has gone to stay with his mother's family in France for the summer. Ezra and I will oversee Saor-Éire until he returns. We couldn't make such a crucial decision without Finnbar's approval.'

Brigid felt relief that Finnbar would not disturb her for some weeks. Her spirits calmed.

CHAPTER 17: FINNBAR

Ezra often ate with the McGraths that summer. He sat in their garden discussing Saor-Éire matters over a glass of Guinness with Niall or eating up Brigid's home-cooked meals with relish. 'I often make do with a pie at my local pub,' Ezra said, winking at Brigid. 'This cold summer collation is much healthier food.'

On one occasion, Ezra arrived at the gate when Brigid returned with Caitlin from Dermot's afternoon walk. He helped the woman manoeuvre the perambulator along the path, and his eyes lit up upon being introduced to Caitlin. He took off his hat and bowed to her, which amused Brigid. She detected some spark between them as they sat side by side in the garden, engaged in animated conversation.

Curious, Brigid asked Niall where Finnbar lived when he was in Dublin. 'He seldom comes to our home, like Ezra. He is a secretive man.'

'Finnbar knows the British authorities will arrest him for clandestine activities with The Artemus Society- the cover name for a Fenian movement started by academic Ronan O'Brien. It conducted anti-British actions during the famine. Saor-Éire began life as a Dublin branch, though it is now independent, so when in Dublin, Finnbar changes his lodgings often. Ezra says he has assisted O'Brien's agitation in England, and that's why he has gone to France. He rarely informs us of his non-Saor-Éire activities.'

Brigid picked up Dermot, who was crawling towards her across the grass. 'Finnbar has a penetrating stare and appalling manners. He is brooding and unpleasant one minute and enthralling the next. I'm unsure which character will emerge when I meet him.'

'He has no time for fun. Life is all about work for Finnbar. He has fierce intelligence and is intolerant of foolishness. His mother died when he was a child. His father, a doctor wedded to his vocation, became a distant and uncompromising parent.'

Niall took a long drink of Guinness, left foam on his moustache, and Brigid took out her handkerchief to wipe it.

'Finnbar is fluent in several languages,' continued Niall, 'including Gaelic, Russian, and French. He is composing a book on the impact of the famine on peasants. He authored an article on the brutal famine after spending time on the West Coast.'

'If you were poor, the famine was brutal wherever you lived. Remember, famine fever took three of my brothers.' Brigid's brain flooded with memories of that dreadful time.

'Finnbar wants to write about famine-suffering peasants. He will write a series of articles under a pseudonym.'

Brigid's memories became more vivid. 'I doubt his reports will be accurate enough for me. They will be second-hand.'

'I have seen some of his work, and he writes eloquently,' Niall jumped to his colleague's defence.

Feeling uncomfortable discussing the famine, Brigid deflected the conversation. 'He wears such dowdy and worn clothing. I wonder if it is a cover for his affluent upbringing and education. What subject did he read at Trinity College?'

'His first degree is in French and German. But when I met him, he was researching for a doctorate in history, examining how mythical stories become woven into truth.'

'Like bog sprites,' said Brigid in a condescending tone.

'That's far-fetched, Brigid, even for Finnbar, but along those lines.'

Recalling their initial meeting, Brigid could not shake off the disturbance caused by his voice and piercing, ice-blue eyes. Finnbar stared through to her core. It fertilised the withered thistle in Brigid's mind. That had first grown over Da's behaviour.

In contrast, Ezra was a warm, engaging man who showed much interest in Caitlin. Brigid learned he walked with her and Dermot to the park when she was at work. He invited Caitlin to the opera, and on taking Dermot up to her one morning, Brigid found her in a fluster, dresses strewn about the room, not knowing which to wear.

'I'll introduce you to my friends Irene and Amy. Amy will find an excuse to 'borrow' a Clery's dress for the occasion,' said Brigid.

Amy chose a midnight blue gown that enhanced Caitlin's alabaster complexion. With delicate white and purple silk flowers woven through her hair, she looked younger. The evening went without a hitch, and Ezra invited Caitlin to dine at a fancy restaurant. I think Amy will need to borrow many dresses.

Caitlin had stars in her eyes and roses in her cheeks when she told Brigid how much fun she had had, and a beaming Ezra became a regular visitor to Caitlin's apartment. Brigid's fingers ached from being crossed in anticipation.

Finnbar returned from France in the autumn of 1857 but avoided Dublin and went to stay with his sister's family in Waterford. The first of his articles, handwritten by Edward Woodward, appeared in the Dublin Gazette.

Brigid found the article a cutting damnation of landlord evictions. It gave harrowing details of how people had suffered, including the terrible conditions on the boats that transported them to the Americas. Literate survivors had written to relatives to explain their suffering, trapped in the ships' holds without food or proper sanitation.

Brigid thought about writing from personal experience. But now, with free time limited by work, she continued to document Dermot's development in her journal, contemplating how it could serve as a background for a future article.

Niall invited Finnbar to dinner without consulting Brigid, adding that he wished to invite Caitlin too. This insensitivity at omitting her annoyed Brigid.

'Why, Caitlin?' she said.

'Ezra and I hope Finnbar will agree to her becoming a covert female member to help Cecilia. We want her to meet Finnbar and speak in Gaelic with him.'

Brigid wondered how friendly Finnbar would be towards Caitlin and coached her. She explained about Finnbar's abrupt and rude manner and suggested she wear plain clothing.

'He likes my apple pies, and as our apples are ready to pick, I shall cook one to help soften his manner.'

Finnbar came to supper on a Monday evening, and Brigid prepared roast pork and roast potatoes with green vegetables supplied by Ezra from his allotment. Caitlin arrived early to prepare Dermot for bed and helped Brigid prepare the table. Caitlin wore an unadorned dark red dress and put her thick hair in a simple bun.

When Finnbar arrived, Niall guided him into the parlour, where Caitlin waited to be introduced. Caitlin curtsied. 'I'm delighted to make your acquaintance,' she said, mentioning she had heard much about him.

Finnbar gave her an icy stare, then looked her up and down before a slight smile twitched his lips.

'It's gratifying to meet a woman whose countenance and clothing show she isn't conceited.'

But Niall deflected any retort by pouring Finnbar a cream sherry. 'What a pleasure to see you, Finnbar. We understand you author articles on the famine. Caitlin comes from Donegal and will explain her experiences if you wish.'

Finnbar's eyebrows shot up his forehead, and Brigid noted he had done something with his untidy hair. 'When did you leave Donegal?' he said with eyes of penetrating intensity,

Caitlin gave him an abridged version of her famine experiences, and Finnbar relaxed while conversing about a matter that interested him. He commented on Caitlin's story, which tallied with those he had heard on his travels. He treated Caitlin with his version of respect, which meant he did most of the talking after her speech. Supper progressed in amiable conversation, and Caitlin expressed sympathy with Finnbar's goal of "Freedom for Ireland."

'When he learned she had been a teacher in Donegal,' Finnbar said, 'Did you teach in English or Gaelic?'

Caitlin replied in Gaelic. 'In both languages. Although my pupils' first language was Gaelic, I introduced them to English so they could learn to read and speak it in the future. Donegal citizens have an English member of Parliament who is keen for children to learn the language.'

Finnbar questioned Caitlin about her husband's background. Brigid thought he was probing too far and cast Niall a questioning look that implied Finnbar had overreached propriety. Niall raised his eyebrows and shook his head.

However, Caitlin was unfazed. 'My husband was a farmer, and we met when I became a pupil teacher in Donegal. Gaelic was his initial language, though he learned to speak English from me. But he died long ago. Then, our daughter and her family succumbed to the relapsing fever in the famine. Somehow, I eluded it.'

Grief briefly filled her eyes, but she recovered her composure and asked Finnbar about his background.

'My father is Irish, but my mother's family is French. I have a sister and a brother, and my mother lost her life while giving birth to him. I don't remember her because I was only two years old. My father, a doctor, is a distant man whom I dislike. Father employed nannies to raise us. When I was eight, my father sent me to board at a Christian Brother's school in Skibbereen.'

Brigid thought he had inherited his father's coldness. She wondered if his mother's death had anything to do with his dislike of women.

'What led you to work for the Fenian cause?' Caitlin pushed his boundaries.

'My best friend at school set up a covert Fenian Group in Waterford.' Finnbar's tone became cautious. 'Our boyhood association puts me in danger because my friend is a violent man who may end up in prison.'

'Do you meet your friend when you go to Waterford?' Brigid asked innocently.

Finnbar's cheeks grew red, and Brigid knew she had put her finger on the truth. 'Sometimes I do. He wanted to marry my sister, but she refused his proposal, saying he was too violent.'

He blinked fast, and Brigid knew he had not given them the entire story.

Brigid's pulse thrummed. 'Is Saor-Éire at risk by this association? It could explain the attacks on members and infiltration by spies.' Then she got up without waiting for his answer and cleared the dishes. After composing herself in the kitchen, she brought through the apple pie.

Finnbar's eyes widened when he tasted it. 'This is excellent pie, Brigid. Where did you get the apples?'

'From our tree,' Brigid gestured towards the garden, now bathed in moonlight and the tree a mere shadow.

'May I have a second helping, please? I don't get such tasty food in my lodgings.'

His eyes held Brigid's a moment too long for decency, and she blushed.

After the guests left, Niall sat back in his chair, putting his hands behind his head,

'That was a delightful meal, mo stór. You coached Caitlin well, and I knew when Finn began asking questions about her background that he had taken the bait. I shall follow it up.' He paused. 'I noticed Finnbar's jaw clenched when you asked him about Saor-Éire's risks. You came too close to uncovering the truth.'

Brigid had no intention of discussing Finnbar any further. 'Caitlin will manage most of the washing up tomorrow while Dermot naps. I'll clean the cooking trays now, and then it is bedtime. I'm drained.'

The following evening, Brigid pressed Niall about Finnbar's associates. 'This man, O'Brien, must be in contact with Finnbar. I worry about our safety and your likelihood of being a permanent target for British Army attacks.'

Niall's gaze turned distant. 'Brigid, it is the price Saor-Éire members must face for Ireland's freedom. The British understand nothing but dominating other nations and their citizens. They believe they are invincible after conquering half the world.'

Niall did not meet her gaze, and Brigid guessed Finnbar planned another raid. Her gut tightened.

Brigid visited the library the following week to see if Edward Woodward had published an article and found it. The wording showed Finnbar had used Caitlin's story to illustrate the British desire to Anglicise Ireland. A further four articles appeared as second-hand reports. His cold personality and incisive empathic writing were at odds, which puzzled and fascinated Brigid in equal measure. Against her will, his mind drew her deeper into his with each article.

CHAPTER 18: A TEST OF STRENGTH

The family enjoyed a warm October in 1857. A gentle breeze from the open kitchen window caressed Brigid's skin. She recalled the sunset from the kitchen window in Ballyconstór. Tears sprung to her eyes. Trivial things reminded her of the past: a clock ticking, someone coughing, or the smile on Dermot's face, like that of his uncle. The memories made her gut twist.

After hearing about his father's suicide, Brigid did not enquire further about Niall's early life. Still, as winter drew in and they sat around the dancing flames of the kitchen fire, she found the confidence to pose the question.

Niall gazed to the middle distance, leaving Brigid uncomfortable. 'My father was an accountant, and like Finnbar, I attended a religious school operated by the Christian Brothers. It is where I met Stephen.' He resisted divulging more information.

The autumn days passed, and the distant look intensified. Brigid wondered if he had experienced an unhappy childhood and had no intention of discussing it. His lack of focus increased in unguarded moments, adding to Brigid's growing discomfort. As frosty November encroached, and he was often late home, Brigid became filled with dread, wondering what ailed him.

One evening, after visiting Caitlin, Ezra peeked into the room and requested a private conversation with Niall.

'I'm sorry he isn't home yet. These days, he seldom arrives home before Dermot goes to bed. Do you know if he is working on a Saor-Éire raid?'

Ezra shook his head, but his eyes would not meet Brigid's, and she suspected he was lying. Her dread increased as Ezra turned on his heel and headed for Caitlin's apartment. *Why does Ezra need to speak with Niall?*

Niall did not return home for supper on the third Tuesday in November. With Dermot in bed, Brigid waited for the front door to open, her anxiety growing as the minutes ticked by. At eight-thirty, Brigid served her meal, covering Niall's with a plate and putting it in the warm oven. Anxious thoughts intruded and caused such knots in her gut that she couldn't eat.

After ironing the bedsheets, stitching some embroidery, and checking their household accounts, Brigid got into bed with a book. But she couldn't concentrate. Visions of Niall lying in the street, a victim of violence, disturbed her. *A cat on a hot chimney pot would have more rest than me,* she thought as the church clock chimed ten times.

Brigid must have succumbed to sleep because the front door banging open woke her with a start. Dermot woke too and cried. Brigid rushed to soothe her son before opening the apartment door. At the base of Caitlin's stairs lay Niall, and at the top stood Caitlin, in her nightgown, frozen.

Brigid gathered her wits. 'Don't worry. Niall must have lost at cards, and I fear he is drunk.' Brigid doubted Catlin believed the feeble excuse. But she had to keep calm for Dermot's sake.

'Do you need any help?' Caitlin, her face full of concern, wrapped her shawl around her shoulders and descended the stairs.

'I can take Dermot to my flat if you wish.'

Brigid did not want Caitlin to see Niall's probable injuries. 'Thank you. If I need your help, I'll ask. Dermot has stopped crying. I have dealt with situations like this in the past.' Brigid did not elaborate.

Caitlin hesitated, shaking her head, 'If you are sure,' she said, climbing upstairs and closing her door.

Brigid breathed out with relief. She helped Niall to his unsteady feet, and her heart rate rose to the roof when she saw a wound in his leg, blood dripping down. 'The feckers waiting for us,' Niall said with a rasp.

Oh, not another raid gone wrong. Brigid helped Niall to his feet and then saw the size of the wound. Slashed in mid-thigh, a gaping hole leaked blood. Brigid fetched a towel to stem the flow and helped him into the apartment.

Brigid had seen nasty wounds on her brothers, but none as bad as this. When she got Niall to their bed, the towel was bright red with blood. Brigid removed it and put another towel under his leg, elevating the limb on two pillows. Gulping at the sight, she found a leather strap to fasten above the wound and stem the blood flow. Niall's face was pale, and beads of sweat had broken out on his forehead. Brigid feared for his life.

'Feck, Niall, I can't deal with this. You must get the wound stitched by a skilled person.' She wondered if the fever had set in or if the pain caused him to sweat.

But Niall refused to have medical attention. 'Secret mission We...' His head lolled, and he lost consciousness.

Brigid swallowed bile and busied herself by finding a clean towel and a small cloth. After washing her hands in hot water from the kettle on the hob, she took a few deep breaths and prepared to stitch the challenging wound.

While Niall remained unconscious, Brigid threaded the curved needle from her sewing basket with tough thread, poured iodine into the wound, and set to work. She sewed each stitch with painstaking slowness to ensure the edges met, expecting him to regain consciousness and scream with pain. Afterwards, she bandaged the wound with clean towelling from one of Dermot's fresh-washed nappies.

Niall groaned, sweat beading his forehead when, at last, he came to his senses. With the fear of infection gnawing at her fingertips, Brigid provided him with a measure of laudanum. She brought another pillow to raise his leg further and removed the strap. Brigid let out a deep sigh when the stitches held. She refused to let her son witness his father's state, so she accepted Caitlin's offer to help when morning came.

While Niall slept, she wrote two letters – one to the bank and another to Saoirse – and left a note for Ezra. Afterwards, Brigid lay beside her husband, unable to sleep. Now a mother, she relied on Niall, and the constant fear of him perishing in a raid gnawed at her mind like a rat in the scullery gnawing a loose board.

'Ruffians attacked Niall on his way home last night,' she told Caitlin later. 'Please give this note to Ezra when he visits. Can you care for Dermot for two or three nights while I nurse Niall?'

Caitlin nodded, her eyes soft with sympathy. Brigid kissed her son's forehead, returning to her apartment before the threatened tears fell. Later, Brigid unlocked the front door to call the police officer to post her letters.

However, much to her astonishment, he was not in his usual spot, and instead, the street urchin appeared, his face streaked with dirt.

'I told thee your man must watch his step. Tell him they got guns; he may not be so lucky next time.'

Shaking with fear, Brigid spoke in Gaelic. 'Er, young man, what's your name, and how do you know this?'

Her heart thumped in her chest, and her eyes searched for the police officer, but he was nowhere in sight.

The boy jumped from foot to foot, looking into Brigid's eyes with a scared gaze. 'I go by Liam as my first name, but I ain't saying more cos it could get me in a fix.'

He turned and sprinted like the wind, his bare feet slapping on the cobbles.

Brigid's body shook at this encounter and, on unsteady legs, crossed the road to post the letters, hoping they would arrive in the afternoon mail. Afterwards, as she shut the front door, the full import of Liam's words hit her like a fist.

Next time, with guns? Oh no, please, not guns. They could kill Niall. Her legs gave way, and she slumped into the nearest chair, tears gushing down her face.

By evening, Niall had a high fever, sweat hung on his brow, and the wound looked red and angry. Brigid poured iodine on it and wrapped it in a clean dressing.

Niall raved with delirium that night, and Brigid gave him more laudanum. The fever continued to burn the next day as Niall raved, thrashing his arms. Brigid dared not remove the bandage but administered more laudanum.

Towards the morning of the third day, he stopped yelling and slept, and Brigid, touching his forehead, thought his fever had broken. She fetched a clean dressing and looked at the wound. The redness had gone down, and the stitches held.

In the morning, Niall woke up and spoke coherently. He recalled nothing after reaching the apartment. With relief sweeping through her fear like a new broom through dust, Brigid gave him chicken broth and another dose of laudanum.

Brigid dozed by the range for most of the day. Then, a sharp knock at the front door roused her. On the step stood Liam. 'What are you after now, child?' Anxiety laced Brigid's voice.

'Listen, I know your man plays cards as a front. I heard my brother, who is in the army, speak about it.' He shuffled his bare feet. 'I'm not one to rat, but the military's paid someone to join your group. It is how they know about the raids.'

He then ran away as fast as a hare again, leaving Brigid rooted in the open doorway. With her pulse beating in her ears, Brigid closed the door.

Caitlin stood near the base of her stairs and hugged her friend. 'I overheard. Finnbar inducted me into Saor-Éire in a ceremony last week. I can help by caring for Dermot while you nurse Niall.'

Brigid felt relief at having another woman with whom to share her concerns.

'I thought it best not to startle you. I'm content to care for Dermot as long as needed. I could help with Niall, too. I learned first aid upon becoming a teacher.'

Overcome with emotion, Brigid fell into Caitlin's motherly arms and sobbed. For the first time since Ma's passing, Brigid felt a mother's comfort and cried water on Caitlin's shoulder.

Niall woke late in the afternoon and said he was hungry, so Brigid heated some more chicken broth and cut hunks of bread and cheese. She sat beside him while he ate and related Liam's words about the spy in Saor-Éire. 'Who could it be? Roberts has scrutinised everybody again. I think Ezra will speak with you about it this evening.'

Niall's spoon had stopped halfway to his mouth. 'Robert never discovered whose handwriting was on message found at the lawyer's office. It did not match our coded documents or the lawyer's writing.' Niall winced, put down his spoon, and lay back on his pillow. 'Damn, leg hurts like buggery, so it does.'

Brigid removed the dressing and examined the wound. 'No change since this morning, mo stór. I'll fetch the laudanum.'

'No mavourneen. I want a clear head when I see Ezra. Give me a dose when he is gone.'

Around five o'clock, the door knocker banged, and when Brigid opened the door, she found Ezra had brought Finnbar with him.

'Is the old devil up to talking, Brigid?' Ezra said, his tone too jovial.

Finn's ice eyes bore into her, making Brigid blush.

'Er, yes. Niall is awake but in pain. However, he wants to see you, so come to the bedroom. Would you like something to drink?'

The men shook their heads, staying with Niall for about twenty minutes, which made Brigid concerned that their conversation had gone on too long.

As they left, Finnbar paused in the doorway to ask Brigid if she had baked another apple pie, and if she had, would she save him a slice? Brigid blushed. 'You are an exceptional woman, and I seldom give such compliments because most women are weak eejits.'

Brigid closed the door, her face burning, musing how she despised the man. He possesses the ability to lower my defences by praising my apple pies. Although I am happily married, I struggle to maintain composure as the man evokes such intense emotions.

Brigid retreated to the kitchen and waited for her nerves to relax before moving to the bedroom and speaking with Niall.

'Did your meeting go well, mo stór? Finnbar and Ezra stayed much longer than I expected.' She shivered.

Niall nodded in reply, but his face creased with pain. 'I'll have that laudanum now,' he rasped.

His wife sat holding his hand till he drifted into slumber. The guilt she experienced over her feelings for Finnbar felt like a brick in her stomach. He returned to the kitchen and attempted to eat some bread and cheese, but the food stuck in her throat, and he gave up. She stitched her embroidery with ferocious fingers, stabbing one with the needle so it bled. The pain blotted out her guilt at Finnbar's hold over her emotions.

The following morning. Niall awoke and said the pain was less. Brigid checked the wound. The injury was knitting, so she poured some iodine over it and put on a clean bandage, thinking Dermot would soon have no nappies.

'I need to do some shopping, Niall. Would you be comfortable if I left you for an hour? Caitlin is caring for Dermot.'

Niall gazed at his wife with such tenderness that it caused her eyes to glisten.

'You have done such an excellent job, mo stór. I would not be here if it were not for your care. Go, do your shopping. I'll be fine.'

Brigid gave him some laudanum first and stood by the bed, playing with a strand of hair eluding her mobcap.

'Niall, now that the British Army is after your blood, please cease being active. You have a family to care for, and I worry for Dermot's safety.'

But Niall's eyes had closed, and Brigid was unsure whether he had heard. She fetched her cape and a basket and left the apartment. To her relief, the police officer was on duty. He apologised for his absence, saying, 'My wife gave birth to our first child, a son.' He grinned, looking like Niall did when Dermot was born.

Brigid congratulated him and hurried away. She bought fabric to dress Niall's wound, nappies for Dermot, and some meal provisions.

At home, Brigid found a letter from Clery's store on the doormat. Amy had explained the situation to Saoirse, who consented to Brigid's having the remaining days of the week off unpaid, but this was the last time she would provide cover for Niall's indispositions.

Brigid suspected Saoirse knew about Niall's Fenian activities, and her determination to end Niall's involvement in raids heightened.

If Niall gets killed or maimed in an attack, I'll become the breadwinner.

Ezra brought a crutch later that day, which someone had pawned, and helped Niall wash his body. After their conversation, Niall returned to bed, and Ezra entered the kitchen.

'Niall has told me you fear for his life because the British Army is spying on Saor-Éire. I'll instruct Robert to increase the guard and inform Finn to remove Niall from the active list for two years.

'Oh, thank you, Ezra. I want that; otherwise, we may have to leave this apartment.' On impulse, Brigid embraced him.

Ezra patted her arm. 'Niall is as stubborn as MacConkey's mule and took some persuading.' He stroked his beard. 'I'm not only watching out for you. Caitlin has become dear to me, and

I care for her safety, too.'

Brigid caught the gleam in his eye at her friend's name, turned to the stew pot, and stirred the contents lest Ezra see her blush. 'Ezra, will you stay for supper?'

'Thank you, Brigid, but I'm meeting Caitlin in a minute.'

Brigid felt relieved because she needed time to discuss the matter with Niall.

In the morning, Niall woke in less pain and got up for breakfast, sitting on a low stool with his leg supported. Caitlin brought Dermot back that afternoon, and the child fell asleep in her arms. Brigid hugged him as warm maternal feelings flooded her body. She thanked Caitlin for her help, tears blinding her eyes.

'Things will work out, Brigid, I promise you. Ezra knows that protection is necessary,'

Over supper, Brigid asked Niall again about raids. 'Dermot and I need you alive, not dead from a British knife or bullet.'

'I have agreed to Ezra's proposal, so please stop worrying, mo stór.' Niall paused, changing the subject. 'Ezra will propose marriage soon. He is a changed man.'

Brigid said. 'You may be right; I can see Caitlin is in love.'

When Brigid left to take Dermot to the park the following Sunday afternoon, a cab with gleaming lamps and horse brasses drew up. Robert alighted to visit Niall.

He bent to the perambulator, and Dermot wailed. 'Oh dear, he does not like police officers.'

Brigid saw a nervous twitch in Robert's temple. 'He is a wary child who is uncomfortable around strangers. I'll return in an hour if it doesn't rain. Please don't tire Niall. He thinks he is as strong as the American boxer John Heenan. He isn't.'

Over supper, Niall related the purpose of Robert's visit: 'He has assured me all members' credentials are under scrutiny. Cecilia had suggested a name we have never considered, yet it makes perfect sense.'

Brigid swallowed a mouthful of colcannon. 'Who is it?'

'Young Connor Conlon, who joined with you. Finn put him in charge of messaging.'

'Oh, feck. Did Connor's age and role blind us to duplicity despite him being right under our noses?'

'Connor has overseen our messages for some considerable time, and being a mere boy, nobody suspected him. We are checking his credentials now.'

As they finished their meal, someone rapped on their door. Brigid ran to open it. 'I must speak to Niall,' Ezra said, his voice strained.

He stepped over the doorway without waiting for an invitation. Puzzled by his rudeness, Brigid showed him into the kitchen, where he addressed Niall.

'We set a trap for Connor, and Cecilia is correct. Two British Army soldiers in mufti were "loitering with intent" outside a warehouse where police officers arrested them. One comes from a family of ten; six are boys, and Connor is one of them. However, the Christian Brothers educate Connor because he wishes to become a priest. So, he lives at the presbytery separated from the rest of his family, and nobody spotted the link.'

Brigid quailed. 'Could Liam be another of Connor's brothers? It would explain why the boy has hung around since we moved in. It will doom the child if the army learns he is an informant.' Brigid's pulse rate ratcheted up several beats.

'If you see the boy again, please warn him,' Ezra said.

Brigid nodded, unable to think of anything but the child's bravery.

The next day. Amy signalled Brigid to meet her at a private table in Sweeney's.

'Why this table?' Brigid said, positioning herself to face Amy.

Amy placed her finger on her lips. 'I saw Stephen last night. The unknown writing on that message at the lawyer's office was Connor's. The man who delivered the message was Connor's brother's friend. Both have vanished, making us think the army deployed their unit outside Dublin. To the Crimea.'

Brigid's appetite vanished. 'Oh feck, what else has Connor spied on?'

'We guess everything. Our work has been compromised. Stephen is livid.'

During her journey back, Brigid thought about the implications of growing unease and, to her surprise, found the street urchin loitering again.

'Liam, what are you after now? You have helped us so much already.'

The boy took off his grimy cap. 'I know your group laid a snare for my brother, Connor. He hero-worships Kevin. I can't agree with them, but I must stop informing them lest my brother finds out. But he leaves tomorrow for Crimea, so I doubt he will. I wish you luck, Missus.'

He turned to run, but Brigid put her hand on his shoulder. 'Thank you for the warnings.' Brigid dug into her skirt pocket. 'Please take this florin as a reward.'

The boy blushed, took the money, and ran off. Brigid's eyes were filled with sadness. So young and yet so wise. Brigid was concerned for his safety.

At home, she found Niall hopping around preparing an evening meal. 'I'm getting into my stride now,' he said, like the Niall she loved.

After supper, Brigid poured more iodine on the scar and bandaged it. To her relief, Niall was putting some weight on the leg. 'The stitches can come out soon,' he said.

'Don't overdo it, or you'll destroy my handiwork.' Brigid removed her boots and rubbed her toes, shuddering at the idea of removing the stitches.

'We have a guest tonight, mavourneen. Finnbar wants to see us. He asked for that piece of apple pie.' Niall grinned, and Brigid felt annoyed at not being consulted, and her heart hammered in her chest.

Over supper, Finnbar explained he thought the family ought to move. 'Stephen has done some house hunting for you and found a property on Heytesbury Street, with an excellent primary school at one end of the road.'

Niall took his wife's hand. 'I'm not mobile enough yet to view it, mo stór. It is best if you go with Finnbar. Will you accompany my wife, please?'

Finnbar fixed Brigid with his mesmerising gaze. Under his scrutiny, Brigid blushed, removing their used dinner dishes. She put apple pie into dishes and a dollop of cream on each and handed Finnbar his dessert first.

'Thank you, Brigid, said Finbar, spooning a piece into his mouth. The pie is splendid.'

Niall beamed at his wife as Brigid blushed. 'She is a grand cook, Finn. I'm fortunate.'

You are. But I doubt you realise how much.

Being treated as a mere woman wounded Brigid's sense of self, and her ire rose, which she quelled with effort, pasting on a smile.

CHAPTER 19: HEYTESBURY STREET

In 1858, the family moved to a new home with three bedrooms on the first floor and two large rooms on the top floor. Brigid offered Caitlin both rooms, but she only needed one because they were of a grand size.

'I can make one into a very comfortable bed-sitting room.' Caitlin's eyes sparkled.

Everyone in the household had fun finding furniture for the house. Brigid's new kitchen had extra cupboards, a superb range, and a more robust water pump in the scullery.

Ezra found a copper boiler. 'I heard it came from a derelict cottage in Wicklow.' He grinned, his eyes twinkling. Brigid blushed.

The McGrath family found moving out of their apartment challenging, as it held cherished memories of being their first home. Brigid missed the old, gnarled apple tree, although the extensive garden at the back of the new property had a less gnarled one.

While Robert couldn't guarantee safety, police officers patrolled Heytesbury Street every hour, a long, straight street with few places for ruffians to hide, giving Brigid more confidence. A nearby enormous park provided a place for Dermot to play with other children.

Caitlin furnished her room with a few items to which she felt attached. Her old employers had bought the rest of her furniture from thrift stores, and Ezra sold them. Despite everyone waiting, no marriage proposal came. Niall suggested their present circumstances suited them.

Brigid said, 'Caitlin will want the security and propriety of marriage. Has Ezra been a bachelor too long?'

'I'll speak to him,' said Niall,

But Brigid, who had been thinking of Dermot, warned against it. 'Think of the consequences. If Ezra proposes, Caitlin will move out, and we'll lose her help. It sounds selfish, but Dermot loves her like a grandmother.'

'Regardless, moving house is the right choice for our family,' said Niall.

The summer months passed, with Brigid and Niall taking their son to the park most evenings. Sometimes, Caitlin and Ezra accompanied them, and the four became firm friends. Dermot, a charming toddler, brought happiness to everyone, with Ezra playing the role of Grandpa with aplomb.

In the weeks leading up to Christmas, Brigid's body felt fatigued, and she struggled to do all her work, falling asleep by the parlour fire. Caitlin spotted the changes and advised her to visit a doctor after Christmas. He confirmed Caitlin's suspicions.

'The child will be born in August.' The doctor congratulated Brigid.

'Me a Da again,' Niall, overjoyed, said, swinging Dermot about the room. 'You'll have little sister Dermot; I know it. Blessed, so we are.'

'Saoirse needs to know. She won't give me maternity leave a second time.'

When Brigid announced her news, Saoirse said, 'I know, I recognised the signs.'

'I'm sorry to have to leave Clery's. I enjoy my work here. But I could earn something by doing small business accounts from home.'

'I have spoken with the manager,' said Saoirse. 'He agrees we can't afford to lose someone with your skills. You have a 'live-in' nanny, I believe. We'll give you six months' unpaid leave, as we did for Dermot's birth, with a return to your current working arrangement.' She clicked her tongue. 'Please don't train your successor so well this time, Brigid. I don't want to lose staff. It reflects on my record.'

The ghost of a smile played on Saoirse's thin lips. Her eyes glistened, and her spectacles slipped down her nose.

Brigid stared at her. 'This offer is beyond generous. How can I ever thank you?'

'By working hard and taking over my position when I retire. No one is better suited or respected. You have earned it.'

On impulse, Brigid hugged Saoirse, tears of joy blinding her eyes. 'You are such a kind person. I owe you a debt of gratitude.'

Brigid continued to work until mid-July. She and Niall enjoyed evening walks to the park with Dermot. Niall's injured thigh muscles needed strengthening, and he had a slight limp. He would have a permanent scar.

'A badge of my determination to free Ireland.' Niall winced and then grinned.

With Brigid's reluctant agreement, Niall invited Finnbar and Stephen to supper so they could thank them for their help in the move. Brigid served roast beef and potatoes with cabbage and lashings of gravy. Finnbar smiled his thanks, as much social etiquette as the man displayed. He gazed at her, waiting for his apple pie as Brigid cleared the dishes. She brought out the dessert, and Finn's eyes shone with glee.

Nobody uttered a word while eating the golden-crusted pie. But, replete, Finnbar wiped his mouth on his napkin, sat back, and congratulated his hosts on their expected child. He reassured Brigid that nobody would compel Niall to take part in raids,

'I have halted them for a year as I plan to travel along Ireland's east coast to learn how families there fared in the famine. I might also take a trip to America, where a Young Irish Comrades group is being formed in Boston. The word has spread among immigrants who want to help the old country.'

'Where are you sailing from?' Brigid asked, avoiding eye contact with his unwavering gaze. They unnerved her less now that she knew him better, but his eyes still had the power to mesmerise her. Although not a person given to sentimentality, his unwavering loyalty to people and the causes he cared about became evident to Brigid. He cared about Saor-Éire, and her opinion of him softened.

'Many ships leave Dublin and Cork for the British West Indies and America. I suspect a higher number of people migrated from the east coast to southern ports.

'More might have left their homes but more knocked on workhouse doors.'

She did not speak further because too many memories surfaced. She fetched the after-dinner port and three glasses and handed them to Niall.

'I'll leave you to talk, gentlemen, and make coffee before I wash the dishes.'

Finnbar's eyes lit up again. 'Coffee, now there is a treat. I drink it when I'm in France visiting my mother's relatives. I'll enjoy a cup. Thank you, Brigid.'

Brigid left the dining room door open to eavesdrop on their conversations. She heard Stephen speak. 'Dammed good liquor, Niall.'

Niall's voice sounded relieved. 'It pleases me to hear we have stopped violent action. The British Army is too close for comfort.'

Brigid trusted the British Army had not caught Liam. When Robert's cab arrived, the men departed to Dún Laoghaire, where Finn lodged with Stephen's family. To her surprise, Finnbar kissed her hand on leaving.

'Thank you for your hospitality, Brigid.'

Feelings of turmoil coursed through her, and she blushed, averting her gaze so Niall wouldn't see. The man had got under her skin, and it had unnerved her.

One Monday in April, sitting outside in the spring sunshine, Brigid wrote to Angela to say the family had moved. She said nothing about Saor-Éire but wrote about her expected child and new house, painting Dermot in front of it. She caught Dermot's smile and gaze so like his uncle's that she knew her sister would approve.

Brigid waited patiently for her sister to reply, keeping busy setting up her new home. Time passed, and Brigid wondered if her letter to Angela had gone astray. Perhaps lost in the foamy depths of the Atlantic Ocean.

Niall told her not to worry because no news could be good news, and Angela might just be busy. But Brigid continued to worry.

Several weeks later, to her nervous relief, she received a reply. Angela wrote she had become a mother to a second daughter and continued with news that shocked Brigid.

Seamus fell victim to a fever while in prison. Before he died, Seamus took over the cottage's tenancy from Da's landlord and gave it to Padraig. However, Padraig must also allow Maura to live there because Da must join her if he survives prison. I heard he had some arrangement with the agent to whom he paid a handsome sum of money.

Brigid gulped and ran her hands through her hair, her shoulders tensing as she read Angela's words. She hoped her father would not survive prison. The rest of her letter contained family news. Angela closed by writing how much she missed her sister and wished for them to meet so she could meet her nephew and the baby when it arrived.

Brigid thought that Angela and her daughters could travel to a neutral venue like the Gallagher's after the baby's birth. She would like to meet her nieces. Tears filled her eyes for the family she had lost. Dermot, a sensitive child, climbed on her knee. Brigid gathered him into her arms and wept. 'Mammy, no cry,' Dermot touched her wet face.

Brigid's second confinement had no problems, and Aisne arrived on August 10th, 1859. Niall, besotted, couldn't resist cradling her. In protest, she cried a piercing sound.

'Aisne looks and sounds like you.' Niall smoothed her downy red hair.

She had Brigid's fierce will but with Niall's deep brown eyes. Brigid felt they looked right through her as Aisne fed at her breast and wondered, *is she a demon sent to torment me? Her cries pierce my heart.'*

Regardless, Brigid loved her daughter with fierce pride.

Dermot adored her. 'My sissa,' he said with self-importance as he pointed to her for visitors.

Throughout the rest of the summer, Brigid enjoyed some fun-filled times. One Sunday, while the warm weather held, Niall took his family to the beach, where Dermot squealed with delight at the waves and enjoyed a picnic on the shore.

Caitlin and Brigid brought the children to the park most days. The two women had grown close, and one afternoon, Caitlin revealed more about her background.

'We often used Gaelic at home to confuse Father, who did not understand a word.' Caitlin's eyes sparkled at the memory. 'Mother and I moved back to Ireland after my father's death when he had just turned twelve.'

Brigid discussed the dilemma of her mother's unknown family and Ma's insistence on her children learning gentlefolk skills. Caitlin suggested she might have English blood since she was a Protestant.

'I have often wondered if Mammy had been orphaned. She had no relatives except Aunt Bessie. My sister and I discussed whether she had been Mammy's employer, who taught her gentlefolks' manners and not a real aunt. It remains a mystery,' Brigid said.

Caitlin's eyes implied she had a different explanation. Yet she remained silent.

One Sunday in December, the family ate dinner with Caitlin

and Ezra. Brigid caught sight of a twinkle in the pawnbroker's eyes. After they had eaten, Ezra said, 'Ye need not worry that you'll lose your nanny, although Caitlin plans to move out in the spring.' His eyes sparkled, and he winked at Brigid, stroking his neat beard.

Brigid's heart leapt with joy. 'You have proposed to Caitlin?'

'Last night, on one knee, after the opera.' Caitlin beamed.

Ezra removed a small container from his pocket. He extracted a sapphire and diamond engagement ring, which he placed on Caitlin's waiting finger. Caitlin held it out for everyone to admire.

'It's beautiful, the colour of your eyes,' Brigid's voice choked with emotion. 'Have you set a date?'

'Not yet, but perhaps in May.' Ezra beamed at his fiancée.

Concerned that reaching the shop required a thirty-minute walk from Heytesbury St, Brigid worried about Caitlin's safety.

'Are you planning to live above your shop?' she said.

'I wouldn't take my bride to live in an old bachelor's flat. I have discovered a lovely house to rent, about a ten-minute walk from yours. I may retire in a few years, and then, God willing, I shall sell up, and we'll move to the country.' His face beamed with glee.

Niall poured the champagne. He and Brigid toasted the happy couple, who glowed. Brigid felt nobody deserved happiness more than Ezra and his bride-to-be.

CHAPTER 20: THE MATCHMAKERS

Niall received a letter in the New Year from Finn, who had gone to America for some months to collaborate with John Stokes of the Irish Comrades organisation. He wrote he had completed the research for his book by interviewing emigrants who had crossed the ocean and survived. So, Finnbar could gain access to its library, he enrolled in some refresher classes in French literature at the University of the City of New York.

'Finn's delayed return means Saor-Éire lacks someone with his razor-sharp intelligence in its leadership. We need fresh blood,' Niall said as he got ready for bed one night.

Stephen came to see Niall a few weeks later with a potential member, Alexander MacDonald, whom he had met on a legal case. Brigid served them coffee and homemade biscuits in Niall's study, left the door ajar and listened.

'My brother studied medicine in Glasgow like our father, but I chose law and studied at Edinburgh University. People's bodies are not for me. I prefer their minds. What makes people engage in activities that get them into trouble?' Alexander's voice held a deep baritone.

'Both are noble professions,' Niall avoided the tricky question. 'Your family must be wealthy.'

'Father's eminence in his profession has brought him success from which we have all benefitted.'

The next day, when Caitlin brought a sleepy Dermot home, the two women sat in the warmth of Brigid's kitchen range and discussed Brigid's opinion of Alexander.

'He is a handsome chap in his late twenties with a neat beard, striking blue eyes, and a law degree from Edinburgh University. It is time Amy settled down. Do you think we could engage in matchmaking?' Brigid said with a gleam in her eye.

The two women hatched a plan. Brigid would hold a dinner party to welcome him to Dublin and introduce him to Saor-Éire. Niall agreed, keen to get Alexander's skills into the organisation. The two women enjoyed preparing a menu and a seating plan. With Niall's approval, they took Cecilia into their confidence. Caitlin informed her that as a valued member of Saor-Éire, she would be a guest, not a servant.

'Niall will tell Robert,' said Brigid. 'I'm certain he will understand. We must show a united front.'

Cecilia nodded and blushed.

The seating plan placed Amy between Ezra and Alexander, with Ezra on her left and Alexander on her right. Ezra volunteered to assist with matchmaking by conversing with Cecilia, who they placed to his right. The two women hired a cook and a server for the night, with payment covered by Saor-Éire.

'We have plenty of free reserves. I can make an exemplary case for this dinner as a business expense. However, whoever I employ must be trustworthy. Do you think Ezra will investigate that for us, Caitlin?'

'Of course. Ezra will enjoy the task.'

Caitlin's smile lit up her face. With Caitlin and Ezra's wedding date in mid-May, they fixed the dinner party date for mid-March.

The dinner was a tremendous success, with Amy and Alexander's animated conversation contributing to its success. Brigid, watching, thought she saw a spark between them.

Several days passed, and Caitlin reported Alexander had taken Amy to the theatre because she and Ezra had attended the same performance and had spotted them. 'They seemed deeply engrossed in each other's companionship, with poor Stephen sitting to one side looking out of place,' Caitlin grinned, 'I'll send Alexander a belated invitation to my wedding.'

Brigid grinned, too. 'Fingers crossed then, Caitlin. They have taken the bait.'

Brigid watched her children's unique development during this idyllic time. She continued to keep her journals and enjoyed comparing Dermot and Aisne. Her entry for Aisne in May commented on her independent spirit. At a similar age, Dermot was gentle and obedient.

In contrast, Aisne resisted her authority. But Aisne became a Daddy's girl, her eyes lighting up when he came home and her chubby arms reaching for him.

You twist him round your little finger, you minx, so you do, Brigid thought,

Brigid's thirst for knowledge grew, but she became frustrated by a lack of information on child development, so she focused on scholarly journals in the library reading room. There, Brigid found an article on evolution by someone called Charles Darwin. His theory stimulated her interest by providing a potential reason for her children's differing characteristics and behaviour.

Upon hearing about her interests, Stephen directed her to the works of the philosopher Rousseau.

'His theory that children are born with a moral sense thwarted by society's restrictions will interest you. I'll lend you my book on the subject.'

When Brigid read it, she saw Stephen as correct because the theory could explain Aisne's tantrums. One November evening, Brigid told Niall she would like to find someone who enjoyed philosophy with whom to discuss her views.

'It's not among my interests, mo stór.' Niall had studied mathematics. 'The best person to speak with is Finnbar. He returns from America in the spring when the crossing is calmer. He will discuss them with you.'

Brigid nodded in meek agreement, but her heart banged at the thought of being alone with Finnbar and did not pursue it. Christmas 1860 arrived, and Dermot turned three. Ezra made him a more intricate train to play with and gave Aisne a music box. She loved it when Brigid played the instrument, clapping her tiny hands together. Music soothed the child's mind. The family ate a Christmas feast with a large goose and a Christmas pudding, in which Brigid hid a silver sixpenny piece. Caitlin and Ezra joined them, and Ezra bit into the coin, which almost cracked a tooth.

Everyone laughed at his grim face, so unlike his usual jovial expression.

Brigid recommenced employment in February. Aisne screamed on the first day, and Caitlin looked exhausted upon Brigid's return. The child had been uncooperative, refusing to accept that her mother must work. Brigid recorded it all in her journal.

Since she now earned a salary, she subscribed to the science periodical in which she had read the article on Darwin's theory. In its March edition, she saw an advert for a lecture on Darwin's theory at Trinity College. Brigid recalled the newspaper cartoonists' caricatures of Darwin's face like a monkey. The establishment's attitudes disturbed Brigid, who, as a married woman, needed Niall's permission to attend. That she needed permission irked her.

'I'm proud of your enquiring mind. Still, in these times, we must protect women from ruffians, especially the wives of our group's leaders.' Niall's eyes held an uncompromising gaze.

Brigid nodded but chafed at the chains of a husband's right to control his wife. She learned from a glowing Amy that Finnbar had returned from America and was living with the Gallaghers. When she sat in the lecture theatre, Finnbar had the seat beside her. Brigid's pulse rate increased when he greeted her with unmistakable warmth in his tone. Brigid thought it planned and suppressed her growing anger.

However, the lecture was riveting, confirming some ideas Brigid had amassed in her journal. Afterwards, Finn invited her to join him at a nearby coffee house and paid the cabby to wait for half an hour. He discussed the lecture's content with Brigid, who warmed to him after listening to his deep-thinking views.

Finnbar lost some of his mystique when talking about something that interested him. A gleam appeared in his eyes as he extended an invitation.

'Please join me as my guest at the upcoming lecture on fossils. For a woman, your company is most agreeable.'

The slur on womanhood disturbed Brigid, but so did the slight gap between Finnbar's front teeth, which was visible when he smiled. Her emotions surged, and she accepted his invitation despite misgivings. Finnbar bowed and helped her into the cab. Polite etiquette from Finnbar?

Brigid felt dumbfounded as the cab rattled onwards, and her thoughts raced. She was sure Finnbar's presence at the lecture was deliberate for protection. Despite this, she arrived home late and had to justify it to Niall. This frustrated her because a man would stay silent in a comparable situation.

Niall, seated by the dying embers of the parlour fire, looked at his wife with brooding eyes. 'Please don't linger alone after a lecture. I'll tell Finnbar that I permit him to take you for a coffee and a chat about the lecture, but I'll allow nothing else.'

Brigid nodded and blushed. Chastened, she took herself to bed, where she struggled to sleep, resentment lurking beneath the surface. Finnbar's more open-minded perspective, considering Brigid worthy of his attention regardless of gender, brought satisfaction.

Some weeks later, following a Saor-Éire meeting, Niall came home with the news. 'Finnbar's trip to America opened his eyes to the funds Americans can amass for the cause. He wants to combine forces with the American 'Irish Comrades.'

'I bet Stephen won't approve of being under the control of the Irish Comrades. Alexander's recruitment needs to be speeded up. If he is on board, you could outvote Finn and ensure Saor-Éire remains a local movement,' said Brigid with a sigh.

Niall's growing negative view of women's freedom came to a head in the coffee house on Monday evening. Brigid joined the meeting after Caitlin babysat for them. Niall demurred when Amy said she had an interest in women's suffrage. However, Finn thought women who contributed to society, like Florence Nightingale, should have the chance. Niall commented such women were rare creatures who did not marry.

His point of view annoyed Amy and Brigid.

'Cecilia and I have joined a women's suffrage group. We want Brigid to join us,' said Amy, gazing with a severe face at Niall, who shook his head.

Brigid seethed inside and, thinking, *I'll show you, Niall,* joined Finnbar at the lecture on fossils. The museum curator presented specimens of ancient snails for the audience to observe. The lecturer explained their millions of years of existence buried in Dorset cliffs in England and opined they provided valuable objects for research into the past.

After the lecture, their discussion led Finbarr to remark, In the library on the top level, you'll find books on fossils. With Niall's permission, we could visit the museum's collection together. It is gratifying to speak to a woman with similar interests.'

He smiled, revealing that tooth gap, unnerving her. Brigid could sense the blush creeping up her cheeks.

Before he helped Brigid into the cab, Finnbar clasped her hand, and the tingling she recalled from her early days with Niall assailed her. When she reached the entrance, her shaking hands had trouble retrieving the key from her reticule. The nearby church bell tolled at ten o'clock, and Brigid hoped Niall would be asleep in bed. But she found him reading beside the parlour fire again.

'You are late home, so you are. A riveting lecture then.' Although he smiled, it failed to reach his eyes, which were as cold as silver sixpences.

Brigid felt an icy chill descend her back. 'I apologise for my tardiness. Finnbar and I had such an interesting discussion. He suggested escorting me to the College Museum to see a fossil collection if you permit it.'

Niall stood. 'Finn is well-read. He has many interests. I'll discuss the idea with him. Come mavourneen, it is time for bed.

I'll make you a mug of steaming hot cocoa.'

Brigid's passion for her husband proved extra intense that night, and he remarked on it. 'Fossils must be fascinating if they make you so passionate in bed. Mavourneen. I'll accompany you and Finn to the museum.'

His wife's blush lay hidden from him in the darkness. But Brigid knew in her heart that fossils did not stir her passions. Niall couldn't observe her deceitful eyes in the darkened bedroom.

Despite the impropriety lurking in their liaisons, Brigid continued to meet Finnbar as if some invisible thread pulled her to him. The man appeared from nowhere, bewitching her. She became further unnerved when he suggested what books to read and questioned her afterwards.

Under his spell, guilt dogged Brigid's footsteps whenever she stepped into the library and dogged her at home, too. She felt as if she were a helpless fish on a fishing line, overpowered.

Brigid mused, *If I had faith in God, I would seek support in the confessional.* Yet guilt needed an outlet somewhere, and Brigid found it challenging to cope without one.

Then Amy reported Cecilia had left Dún Laoghaire and had taken lodgings near a local school where she had a teaching post. Brigid wondered if independent Cecilia might be a sympathetic listener. So, she invited the young woman to join her for coffee one Monday during the Easter holidays.

Cecilia listened intently to Brigid's concerns. 'I know what you mean. Finnbar mesmerises me, too. The news of his return caused me such turmoil I moved out of the Gallagher home. When Finnbar had stayed with them, I feared he would try to kiss me, or worse, and my sleep became disturbed. So, I thought it best to leave.'

'Female attention feeds his mind somehow,' Brigid said. 'An attractive woman in his line of sight feeds his desires. Like you, I'll keep my distance in the future.'

She recalled his comment on vacuous women and knew that she reciprocated Finn's desires in her heart. She must get a grip on her emotions. She threw herself with vigour into caring for her family. But despite her efforts, she failed to notice the physical manifestation of her inner turmoil until Caitlin pointed it out.

'You have lost weight, Brigid, so you have. Is your workload overwhelming you? Managing a home, family, and work is challenging, even with help.' She paused, appraising her friend. Brigid. 'Are you eating well or skipping meals?'

Brigid stammered her reply as Caitlin took her by surprise. 'I'm not conscious of poor eating habits, but perhaps you are right.'

Dermot ran into the kitchen, 'Mammy, I heard Caitlin tell you to eat. Have my dinner.'

Brigid ruffled his hair. Such a sensitive child and pondered how long it would take for Niall to notice. She concluded she must cease attending the reading room, although she pined for Finnbar's mind and those bewitching eyes.

Before everyone knew it, Caitlin and Ezra's wedding day arrived. Caitlin wore a dress made of soft blue silk, which enhanced her ivory complexion and placed fresh spring flowers in her hair. She also carried a bouquet of them. The service included a splendid nuptial Mass, redolent of incense, uplifting hymns, and tender moments of affection. To Brigid's relief, Finn did not attend the ceremony. Niall said he had urgent personal business in Skibbereen. Brigid held back from asking what business, as she feared that knowing might open

Pandora's box.

Ezra closed his shop for the first time in thirty years and took his bride on a honeymoon to England. Their carriage, pulled by a grey stallion with a blue feather plume, took them to catch the ferry to Liverpool on the wedding night. A delightful day for all, and Brigid's fears were allayed.

While Finn stayed away from Dublin that summer, Brigid continued to use the reading room. She tried to put him from her mind but failed, and anxiety continued to nag at her conscience.

CHAPTER 21: THE ASSAULT

Ezra arrived uninvited one night in August 1861. He and Niall retired to the study and talked for over an hour. But Niall refused to reveal the nature of their discussions. Brigid thought it must be a grave issue for Ezra to bow and leave without imparting some irreverent comment. He was too serious, and Brigid's pulse beat fast with anxiety 'Niall, please tell me what has happened. I'm scared.'

Even though Brigid's eyes implored him, Niall shook his head and refused to be drawn. Brigid worried about the possibilities: another raid gone wrong, another spy in Saor-Éire? Before leaving for work each morning, she scanned the street, half expecting to see the street urchin. Continued worry caused insomnia and headaches, but Niall remained implacable, and it took Amy to relieve her distress.

She beckoned Brigid aside one dinner time. 'Did you hear about Cecilia's assault?' Tears glinted in her eyes.

Brigid gasped. 'Assault? No, what has happened to the poor girl?' Her pulse rate increased, remembering how Seamus had attacked her, the weight of the heavy body and hardened member.

'Someone attacked Cecilia on her way home from a suffrage meeting I did not attend. She walked to save money, and a man used a stick to push her to the ground. Then, he dragged her into some bushes and...and assaulted her.' Amy's voice faltered.

Brigid was powerless and had the terrifying premonition that Finn had attacked her. Drops of perspiration formed on her brow forehead.

'Heavens. Is the poor girl hurt?' she said.

Amy replied, 'Cecilia is distressed and at my father's house under Mamma's care. A street urchin found her and ran for a police officer who hailed a cab and accompanied her to Dún Laoghaire. Cecilia has described the man as well-dressed, wearing a black cape and a stovepipe hat and carrying a silver cane. She said he possessed a thick but well-trimmed beard and a swarthy complexion.'

Relief washed over Brigid. The description was not one of untidy hair and pale-skinned Finn. The attacker sounded far more sophisticated.

'Father has forbidden me to attend any more suffrage meetings and has threatened to stop me from working, too.

Brigid's eyes widened with shock. Amy's words tormented her because she enjoyed the freedom of work, and she feared Niall might forbid it. But she recognised the attacks provided an excellent excuse to avoid associating with Finnbar.,

That evening, Niall announced Alexander would rent Caitlin's vacated room. It bothered Brigid that Niall did not discuss it with her first, and her pulse rate rose as she asked why.

Niall said, 'The attack on Cecilia has made the Saor-Éire leadership review how Robert's men can provide more effective surveillance of women. With Alexander in the house, we can improve protection for you and the children. We have agreed all Saor-Éire wives must cease going out unaccompanied after dark until the police catch this odious attacker.'

Brigid blanched; she found a young teacher from a nearby school to rent the other vacant upstairs room. Twenty-five-year-old Eileen had to bring up her seven siblings when their parents perished in the famine. But the woman possessed a demeanour of quiet strength and revealed a lifelong teaching ambition. Brigid welcomed her into the household and viewed her as a kindred spirit.

A week later, Caitlin arrived wringing a wet handkerchief as she entered the hallway.

'Whatever is the matter, Caitlin, have you and Ezra argued?'

Caitlin's face crumpled, and she pulled a clean handkerchief from her reticule. 'It isn't an argument, though Ezra isn't his usual jocular self. He refuses to discuss it, and I'm filled with a profound sense of foreboding.'

Brigid tried to comfort her friend and resolved to ask Niall what had warranted such strange behaviour from Ezra. *I hope it isn't another botched raid.*

Niall remained resolute and tight-lipped until Stephen came to see him two weeks later.

Afterwards, Niall said. 'I know you have been worried about the secret meetings, but I could disclose nothing until tonight. Cecilia is pregnant, and Stephen has offered to marry her to hide her shame.' Brigid sat speechless with shock, and Niall continued. 'When she suspected, Cecilia saw a doctor who confirmed the pregnancy. She needed time to think about Stephen's proposal after she learned about his sexual orientation, but she has now accepted his proposal. The marriage will lend some credibility to Stephen and end any gossip surrounding him. It seems an ideal solution for both.' Niall smiled, but it did not reach his eyes.

Brigid's stomach churned, and her mind raced, but she still found her voice. 'When are they to marry?'

Brigid's tongue felt like old leather, imagining herself in such a dilemma. It did not bear thinking about.

'So, Stephen asked me to be his best man tonight, and I agreed. Ezra will supply the wedding ring and a place to live. The apartment above his shop has no tenant, so Cecilia and Stephen can move in.'

'Will Stephen bring up the child as his own?' Brigid asked.

'Yes, Robert made his son swear under oath that he will remain celibate so the child can bear the name Gallagher.'

The news rendered Brigid speechless once more. Before

Cecilia's attack, she couldn't have imagined such a scenario. A few days later, the pair wed by a special licence. The bride looked radiant in a smart suit of heather-mixed Scottish wool and a matching hat. The wedding party then retired to The Three Peacocks, where Niall ordered champagne. Stephen presented Cecilia with a betrothal ring. Robert welcomed her to his family, and Diedre kissed her cheek.

During the meal, Caitlin told Brigid that Ezra had a couple of Saor-Éire members decorate the apartment. Diedre provided new curtains, and Ezra found a three-piece suit to replace the shabby brown sofa.

'Cleaned up, the place feels comfortable and very welcoming,' said Caitlin, who had supervised.

At three, a cab picked up the newlyweds and took them to their flat. Once they left, Amy took Brigid aside.

'Please say nothing, but Alexander has proposed, and I have accepted. My parents want us to marry soon because Alex can protect me from this odious man. I shall leave Clery's and Mrs O' Keefe after a formal notice appears in the Dublin Gazette next week.'

It did not surprise Brigid when Alexander gave Niall a month's notice before Christmas. 'I have found a house Amy likes, and we shall marry on Burn's night, 25th January 1862.' He grinned at Brigid. 'I adore Amy, and I'm eager to care for her as my wife. Our wedding won't be as grand as Amy wished, but most guests, including my parents, brothers, and sisters, can attend. Since it is Burn's night, too, I have engaged a Scottish piper.' His wide crinkled the corners of his eyes.

Around the time of Brigid and Niall's anniversary, Brigid learned Finnbar had returned, having been gone much longer than anyone had expected. 'I wrote to him to ask for help to find the attacker. As members of Saor-Éire, we must support Cecilia and help the police bring the bastard to justice. He may be a spy and a murderer, too.' He paused, watching his wife's expression of dismay at the news. 'Finnbar will rent

Alexander's room after the wedding,' he said.

It dumbfounded Brigid as Finn's presence in the house would torment her. 'You rented the room for the second time without consulting me. Can't I have a say on who lives in our house?'

Niall replied caustically. 'You did not consult me about Eileen, did you?'

Brigid's face burned. 'Eileen is my companion and a woman. Most nights, you are out for bank or Saor-Éire work. These days, the children are in bed when you get home, and Aisne cries for her Da to kiss her goodnight. Bringing strange men into our home should be something we discuss beforehand for the children's sake. I need to ensure the man won't harm them or us. Finnbar consorted with some dangerous people and used to hide his location. Won't his presence put us in more danger?'

'No.' Niall remained implacable. 'Robert has promised to step up the guards on all senior Saor-Éire officers. Someone will stand outside the house on watch, not patrol. Having Finn in one place means officers can shadow him.'

'But won't the Army pick up his movements, too? persisted Brigid.'

'We take that risk or move. Robert assures me we can better protect women with another male person in the house. Given the circumstances, I prefer having Finn live here over a potential undercover spy.'

That night, as Niall snored beside her, Brigid thought of Finn's movements in the past. He often stayed with Stephen's family when he first returned to Dublin from some trip. Did his attitude towards women hide a secret? If so, it would resolve her emotional problems. But her nerves were strung like violin wire because inside, she knew that if Finnbar called, she would answer. Is this evidence of Da in me? she wondered, disgusted with her unfaithful mind. Sleep did not come until the church clock struck three, and her dreams were of her childhood home and Scamp, the dog, dashing through the fields on a warm summer's day, heading for the cool lough.

CHAPTER 22: GUILT AND LOSS

On the eve of Amy and Alexander's wedding, it snowed. The streets of ordure and mud, typical for the time of year, disappeared under dazzling white crystals, the perfect backdrop for a winter wedding. The bride looked resplendent, shimmering in a white lace ensemble, coordinating cape, and crimson silk lining. Over one hundred guests were in attendance, and although on the guest list, Brigid did not spot Finnbar until after the wedding. They locked eyes while circulating among the guests. He gave Brigid one of his alluring gazes before nodding his head. Brigid's cheeks grew hot.

Finnbar and Brigid sat at separate tables for the meal, but Brigid could feel Finn's eyes burning into her back. She drew her white shawl closer to her bare shoulders and quivered. A dessert of some creamy concoction completed the meal. But knowing Finn could see her, Brigid's appetite vanished.

After the wedding feast, everyone enjoyed Irish and Scottish dancing. The piper, clad in the vibrant scarlet and black tartan, arrived at nine o'clock to play Highland Wedding and a soothing lullaby before the newlyweds left for their honeymoon. Brigid returned home at eleven, for the children's sake. Niall did not return until dawn after enjoying drinks with his Saor-Éire friends. He woke Brigid up, his face contorted with pain, 'My head hurts something fierce.'

'You can't manage strong liquor, then.' Brigid grinned, but she recalled her father returning home drunk and collapsing.

Niall ate little the following day, which Brigid attributed to a hangover. But she grew concerned when he displayed a pale complexion and ate no breakfast before work for several days.

His appetite had vanished, and he continued to complain of headaches.

Meanwhile, Brigid prepared to take Finnbar as their lodger. On Saturday, she kept busy amusing the children and rearranging the room. Brigid felt unsure what changes she ought to make for a man's spartan tastes. She stood by the bed, musing on the matter, holding her best sheets.

'Dermot, fetch the periodicals from my bedside table, sweetheart.'

Dermot, ever eager to please his mother, obeyed. Brigid brushed the rugs and furniture, changed the bed linen, and added new candles. The inner turmoil of having Finn living with them left her drained. She noticed the need for peat in the fire and rested in the armchair before descending to fetch it.

A tiny voice called out, 'Mammy, someone's at the door,' making her stomach churn.

Brigid leapt from the chair, wondering, *could it be Finn? I expected him this afternoon.*

She hurried down the stairs, tossed the duster into the scullery, tidied her hair, squeezed her cheeks, and straightened her skirt. With a valise and a wooden walking stick in hand, Finbarr stood on the doorstep as she opened the door.

'Good morning, Finnbar,' said Brigid in a faint voice. 'Welcome to our home.'

Finnbar bowed. 'I apologise for arriving early, but I had to vacate my previous accommodation by ten o'clock. At the wedding feast, I wanted to tell you, but your premature departure prevented me, so here I am.' He disarmed Brigid with a gap-toothed smile.

Brigid pasted a smile on her face. 'It is no bother, Finnbar. I have finished preparing your room.'

As her heart thumped, she made way for him to enter the hallway. Dermot appeared behind her skirt, and his shy expression and down-turned mouth showed his discomfort at having a new lodger in the house.

Aisne appeared from behind her mother's skirt, a finger in her mouth.

'This is Finnbar, sweetheart. He is to lodge with us as Alexander did.'

Aisne toddled in front of Finnbar, hands on hip, with a pout on her face. 'Man, up,' she said, pointing to the stairs.

Brigid sensed the rising heat in her body, and her hands perspired. 'I apologise for Aisne. She has yet to learn her manners.'

'Seeing young ones in the house is a joy. My sister has five children, and we have jolly adventures when I visit.' He gave Brigid a mesmerising grin, which, with his musky scent, unnerved her.

Brigid collected herself. 'Your room is on the third level. Please follow me.'

She had not climbed many steps when a cry from beneath halted her. Flustered, Brigid had forgotten Aisne, whose face had turned crimson as she wailed beneath the staircase.

Finnbar collected her, saying, 'Ups-a-daisy,' and hoisted her onto his shoulders.

Brigid had never seen him display a child-friendly side to his character before. His actions resembled those of a father, not an intellectual, and Brigid experienced unexpected affection. She felt like a lost puppy as the four squeezed into Finnbar's room.

'Shall I fetch the peat?' said Dermot, who turned to scurry down the stairs.

'No, I'll deal with that later, mo stór. Finnbar, I'm unsure what Niall told you about rent. We supply peat and fresh bed linen, but if you require meals, which is an extra charge.' Brigid spun her wedding ring.

'Niall and I settled on the rent for a pleasant room.'

'You are welcome to eat with us like Alexander did.'

'Brigid, you are kind, but I would not want to impose on your generosity. I shall dine at my club.'

While speaking, his eyes roamed over Brigid's body, and she grasped the implications of his words. She longed for the walls to swallow her up and averted her eyes to mask her emotions.

But Finn stepped towards her. 'We both understand why I'll not intrude. Still, I did not wish to upset Niall by rejecting his offer.'

His lingering gaze made Brigid need to escape. Her hand shook as she retrieved a key from her skirt pocket and set it down on the small table.

'Your key, Finnbar. Because of our busy work and children's schedules, we retire early, while you may come and go as you, please.'

She pivoted, picked up Aisne, sent Dermot ahead, and hurried downstairs. Her heart beat rapidly until the front door's opening and closing reached her ears. Then she breathed out, unaware she had been holding her breath, too.

Niall came home at noon on Monday, a week after Finnbar moved in. Headaches had continued to bother him since Amy and Alexander's wedding, and Brigid could no longer attribute them to alcohol. She observed his exhausted face etched with profound furrows on his cheek and the evident dark circles beneath each of his eyes. His appearance reminded Brigid of Ma during her illness.

'You are home early. Are you feeling unwell?' Brigid squeezed her hands, anticipating an unpleasant response.

'My head is pounding. In truth, my whole body is throbbing with pain. I'll rest in bed for a couple of hours.' Niall struggled to smile at his wife, but it distorted into a grimace, causing Brigid's pulse to race.

Brigid pondered whether he had caught the circulating winter fever and felt his forehead: hot, he had a fever. Brigid's anxiety grew. 'Yes, sleep mo stór. After I have given food to the children and put them to bed, I'll bring you some broth.'

She hurried to the kitchen and began working. When she opened their bedroom door a couple of hours later, her breath caught. Niall had beads of sweat upon his brow. His face flushed, and his gaze fixed. His fingers plucked the coverlet as he mumbled incoherent words. A severe infection had developed.

Startled, Brigid filled a bowl with water from the scullery and returned to sit beside her husband. She bathed his fevered brow, cooling it for two hours as his face sunk before her eyes, and he mumbled to himself. Brigid had dashed to the scullery to collect fresh water when she heard Finnbar open the front door and enter the hall.

'Finnbar, Niall is sick with a high fever, and I fear he is delirious. Could you please contact a physician?' Her voice sounded loud in her ears and filled with apprehension,

Finnbar poked his head around the door, saw Niall's condition, and agreed with a nod. Another hour passed, and Niall's fever worsened. Brigid's heart raced with concern when Niall complained of pain in his stomach, curled up, let out eerie, gut-wrenching, primal cries, and threw up into the chamber pot. Brigid wiped his brow and stroked his hand, but he seemed oblivious. She became alarmed when she recalled how the famine fever had caused hallucinations.

Brigid had emptied the chamber pot when the front door opened. Her heart raced, and she inhaled short, rapid breaths. Finnbar had returned an unfamiliar doctor. The physician wore a black cloak, a silver cane, and a neat dark beard. He emitted an aura of importance as he examined Niall. In Ulster-accented English, he asked Brigid where Niall worked and what pubs or restaurants he patronised.

She said, 'My husband is the Assistant Manager at the National Bank in the city centre. He often eats dinner in the Stag's Head but takes some customers for evening drinks at various pubs.' Brigid felt uneasy by the questions because she knew the water to be unsuitable for drinking in some areas of Dublin.

The swarthy doctor stroked his beard. ‘Has he shown any complaints of nausea or diarrhoea?’

‘We attended a wedding three weeks ago, and he had much to drink. Headaches have plagued him ever since. At the start, I attributed it to the overconsumption of alcohol. However, he has eaten little food recently. Today, he is experiencing stomach pains and has vomited.’

Niall screamed, clutching his abdomen, and vomited into the chamber pot that Brigid had replaced on the bed. Then, the stench of a foul excretion, redolent of the odour of fresh cow manure, assaulted Brigid’s nostrils.

The doctor’s wrinkled nose and intense gaze intensified Brigid’s fear. He beckoned her to his side.

‘I am concerned that your husband may have visited a pub where typhoid fever is present.’

‘Typhoid? The disease that killed Prince Arthur?’ Brigid’s heart leapt to her throat.

‘Yes. I must admit your husband to a fever hospital, as the disease is contagious. Keep your children from him, Madame.’ The doctor turned to Finnbar. ‘Please ask the cabby to fetch an ambulance from the hospital.’

He turned back to Brigid, whose legs shook. ‘Once your husband departs, wash all the bedding and clothing with lye soap and any crockery he has used. Refrain from sleeping on the bed until the mattress is clean. Cover your hands with gloves for all this work and destroy them afterwards.’

Brigid’s face blanched, and she glanced at Finnbar, whose eyes met hers, wide-eyed and staring with terror, too. The doctor examined Niall’s pulse and expressed his thoughts with a head shake. Finnbar left as soon as an ambulance arrived. Two men carried a raving Niall from the house. Brigid wanted to accompany him, but the ambulance driver refused, saying,

‘It is a fever hospital, Missus. You can’t go; ‘tis forbidden.’

Finnbar took the weeping Brigid into his arms. Before she knew it, his mouth lay upon hers, and she responded, the sweetness blocking her pain. Then he helped her to his room and laid her on his bed.

'You sleep here tonight, Brigid. I'll use the parlour sofa.' He kissed her again, and her resolve vanished.

'You can't leave us, Niall,' she wailed and wept, her face against Finbarr's shirt.

'Don't weep, mavourneen. I'm here to help you.'

Brigid, her face pale and ravaged, gazed unfocused into Finn's. 'Is this a dream? I want my husband, and the children need their father.' She wailed.

Finnbar kissed her mouth, and the kiss devoured Brigid's senses. Before she knew it, she had taken off her clothes, and they made passionate love. Afterwards, Brigid felt appalling guilt, worse than running away from her brother and Luke. She wanted to run from the bedroom. 'My children,' she wailed, flinging on clothes, and rushing down the stairs.

She found the children sleeping. Unable to find sleep in her bed, Brigid wandered the parlour floor and rested on the sofa. But sleep evaded her as images of her deceased brothers filled her mind. She sat up to weep with her face buried in her palms. Hearing a sound, Brigid glanced up to find Finnbar in the doorway. He wrapped his arms around her, and Brigid did not resist as he guided her upstairs to his room, where they slept entwined like experienced lovers.

The doctor called in the morning with his invoice. Brigid showed him inside the parlour.

In a childlike tone, she asked, 'How is my husband?'

'Madame, prepare yourself. Your husband has typhoid fever, and his life is in jeopardy.'

Brigid's eyes misted, and she collapsed onto the sofa. Mute, she gazed at the doctor as if she had witnessed a ghost. Finnbar took command, paid the doctor, and escorted him from Brigid's home. She sat motionless, staring out the window, and then cried tears of remorse and loss in Finnbar's arms.

'What have we done? Did we share a bed last night?' She pulled a strand of hair from her head and chewed it, her eyes brimming with frenzy. Then she sat stock still like an apparition, unable to breathe until a wail pierced the air.

'That is Aisne. I must see her,' Brigid hiccupped as she swallowed the vast lump of fear now occupying her throat.

'I'll take care of everything, Brigid,' Finn said, his eyes tender. 'You see to your children.'

'No, Finbarr, the bedding, I must wash it. Please feed the children some oatmeal and milk and keep them from the bedroom. Eileen can help you before she goes to work.'

Brigid fetched her children, her face white and lips pale. 'Mammy needs to do some laundry, and Finn will prepare your oatmeal. Be helpful, please,' she said.

Dermot's tiny face wrinkled as if he knew the truth, and he nodded.

As if powered by a steam engine, Brigid stripped the bed. She cleaned the sheets with lye in the scullery, reminiscing about Ballyconstór. Brigid found some cotton gloves and cleaned the mattress with her doorstep brush and lye soap. Then, after rewashing her hands, she joined her fractious children and relieved a stressed-looking Finnbar, who thrust his hand through his disordered hair.

'Man says no see, Da,' Aisne said, her eyes blazing.

'Daddy is sick and is in hospital with a fever we can catch.' Brigid had difficulty keeping her voice level when every fibre of her being wanted to wail.

Aisne poked her brother with her spoon and wailed, 'Me, me, go see Da.'

'Aisne, stop banging that spoon, or you'll go to bed with a smack,'

Brigid held back her tears until the children had finished their porridge and gone to the parlour to play while she washed the dishes. She could eat nothing and shed bitter tears of fear and guilt in the scullery. Confused, she looked upwards without knowing why. 'Please don't let him die.'

Until a dire message saying she should come at once arrived on Thursday, the hospital denied Brigid access to her husband, his infection too severe to permit visitors. The cab ride to the hospital passed Brigid in a haze of anguish. The nurses allowed Brigid a few minutes with Niall, who was lucid.

Like a baby for the breast, Brigid caressed his cheek, and he turned his feverish, hollow-eyed face towards her; his dying face was brimming with affection.

'I love you, my darling wife. My life with you has been filled with joy. You have given me such beautiful children.' Niall managed a wan smile and whispered as Mammy had done, too. Take care of our children for me, Brigid, and wed again if you meet someone who loves you as I do. You have so much to...'

His eyes closed, and his head drooped to the side. Gone. Brigid sat transfixed by her husband's features, searching for any sign of life as she plunged into an abyss of grief. She called for a nurse, who hurried in and took his pulse.

She shook her head. 'Madame, a priest came earlier and gave him the last rites.'

The nurse led Brigid to a tiny office, where someone brought her water. But choked, Brigid was oblivious to all but Niall's deathbed face, which stood before her like a sentinel, unmoving but full of love. After some time, a cab arrived to take Brigid and her empty heart home. She stared at the wet streets, too overwhelmed to cry, her heart as heavy as the dark clouds scudding across the sky. Caitlin met her at the door, but Brigid didn't appear to recognise her friend.

'I must see my children and explain their father has died,' Brigid said, her eyes bright with unshed tears as she pushed past Caitlin.

'Ezra has taken them for a walk. We'll take care of them

while you rest. Ezra prepared your bed with a new feather mattress and bedding,'

'Rest? How can I when my husband has died and taken my heart with him? I shall never rest again.' Brigid broke into heartrending sobs.

Caitlin held her friend before steering Brigid to the bedroom. There, she helped her undress and lie down. Lifting her head, Caitlin gave the grieving widow a dose of laudanum. Brigid rested against the pillow and fixed her gaze on the ceiling, uttering incomprehensible words until the laudanum worked.

Upon waking, Brigid found the room in the dim light of one candle. 'Niall, my beloved husband, wait for me.'

Caitlin brought her a bowl of soup, but Brigid declined it, picking at the blanket as she attempted to rise.

'Dermot, Aisne, where are you?' she howled like a stricken animal while tears streaked her cheeks.

'Hush, you must rest.' Caitlin pushed her back into the pillows and administered another dose of laudanum.

Sunday came before Brigid lucidly reacted to her surroundings and called for her children without a banshee-like howl. In an instant, Caitlin arrived with a bowl of broth. She took her hand as Brigid turned her head and said,

'I dreamt I was in a pit of vipers. Their fangs dripped, and their squirming bodies reached for me.' She shuddered. 'I must organise a funeral.'

'Don't worry. Ezra has taken care of everything. Please drink some broth.' She ladled a spoonful into Brigid's mouth and persuaded her to eat some bread.

The door opened, and Finnbar walked in. He removed the bowl from Caitlin's hands.

'Ezra has brought the children into the kitchen, Caitlin, and they need feeding. I wish to speak with Brigid alone, please.'

Caitlin nodded and left the room. Finnbar closed the door

and pulled Brigid into his arms. She pressed her head against his shoulder before fighting to escape.

'No, no, Finn, I can't do this. Niall is dead. I must mourn alone.'

'You are not alone, Brigid. Ezra and Stephen have prepared funeral arrangements for tomorrow. The doctor urged for Niall's burial to be done without delay. The risk of contagion, you see.'

Brigid disengaged from his hold. Her heart longed for Niall, not Finn. She yearned for the embrace that had enveloped her on their wedding night and cradled their newborn children. Her heart felt like a lump of lead in her chest. Overwhelming feelings of regret and grief enveloped her senses, preventing her from concentrating on more than one footstep or one word at a time. Yet Finn held her as she sobbed.

Brigid got up the next day, appearing pale after a sleepless night. Cloaked in black attire with a black mantilla veiling her features, she embraced her children at the funeral service. At the graveside, Caitlin took a squirming Aisne into her arms. But Dermot stood by his mother, holding her hand. No longer a child but still a young boy.

The priest intoned his prayers for the dead, quoting the surety of new life in heaven. The words did not comfort Brigid. Dry-eyed, she drew Dermot to her side, knowing the loss would consume her for many months. As the gravediggers covered the coffin with soil, Dermot turned and wept into his mother's skirt.

Aisne, too immature to comprehend, tugged her brother's arm and pointed out the grave. 'No cry, Dermot. Da, dere.'

Brigid gazed into the grave. Aisne was right. It was Niall's place of eternal rest, the man who had taught her love. Tears flowed then.

Three days following the funeral, Finnbar enquired whether Brigid wished him to vacate his accommodation.

'Not at present, because I need your rent. Having lodgers

in the house will help me pay my bills, but I must work full-time. My first task is to take the children on a holiday in the countryside, away from death scenes.

'A relative of my father has a farm with a cottage he rents. Take the children there for a week. I'm sure Caitlin will help you.'

Caitlin persuaded Brigid to go, and Ezra organised a carriage. Brigid paid no attention to the frigid temperature in the cottage despite her limbs feeling as chilly as ice on Daisy's cow trough in Ballyconstór. She embraced the cold. It pushed out other sensations like it had in the famine.

Caitlin built peat fires and cooked stews, colcannon, and potato cakes. Food appeared before Brigid as if by magic, causing her to ponder if her friend had help from leprechauns. Caitlin took the children for long walks in the crisp, dry weather. Sometimes, Brigid accompanied them, oblivious to her surroundings, steeped in a more profound pool of sorrow than after Ma's death. Desolation lingered with every step, even when Aisne sought her mother's attention.

'Mammy, Mammy, me see a cow, me see a horse.' 'She needs her Mammy, so she does.' Caitlin looked at Brigid's ice-cold and unmoving face and sighed.

One afternoon, Dermot took his mother's hand. 'Mammy, we need you more now Daddy is gone. Come back to us, please.' His sweet voice and his tiny face beseeched her.

The expression touched Brigid's heart, and she responded to him for the first time that week.

She clasped his hand, thinking, *Dermot is right. I need to gather myself for the sake of the children. They need me, and I need them.* Knowing her duty lay with her children now, she sighed with resignation.

After returning to Heytesbury Street, Brigid evaluated her life by reviewing the family's finances. She had a mortgage and school fees to find for Dermot, whom Niall had wished to attend a Christian Brothers School. Brigid listed her income and expenditures. The figures showed her financial situation to be precarious. With regret, Brigid concluded she couldn't meet the cost of private schooling for Dermot. Eileen reassured Brigid he would obtain a grand education at her school and offered to accompany him. However, both children would require supervision on Saturdays, and Aisne would be necessary on Mondays, as Brigid concluded she must work full-time.

Caitlin advised Brigid not to worry. 'I'll work the additional weekday with no salary raise. We also have a solution for Saturdays. Ezra talked with Eileen and Mary-Ann, a pupil teacher living with us. Eileen has agreed to supervise the children on Saturdays, with the support of Mary-Ann, in exchange for a shilling reduction in rent.'

Their generosity overwhelmed Brigid, and tears streamed down her face. Caitlin held her close in her arms. 'Ezra has discussed things with Saoirse, and she has arranged for you to work full-time starting next Monday.'

'How can I repay you all?' She said, staring into the distance, distress glistening on her lashes.

'To see you smile will be enough thanks for me,' Caitlin said.

Brigid felt a small measure of composure and gave a wan smile.

CHAPTER 23: BRIGID'S SECOND MARRIAGE

Brigid confided in Saoirse upon recommencing her employment. 'It is hard to cope alone, but the lodger helps us with the children on Saturdays and Caitlin on weekdays.' Brigid's voice quivered, and her eyes misted.

Saoirse hugged her. 'I was married twenty years ago. My parents disapproved of the match because of my husband's Protestant faith, and we parted company. A runaway horse killed him as he crossed the street. We had been married for three months, and I miscarried our child.' Tears filled Saoirse's eyes. 'Grief catches you when you least expect it, Brigid, but you have children to raise, and they will comfort you.'

Brigid hugged her back. Knowing Saoirse's secret, she found solace in someone who understood the pain of losing a loved one.

Mary-Ann proved an excellent helper. She tucked the children into bed at night. Then, the women ate supper together before Ezra collected Mary-Ann at eight. After supper, Eileen retired to her room while Brigid relaxed in her chair by the kitchen range, reading or sewing.

Tears often threatened while she gazed at the empty chair opposite her. But Brigid found solace in her journals and re-read her notes. She wondered whether she would make some money by authoring a series of articles on child development, so she had Niall's desk moved to the parlour, where a coal fire blazed in winter. She couldn't afford to heat two reception rooms.

The unidentified attacker who had harmed Cecilia struck again, committing another heinous act against a woman. Brigid worried about Mary-Ann going home alone if Ezra could not accompany her. However, the emptying of Niall's study gave Brigid an idea. It could become Mary-Ann's room to sleep in on nights when she would otherwise have to return home without an escort.

Ezra approved the plan, a smile spreading across his face. Brigid wondered whether to broach the subject of Mary-Ann moving to live with her full-time. But she was reluctant to remove the income her rent gave Ezra. While writing letters to thank people for their condolences one afternoon, Brigid searched the desk for more blotting paper. She found a letter addressed to her instead, written in Niall's hand. She broke the seal with trembling fingers and read the note.

Dublin. 1857

My Darling Brigid,

Please forgive me if I have lost my life. I shall watch over you from heaven forever, and we'll meet again one day. Take care of the children and ensure they attend church and are confirmed. Find a suitable governess for Aisne, whose character and intelligence need moulding. Dermot has much to give, so send him to an excellent school where he can flourish.

Mavourneen, I loved you when we met and knew I had found the right girl. Your beauty is both internal and external. Please marry again if you meet someone who will love you as I have. I wish for nothing more than your pure happiness.

Your devoted husband, Niall.

Brigid wept the bitter tears of her betrayal and loss on reading the letter. The thought she had deceived him on the eve of his death was unfathomable. Brigid concluded that her mind had unhinged and must forgive herself. She did so by caring for Niall's legacy: their children. However, Brigid found managing without Niall harder than expected, although working full-time left her mind too tired to brood.

Ezra helped Caitlin with the children as much as possible. Aisne tugged his beard, saying, 'Ezra, long beard,' which made him laugh.

During the first weeks of mourning, Dermot would crawl into bed with his mother at night and cry as she cuddled him close. But in time, he became more settled and left Brigid undisturbed. Brigid saw little of Finnbar, who did not disturb her either.

Alone in her bed, she would hear Finnbar's step in the hall or on the stairs, and sometimes, the silence of his hesitation on her landing told Brigid he was thinking of her. As the months passed, Brigid listened to that hesitation. Desire overrode the guilt, but she issued no invitation, and Finnbar left to visit his sister.

Stephen and Cecilia found a house and moved out before the child's birth, leaving Ezra's flat empty again. But Ezra found an assistant whose wages he supplemented by free accommodation.

This freed up time for him to spend helping Caitlin with the children. Finnbar showed fatherly affection for them, playing games or taking them to the park, and he joined the family for Sunday dinner. He showed particular interest in Dermot and took him fishing, which delighted the child. But Aisne gave him no quarter and acted with restrained coolness, unlike her boisterous personality with Ezra.

'She's stubborn like her mother,' Finnbar said, and Brigid blushed.

The summer weather that year was pleasant. Brigid found peace watching her children play. Ezra and Caitlin volunteered to take the children to the seaside for two weeks in early August. Brigid intended to help Cecilia with her baby's delivery during that time.

When they worked on Saor-Éire matters together, Cecilia

said, 'Stephen is fond of me, and we share a bed. He does his best to be a husband, even making love, although he cannot complete the act. But he will be a good father, I'm sure.'

To everyone's dismay, the assaults on women did not stop but increased. Despite investigations, Robert reported that the man left no clues, resulting in no leads for the police. Concerned for his wife and sister, Stephen repeated Cecilia's description.

'The man is tall, swarthy, and bearded. He uses a silver-topped cane to hit the woman he attacks and has an air of authority about him that disarms the woman. He has a northern accent, too.'

Something clicked in Brigid's brain. The doctor Finnbar brought to see Niall fitted the description. 'I need to speak with Finnbar when he returns,' she said to Caitlin.

'Ezra tells me he won't return until September.' Caitlin watched Brigid's face, which she was careful to keep impassive.

In the meantime, a fourth assault occurred, and this victim died, strangled with her shawl. *The man's audacity has become too much, turning into murder. He may strike again.*

Upon his return, Brigid wasted no time inviting Finnbar to join her in the parlour. She lit a coal fire against the cold and wet weather that had set in and prepared coffee and biscuits.

After pleasantries about his visit to Waterford, Brigid said, 'Finnbar, another attack on a woman occurred this summer. The criminal strangled a woman in broad daylight. The fear of women leaving the safety of their homes is such that I have resorted to taking a cab to Clery's. Do you recall the name of the doctor you brought to see Niall?' Brigid sipped her coffee, waiting for his reply.

Finn's eyes locked onto Brigid momentarily, causing her cheeks to flush. 'Yes, I do. He is a member of the gentlemen's club I use at Trinity College. You need a degree to join. His name will be on the bill I paid.'

'Cecilia's description fits him, although I recall little except for his beard and silver-topped stick. But Roberts says the stick is crucial evidence as he beats his victims with it.'

Finbarr, his brow creasing, excused himself and disappeared into his room. He returned a few minutes later, holding the bill.

'His name is Richard Perry, and he is a doctor from Belfast. If I recall correctly, he is on a year's secondment at the Royal Park Hospital. I'll contact Robert tomorrow.'

As he finished speaking, a piece of coal fell in a shower of sparks. Brigid bent to pick it up with the tongs before the coal burned a hole in the rug. But Finnbar was quicker, and their eyes met and locked. Then, as he tossed back the coal, Brigid's stomach flipped. Finn kissed her and undid her self-control.

Finn carried Brigid to her bedroom and laid her on the bed. There, he kissed her again with more passion. They undressed, and their lovemaking burned with slow desire until Brigid could bear it no longer. She took his erect member and pulled it into position. He entered and moved within her. Finn's groans of pleasure joined Brigid's moans. In the next few hours, they made love again, and Brigid's orgasms surpassed any she had had with Niall. Then Finn withdrew.

'I've never known a woman so passionate.'

Her hand traced his features as she said, 'Have you had many romantic partners?'

'You are number eight, and I have fallen in love. You captured my heart during the lectures.'

'You are in love with me?'

'Yes, I am. I want to marry you and care for your family.'

'I need time, Finn. It is still too early after Niall's death. I'm in mourning.' Brigid attempted to sit up, her emotions in turmoil.

Finn stopped her and twirled a braid of hair, which had fallen from its pins. 'I'll wait for you, Mavourneen. I know you love me, even if you do not.'

Finn sent a message to Robert the next day, who came

to see them. He asked questions about the doctor and their recollections of him. Brigid could remember little, but Finn described the man. He enquired at his club about the lodgings where the doctor lived. Two police officers detained him for questioning as he ate breakfast the following day. Fortunately, they had caught him in time because his tenure ceased at the end of October.

Robert enquired in Belfast and learned similar attacks had also occurred but had stopped a year ago. A few days later, Robert explained the doctor had confessed, and the police imprisoned him for trial. Robert asked Cecilia to take part in an identity parade, where she identified the doctor. While they waited for his trial, Finn did some investigations. He learned the doctor was a member of an Orange Order Lodge, and his work included spying on Saor-Éire.

'Thank God, we caught him. The man is a murderer and a spy.'

Caitlin and Brigid felt inordinate relief, although a lingering fear kept many Dublin women indoors that winter.

Saor-Éire sent a spy to learn more about the doctor's Orange Order Lodge and learned the lodge was seeking Ronan O'Brien's and his group's whereabouts. Finn smirked, claiming that the man would not be found as O'Brien had escaped to America.

The close encounter with "another beast" made Brigid uncomfortable. Visions of Seamus swam into her dreams. Finn stopped avoiding Brigid and became more, not less, passionate. He repeated his marriage proposal, and Brigid repeated her refusal until the day came when she experienced the unmistakable signs of pregnancy. A doctor confirmed her suspicions, and the decision was inevitable.

Finnbar and Brigid married in a small ceremony at St Catherine's Church just after Christmas 1862. Since she was still mourning, Brigid was unsure what to wear. Caitlin took over and found a plain, deep purple silk dress that Caitlin knew would suit Brigid. She found a matching ribbon for Brigid's hair. Aisne wore a lavender frock as the flower girl, and Stephen was Finn's best man. They ate supper in a private room at Finn's club, the occasion subdued by convention.

The newlyweds took a few days' holiday with the children, staying in Finn's cousin's cottage. Robert lent them his carriage to transport them. They stumbled in, completely drained, the children squabbling and Finn desperately trying to impress. It tried Brigid's patience and her temper, but conscious of the need to build her new family into a unit, she did her best to stay calm. The family's new formation needed to be cemented.

CHAPTER 24
CEMENT MIXING

Once the family was ensconced in the cottage, Finn started a blazing fire and dangled a kettle over it. The children complained of hunger and tiredness. After feeding them, Brigid put the children to bed. Finn then made Brigid put her feet up while he served a ham, cheese, and bread supper.

The newlywed couple's conversation veered to the famine when Brigid said the cottage reminded her of where she lived as a child. As Finn discussed the material he had gathered for his book, Brigid became fascinated by the depth of his research, remarking he should have interviewed her.

Finn nodded. 'Considering it, I decided the required closeness wasn't worth the risk.'

Brigid acknowledged he was right. 'But perhaps we could collaborate now.'

Finn nodded again. 'There are many things we can do together now we are wed.'

Brigid blushed, knowing what he meant. Despite her mourning period, Brigid had kept up the Saor-Éire accounts but had shown little interest in anything else. Now married to its top leader, renewed interest in Saor-Éire ensued. Finn raised the subject of the Ulster Orange Lodges.

'Members of the lodges are Protestant, not Catholic. Fenians are Catholic, and people separate along these sectarian lines.'

'Tell me more about O'Brien,' said a curious Brigid, concerned for Niall's precious children.

'He is violent, as I once told you, and the British military are in pursuit of him, but without knowledge of his location. Ronan left six months ago for America and travelled under an assumed name. He can't return to Ireland for at least a year, so he has asked me to help purchase more arms and ammunition for an uprising in England funded by American sympathisers.'

Brigid's pulse rate rose, though she kept her tone level. 'Why join such a violent Fenian as O'Brien when you have plenty of chances to cause trouble in Ireland?'

Finn, who had taken to smoking a pipe, knocked out some ash and refilled it. 'I'll discuss it with Stephen and Ezra to see what they think. I understand your concerns. I have a wife and family to consider now while O'Brien is unmarried.' Finn paused, staring into the dancing flames. 'He remains devoted to my sister, even though she has married someone else.'

Brigid stared into the fire, too, the shadows leaving patterns on the whitewashed wall reminiscent of her childhood home. When she looked up, the sparkle in Finn's eyes disturbed her.

She yawned, now unwilling to discuss violence. 'I'm tired, Finn. Can we forget Fenian activity for tonight, please?'

Finn got up in a flash, 'Of course, mo stór. I found a stone hot water bottle and filled it to warm the bed. You get undressed, and I'll bring you a cup of hot cocoa.'

Throughout the week, they made slow-burning love at night while focusing on Brigid's children during the day. She wanted to cement the family unit and get her children to accept Finn as their stepfather, which she knew would not be easy.

However, while Dermot and Finn bonded over a mutual liking of fishing, winning Aisne's trust was much more challenging. One morning, while preparing the family's oatmeal for breakfast, Brigid asked Dermot to get Da a spoon,

Aisne responded with fiery eyes, like Niall's. 'Finn, not Da.'

Brigid felt choked and stirred the oatmeal vigorously until she composed herself. She turned towards Aisne.

'Yes, sweetie, you are right. But your Da wanted Finn to take his place in our life.'

Aisne's eyes still blazed. 'Won't call him Da. Da's in a grave.'

Brigid knew not to provoke her wilful daughter further and did not reprimand her. She would manage the issue at home if the child persisted in showing dislike for her stepfather. Aisne was noticeably young and might never accept Finn, but she needed to be polite.

As Brigid planned, they spent the remainder of the week cementing a family. Finn took Dermot fishing and one day returned with three trout for supper.

'I caught one, Mammy. He was strong, and Finn had to help me reel him in.' Dermot's eager eyes sparkled, and his treble voice rose.

Brigid hugged her son and told him she was proud of him. Aisne refused to be second best. She pouted and toddled off.

Brigid picked her up and kissed the top of her head. 'I'm proud of you, too, my clever little lady.'

That evening, Brigid baked the trout in the range's oven. Everyone enjoyed the meal, even Aisne, who, with eyes ablaze with daring, turned her attention to Finn.

'We have Dermot's fish tonight. 'Morrow, I catch fish.'

Finnbar glanced at Brigid for confirmation, who shook her head.

. 'Finn will take you fishing when you are big enough to hold a rod.'

Aisne banged the table with her spoon. 'I am big now. Finnbar takes me fishing 'morrow.' She hit the table again and glared at Finn, her tiny body rigid with suppressed anger, which Brigid feared would soon erupt.

Brigid saw the frustration in Finn's furrowed brow and the tic in his temple as he maintained his composure. Brigid knew she must deflect the antipathy. Scolding Aisne would do no good. *It will make things worse,* thought Brigid, who said,

'Tomorrow, we'll see some cows; I used to milk them.'

'Where did you learn to milk cows in Dublin?' Dermot's brow puckered.

'I grew up in the countryside, not in Dublin.'

Before her son could ask more awkward questions, Brigid cleared their used plates and produced dessert with a flourish.

'Apple pie baked at home.' Finn's eyes lit up as Brigid put a substantial slice before him and smaller portions in front of her children. 'Eat up. I want you children asleep in thirty minutes.'

Once the children slept, Finn broached the delicate subject of who should succeed Niall in the Saor-Éire leadership. He suggested Alexander. Brigid fixed her eyes on the flames; Niall's face took shape within them, and he nodded.

'Well, Alexander is degree-level educated and would add much knowledge to the team. He is a deep thinker who comprehends the concept of losing one's sovereignty. Scots hate the English as much as the Irish do. However, it is right to ask Amy for her opinion. If Alexander becomes a part of the elite, she could become a focus of spies' attention and require extra protection, like me. Have you spoken to Robert? You need his agreement, too.'

'I know Ezra will put the idea to Alexander, and Stephen will talk to Robert,' said Finn.

'I'll visit Amy. It is time we had a chat.'

So, on their return home, Brigid sent her friend a note saying she would visit. Curious about Amy's lack of communication, she hoped for her well-being. They had bought a splendid Georgian House near Mountjoy Square, a few streets from Dublin's prison. The location made no sense to Brigid. But Finn explained Alexander had bought it on Robert's instructions as the likelihood of attacks was less where properties sat in well-patrolled city areas, like those near the prison.

Brigid was relieved to see nothing of the prison visible as she climbed from the cab. A housekeeper admitted her to Amy's home and showed Brigid to the drawing room. The house had well-proportioned rooms, lofty ceilings, and elaborate cornices. Tapestries hung on the sky-blue silk-covered entrance hall. Emerald and gold damask curtains hung at the drawing room windows, matching the deep pile of the green and yellow patterned carpet.

Amy welcomed Brigid with a hug. 'It is gratifying to see you looking well, Brigid. The countryside air agrees with you. Please make yourself comfortable.'

Brigid noted Amy was in the advanced stages of pregnancy and wondered why nobody had informed her. But it explained why Amy had not attended her wedding to Finnbar. Amy directed her friend to a pale green sofa on one side of a roaring fire.

Amy pulled a cord and rang for the maid. A girl dressed in an elegant dark frock overlaid by a frilly apron brought tea and cakes. 'To what do I owe this visit, Brigid?' said Amy, pouring the tea.

'I know Stephen has spoken about this matter, but I want to know your opinion about Alexander joining the leadership of Saor-Éire. It may expose your family to danger.'

'My role is to bring contentment to Alexander. I'm no longer the wild and impulsive person people once knew. I obey my husband. I made that vow before God.'

Noticing Amy's transformation into a society wife, Brigid congratulated her on the pregnancy and asked about the due date.

Amy said, 'In March. Because of a challenging pregnancy, the doctor has advised me to be on bed rest for much of the time.'

Amy's beautiful ringlets sat still on her head. She looked stunning with soft skin, manicured fingernails, and a pale pink silk dress that suited her complexion and disguised her bump. She shone with the unmistakable luminosity of late pregnancy. After chatting for an hour, Brigid took her leave, noting Amy had become fatigued.

'I'll visit again before your baby is due. I shall have my hands full with three children and my job at Clery's store after mine is born.'

Marriage to Finnbar, who now made an income from writing and lecturing at the university, meant Brigid had fewer financial problems. *We can afford a maid,* thought Brigid on her way home. She wondered whether Mary-Ann would be suitable. She knew the girl was not happy in her pupil-teaching role and put the matter to Finn and Ezra. Brigid suggested another pupil teacher could rent Mary Ann's room. The two men agreed, and the girl was overjoyed by the plan.

'Your lodgings, food, and uniform will be free, and we'll pay you a fee of £22.00 per year, including remuneration for your help caring for the children on weekends,' said Brigid, smiling.

'How soon can I start?' Mary-Ann's shoulders straightened, and her body tension eased.

'You can give the school a week's notice when Ezra has redecorated your room and found some furniture.'

But Brigid needed to explain the matter to Eileen. She wondered if she and Mary-Ann did not get along, judging from Eileen's furrowed brow and pursed lips when she told her. After a few days, she questioned Dermot about the two women.

'Who takes care of you on Saturdays?' she said.

'Mary-Ann takes care of us. Eileen goes off with a man somewhere. I don't think she likes Aisne. She gets cross with her.'

Where Eileen went in her off-duty time was not Brigid's business. However, she had agreed to care for the children, and leaving the task to Mary-Ann was deceitful. Neither did Brigid appreciate the woman's changed, cold, condescending manner. It conveyed something unpleasant, and Brigid was eager to get rid of her. She discussed with Finn whether to give Eileen a week's notice to leave. 'Her unfriendly attitude gives me cause for concern,' she said.

But Finn suggested leaving it until the end of the school

term, to which Brigid agreed with some reluctance. She did not visit Amy before her child was born because the baby, a girl, arrived early. Amy wrote in a note that she and the child were well, but they would need time for recovery from what had been a traumatic experience.

CHAPTER 25: DANIEL

Brigid gave birth to her third child on 5th June 1863. The delivery was difficult because the child was in the breech position, and Brigid lost a lot of blood during the procedure. Despite his serious tone, the doctor's eyes conveyed genuine kindness as he said, 'I advise you not to have another child. You were fortunate to avoid a risky Caesarean section during childbirth. We do not know how much damage your womb has received.'

Brigid gave him a weak nod and wished he had used chloroform to make her unconscious during the birth. The physical effects were evident in her pale, drawn face. Her eyes lacked lustre, too, and because of the blood loss, her recovery was slow, her appetite poor, and she remained bed-bound for four weeks.

Concerned about her fatigue, Caitlin asked the doctor to visit.

'Mrs Hayes, the blood loss, coupled with your age and a traumatised womb, is causing your fatigue. Rest and food such as liver will rebuild your strength. You are making progress and will recover for your son's baptism.'

Baptism? Because Brigid had lost her faith, she had forgotten Finn wanted his child baptised, just as Niall had. Despite the fatigue, she followed the doctor's instructions, carried her son down the aisle, and took her seat in the front pew.

The priest's voice echoed around the congregation as he baptised her son, naming him Daniel after Finn's brother, who had died in the famine. Despite her lack of faith, Brigid felt joy fill her heart.

The child resembled his father, with dark hair, piercing sea-green eyes, and a fierce disposition. He looked right at Brigid, and despite her previous experience as a mother, she had lost confidence with the difficult birth. As the oldest of six, Mary-Ann knew how to manage the situation. Brigid was thankful to the girl and rewarded her with a bonus.

But given her lack of trust in Eileen, Brigid was pleased when the woman gave her a month's notice because she was getting married. Mary-Ann had confirmed that Eileen did little to help with the children's Saturdays.

'My experiences with that woman were unpleasant. She could be a bully and a telltale. That is why I left teaching.'

'Well, she is out of your life now, and I won't bully you.'

Mary-Ann said, 'I know you won't; you are far too kind-hearted.'

Caitlin had news that alarmed Brigid. 'Ezra thinks Eileen's fiancée is from the North. He followed them to your house one Saturday afternoon when he returned to collect my shawl and caught the man's Northern accent. He now wonders if Eileen is a spy's informant.'

Finn's anger was palpable because if Ezra had accurate suspicions, Eileen had sabotaged Saor-Éire's operations. He ordered a membership review. Robert stepped up surveillance and sent a young officer to follow Eileen before she left Heytesbury Street one evening and discovered she walked to a house near the docks.

Further enquiries revealed her fiancée was from Armagh. Finn was sure Robert had identified the spy. *How had Eileen obtained information to pass on to her fiancée?*

Finn had moved Niall's desk back to the study. He examined the desk and found scratch marks on the lock. He called for Brigid to inspect it. 'Did it have scratch marks when you had it in the parlour?' She shook her head, her heart pounding with fear.

'Then Eileen must have opened it, perhaps with a knife or

something,' Finn's fury was evident in his burning eyes. But she was soon gone, and Finn found a young man, Rory, who had joined Saor-Éire and needed lodgings. However, for Finn, salvaging Saor-Éire's plans became the top priority, and he worked hard to implement new ones. Finn met Stephen and Alexander to discuss matters. After the meeting, Finn said he and Stephen agreed that the family should move.

'The house is no longer safe. Eileen has revealed our work to the Orange Order and the British Army.'

Overwhelmed by everything that had happened, Brigid couldn't think of moving.

'I don't wish to separate the children from their familiar home yet. It is too soon after their father's death. I don't want Dermot to change schools before he turns eight.'

'Upon your head be it, then. That fecking woman and her associates know every detail of our home and life.' Finn's tone would cut a loaf of stale bread.

But nothing happened, no raids or blatant spying, and Brigid dropped her guard. Caitlin and Ezra came to supper in September to celebrate Finn's birthday. Finn admitted that O'Brien's group planned an attack on English soil.

Caitlin's face turned white. 'Men will die if they attack English soil, so they will.'

'The American Fenian Group, Irish Comrades, have merged with O'Brien's group and put me in charge of Irish and English actions. O'Brien intends to steal guns and ammunition from under the noses of the English militia and wants the help of Saor-Éire to make bombs.' Finn glanced at Ezra.

I fear for Ezra's life if caught; they could imprison him, or worse.'

Caitlin's eyes glittered, and her voice trembled. She took out her handkerchief and patted her eyes.

Finn's knuckles showed white as he gripped the table, and his jaw clenched. 'Saor-Éire agreed to help on Irish soil, so I have a raid planned in Ulster.' His ice-cold eyes glared with menace at Caitlin.

Brigid's pulse thrummed, and her mouth dropped open. 'Does this mean Saor-Éire is also collaborating with the American Irish Comrades?'

'Our ethos to remain local has not changed, but we can't sit idle while others fight for our freedom from British rule. We must help those who share our aims. I have a serious grudge against Ulster Orange Lodges. That evil woman, Eileen, opened my desk. I want to kill her, so I do.' Finn's sea-green eyes blazed.

'You don't mean that, do you, Finn? If they caught you, you'd hang. I couldn't cope with a second loss. I have three children to raise.' Brigid's face turned a shade paler than alabaster, and she dabbed her eyes.

Ezra and Caitlin left around ten o'clock. Brigid wondered how much Amy knew about their plans as she shut the door behind them. The next day, Brigid sent a note inviting her to tea.

Amy arrived looking mature and self-possessed. 'Thank you for inviting me. It seems ages since we last met.' Amy kissed Brigid's cheek.

They sat in the parlour, and Mary-Ann brought Darjeeling tea and small cakes. Brigid broached the subject of Saor-Éire's plans. Amy explained Alexander had locked his study and that she had never seen his correspondence.

'Our cellar has become a secret meeting place for conveying information. They are planning something dangerous because Alexander goes out at night dressed in old clothes and returns with muddy boots. I wonder if he has been down to the docks.'

Brigid studied her friend's face. 'Finn has been doing the same thing. He has always been secretive, so I paid scant attention.'

'But what if something goes wrong? The men are risking not just their lives but ours, too. I have spoken to Alexander about it, but he won't listen.' Amy sighed.

'Finn is just as determined. I think his dedication to Irish independence has made him reckless, to the point of considering joint action with Ronan O'Brien. They won't inform us of any raid's timing or location.'

Amy's hand shook, slopping tea into the saucer. 'O'Brien? One day, a raid could bite them like a rabid fox.' Tears filled her forget-me-not-blue eyes.

Brigid placed a comforting hand on Amy's arm and changed the subject. 'How are Cecilia and her son, Alastair, getting along? The boy must be talking by now.'

'Alastair is an adorable little boy. Mamma dotes on him, and he wraps Papa around his little finger. Cecilia is an excellent mother and homemaker.'

'How is Stephen?' With her brow furrowed and gaze direct, Brigid hoped Amy would read the implicit message.

'He keeps his promise, but we never speak of it. He qualified as a solicitor last year, and with it came a salary increase, which pleased Papa. Qualifying has given Stephen a better understanding of the penalties for infringing the law if you grasp my meaning.'

Brigid inclined her head. 'How does he get on with Alexander?'

'Alex is a barrister, but he and Stephen have worked on several cases. They seem to work well together, and Stephen's standing in the legal world has grown. I don't think he wishes to jeopardise it.' Amy blushed. 'Brigid, we have told no one yet except family members, but I expect another child in the summer.'

'That is grand news, congratulations. How is your daughter developing?'

'Isabella has a strong will, Brigid. We have engaged a nanny who spares me from tussling with her. The cook exempts me from cooking, as I never enjoyed it.' She paused, stroking her belly. 'I hope this pregnancy is less complicated than my first. I am better equipped to manage my condition than last time.' Amy glanced at the clock. 'My cab will arrive soon. It has been lovely to see you, Brigid. You must join us for supper in the Christmas season when I am strong enough to host a party. I have yet to show you the pictures we brought back from Switzerland.'

Brigid hugged her friend as she bid farewell and reflected on how their lives had diverged. Amy had household staff, including a cook and a nanny. Judging from her fine clothes, she had the money and time to visit hairdressers and expensive dressmakers. Meanwhile, Brigid dressed her hair without help and went to work to earn money.

That night, Finn and Brigid discussed whether they could afford to enrol Dermot in the renowned Christian Brothers' school in January 1865. Brigid opined it would stretch their finances, and as he seemed to do well at his current school, they shouldn't move him. Mary-Ann accompanied him each morning and afternoon as part of her duties, and the arrangement worked well. So, Finn agreed to leave the status quo until September.

A few days before Christmas 1864, Dermot came home complaining of a headache and stomach ache. He had taken part in a nativity play where he played Joseph's role. Believing his complaints were a reaction to the day's tension, Brigid sent him to bed early.

In the morning, Dermot complained that his neck glands hurt. Brigid recognised their swelling from her childhood. Dermot had the mumps. She tucked him back into bed, hoping the disease would pass with no problems. However, she felt anxious because neither Aisne nor Finn had ever caught the infection. Before long, Aisne complained of a sore throat and neck. She was far less compliant than Dermot and refused to stay in bed. This worried Brigid, as she feared for Finn's health and tried to keep him away from the children. But he visited Dermot to read him a story he had written about fishing, and in no time, Brigid had another patient who, like Aisne, would not stay in bed.

'I'm not ill. I have a sore neck.' Finn said with annoyance when Brigid suggested he should rest.

But she had to cancel the season's plans, including Amy's supper invitation, and Christmas was a subdued event. Brigid made bread poultices for her patients' necks. Still, Finn would not use one and wrapped a scarf around his instead. He continued with a light work schedule until his temperature soared, which forced him to bed. The family doctor came to check on him and warned it was unlikely he could father more children.

'That isn't an issue,' he responded in a tone Brigid couldn't comprehend. 'I have enough children already.'

Brigid felt disturbed by this comment. *What did Finn mean?*

The doctor had warned her against having more children anyway, so this was, in one respect, a relief. However, Brigid chooses not to question Finn, for she knows he would give an unsatisfactory answer. She wondered if he could have fathered other children on his travels, in France or on the West Coast. But she has no evidence that anything like that had ever happened.

CHAPTER 26: TOWARDS THE FUTURE

In the summer of 1865, Dermot came home from school with a glowing report, pleasing his mother. Aisne and Finn finally bonded because they both had had the mumps. Aisne spent hours painting pictures, and Brigid was rocked by the maturity of her daughter's art. She attended Dermot's school and wished to exhibit her work on the bedroom walls.

'Mrs Hayes, I'm unsure whether you are aware, but Aisne learned to read independently before attending school. I caught her with one of Dermot's books, and upon reading a passage, she was word perfect,' said Mary-Ann.

Brigid's jaw dropped. 'Goodness, she will be off to Trinity College soon.'

Embarrassed, she laughed at her own joke. But soon, Aisne authored simple stories illustrated by her paintings.

Curious and wanting to learn about his world, Daniel had his fingers in every nook and cranny. Fascinated by coins, Brigid and Finn had to be careful not to drop any. Finn counted farthings and played with his son,

'He'll be a financier or something when he grows up.'

'He will be tight-fisted,' Brigid said as she recalled wrestling a coin from his chubby hand before he could put it in his mouth.

But it was soon clear the boy liked to count. 'I wager it will be more than pennies you'll count with one day, my son,' said Finn sagely, ruffling his son's hair. 'Having a few farthings in your pocket will teach you the value of money.'

Amy gave birth to a son in early August, just before Aisne's birthday, and this time had an uncomplicated delivery. Brigid travelled to see her and the child, whom they named Douglas after Alexander's grandfather. A healthy boy, he was the image of his mother. Brigid was pleased to see Amy looking well and happy.

Summer gave way to a wet autumn and muddy streets clogged with wet leaves. Life wore shades of grey in the foggy, dank November, and Brigid looked forward to Amy's festive celebration. But Amy became sick with a strange fever after Christmas. Doctors puzzled over the unusual rash and other symptoms of aching joints and swollen glands and took some time to diagnose her disease as rubella, a disease that resembled measles.

Nobody in Amy's family or friends had ever suffered from rubella, and doctors couldn't discover where Amy had caught the infection. The doctor transferred Amy to a fever hospital, where they isolated her. Brigid pondered the possibility of it being caught at her mother's soup kitchen. Still, the disease ended plans for holiday celebrations for a second time. *Is the event doomed*? Brigid wondered.

Isabella, along with Brigid's two older children, had caught measles in an epidemic around the time Brigid weaned Daniel in the early winter of 1865. But for safety, Brigid sent Daniel to Caitlin. She had nightmares about Joseph's death, and Daniel was too young to fight the disease.

Before they knew it, the spring of 1866 came upon Ireland. The Hayes family visited the park on the first day of the season. Clumps of bright yellow daffodils adorned the park, their petals glistening in the sunshine. Aisne pointed to the sky, where a magnificent hot-air balloon hovered overhead, its emerald and daffodil-coloured stripes glittering in the sun.

'Look Mammy. Can we go up in one, please?' Aisne's animated face filled her mother with joy, wishing Niall could share it.

'I went up in one when I last visited my sister, accompanied by my nephew. We had a lot of fun,' Finn said.

Finn's claim of having fun going up in a balloon met with disbelief from Brigid. But despite his encouragement, she felt too uncertain about joining them. 'It will topple over.' Her voice quivered with apprehension. 'Daniel is too young, anyway.' She clasped her son's hand.

Finn paid the fare and climbed inside one of the stationary balloons with Dermot and Aisne. Soon, they rose above the park, and the children waved at Brigid, whose heart fluttered with fear.

She waved back at them and recorded the venture in her newest journal. Finn had urged her to publish them all, but Brigid would not. The precious memories now felt too private to share with the world.

In May, when the Irish Comrades began an armed uprising, Saor-Éire obtained valuable information. Alarmed at the civilian casualties, Brigid asked if the rebellion had finished.

'Not yet. We plan more action for later this year.'

Finn gave no further details, and Brigid quailed, her thoughts overwhelmed with foreboding.

The summer came and went without incident, and Brigid relaxed. She took a brief period of unpaid leave to prepare Daniel for school. This gave Caitlin time off to finish working on the Ulster documents collected in May. Finn went on a journey to see his sister in August, leaving Brigid and the children behind, which irked her. Balancing her Saor-Éire work with childcare, Caitlin took them out as much as possible during the summer.

'Cecilia has returned to teaching and does less work for Saor-Éire now,' Ezra revealed during a September supper, looking with a pointed gaze upon Finn, who did not react.

Caitlin turned to her husband. 'I'm anxious about what you do since you have employed an assistant.' She raised her eyebrows at Brigid and, with a light shake of her head, warned

Brigid not to question.

An answer came in December when a group of unnamed Fenians exploded a bomb to free members held in an English prison. The explosion damaged nearby houses killed ten people and injured many more. The prisoners couldn't escape as the prison authorities had moved them before the attack, raising suspicions of espionage.

Brigid wondered if Finn and O'Brien worked as a team and suspected Ezra had manufactured the bomb. Her body shivered when she thought of the danger Ezra had put himself in, and she thought, *did he know his bomb would kill civilians?*

She questioned Caitlin over coffee. 'Do you know why no prisoners escaped on the Irish Comrades raid? I can't get much out of Finn.' She chose her words with care to avoid upsetting her friend.

'I don't,' Caitlin said, her face solemn. 'But I wish Ezra would stop making bombs. I hate the thought of civilians being hurt.'

Brigid drank her coffee, thinking, *she knows.* Then she spoke aloud her thoughts. 'Civilian casualties were never part of the plans when I joined Saor-Éire. I can't say I like how matters are developing. Finn is getting in too deep with O'Brien's group.' Brigid then recounted her first meeting with Finn in the coffee house. 'I disliked Finn for his lack of manners, but he has a way of bewitching women. However, I never envisaged Finn would turn to such violence, nor that I would bear him a son. Sometimes, he can be cheerful and play with the children ... but at other times...' She left her words unfinished.

Caitlin refrained from commenting. She and Ezra joined the Hayes for a family Christmas in 1866. Everyone stayed healthy, and Brigid and Finn attended the long-promised New Year's Eve party. Upon returning from the party, Finn and Brigid could spend a night alone at home. with everyone else, including the children, away overnight,

Amy decorated her home in a German Swiss fashion, complete with a decorated fir tree bearing red and gold bows and candles. Over a meal of roast pheasant, she recounted their honeymoon trip to Switzerland. She repeated their attempts at skating and the sleigh rides through the snow. 'To warm ourselves from the frigid air, colder than here, we enjoyed spiced glühwein. We'll drink it at midnight.'

'Where do you obtain the spices?' asked Brigid.

'I get them with stollen, a Germanic spiced cake, from a German goods store. It's one of Dublin's new specialist shops. I'll serve both at midnight.'

Brigid felt the warmth of the house when they sang songs around the piano played by Amy. Alexander disappeared outside as the nearby church clock struck midnight and church bells rang. He returned carrying a lump of coal in his gloved hands, and Brigid's eyebrows rose, wondering if it was a strange Swiss custom.

'It's called first footing in Scotland and is supposed to bring luck,' Amy said, linking arms with her friend. Everyone linked arms to sing *Auld Lang Syne*. 'Another Scottish custom,' Amy explained when they sat down to stollen and glasses of glühwein on 1st January 1867.

'Have you seen Stephen and Cecilia?' Brigid said with apprehension. 'I note their absence from the evening.'

Amy blushed. 'I was hoping you wouldn't ask. Doctors say Stephen has developed alcoholism. Has Finn not told you? He may lose his career if he doesn't stop drinking.' Amy turned her wedding ring.

'He hasn't, and I apologise deeply.' Brigid touched Amy's hand. 'What will become of Cecilia and Alastair?'

Amy did not know. 'He is still living in their home, and our mother is doing what she can to help. But it is exhausting her.

Alastair is a demanding child.'

There was no more questioning from Brigid. She stilled her tongue, itching to remark about Da and his alcoholism.

The party broke up around one o'clock in the morning, and Finn had a cab waiting to take them home. When they left Amy's house, the sky was starry with a waxing moon. Brigid's mind recalled another such night long ago. She shivered as she breathed in the crisp winter air and was glad of the muff Finn had bought her for Christmas. The stars glowed, and fallen snow sparkled like diamonds in the cab's light as Brigid climbed inside. She could hear the horse's hooves muffled as it clomped along the cobbled streets and snuggled up to Finn for warmth.

With a captivating smile, Finn mentioned he had placed a warming pan in the bed before they left last night. Brigid yawned and snuggled closer, thinking of that warm bed.

But to their dismay, they saw dark smoke billowing in the distance as they drew near Heytesbury Street. The horse whinnied and raised his forelegs, so the cab bucked, dislodging the passengers. Brigid's heart missed a beat and jumped to her throat. She knew which house was on fire.

'The warming pan, Finn. Did you close the lid tight?' Brigid gasped, not believing her eyes. All her possessions, the children's toys, and life with Niall could be consumed by the flames.

The cabby tried to coax his horse nearer, but the animal would not move and neighed with fright. Brigid attempted to get out of the cab but discovered she couldn't move either. Finn paid the cabby while Brigid stared wild-eyed at the scene, her heart thumping harder than it had when she and her siblings buried Scamp.

Finn tucked her arm into his, stroking her hand. 'Come, mo stór, let's find out what happened.'

Brigid saw flames licking their way through the house's hallway and the parlour towards the kitchen. Water dripped from the upper windows as fire officers battled to control the flames below. Brigid thought her whole life was disappearing before her eyes, which misted over.

The Chief Fire Officer came to speak with her. 'You are lucky, Missus. Your neighbour spotted the fire before it took hold. The brave man sent his son for us while he broke in and dumped gravel and water on the flames.'

Brigid gasped and shuddered as an icy chill ran down her spine, watching the conflagration, her heart hammering.

The fire officer addressed Finn. 'Was anyone at home? We have found no one.'

Brigid spotted the ladder extended to her bedroom and the broken window. 'Nobody, officer. We have been to a New Year's Eve party.' The words stuck to her throat, and she sounded like a frog when they emerged.

'Do you know how it started?' Finn said.

'We suspect arson. When we arrived, we found a piece of rag lying on the path. It smelt of a new flammable product called paraffin.'

The fire officer's wrinkled face had a solemn expression as Finn strode off to inspect the damage. 'Madame, I must ask you, does anyone in your household have enemies who might wish them harm?'

Brigid watched the scene and shivered, but not from the frigid air. 'You must ask my husband that question, officer, not me.'

The officer studied Brigid's face, his expression one of concern. 'I will, Madame.' He shook his head before striding over to join Finn.

Brigid was alarmed when a figure emerged from the shadows after he had left, calling out to her.

'Missus, Missus, it's me, Liam. My other army brother, the one billeted in Dublin, and two army friends have done it. I came to warn yous. But nobody was home, thank God.'

Brigid opened her mouth to speak, but Liam disappeared into the shadows again. Brigid, rooted to the spot for a few seconds by the news, hurried to join Finn and Robert.

'Liam has just told me that his brother is the culprit.'

Finn's face darkened with rage. 'You mean that fecking street urchin that Niall told me about years ago?'

'Yes. Liam has grown up but came to warn us.'

'Who is this boy?' The fire officer said, his mouth set.

'His first name is Liam, although he never told me his last name. He lives in the dockside tenements. He knows we are members of a Fenian group, and when my first husband was alive, he became an informant. I have not seen him for years. But Liam has two brothers in the British Army. He says one of his brothers and a pair of army friends set our house alight.'

The fire officer's face paled, and his eyes glittered with disbelief. 'Someone does wish you harm. How did Liam's brother find out that you were not at home tonight, or was their intention to burn you in your bed?'

Brigid's icy hands shook, and she pushed them deep into her muff. 'I don't know.' She paused, controlling her teeth, chattering from shock and cold. 'I had forgotten about Liam. He must have watched this house like he did the apartment I lived in with my first husband in the neighbourhood of North Reading Street. We would have owed our lives to him had we been at home. He is a sympathiser for our cause and a courageous lad.'

Finn put his arm around Brigid's shaking shoulders and turned to the officer. 'We'll need police to find these feckers. I'll use my small pistol to execute them if I catch them.'

The fire officer shook his head. 'Don't talk like that, sir. It could get you hung. I'll contact Inspector Gallagher today. I suggest you find a hotel for the rest of the night while we clear your home. We confined the fire to the lower floor, but there is smoke and water damage on the upper levels.'

Brigid walked up the short path and looked inside. Despite her need to see the damage, the fire officer advised her not to check the kitchen. 'Your kitchen is so damaged it will need rebuilding, and the hallway floorboards are gone. It is dangerous to enter.'

Finn woke the snoozing night manager of a nearby hotel. Once in a room, Finn paced the floor, muttering about the feckers, repeating his threat to execute them while running his hands through his hair.

Brigid, her nerves in shreds, said, 'Finn, please keep your voice down. Your pacing is giving me a headache. You'll wake other guests and have us thrown out. Wanting them caught does not justify taking matters into your own hands.'

Brigid's mind was in turmoil, filled with the forgotten spectres of death, and a lump grew in her throat. She couldn't rid herself of the sensation that the British Army wanted her family dead. She repeated her request for Finn to calm down twice before he got into bed. He looked at Brigid in the candlelight while his head lay on his pillow.

'Thank God everyone went elsewhere tonight. The soldiers must have acted fast but dropped a rag in haste. Mo stór, we must move house.'

Brigid's aching head and shredded nerves left her exhausted.

'Let Robert investigate first. I must contact the insurance company and get the repairs done before we can move. Until they confirm the cause, the insurers won't pay out, so we can't repair the damage. Yet.'

Her body shook as the shock set in, and the lump in her throat grew. But Brigid must have fallen asleep, for Finn, shaking her shoulder, awoke her with a start.

'Get up, Brigid; it is eight o'clock. We must collect the children.'

Neither Brigid nor Finn could stomach breakfast, so Finn paid the check, and the concierge called a cab. When they arrived at Caitlin and Ezra's home, Caitlin held Daniel on her hips as she let them in. 'You are early. Dermot and Aisne are still eating breakfast. Did you have fun at the party?'

By shaking her head, Brigid caused Caitlin's eyes to widen. 'What's happened?'

'May we sit down somewhere, and would you fetch Ezra, please? We have something serious to tell you.' Brigid remained composed to protect the children.

Caitlin's face paled, and she stammered. 'Ezra is dressing.'

She led them to the parlour, handing the squirming Daniel to his mother. With a frown and widened eyes, Dermot entered the room. as Brigid pasted on a smile. 'What's happened, Mammy?' he said.

Brigid saw fear reflected in his eyes. The child was too wise to be fooled.

'Dermot, watch your sister and finish your breakfast, please?' Brigid said, and the boy nodded, but his solemn expression showed he knew the matter was serious.

Finn related their story in as much detail as possible when Ezra joined them while Brigid sat pale-faced and teary-eyed.

'The flat above the shop is vacant. Live there while you have repairs done. I'll find bedding for the children,' Ezra said, his face uncharacteristically solemn.

Brigid asked if Caitlin could care for the three children for several days. 'I'll deliver a message to Mary-Ann to come and help you, but it is my responsibility to find her a place to live,' she said in a resigned tone.

'She is welcome to live here, and the lodger is, too. The house has an attic bedroom we don't use. Leave these matters to us, Brigid. Shall I despatch a message to Clery's?'

Brigid nodded and gulped. 'Caitlin, I can't express enough gratitude for your and Ezra's help.' Then, her self-control gone, she burst into tears.

'Shush colleen. What are friends for if they can't help in need?' Caitlin wrapped her arms around her friend, who sobbed into her shoulder.

Later that day, they visited the house to assess the damage. Brigid needed to know what had burned to find peace – her anger at the destruction burned like a dozen candles. Robert arrived and said he had sent the rag to Trinity College's chemistry department.

'If the university confirms the substance as paraffin, it is arson.'

Finn gave him a stern look. 'I swear Saor-Éire will find the feckers.'

'I'm aware of your connection with the Irish Comrades,' Robert said. 'Have you or Saor-Éire members taken part in any raids on British Army bases?'

Brigid held her breath as Finn's face paled and his fist clenched. With her anger close to eruption, she said, 'You have, and you supplied the bomb. Caitlin told me Ezra makes them.'

Robert said, 'You fecker Finn. By joining with O'Brien, you have risked all our families' lives. Saor-Éire agreed we would hold no action on English soil.'

Finn gulped, and his voice sounded strained. Saor-Éire did not attack English soil, but we helped O'Brien by supplying ammunition.' He ran his fingers through his hair in agitation. 'Ronan O'Brien is an old friend. We grew up together. Ezra was unaware of the reason I needed the bomb.'

Brigid guessed Finn was holding back some information from his guarded look. She averted her gaze so he couldn't see her tears.

Was he involved in the Cheshire Armoury raid in England too? God knows what the army will do to him if they find out. Her mind refused to contemplate the thought further.

Brigid heard Robert say, 'That is the link, Finn. It is a deliberate military reprisal. Saor-Éire must discuss it and your future as a matter of urgency.'

Brigid turned to face her husband. 'He is right, Finn. You have put all Saor-Éire families' lives in danger, and they could target anyone next. Why would you subject us to such an attack?'

Finn's eyes looked guarded when he said, 'Independence for Ireland is a struggle for freedom. We are fighting the fecking English, and there are casualties in any war.'

Brigid looked at Robert, who shrugged his shoulders. 'You are our leader, Finn, but you may face deposition after this fire.'

Brigid's heart filled with dread. She had no illusions about his killing potential and wondered, *where does he keep the small pistol, he mentioned? It must be inside his locked desk.*

The Hayes met Ezra and Caitlin at the flat to prepare it for the children. Brigid cleaned the place, put clean sheets on the bed, and shopped for food. Brigid thanked Ezra, her eyes glistening, and they moved in the following day.

Three days later, they received a cryptic note from Robert: *Arson confirmed.*

Finn then sent a note to Brigid's insurance company, which sent a loss investigator. As expected, he interrogated Brigid and Finn, who carefully worded their answers.

The investigator then assured them he had found no evidence of fraud and promised to send a detailed report to the insurance company. 'After my manager reviews the report, the insurers should release your funds.'

Brigid addressed Finn, 'I know you want to move, but I can't face it now. It will disrupt the family's routines beyond what I could offer Robert. Please step up the patrols and station an officer on watch.' Robert gave way and agreed despite the strain on his police budget it would cause.

The repairs took three months to complete. Brigid remodelled the parlour and repainted the entire house. Once able to climb the stairs, Finn worked on his book, desiring uninterrupted focus. Brigid's anxiety grew; something seemed amiss.

Ezra and Alexander visited one evening for information on Liam. Brigid told them what she knew, emphasising the boy's affiliation with Saor-Éire's ethos. But it bothered her that the boy knew where her family lived. Brigid's head filled with unanswered questions, pushing aside other thoughts like a cuckoo. Unable to shake, feeling watched, she began hailing a cab to work. Two weeks after they had all moved in, Mary-Ann said something pleasing.

'Rory and I are courting. We have been together since the fire, and he has requested my hand in marriage. We don't wish to move Mrs Hayes, and if we marry, we wish to convert the two top rooms and attic into a flat. Would that be acceptable to you?'

Brigid assured her the idea would be acceptable. 'Do you have imminent wedding plans?'

'No, not until next year. Rory proposed marriage a couple of weeks ago. I would not give him my answer until I had spoken to you.'

'If you love him, say yes. Something good has come from this unfortunate incident.'

Despite extensive searches, Robert couldn't find Liam. Brigid grew concerned that his brother knew he was an informer, and harm had been done to him. The fear something had happened to the lad strung her nerves out, and Brigid suffered excruciating headaches.

She lied about the cause of the fire at work, saying a burning candle lit a curtain. The headaches became so disabling Saoirse sent her home and advised her to rest.

But Brigid couldn't sleep, with Liam's safety at risk. She visited Diedre's soup kitchen and asked to help her for a few days. *Someone who lives there might know Liam.*

Dressed in old clothes, Brigid set off the next day and discussed the boy with a buxom woman from the tenements. Norah listened to Brigid's description.

'Few families will have a boy named Liam and two brothers serving in the British Army. I'll enquire.'

A couple of days later, Norah had news. 'The family lives in two filthy rooms in the worst area of the tenements. The slattern of a mother has little control over her children, but one is called Liam and fits your description. My husband says Liam is eighteen and has been working down the docks for six years. He is a strong, well-liked lad, looked after by his friends, and remains unharmed. I hope this puts your mind at rest as my family is emigrating, and I can't make further enquiries.'

Brigid felt an enormous burden lift from her chest. With Liam safe, she would find the strength to help her family construct a life from the remains of their old one. 'Thank you so much.' Brigid pressed a florin into Norah's hand. 'Where do you intend to emigrate?'

'We seek a better life in America, so to Boston Missus. They say we Irish are building the city, and there is plenty of work for tough men like my man.'

Six weeks later, Alexander, considering Finn's question about the possibility of prosecuting the British Army for arson, opined Liam had the only testimony that would stand up in court. Brigid, adamant she would not implicate the boy, refused to contact him. Then Robert's enquiries revealed the British Army posted its Dublin battalion in Guyana, so Brigid told him to close the investigation. Brigid wished for a happy future for Liam, a boy who risked his life for little gain. *I'll be forever grateful,* she thought.

CHAPTER 27: BONDS MADE & BROKEN

Saoirse caught a chill in February, and in Dublin, smog went to her chest. Mrs O'Keefe called for the doctor, who diagnosed double pneumonia and transferred the woman to the hospital. But her condition worsened, and she passed away. Brigid grieved the loss of a compassionate mentor and friend.

A few days after her funeral, the manager called Brigid to his office. 'Saoirse had a last request. She wanted you to take over her position. At a meeting this morning, the board approved your promotion to Head of the Accounts Department. I recommend you as a diligent employee who manages personal issues without permitting them to affect the quality of your work. It is rare to find a married woman with such skill. You'll be pleased to hear it comes with a substantial salary increase.' He held out his hand. 'Congratulations, my dear,'

Brigid took his hand, tears clouding her eyes. 'Thank you,' she said, seeking her handkerchief.

'I have had Saoirse's desk cleaned and polished for you, and I'll make a staff announcement this afternoon.'

When Brigid told Finn, he congratulated her. 'Your intellect is exceptional. That is why you captivated me.'

Brigid's cheeks burned, and she felt like a peacock with such praise. But by the spring of 1867, the family had bonded into a tight-knit team, and Aisne had connected with Finn, but unlike Dermot, she refused to call him Da. Brigid reflected the fire had brought the family closer.

Finn submitted his thesis to the university that spring and obtained his doctorate in history. He took on more teaching at Trinity College, where he had a salary increase. With their finances improved, Brigid engaged a well-qualified governess for Aisne, who specialised in art but could teach French and English too. The girl danced around the floor when she heard this news. The idea of a school regime had never appealed to her. She wanted to paint, not do arithmetic.

'You must do some mathematics,' declared Brigid. 'You need to manage money and household accounts.'

Aisne pulled a face and flounced off to paint.

Nobody could doubt Daniel's parentage: an authentic copy of his father, with the same eyes, fierce intelligence, and an ability to command respect. But Brigid hoped he would not have any propensity to violence. Finn planned for Daniel to follow Dermot to the Christian Brothers' school when he was eight.

Mary-Ann and Rory had married in the spring, and Mary-Ann soon expected their first child. Brigid cleared the box room on the third floor, and Rory transformed it into a nursery, whitewashing the walls and obtaining furniture from Ezra. Brigid lent them the rocking cradle and press.

On the surface, life for Brigid's family looked grand, but her fears never disappeared. She put up an emotional barrier against Finn's wish to remove British rule from Ireland. At the next meeting of Saor-Éire, Finn explained to the members the organisation must focus more on the north of Ireland and the threat posed by the Orange Lodges. He made plans to travel in the Ulster region that summer and use collecting material for another book as a cover to investigate lodges.

Alexander was now Finn's second in command, and few people outside Saor-Éire's leaders knew he had organised for interrogations to take place in Alexander's cellar.

Upon learning this from Finn, a horrified Brigid, fearful for Amy's safety, took a cab to visit her friend. Amy welcomed her with surprise until Brigid explained the reason for her visit.

'Don't these interrogations scare you? Before your marriage, your father viewed your security as so important that Alexander brought forward the wedding.'

With a sanguine attitude, Amy distinguished those attacks from Saor-Éire's activities.

'The maid's and nanny's rooms are on the third floor, with instructions to keep the children away from the cellar. The cook, a Saor-Éire member's wife, disguises the room as one for storing pots and pans. Interrogations are infrequent and occur at night.' Amy paused. 'I have accepted that freedom for Ireland comes at a price.'

Brigid had once doubted Amy's resilience, but she now held her in high esteem. She took her leave, and Amy promised to visit her soon. In the cab home, Brigid sighed. *Will I ever find a peaceful life*?

When Finn returned from Ulster, Brigid felt compelled to ask if he had planned any action, but Finn refused to enlighten her. An attack came one foggy night in late November 1867, and two Orange Lodge premises burned. Brigid expressed her horror at the potential for civilian deaths,

'I set up a northern arm of Saor-Éire under another name in Ulster in the summer. They led the action, and my informants assure me they checked the buildings for occupants before attacking,' said Finn.

Brigid accepted this explanation. But then came the news that civilian deaths had occurred, and Brigid, who had seen enough death to last a lifetime, inferred Finn's being more deeply involved than he had led anyone to believe. She felt waves of fear crush her body as the truth dawned.

'You organised it all in the summer, not just set up the Ulster arm. If I'm right, the military will pursue you like a stray dog.' Brigid averted her gaze to hide her glistening lashes.

'I understand your concerns, mo stór. O'Brien led the raid,

not me, and we took precautions to avoid collateral damage. But it is out of our control. O'Brien has returned to America to avoid capture. I hear he has a woman in New York.'

Brigid turned back to face her husband, her fists clenched.

'But regardless, you are a marked person. It's in my bones. The military will attempt to capture or kill you. What will we do then?'

Her eyes blazed with anger at her husband's implacable stand on extreme violence.

Three weeks later, Caitlin warned Brigid she had reason to be fearful because all her family's lives were in danger. Brigid's heart fluttered when she heard this. 'What do you mean?' she stammered.

'Ezra told me Robert Gallagher has information about an attack planned on Finnbar's life by some Orange Order Lodge.'

'Feck, does Finn know?' Brigid's voice rose a semitone and held a note of disbelief.

'Yes, he does. You are not aware of Finn's activities. If he sets foot on English soil, he will get arrested and imprisoned because of a bounty the army has placed on his head. Ezra believes that the sooner Finn follows O'Brien to America, the better.'

The news stunned Brigid, and her mind spun as the gravity of the situation sank in. 'Then the options are Finn and I separate, or the whole family leaves Ireland.' She set down her cup, clasped her hands over her face, and wept. 'All my life will vanish if we must flee. I'll never visit Niall's grave or meet my siblings again. The children's schooling, my house, my job...' She couldn't finish as sobs wracked her body. Caitlin comforted her distraught friend, but Brigid's heart rent in two.

That evening, spinning her wedding ring, Brigid raised the matter with Finn. The anger about what she had learned from Caitlin made her cheeks burn, and she wanted to knock out his gappy teeth. Finn did not deny the gravity of their predicament. He explained they must all emigrate.

'The British Army, Ulster Orangemen, and the British police know they can get to me through you.'

Brigid's face paled. 'Do you know what you ask of me? How can I abandon my whole life?' Brigid lay her head back in her chair, stifling her sobs in her handkerchief lest the children wake.

Finn said, 'They have offered me the position of Head of the Irish Comrades Division in Boston. They have plenty of money in America, so I will have a decent salary. The Comrades have agreed to let me find a suitable teaching job and have taken responsibility for finding us a home and covering the rent.'

Tear-stained, Brigid gazed up at Finn's determined eyes. She understood she couldn't resist him. She had the children and their welfare to consider.

Ezra advised Finn to avoid sailing from big ports like Dublin, Cork, or Belfast. 'You have a face that is too well known, Finn. Wherever you sail from, you'll need a disguise.'

Finn sailed from Moville in Donegal. In preparation, he grew his hair longer and beard and wore spectacles. On Caitlin's advice, Finn wore tattered clothing to give the appearance of being a poor migrant. With Brigid's permission., he used the alias *Joseph McGrath*. Before leaving, Finn told his wife that the Irish Comrades had found a house in Boston's Back Bay area. He gave her twenty dollars for use when she reached America. Brigid took them with a trembling hand and did not ask where he had got the money.

With tears and hugs, the family said their goodbyes as he set off for Donegal on a donkey cart provided by an acquaintance of Caitlin. Daniel sobbed himself to sleep that night. Then he woke and crept into bed beside Brigid. 'Will we ever see Daddy again?'

Brigid hugged her son to her breast, wondering the same thing. Daniel cried into his father's pillow and found comfort in Brigid's embrace until he fell asleep. But sleep eluded Brigid until the early hours, and she woke at seven when Aisne entered her bedroom.

The girl stood with a hand on her hip, glaring at Daniel, who sat up, rubbing his eyes. 'Mammy, it's time to get up. What is Daniel doing in your bed?'

Daniel burst into tears, turned, and buried his face in his mother's breast.

'You are a cry-baby, so you are.' Aisne's voice dripped with disdain. 'Your Da is alive, isn't he?'

Brigid sighed. Aisne resented Daniel having a living father while hers lay in a cold grave, never to be seen again. But Brigid decided she must plan for their future.

'Set the table for breakfast, Aisne, while Daniel and I get dressed. Ask Dermot to light the fire and get the kettle boiling.' She used English and gave Aisne a stern look when the girl replied in Gaelic. 'We must speak English to prepare for life in America, so please do not use Gaelic again.'

Aisne flounced off and, after defiantly speaking in Gaelic to Dermot, refused to talk at all until supper time.

The following morning, Brigid observed a cerulean sky from the bedroom window, evoking memories of that day at Aunt Bessie's in Bray. The beech tree across the street stood in full leaf, and it made Brigid wonder if there were similar trees in Boston. Not knowing the answer, she turned away and sighed, her mind on the immediate future.

At Clery's, she gave a month's notice to the manager.

'My husband has a job offer in America that is too good to refuse. So, with reluctance, I have agreed to emigrate.' Brigid had difficulty holding back her tears.

Despite his emotions, the manager agreed that the family would have better opportunities in America. He wrote Brigid a glowing testimonial.

'If you ever return, a job will be open for you here.' He dabbed his eyes with a large white handkerchief.

Brigid asked Caitlin if Ezra would like to rent her property and keep Mary-Ann and her family in their home.

'You honour us. It is a lovely house, and I have always admired it.' Caitlin's eyes clouded with tears.

Brigid decided not to inform the boys' schools about leaving and asked Caitlin to send them a letter once the family had sailed. She had trouble finding a boat sailing from Ireland to Boston with a cabin for four at short notice. Ezra found a suitable cabin on the steamship Apollo departing for New York from Liverpool in August. The cabin cost five guineas, a reduced price because it had an obstructed view.

'The shipping clerk advises you to take plenty of food that won't spoil, like cheese, nuts, and dry biscuits. Pack suitable clothing for a sea voyage because the weather can be brutal at sea. I have found a trunk and two suitcases for your belongings.'

Bridget tried to see the changes as a new chapter in her family's life. But it broke her heart to leave the graves and her living sister and brother, whom she met at Robert Gallagher's home. She did not want anyone local to associate them with her.

It was a tearful occasion, and Brigid hugged her siblings so hard that Angela complained of being unable to breathe.

Padraig had to blow his nose after he had embraced his sister. 'You are the bravest of us,' he said in Gaelic. 'Ma knew it, so she did. We all wondered where your strength came from.'

Brigid gazed upon them both, etching their features into her mind.

'I shall never forget you or the beauty of Ireland's green fields and blue mountains. Her eyes misted.

It's the end of an era, and I must flee for the second time in my life.

PART TWO: EMIGRATION TO THE AMERICAS

CHAPTER 28: THE APOLLO

The family left Ireland in August 1867 on the night ferry to Liverpool. The family endured a rough passage to Liverpool, and the children, who had little sleep, were exhausted. Brigid sighed with relief when she saw the sturdy, sea-going wooden emigration vessel, her sails being unfurled by sure-footed sailors in wide-legged trousers who climbed the rigging. This fascinated Dermot, who waved his hand at those at the top. 'Mammy, I want to join them.'

'It is far too dangerous. Watching the sailors makes me feel queasy, like witnessing you going up into the sky in those hot-air balloons.'

Brigid moved from the rail to face the dockland, recalling her arrival in Dublin twelve years earlier. *How green I was then,* she thought with nostalgia.

The Apollo's passage began with the evening tide, the land receding into the hazy, pink-tinged horizon as dusk fell. The yawing vessel sailed out of the River Mersey into the wide estuary, and the children were fascinated by the building-lined shore and the ship's foaming wake.

'What makes the water so frothy, Mammy? It looks like dirty soap-suds-filled washing water.' Dermot grimaced.

Brigid suspected the paddlewheel's movement caused it, although she wasn't sure. She sighed and leaned on the ship's rail, feeling exhausted in body and spirit. The children became sleepy after losing sleep the night before. Brigid took them back to their cabin and settled them down for the night. Brigid could trust Dermot to keep the cabin door shut at age eleven.

'Open it to nobody but me. I'll rap on it three times, two knocks close together and another two seconds later. If the knock isn't as we agreed, don't answer it. We must be careful because there are ruffians on board the ship.'

Dermot nodded, and as his eyes closed, Brigid shut and locked the cabin door and went on deck. The breeze blew hair about her face. Childhood memories crowded her mind as the ship sailed into open water. She shivered with apprehension, thinking of what lay ahead. She walked along the deck, breathing lungs full of British sea air for the last time.

Expenditure on a cabin proved a wise decision because measles broke out among the children in steerage. Since Daniel had not contracted the disease, Brigid kept her family from that part of the vessel and spent as much time on deck as possible.

The captain, a tall, lean man in his late thirties, commanded his ship with evident skill. He steered it between storms, sought the calmest waters, and navigated by the North Star and his compass. He devoted a large part of the passage to conversing with Brigid. The captain explained the boat had been clinker-built and well-ordered to prevent water seepage. The provision of steam improved the ship's speed compared to sailing ships. Both boys showed interest in the paddlewheel's role, which the captain explained to Brigid's relief. Dermot was obsessed with the sea, spending hours watching for flying fish, dolphins, and whales. The captain's spyglass fascinated Daniel, and he looked through it whenever he could.

One day, Daniel asked to steer the ship. The captain put the child on his knee. 'Your son reminds me of my son, George,' he said, his grey eyes wistful. 'I have two children. Annie is twelve and has begun work as a pupil teacher in Exeter. I cherish my brief time with them, but it's never enough.' His lips pulled into a thin line as he helped Daniel steer the ship.

'Being separated from your children for extended periods must be challenging.'

Brigid mourned the loss of her own loved ones, her lashes glistening with sadness. The captain's expression softened, and he smiled.

'Their mother is deceased, and they live with my sister-in-law. I write whenever I reach land and compensate for time lost when I dock in England. But I worry about them growing up without Jenny or me.'

The sight of pain in his eyes caused Brigid's heart to ache. 'I'm sure you are a fine father,' she said, sensing his distress but hoping to see him smile.

But he did not smile. He peered at dark storm clouds billowing on the horizon. 'Take your children to their cabin. The Atlantic storms are erratic and brutal. Make sure everything is secure, and lie flat in your bunks. I'll have a steward bring slices of ginger to suck. It can help with seasickness.'

Brigid found Aisne in a deck chair drawing the horizon, and she had to be persuaded to leave.

'The captain says the seas may get rough.' Brigid held out her hand to her daughter, who didn't move.

'You don't wish to be washed off the deck, do you?' Dermot's brow creased with annoyance.

Aisne's brow furrowed. 'I wanted to sketch the atmosphere in those clouds.'

Brigid grabbed her hand and explained why she must come to the cabin. 'On the Captain's orders,' she added.

The family lay on their bunks for hours, fighting seasickness. The sun had vanished behind the horizon before the waters calmed. The boys were hungry, while Aisne remained pale and listless. Brigid took them all up on deck, where they watched the stars emerge, their flickering brightness lighting the night sky.

Aisne, awed, said, 'The stars provide sparkling beauty and calm my spirit.'

Brigid felt a wave of love envelop her as she watched her children's star-struck faces and wished she could give the captain her joy. *I guess I'm lucky not to be separated from my children. I don't think I could bear that.*

One sunny day, about halfway through the voyage, Brigid found the captain seated in a deck chair. 'Hello, what a surprise to see you here, captain,' she said, taking the seat beside him.

'I'm off-duty,' he said with a wistful smile.

Brigid smiled back. 'Are you indeed off-duty or resting between turns at the helm?'

'I have limited time off-duty, but I take it when the weather is calm. My name is John Lansdowne, by the way.'

He offered his hand, and after a moment's hesitation, Brigid laid her hand upon it. A tingle ran up her arm.

'Mine is Brigid McGrath,' she said.

'Why have you come aboard my ship, Mrs McGrath?'

'We are emigrating to America. My husband has a job in Boston. He emigrated two months ago.'

'A brave decision for your family to take. I have escorted many a family to the Americas.'

He picked up the spyglass on his lap and studied the rosy horizon. 'My home is in the West Indies on the island of Barbados.' As he lowered the spyglass, a faraway look in his eyes told Brigid he missed his home.

'Why did you send your children to England if your home is in the West Indies? Do you not have a family member who could help you?'

The captain took a portrait locket from his pocket. 'This is a picture of my wife. I carry her close to my heart. She succumbed to a fever in Barbados while I was at sea. My sister helped me for a time, but when she died, I couldn't provide for them alone, so I sent my children to England to my wife's family.'

His eyes held a sadness that melted Brigid's heart.

I became a widow, too. I know the anguish such loss causes.'

John gazed up at her with a grateful smile on his weathered face.

A shiver ran down Brigid's back despite the warm sun. *Is*

it my imagination, or did I experience a spark of something more than friendship in our mutual loss?

'My father had to sell much of his plantation following the Act of Emancipation in 1832, and so I joined the militia. I guarded cargo bound for England and met Jenny when we docked in Bristol. She enchanted me with her blonde hair and blue eyes.'

'You must have loved her very much.' Brigid paused, gazing at the horizon. 'New love can appear at any moment. Daniel is my second husband's child. My first husband and I met when I moved from the countryside to Dublin. He died a few years after we wed. Dermot and Aisne are his children. This voyage at sea is the longest I've gone without working or caring for a baby since I turned sixteen.'

She averted her gaze from the captain, the conversation evoking too many memories. She stood, her heart hammering, and gave a hollow laugh.

'I need to find my children before they misbehave.'

John induced in Brigid the odd sense of feeling virginal - too much emotional turmoil for a twice-married mother of three.

John gazed at her face, his voice husky. 'You are a beautiful woman, Brigid. You have the most gorgeous green eyes I have ever seen.'

'My first husband used to say that.' Brigid sensed a warm blush on her cheeks, and an uncomfortable silence followed. The captain stood up, hunger evident in his eyes, and held out his hand.

'It is a pleasure to voyage with you, Mrs Mc Grath.'

Brigid wanted to run, but her feet refused to move, and shaking hands, they held each other's gaze, exceeding that acceptable in polite society.

Then Daniel called from the nearby rail, 'Flying fish, Mammy, look.'

Brigid excused herself and called to her son. 'I'm sure

Aisne will sketch them. Let's find her.' The encounter with the captain caused Brigid to have such tumultuous emotions that her equilibrium was disturbed. In her heart, she knew she should keep her distance. However, the measles so afflicted passengers in steerage that some children passed away. So, Brigid kept Daniel from steerage and spent much of the voyage near the bridge, carefully avoiding unsettling gazes and keeping conversation business-like.

After twenty-five days, the ship sailed through the narrows to Manhattan, and they reached New York. Brigid was fascinated by the skyline of prominent buildings and the Statue of Liberty, her stars glittering in the sunshine. Aisne had filled her sketchbook, yet she found space to sketch the awesome statue. Passengers lined the deck rails, even some from steerage, causing Brigid to move to join the captain again, for Daniel's sake. People waved and cheered, having reached their destination. The captain ruffled Daniel's hair and let him pretend to steer the ship while Brigid's legs trembled under her skirt.

'We must drop anchor soon, and officials may board because of the measles. Have a safe journey onward, Brigid, and much luck in the future.'

He extended his hand and kissed her fingers, which tingled, and Brigid felt relief at reaching their destination. She doubted they would ever meet again, and a door closed in her heart, but Brigid found she could not lock it.

After disembarkation, officials directed Brigid to a shed. An officious-looking woman sat at a table inside it. The air felt humid and hot as sweat dripped down Brigid's back. 'What brings you to America? The woman enquired with a strong drawl in her accent.

'My husband works in Boston, and we plan to join him.' Brigid's face remained impassive. Given Finn's reason for emigration, Brigid felt uneasy.

'Can you read and write, and have your children had any education?'

'I am a qualified bookkeeper, and all my children can read and write. The youngest shows an impressive aptitude for numbers.'

This information seemed to satisfy the official, who smiled, showing two missing teeth. She gave Brigid a slip of paper bearing an official seal. 'Welcome to America. Do you need a hotel in New York, Ma'am?'

'No, thank you for asking. My husband has arranged for us to be escorted to the next train for Boston. We have open tickets.'

Finn had arranged for a cabby to meet his family on the dockside, and Dermot spotted him.

'Welcome to New York, Ma'am. We can head directly to the train station, or you can take your time shopping if you prefer. Most visitors wish to spend time in Bloomingdale's store.'

Aisne and the man exchanged glares and grins as they returned to his cab. Once they set off, Brigid's clothes stuck them to her like wallpaper paste.

'How do people stand this heat?' She waved her handkerchief like a fan.

'You become accustomed to it after a few summers here. But winters can be brutal, too,' said the cabby in a strange accent not unlike Ezra's.

'Cold I can take, but not this New York sun, which is heating my blood like water in a kettle over a roaring fire.'

Brigid couldn't believe the height of the buildings as they travelled towards the train station. The buildings trapped the heat in such confined spaces. The sun shimmered on the metalled roads and glinted off the windows and ornate gilded signs. Everything felt larger and busier, and the children's excitement grew with each turn of the cab's wheels.

Brigid had difficulty keeping the children in their seats, as they wanted to jump up for a better view. The carriage continued its journey through Central Park, with its green spaces and foliage. The driver stopped outside the new Bloomingdale store on New York's East Side.

'You have plenty of time to stop, Ma'am. Every woman wants to shop here.'

Brigid could see his point, observing the finery displayed in the windows. Inside the store, her eyes widened in amazement at the luxurious items surpassing anything in Clery's merchandise. She bought a colossal hat adorned with feathers and a Chinese fan to cool herself.

The store had a children's clothing department where Brigid found knee britches for her sons. Aisne, independent as usual, found a green dress with ruffles that suited her colouring.

'So much expense. People must earn big wage packets over here,' Brigid said, worn out, her nerves frazzled. Let's return to the carriage.'

As she stepped out of the revolving doors, she met an oven-like heat on the street. Weary, Brigid climbed into the carriage, with the children tumbling after her,

'Sit down, will you please, children, or you may damage my new hat.'

As they trundled towards the railway station, Brigid stared at the majestic brownstone buildings, more splendid than anything in Dublin.

Top-hatted men in tailored suits accompanied women dressed in exquisite clothing. Children ran around chasing hoops and balls, and the atmosphere was prosperous.

However, the driver said, 'Many immigrant families occupy tenement apartments in Manhattan - like Five Points, a rough place with immoral women and roaming gangs. Steerage passengers on your ship will face a harsh reality in disease-ridden tenements.'

Brigid sensed he had lost somebody dear to him, and she shivered despite the heat. Aisne glanced at her mother with a furrowed brow. Brigid wondered if her daughter understood the cabby's comments. She waved the fan with vigour, expelling the Irish cobwebs and the New York heat. *Does Aisne know how lucky she is? A fresh start for us all awaits, and we will not live in a New York tenement but in a house near the sea in Boston.*

CHAPTER 29: THE IRISH BUILD BOSTON

Finn had booked his family a sleeper couchette for the twenty-hour journey to Boston, and he promised to meet the train. Brigid was overwhelmed by the American experience. With the Civil War ending only two years earlier, construction for the new United States was in full swing, with scaffolding dotting the skyline everywhere as the cab made its way to the train station.

The children complained of being hot, tired, and hungry. Brigid found the stationmaster asked about the train timetable and telegraphed. Finn's office to let him know their estimated time of arrival in Boston. Then, exhausted, Brigid found the station restaurant or diner, as the gilded sign announced.

While the children ate steak and fries, the waiter brought ice-cold water along with Brigid's cheese sandwich. 'Would you all like to try the new non-alcoholic ginger beer, Ma'am? We keep it cold.'

Brigid nodded, too hot to think what the drink would taste like. The new experiences excited the children, who chattered among themselves and peppered their mother with questions she couldn't answer.

'How do they keep drinks so cold in this city?' Aisne said, sipping her ginger beer.

'Have you seen the size of that train's engine?' Dermot cut across his sister before Brigid could open her mouth.

Brigid sighed as the children chatted with excitement. A hovering waiter refilled their glasses and provided a finger bowl for the children's hands.

Once aboard the train, the family settled into their four-berth couchette and slept much of the journey. They reached Boston on September 10th, a month after leaving Dublin. It seemed a lifetime ago to Brigid.

Finn waited for the train on the platform, and the boys threw themselves at him. Finn kissed and hugged his wife when he untangled himself, and Brigid returned his kiss. She wrinkled her nose because her husband smelled of expensive cologne. However, Aisne stood back, unsmiling, but her stepfather kissed her hand and patted her head.

'I'm glad to have made it here, Finn. We have all missed you, and I look forward to sleeping in a proper bed tonight.' Brigid appraised her husband. 'Finn, you seem changed. You have an unexpected air of prosperity.'

'Is this all your luggage?' Finn said, as his eyebrows rose on his forehead, eyes gazing at the cases and boxes.

Brigid looked down at them, an apology on her lips.

'We set out with less luggage, but our New York cab driver said we should shop in Bloomingdale's store. I got carried away by the overwhelming range of goods on sale.' She felt her cheeks burn and lowered her eyes.

Finn had walked to a nearby cab driver when she looked up, and Brigid heard him joke: 'If you can't fit the luggage in, my wife will have to walk; I doubt she has a dollar left.'

Brigid's mouth gaped at this display of humour since he seldom displayed it. She thought her husband stood taller, as if a heavy weight had dropped from his shoulders.

He helped everyone into the carriage, his behaviour being that of a gentleman, unlike the violent Fenian to whom Brigid had said goodbye two months ago. *What has changed him? I hope it isn't another woman.*

The horse trotted along smooth, cobbled streets, thronging with people. Brigid discovered Boston to be a more compact city than New York. She liked its park, terraces of houses, and the smell of the sea that reminded her of Dublin. But she guessed the carriage had driven away from the coast when the salty air became more like the countryside.

'Finn, where are we going? The smell of the air does not chime with "Back Bay." The salty sea odour has vanished. Are we travelling inland?'

'Well spotted, Mavourneen. I have a surprise. When I arrived here, I discovered that Harvard University sought an Associate Professor of French Language and Literature. I spent time with my aunt in France, so I'm fluent in the language. And, of course, I have my undergraduate degree in languages, my doctorate in and experience at Trinity College. To my astonishment, Harvard offered me the post. So, I eschewed the residence in Back Bay for a house I've rented in the city of Cambridge near Harvard.'

Brigid studied him with awe. He had transformed before her eyes, like a chrysalis turning into a butterfly. She couldn't comprehend it.

Finn grinned. 'I have arranged for Dermot to attend the highly regarded Latin School. Aisne will join two other girls and a governess, while Daniel will attend an excellent Dame school. I have been to soirees and dinner parties and joined a gentlemen's club. Everyone is dying to meet you.'

His eyes glowed with pride, something Brigid had seldom seen since they more often blazed with fury. Her heart rate increased with unaccustomed pleasurable anticipation. Thinking of the house, Brigid pondered on its size.

'Do we have any servants?' she croaked, frog-like, licking her heat-dried lips.

'Yes, we have a housekeeper, a cook, and a housemaid. We also have a stable of two gardeners but no horse. Oh, a laundress comes in once a week; she is grand.'

'A cook? But I cook.' Brigid's eyebrows shot up towards her hairline, thinking she would lose the role.

Mrs Klocke is a superb cook, and she and our other

servants will assist you in your new life as a professor's wife by relieving you of the responsibility of preparing meals and running the household.

But I don't want to stop preparing meals or running the household, thought Brigid, her inquisitive heart filled with apprehension at what other roles she might lose. *How can I occupy myself when I have servants to do my work?* Tears pricked at her eyes as she contemplated this changed existence.

'You'll have a busy social life, my dear. Professors' wives host tea and supper parties and afternoon card games. Wives engage in philanthropic enterprises, which you can join. They are too busy to be running the household.'

Brigid, the daughter of a drunken Irish peasant farmer, found the society life overwhelming. Villagers had gossiped that the Manor House had many servants in its heyday when the lord and his family lived there each summer. *Is being the Lady of a Big House my role now? Feck, no.* Brigid's stomach twisted at the thought of an idle life, an anathema to any previous experience.

The cab rumbled along rutted roads, passing elegant properties with neat gardens but no fences until the carriage turned into the curved gravel drive of a vast three-story property. Two men working on the flower beds and lawns paused when they heard the carriage, catching Brigid's attention.

A white, wood-clad house featured a porticoed entrance and a wrap-around porch with a swing sat well back from the street. It had extensive grounds filled with bushes, trees, and other plants Brigid couldn't name. Shocked, her eyes opened wide. 'Is this grand house our new home, Finn?'

Finn nodded and grinned. 'Wait 'til you see the rear garden or yard, as they say here. We have a paddock, too.'

'You're saying we'll live here, Father?' Aisne's eyes practically popped out of her head.

'Yes, I moved in last week. The house belongs to a family

living in Toronto, Canada, for two years. The agent told me the family had left their furniture behind, so I rented the property the day I viewed it. It is magnificent.'

Brigid marvelled at the house while the boys explored the front garden and street. Several seconds went by before she felt able to speak. 'Finn, the rent on this house must be exorbitant. How can we afford it?' She gazed from the carriage through the vast open double doors to the house and upwards at a winding, balustraded staircase.

'I'll explain the finances later, Brigid. But first, as the Lady of the House, you must meet the staff.'

Lady of the House? So, my role is to oversee household matters. What will I do to prevent idle hands? The thoughts filled Brigid with trepidation, which increased when she saw the staff assembled on the gravelled drive by the porch.

Finn introduced each one, and the women bobbed a respectful curtsy. The two gardeners bent their heads and doffed their caps. Brigid recalled her brothers standing before Da, awaiting his wrath. Finn gestured to one gardener.

'Scott doubles as a manservant and Ulrike as a lady's maid,' He gestured to the youngest woman, who bobbed a second curtsy.

Observing Finn's excited eyes and animated voice, Brigid wondered if inferior status had troubled him in Ireland. He appeared to have turned into a gentleman in America. His carefree approach to appearance had vanished, and Brigid felt he had thrown it into the ocean upon disembarking the ship from |Moville.

The housekeeper, Mrs Frankel, spoke first. 'We look forward to serving you and your family.'

She looked at Aisne, who, awestruck, gazed back instead of politely lowering her eyes.

'I'm sure you ladies want to freshen up after your journey. Please follow me.'

The woman lifted her skirts and guided Brigid and Asine

to the first indoor privy room they had ever seen. It had a sink with gold taps and a porcelain bowl. Brigid washed her hands, drying them on the fluffiest of towels and exited, shaking her head with disbelief. Aisne's turn came, and afterwards, they stared at each other dumbfounded.

The overpowering sense of opulence caused Brigid's legs to turn to jelly. Sensing her feelings, the kind housekeeper guided her to a well-proportioned room with a sunny view and invited her to sit.

'I will bring some refreshments, Ma'am,' she said.

The room had various seats, and Brigid settled into the most enormous armchair she had ever seen, with a navy blue and cream striped cover. The scent of lilies from a cut glass bowl on a polished mahogany centrepiece table brought memories of Mrs O'Keefe's house.

Brigid took careful note of her unfamiliar environment. Amy's home, though elegant, couldn't match this vast house. She studied the tall ceiling and elaborate cornices, the thick pile of deep blue carpet, and matching wallpaper and drapes. *I must be dreaming.* Brigid's heart fluttered like a caged bird, recalling how far she had come since fleeing Seamus. She glanced at Aisne, whose wild-eyed gaze told Brigid her daughter was overwhelmed, too.

The housekeeper brought in a silver tea service and bone china cups. Arrayed on a plate lay small cakes, their aroma of marzipan. She poured tea into two cups, leaving milk in a jug, sugar lumps in a bowl with tongs, and pieces of lemon on a plate. Two napkins in silver holders lay on the tray. She curtsied and exited the room, closing the double doors behind her.

Long-windowed doors lay open to the garden, letting in a pleasant breeze and allowing the smell of freesias to mingle with lilies, an intoxicating mixture. The entire scene was overpowering in its array of colours and odours. The soft breeze caressed Brigid's skin, cooling the cloying outside air.

'This luxury quite overcomes me. Please add some milk and sugar to my cup, Aisne,' she said.

'I'll speak English all the time, Mammy. Mrs Frankel has a strange accent. I don't believe she will understand Gaelic.' Aisne handed her mother the cup. 'Why has she left lemon?'

'Perhaps Americans drink tea with lemon?' said Brigid, perplexed.

Aisne gazed at the exquisite blue deep-piled carpet from her seat on an enormous sofa matching Brigid's chair.

'I'm sure you won't allow us to play in here, Mammy. Will I have to call you Mamma like Isabella?'

Brigid shook her head, picked up a plate, and chose a cake. Then she leaned back into the soft contours of her armchair. The cake tasted delicious, a lighter sponge than even she could make.

Brigid gazed around the room again and spotted the surfaces adorned with ornaments. The shining brass fire tools stood ready for use. A peacock-embroidered screen concealed the dark cavern of a massive marble fireplace. The aria *I Dreamt I Dwelt in Marble Hall* from the Irish opera *The Bohemian* came to Brigid's mind.

A pair of full-length white lace curtains hung behind magnificent blue velvet ones. *Two sets of curtains? Such extravagance: it is unbelievable.* The walls were hung with expensive artwork, and several small mahogany and rosewood tables stood around the room where Brigid could see her reflection.

As Brigid sipped her tea, the tension in her shoulders from travelling melted, and the peaceful room soothed her apprehensive mind. She placed her cup on a nearby table as her eyelids drooped.

Aisne jolted her awake with a shake of her shoulder. 'Mammy, have you noticed the lamps on the walls? They are lit by gas. We don't need candles or oil lamps in here.' Aisne couldn't contain her excitement and jumped up and down with glee. 'I want to see my bedroom, please, Mammy. It may have gas lights, too.'

'You need to ring for the maid to show you. I'll pull this velvet cord as I recall seeing one like it in Amy's house.'

'Do I need to ring for the maid all the time, Mammy? Can't I do things for myself?' Aisne nibbled her nails.

Brigid, about to reprimand her daughter, stopped her when the doors opened.

The housemaid bobbed a curtsy. 'Yes, Ma'am. How may I help?'

'I wish to view my bedroom, please,' said Aisne with her characteristic directness.

The housemaid curtsied again and said, 'Would Missy like to follow me upstairs? You too, Ma'am, if it pleases you.'

'Are those gas lamps? Miss ... er' Aisne's face reddened, not knowing what to call the housemaid.

'My name is Ulrike, Miss, and yes, they are gas. Being one of the first residents in the city to have a house linked to the gas supply made Professor Schmidt proud. We are fortunate to live in such a modern home.'

Brigid nodded and got up to join them, thinking she would take root in the chair if she stayed longer. Upstairs, Brigid found three bedrooms and an indoor bathroom with a separate privy along the hall. The master bedroom, up another floor, had a double aspect with an enormous four-poster bed, a private bathroom, and a dressing room. The ruby wine-coloured velvet curtains matched the velvet sofa under the window. Brigid evaluated the mattress for softness and, exhausted, drifted into sleep.

Aisne banged the bedroom door and woke her mother from a dream about her childhood cottage. 'Sorry, Mammy, but you must see my room. The girl it belongs to has pretty dolls dressed in fashionable dresses. She has left me a note saying I can play with them.'

Brigid had not seen Aisne's face so animated since they

left Dublin, so she followed her daughter. The Schmidt's had decorated the room in pastel pink, containing an exquisite doll's house. It also held a small four-poster bed and bookshelves with children's books. 'Look, Mammy, it does have gas lights.' Aisne jumped up and down excitedly.

Brigid gasped, 'It is an exquisite room. You must take much care of it.'

Brigid next visited the boys' rooms. One looked masculine, with posters of football matches and rowing scenes suitable for Dermot. A rocking horse and a low bed furnished the smaller room designed for a younger child. *Daniel will love this room.*

Brigid found two guest suites along the corridor from the master bedroom and, between them, a magnificent bathroom and privy, the sink, and a lavatory bowl decorated with roses. Brigid couldn't believe her eyes. *Opulence after opulence.*

Brigid found the stairs to the servants' quarters by opening a door far from the window in the corridor. *Aha, I expect the backstairs to the servants' quarters.* But Brigid closed the door lest she meet a servant. Instead, with her heartbeat pounding in her ears, she tiptoed down the elegant cream and navy-blue swirl-patterned carpet on the curved mahogany staircase to explore the remaining areas of the house. A stunning crystal chandelier adorned the entrance. It was designed for candles, and someone had adapted it to use gas. Brigid's thoughts were filled with questions, and curiosity drew her gaze to the ornate ceiling where she guessed the pipework was concealed.

A magnificent sixteen-seat dining room with mahogany furniture and another chandelier lay off the entrance hall. The hall ended at the library. Brigid guessed it was Finn's territory, so she did not pry. Next to the library, a smaller room held a mahogany desk, a damask sofa, and three chairs. Photographs of children stood on the desk, and Brigid found a box containing calling cards. *Is this room for my use?* Thought

Brigid with awe.

A well-furnished parlour with sofas and chairs lay next to a huge formal dining room containing a mahogany table and sixteen elaborate chairs. A family-sized table for six people sat to one side, and doors opened to a large terrace overlooking the lawns and pond in the backyard.

Through double doors, Brigid discovered a children's playroom connected to the entrance hall. Her nostrils picked up the familiar smell of baking bread wafting from the lowest floor. The kitchen and scullery must be below her. She crossed the hall, reached for the kitchen doorknob, and to her surprise the housekeeper opened it, giving Brigid a sharp look.

'Ah, Ma'am. I hoped to give you a guided tour of the house, but I think you have been doing it yourself.'

Brigid's nerves jangled. *Oh dear, have I overstepped the mark?*

The housekeeper drew her lips into a thin line. If you wish to tour the kitchen, Ma'am, Mrs Klocke will show you around.'

Brigid knew from the housekeeper's tone she had indeed violated her sense of ownership. 'Mrs Frankel, when possible, please show me how these modern conveniences work. Everything here is so advanced compared to Ireland.'

Mrs Frankel said, 'With pleasure, Ma'am. Compared to many other Boston houses, this one is very modern. Herr Professor Schmidt insisted on being up to date.' She paused. 'Will tomorrow at eleven be acceptable to you? Ulrike will have finished cleaning the bathrooms by then.'

Brigid nodded her assent, hearing youthful voices and laughter coming from the playroom. She wondered if Finn sat in the library, where the door stood ajar. She knocked.

'Come in,' said Finn's voice. He sat behind a grand mahogany desk, writing with a gold nib pen. 'I mistook you for Ulrike with my coffee, but please come and join me.' This room is such a pleasure to work in.'

Ulrike arrived and placed the coffee on a small table near

Finn's desk. 'The cook has announced supper is at eight tonight in the small dining room.' She turned to Brigid. 'Mr Klocke said to tell you she is used to feeding younger children in the playroom at six. Is this a suitable arrangement for you, Ma'am?'

'Yes, please tell the cook her everyday arrangements sound perfect. I'll supervise the children.'

The maid curtsied and left the room, saying, 'Good day, Ma'am.'

'Why do I have the sense I'm on a job interview?' Brigid's discomfort caused heat to rise in her cheeks.

Grinning, Finn said, 'The staff are used to Teutonic strictness. There is no room for slackness here. I learned that last week when Mrs Frankel asked me not to enter the front hall without removing my boots. A scraper with a lion's head stands on the porch, and house shoes are in a box beside it. We have labelled containers.

'Are you using your correct last name? I must explain why Aisne's and Dermot's last names are different and why.'

'I explained that yesterday, so don't worry.'

'I notice the house seems taller at the back. What do they call the lowest floor? The cellar?'

'The basement. It has a massive kitchen with doors that open to the garden, which is Mrs Klocke's territory. She guards it like an animal over its prey. I dare not enter because she gives me disapproving looks. Have you seen the terrace? It has a teak table, chairs, and steps down to the garden. It is a pleasant place to sit, drink coffee, and smoke after supper. I have gazed at the stars every night since I arrived here.'

Brigid could think of nothing to say. She had a tough time taking in all she had seen.

After supper, when the children had gone to bed, Brigid and Finn sat on the terrace with their coffee. Curious about their financial status, Brigid said, 'Finn, are you still working for the Comrades since you have a professorship, or have you given it up?'

'Oh no, I am still its leader. I have a small studio apartment above a barbershop on Boylston Street. I used it as my lodging when I first arrived in Boston. Now, I use it as my Irish Comrades office. It has a back entrance, and on O'Brien's advice, I organised women of a specific type to visit and give the impression they used it for liaisons. Such activity makes suitable cover for potential spies. But our receptionist, Carmel, is Irish and most efficient.'

Brigid perused her husband's appearance and demeanour, wondering if he was engaged in an affair with an unknown woman. She concealed her suspicions and said, 'You look fashionable, Finn. You must have spent a substantial sum of money to look so groomed. What is our financial situation?'

Finn took a fish-tailed pipe from his pocket and tamped down the tobacco. 'My Harvard salary covers the rent. I have a commission to author articles for the New York Times, which helps with other costs, like the servants. They pay me fifty cents per column, and I intend to publish my second book on the famine soon, bringing in more revenue. As my position is an associate professorship. I must achieve tenure and, thus, a full professorship. I gather success depends on your publications and the donations the work attracts, so I must write.'

He paused, lighting the tobacco with a long match from a pot on his desk. He puffed with fury, clouds of smoke filling the surrounding air, and Brigid batted the smoke, coughing.

'The Comrades pay other expenses like wood, gas, and school fees. I concluded this house was affordable to the Irish Comrades' finances if I paid the rent, and they agreed.'

Brigid's heart sank. 'I hope they won't use the savings to buy guns and ammunition.'

Finn raised his eyebrows, appraising his wife, and shook his head. as he puffed his pipe. 'Brigid, people are fashion-conscious here. A colleague warned me that winter would arrive fast after this warm autumn, bringing bitter cold and heavy snow. You must buy new winter clothing for yourself and the children.

Most shops are small retailers, and I have visited a gentleman's shop and ordered two suits for the winter. Faneuil Hall and Quincy Market are two popular food markets with ladies. I'll escort you there next week. On advice from a colleague, I have subscribed to two ladies' magazines for you, Godey's *Lady's Book,* and Ballou's *Pictorial*. Most society ladies take the former.'

Hearing about ladies in Boston society bored Brigid. She hoped to work, not to become one of them. She yawned as exhaustion overwhelmed her.

'Finn, I'm feeling drowsy after such a long day. I think I'll go to bed.'

Finn rose and took her hand. 'I must be up early because many colleagues are at their desks by six. Lectures start at seven-thirty, and we work long hours. A relic of the country's agrarian and pioneer past, I believe.'

Brigid recalled how she used to wake up early to clean up after her father's drinking, and the memory sent shudders down her back. In the bathroom that adjoined their bedroom, Brigid gazed bewildered at the bath's brass taps, the jars of crystals and bars of soap on the windowsill. Such luxury awed her, so she waited for Mrs Frankel's tour before tackling them.

She had a strip wash, got into the luxurious feather bed with its ivory silk sheets, and drifted off into a dreamless sleep until the sun streamed through the undrawn drapes in the morning.

Mrs Klocke arranged hot food trays for breakfast on a side table in the parlour. Dermot, dipping fresh bread into a boiled egg, asked if he could go fishing with Brad.

'Brad, who is he?' Brigid's brow furrowed. 'I must meet this person before agreeing.

Dermot frowned, his brow puckering. 'He is the younger gardener. I met him yesterday. You'll like him.'

Brigid tried to recall his face, but it was a blurred picture. 'I'll seek him out this morning, Dermot.'

Breakfast ended, and Aisne left the room to use a new sketchbook and pencils Finn had gifted her. Daniel expressed his desire to play with the toys in the playroom, his child's face full of joy. Brigid set Dermot to read a book and supervise his brother, and then she went out to search for Brad.

A large pond with fish that looked like larger cousins of the goldfish Dermot had won at a fair in Dublin stood on the rear lawn, surrounded by paving stones. Statues, their smooth surfaces gleaming in the sunlight, stood around the gravel pathways. Many trees graced the garden, especially conifers, plus some vast trees with which Brigid was unfamiliar. They had large leaves bearing lobed indentations. *Boston does have leafy trees,* she thought. *These are magnificent in their autumnal russet and gold colours.*

When she found Brad, she asked what the trees were called.

'Maple trees, Ma'am. They grow well here. People make pancake syrup from the sap.

Brigid enquired about the kitchen garden, which was full of herbs and vegetables. She recognised parsley, sage, and rosemary, and the odours brought back many memories of Ballyconstór. Beyond it was an area of fruit trees and bushes, with blackberries sagging down the branches. Brad showed Brigid the entrance to a vault. Brigid saw ice blocks glinting like diamonds in the shaft of sunlight entering the cold bunker. She closed the door.

'Brad, where do we get the ice from?'

'We get it from frozen ponds in the winter.

Brigid noticed the sun had risen high in the sky and, glancing at her lady's pocket watch, saw the time was close to eleven. Brad had impressed Brigid as an intelligent young man.

'You may take Dermot fishing, but he is still a boy and needs a firm hand, please, as he can become overexcited.'

'Yes, Ma'am. I spotted that when we discussed fishing yesterday. He's a fine boy.'

Flustered by the gardener's evident confidence, she hurried back for Mrs Frankel's tour.

The housekeeper took Brigid down to the kitchen, where the ceiling was hung with many copper pots and pans interspersed with bunches of herbs – lavender, basil, and oregano. A large, scrubbed wooden table sat in the centre with six chairs. The cook was busy rolling pastry, and a wonderful, familiar appetite-stimulating smell hit Brigid's nostrils – apples. 'Good morning, Mrs Klocke. Are you cooking my favourite pie?' Brigid grinned.

The cook turned and bobbed a curtsy. 'Yes, Ma'am. Herr Professor asked me to cook it special.'

With a hint of foreignness, she drawled the word "Marrm," a sound Brigid found grating. The woman wore a clean apron and mobcap, and the kitchen was spotless despite the cooking.

'I'll set a cold luncheon on the parlour and dining table for one o'clock if it pleases you. Do you wish to have children's lunch in the playroom or parlour?'

'Please set it up at the table in the parlour. We are used to eating as a family,' Brigid said, thinking, *I need to persuade Mrs Klocke to let me cook, too.* Brigid's hands itched to prepare colcannon and potato cakes on a magnificent range that burned gas. Then Brigid spotted the scullery, where a sizeable dark-haired woman with meaty forearms turned sheets through a mangle.

Mrs Klocke sniffed and inclined her head. 'Ma'am, the laundress is working today. The housemaid washes undergarments between her visits, and you can send the professor's shirts to the laundry at the university if you wish. Professor Schmidt sent his shirts there.'

Mrs Klocke's evident dislike for the laundress made Brigid wonder if the woman was usurping the cook's role in the house. She left the matter until she learned more about the cook. Brigid observed a servant hierarchy she had not met before. *I need to tread with care until I understand it.*

When they had climbed back to the first level, Brigid said, 'Mrs Frankel, please accept my apologies for yesterday. I have never had a housekeeper to help me before.'

'Well, thank you, Ma'am. Do you wish me to show the bathrooms now?'

'Thank you.' Brigid felt the censure in Mrs Frankel's tone. 'I did not bathe last night. Exhaustion prevented me from understanding the workings.'

Mrs Frankel smiled. 'Follow me, please, Ma'am.' She ascended the stairs and almost collided with a running Aisne.

'Aisne, you must not run downstairs, as you might not see someone coming up and bumping into them,' said an embarrassed Brigid.

'Sorry, Mamma,' Aisne used a voice that copied Isabella and Brigid knew she was being mocked. But she stilled her tongue, thinking, *I must teach the children house etiquette. The family has much to learn.* She fixed on a stern expression.

'Apologise to Mrs Frankel, please.'

Aisne, her cheeks burning, reluctantly obeyed.

After ensuring Brigid understood the plumbing, Mrs Frank guided Brigid back to the first floor of the house.

'Please, Ma'am, may we go to the morning room? I wish to discuss the rest of this week's menu?' She paused. 'Er, Mrs Schmidt and I discuss the week's menu on Mondays.'

Morning room. Does she mean the smaller room where I found Mrs Schmidt's cards?

Mrs Frankel opened the door. 'Mrs Schmidt deals with her correspondence here, too. I bring her mail each morning and place it on the desk. Then I post any letters for her by luncheon.'

Brigid spotted Mrs Frankel's use of the present tense. *I must prove my worth as Lady of the House.*

'I have prepared one for this week after consulting Herr Professor. Can we check it now, please?'

Mrs Frankel directed Brigid's attention to a sheet of paper on the desk, and Brigid sat to study it.

'Please join me by taking a seat, Mrs Frankel.'

'Excuse me, Ma'am, but I don't sit with Mrs Schmidt. Professor Hayes suggested fish for tonight's supper and pork cutlets for Saturday. On Sunday, Mrs Klocke will cook a roast beef dinner.'

Brigid read the menu and nodded her head. 'The menu is pleasing. You have thought through it well.' She paused. 'Mrs Frankel, it will take time for me to relinquish control of running the household since I'm accustomed to doing things myself. I appreciate your patience as I adapt to this new life.'

'With pleasure, Ma'am. Shall I bring today's mail and ask Ulrike to bring you some coffee?'

'Thank you. That will be most helpful.'

Mrs Frankel curtsied and left the room. That she had spoken of Mrs Schmidt in the present tense was not lost on Brigid, who knew she was being tested. The mail and coffee arrived within two minutes, and Brigid felt Ulrike waiting with it out of sight. For someone used to spies and street urchins, this felt unnerving.

'Thank you again, Ulrike. You are most prompt.'

'My pleasure, Ma'am. Do you require anything else?'

'No, thank you. Coffee is all I need.'

'Mrs Klocke rings the luncheon gong at one o'clock.' Ulrike curtsied, departed, and closed the door behind her.

Brigid sighed with relief. Servant behaviour and unfamiliar names overwhelmed her. It felt like being on a week's trial before being offered a permanent job. The feelings made Brigid wonder again, *how can I persuade Mrs Klocke to let me do some cooking?*

She turned her attention to a pile of mail. When one piece caught her eye, Brigid was about to throw much advertising material in the wastepaper basket. It came from a philanthropic organisation devoted to educating the children of poor migrants. It sought a tutor for a nine-year-old boy whose native language was Gaelic. His teachers had spotted a clever boy with potential. However, to take advantage of the education in the Boston public school system, he needed to improve his English and arithmetic. Brigid put this advert aside to consider offering her help. *In Cambridge's society, I doubt many women are qualified bookkeepers who have earned a salary. I'll find it hard to fit in.*

By the time Brigid had finished going through the mail, the gong for dinner rang. Mrs Klocke had arranged a bewildering array of cold meats alongside a large bowl of salad and two dressings. 'Caesar and French dressing,' explained Ulrike. 'Mrs Klock has a set out a bowl of strawberries with a jug of fresh cream and a pitcher of ice-cold lemonade.'

'With delicious food like this, I must watch my waistline,' said Brigid.

The children tucked in with relish, the boys hungry from their morning's activities.

Finn arrived home and joined Brigid. 'How are you doing, honey?'

Honey? Brigid's eyebrows rose. 'Fine. However, letting go of the responsibility for housekeeping will require time. But I'll get there.'

After lunch, an eager Dermot got ready to go fishing. 'I think I'll join you.' A grin spread across Finn's clean-shaven face. 'Aisne and Daniel can come, too.' He gazed at his wife. Will you join us, Brigid?'

She shook her head, thinking she would have had the dishes to wash in Ireland. Still, with Ulrike clearing the table and washing up, she ascended the grand staircase to her bedroom. She rifled her wardrobe for a dress for supper. *I might as well have a bath and wash my hair beforehand. Dermot and Aisne can manage without help once they understand the plumbing. But Daniel will need it.* Brigid felt an ardent desire for her help to be needed. After her bath, she rested and must have slept, for she woke to eager children's voices. Aisne came running into the bedroom without knocking.

'Mammy, the river is much cleaner than the Liffey. Dermot is eager to go sea fishing tomorrow. Father gave his permission. I intend to sketch the statues. They are beautiful and so cool to the touch.'

Brigid sat up, bewildered. *Father? When did she decide to give Finn that title?* She swung her legs off the bed. 'Where is Daniel?'

Aisne sat with a thump on Brigid's bed. 'Father had to carry him home as he got tired. He has taken him to his bedroom for a nap. Father says school starts in a couple of weeks, and I have a governess with two other girls, Virginia and Francine. She will teach us in Virginia's house. It is going to be fun.'

Brigid agreed it would be fun for Aisne. But the unfamiliar atmosphere left her bewildered, and she descended the stairs in a daze.

In the next morning's mail, Brigid received several welcome letters, including one invitation to a tea party. She had one exciting letter. A philanthropic organisation that rescued orphaned children needed a voluntary treasurer. The chairperson had heard Brigid had bookkeeping experience and wrote to ask if she could visit to visit to discuss the position. Brigid picked up the tutoring leaflet and wrote to the secretary, explaining that Gaelic was her first language. But her English was fluent, too, and she would like to take the position. She then wrote to the chairperson of the other organisation, inviting the lady to tea. The two got on well, and Brigid accepted the treasurer's role. While unpaid, both gave her a pleasing sense of self-worth.

So, sitting on the terrace after supper one evening, she told Finn about them. 'I got the post as a tutor and took the treasurer's position. The chairperson is a Jewish lady from Hungary. Her husband studied at Oxford in England for his doctorate. I don't intend to start either post until the

children have settled into their schooling. Ulrike told me she functioned as the Schmidt children's chaperone, for which she received a fee. It would be a relief if she took on the job for us. What do you think?'

Finn puffed his pipe, smoke billowing into the light breeze. 'How much is her fee?'

'The Schmidt's paid her twenty cents a month. The extra income will pay the fee if I write pieces on child development for those ladies' magazines.'

Finn said, 'Not all our neighbours have a field for keeping a horse and carriage. I'll inform Professor Andersson, who is visiting from the University of Uppsala in Sweden, that we have an unused and stable field, which I hear he seeks. That will bring in some more income.'

That night, Brigid and Finn made passionate love.

Afterwards, lying in Finn's arms, Brigid reflected they had a place in society where they received respect and were not potential targets for violence. Reuniting with Finn halfway across the world reassured her she had made the right decision to emigrate. Her mind settled, and she slept without stirring through the night.

CHAPTER 30: CAMBRIDGE

The Cambridge Latin School prepared boys to attend Harvard and similar colleges. Daniel's tuition at the Dame school would prepare him to enter the Latin School. After discussing the matter with Finn, Brigid decided Aisne would benefit from additional private lessons in art and music. The governess took the girls to a Boston Symphony concert. Radiating excitement, Aisne exclaimed, 'I adore the violin's melody. I want to learn how to play it.'

Finn added music lessons to her tutoring and bought her a violin. Brigid soon wished he hadn't, as Aisne had the household cringing each time she practised.

Besides her philanthropic work, Brigid enrolled in an accountancy course to be accredited in Massachusetts so she could take private clients' work. She had to work hard because the requirements were more demanding than those in Dublin. But overall, the family's adaptability astounded even Brigid, who couldn't believe the speed with which she had found worthwhile situations that did not require her to play cards, host tea parties, or gossip.

Mrs Frankel said, 'You are a resourceful woman, Mrs Hayes. I congratulate you.'

As they became closer, Brigid told Mrs Frankel a little of her past, enough to open her eyes to her independence and perseverance. The housekeeper's jaw dropped, and her eyes widened in astonishment.

'You escaped from an arranged marriage? Such courage, Mrs Hayes, such courage.'

'A determination to avoid marrying a beast, not courage, set me on the path of freedom. However, after I had stepped toward independence, I continued to tread a successful path. The confidence came from my mother's teaching, I think.'

The children loved their new schools. To Brigid's surprise, sporting activities took priority over academic work. Dermot enrolled in rowing and ice hockey classes for which he needed to learn to skate. It struck Brigid that he loved life where water was involved, and she pondered how that would affect his life's course.

Daniel, too young for such activities, enjoyed softball. When he entered Latin School, he wanted to join the Charles River rowing team, which his brother planned to do. All three children took skating lessons as the ponds froze.

It soon became apparent that both boys' academic prowess was ahead of their American peers. 'The strict routine of learning to read, write, and reckon in Ireland has paid dividends. The Latin School has put Dermot in an accelerated mathematics programme, and Daniel helps the Dame school teacher teach reading,' said Finn, his voice tinged with pride.

The governess acknowledged that Aisne's knowledge was more extensive than that of the other girls, girls whose parents wanted them educated to become society wives, but this was not Aisne's plan for her life.

'I might never marry Mamma. I wish to be a celebrated artist someday.' Despite being young, Aisne was serious, even though Brigid laughed at her ambition. Aisne's other accomplished subject was French. Learning from her stepfather, she had amassed a significant amount of vocabulary in the language.

Brigid teased her at breakfast one morning. 'See, Da has his advantages.'

But Aisne pouted, returning to the playroom with her sketchbook, 'My Da's in Ireland.' Refusing to speak further, she sketched a Dublin street from memory.

As late autumn, or fall as Americans called it, remained warm, Aisne sketched the sculptures in the garden. Her face became animated as she explained their form to her mother.

'I must discover how to create these statues,' she said, her eyes animated by curiosity.

Aisne's artistic skills developed fast, and at Brigid's suggestion, the governess promised the girls a visit to a museum where Aisne could study other statues. Aisne was bursting with excitement. 'The assistant in the gallery said sculptors make them of marble, and I'm curious about how they do the work.'

Finn thrived on his work at Harvard. One evening, Finn clarified how he had gained the professorship.

'The previous Professor of French had a stroke last May. I heard about the post from an Irish Comrades volunteer–another professor sympathetic to our cause. His parents fled Ireland fifty years ago, and he was born in Boston. My mix of qualifications convinced the interview panel that I had the right qualities. The university liked my qualifications when I suggested I deliver an undergraduate elective course in Gaelic History. Students of Irish descent have expressed an interest. However, I had to revise French literature to teach the material. It kept me busy while waiting for you to join me.' He gestured to several books on his extensive oak desk, then sipped his coffee.

'Does Harvard know of your Fenian activities?' Brigid's pulse quickened as she waited for his reply.

'Yes. I had to explain why I came to America. However, I'm not the sole refugee from tyranny. Two Jewish professors escaped from pogroms in Eastern Europe as Ezra did. One African American Professor came from The University of Georgia and escaped the South via the Underground Railway, as it is called. The German professor is on a sabbatical from the University of Hamburg. Our offices are adjacent, and we have developed a rapport. He introduced me to the Meerschaum pipe. Finn took it out, packed it with tobacco, and lit it, his eyes alight with enthusiasm.

He has academic respect, Brigid thought. *Had it been lacking from his sense of self in Ireland?*

Tutoring Cormac became Brigid's favourite role. She instructed the child in a room within the City Library. The boy told Brigid his two sisters and his baby brother had died of the relapsing fever brought on board their emigration ship by a sick passenger.

'My mother's heart has broken, but my parents agree I must get an education. They view it as my escape from poverty.'

Brigid asked about his accommodation, and the boy explained that most Irish immigrants lived in poverty, even in Boston.

'Some children work in factories while others beg on the streets. They don't go to school. Da is certain my prospects are better in America with schooling.'

'Your father is a wise man. The best way out of poverty is an education which permits a person to get a career with prospects.'

Contrary to expectations, Cormac explained that the lives of many immigrants did not resemble the lives they had expected, and they profoundly missed the familiar landscapes of their homeland.

Brigid felt determined to help Cormac because he reminded her of Liam. She told him something about her past and the power of determination to achieve one's goals. Cormac's solemn face showed he absorbed everything, which pleased Brigid, who wanted the boy to succeed.

The children's social calendars, preparations for invites to supper parties, and a New Year's ball made the weeks fly. Brigid had a delightful time selecting new clothes for herself and the children. A fellow professor's wife, French Canadian Celine, introduced her to a dressmaker in Back Bay.

'I highly recommend meeting Madame Solange,' the woman advised.

Upon encountering the seamstress, Brigid thought *Angela's skills made her competent as the seamstress by age eleven*. But the woman designed a gown of pale green silk with a hooped skirt for the Harvard New Year Ball, and Brigid feared she would have to stand up all evening. *My poor feet,* she thought, remembering those too-tight evening slippers of Amy's so long ago.

On Celine's advice, she and Finn took dance lessons in a small studio in Cambridge. Both laughed at their ineptitude. But by Christmas, the Hayes family had made several friends in Boston society.

Mrs Klocke arranged an authentic German Christmas Eve banquet comprising fish and potato salad. The family ended the meal by tasting a German stollen cake like the one Amy served. Finn presented Brigid with a stunning pale green shawl to match her ball gown, and she gave him some of his favourite tobacco.

The family ate conventional Irish food on Christmas Day and gathered around the parlour fire in the evening to play charades and sing Irish ballads. Brigid felt happy hearing some memories of home, but she pined for the fields of Wicklow.

By the time of the ball, Brigid had eaten far too much food, and Ulrike, who helped her dress, had to pull Brigid's corset extra tight. Brigid felt homesick when she slipped into her gown.

At the ball, an acquaintance introduced Brigid to Beatrice Stone, a leader in Boston's society. Beatrice introduced Brigid to a new group of ladies. Their husbands filled Brigid's dance card, leaving Finn only with the last waltz. 'You look beautiful tonight, my darling,' he said.

Brigid felt the heat rise in her cheeks. She couldn't recall if Finn had ever acknowledged her beauty before.

After the ball, Brigid gave her first dinner party with a guest list of two politicians, a physician, a judge, three fellow academics, and their wives. Mrs Klocke produced a magnificent meal, with servers hired for the occasion. The banquet had a mixed Irish and German theme: red cabbage with roasted potatoes and pork schnitzel. The cook made an excellent cheesecake, which she served with ice cream. Through conversation, Brigid gained more significant insights into the activities of Boston society ladies. The guests' wives showed interest in her tutoring role.

'I have not heard of anyone doing such helpful work,' said a stout, late middle-aged matron. She wore an out-sized candy-striped dress that did little to improve her wrinkled looks. Her ample bosom pushed out of the top of her gown, and her arms looked enormous in the now unfashionable puffed sleeves. Brigid guessed her size resulted from eating too many cakes at tea parties.

In February, Finn and Brigid attended a "stand-up supper," as Bostonians called it, at Beatrice Stone's home; her husband was a wealthy Boston merchant. The childless couple paid close attention to social events. Their house was a tall brownstone near Boston's city park, which looked grander than the Hayes house. The complex menu included boned turkey in aspic, ham, tongue, beef à la mode, and potted lobster. It staggered Brigid. The cook prepared ten different desserts. Expensive wines and champagne accompanied the food. Brigid reflected on the distance she had travelled in her life's journey from the days of nettle soup and weevil bread.

During the winter, Boston had heavy snowstorms, and Brigid understood why Mrs Frankel insisted on boot removal on the covered porch. She valued the marble-floored sparkling hall tiles and the expensive imported Wilton carpets too much to allow dirty, wet snow onto them. But Brigid's growing understanding of Boston society left her with a conscience over the poor Irish living in tenements. She noticed Cormac's significant improvement in English after a few months of tuition. He and Brigid discussed his life in Ireland and in Boston's tenements. Brigid feared they mirrored those in

Dublin.

'The best way to understand tenement life is through a visit. Ma would like to meet you.' Cormac drew a map to direct her to his tenement block. Brigid decided she would visit soon.

On a Wednesday in mid-February, Brigid rifled through her wardrobe. She found her oldest clothes and boots, including a threadbare coat. She hailed a cab to Boston's North End, alighted on Main Street, and asked the driver to return in two hours.

Brigid walked through the snow-covered and rutted thoroughfares where the smell of dirt overpowered her senses, and nausea tickled her stomach. The buildings reminded Brigid of Dublin's tenements, with the scent of fresh air replaced by the smoky pall of chimney smoke. It hung over the dark and grimy streets like a Dublin November fog. People who passed her wore little more than rags, women with torn and dirty shawls, and men in stained britches.

It shocked Brigid to think these poor people had fled famine and disease in the stinking hold of a ship. Their lives have improved little from their past.

Brigid checked Cormac's map and found his block. The authorities housed his family on the fourth floor. Brigid ventured into the stairwell, where a woman with bright red hair sat on the stairs. The two women exchanged astonished glances. She was Norah, the brawny Dublin soup kitchen helper.

'Holy Mother of God, Norah said, crossing her breasts. 'Is it you, yourself, Missus Hayes?'

'Norah, it is an absolute joy to see you. How have you been since your family emigrated?'

'The housing could be better.' Her expression hinted at the irony. 'Women work as domestic servants. Some work with the men. My six children work in factories and don't get fresh air or schooling. Measles, dysentery, and cholera are rife, and people die.' She shot Brigid a piercing glance. 'How come you're here too?'

'In Boston? My husband got a job teaching in the city. He is authoring a book on the Irish Experience in America.'

Brigid chose the most relevant facts. But Norah's sardonic smile hinted she knew Brigid withheld others.

Brigid moved her foot from a rat that ran across the stairs, feeling the creature's presence in her marrow and wondering how many relatives it had. 'Where do the men work?' she said.

'On building sites. I told you once the Irish are building Boston. When a new building goes up, Irish immigrants labour on it. In the future, people will acknowledge that Irish immigrants built the city of Boston despite lacking other employment. Some businesses refuse to employ Irish people. We are ignorant and dirty, they say.'

Brigid couldn't hide her surprise. 'That is unfair. Irish people are hard workers. I have taken a voluntary post tutoring a boy who lives in this block, and I hope to meet his mother. Can you direct me? His name is Cormac O'Connell.'

'They are on the fourth floor – sad case. Maggie lost two daughters and a son on the passage over. I doubt her sanity.' Norah turned and pointed up the grimy stairs. 'Watch your step. People leave all kinds of rubbish about.'

Brigid climbed past Norah and, stepping with care, knocked on the O'Connell's door.

Cormac answered her knock. 'Hello, Mrs Hayes. I hoped you would visit today. Ma has the kettle on, and I brought tea from the docks. They spill packets unloading; if you are quick, you can run off with one. Otherwise, they throw them in the water, saying, 'Here's another for the Boston Tea Party,' I don't know what that means, though.'

Mrs O'Connell looked at Brigid with the sad, defeated eyes of a depressed person. 'Come in, Missus.'

She gestured to an empty chair. 'Cormac speaks highly of you. His school grades have improved with your tutoring.'

Brigid took a mug of tea, gazing at the grimy, untidy room

with sorrow. This couldn't be what the family had expected when they left Ireland.

'Cormac aspires to be a doctor, and my husband wants him to get the education.'

'I understand. I'll help your son as much as I can.'

'It is right generous of ye, Missus, so it is.'

Brigid and Cormac's mother exchanged experiences of the famine, and Mrs O'Connell remembered the women fighting to get into the Limerick workhouse.

'We said goodbye to Ireland that day,' Tears filled the woman's eyes. 'Sometimes I wish we had missed the boat because my babbies might still be alive if we had.'

Brigid doubted it. People like the O'Connell family died of starvation and disease. After watching her for some minutes, Brigid concluded her view to be correct. Mrs O'Connell was depressed. Then, the woman coughed in the familiar way as Brigid had once done. *What is most concerning is that cough,* she thought as visions of her mother crowded her mind.

Brigid could see Cormac's protective but wary eyes watching his mother. When Brigid spoke of her brothers, he shook his head, so she stopped. Cormac hinted his mother had experienced too much death. *She reminds me of Ma,* thought Brigid with sadness. *I wish I could find some cough mixture. I'll ask Beatrice.*

Brigid resolved to give Cormac as much help as she could, too. *Some of Dermot's clothes might fit him, and he could use some decent shoes,* she thought, checking the boy's approximate size. 'Thank you for the tea, but I must go now, Mrs O'Connell. I'll see Cormac on Thursday as usual. You have a fine son.'

Norah still sat on the stairs as Brigid left and gave Brigid another penetrating stare.

'How do men occupy themselves when building work stops for rough weather?' Brigid spoke in Gaelic.

Norah laughed. 'Stop? Except for heavy snow, the overseers don't let them stop until visibility is zero. Then they go down there for a mutton pie and a pint of beer at dinner time, along with the lazy drunks.' She pointed down the street where intoxicated men stumbled out of a bar.

Brigid felt a surge of uneasy recognition as she walked down the street, her heart pounding. She stopped the one man who walked upright to ask about his living experience in Boston. With a suspicious and critical eye, he judged if Brigid's question would be his time. 'We work when we can, but we drink when we can't. 'Tis the Irish way. I rely on Maureen and our kids to bring home some more dough.' He made a maniacal sound.

Do you mean dough to drink away? Brigid's gut twisted at the memory. 'Would you return to Ireland if you could?'

The man's eyes sparkled with amusement. 'What, go through that death trap sea voyage again? No chance. We come to America, and here we stay. There is nothing fer us in Ireland except rotten potatoes, sod 'ouses, and the fecking English.' He walked on, chuckling.

Brigid said goodbye to Norah and returned to the cab rank, where the cabby waited as planned.

'Did you find what you wanted, Missus?' he said. 'I came here in 'forty-eight, and we had a terrible cholera outbreak in 'forty-nine. My wife and two children died. That is why I became a cabby. I worked with horses back home in Ireland.' He coughed, flicked the horse's reins, and they trotted off, hooves clattering on the cobbles as light snow fell.

When Brigid got home, she bathed and changed. In the bath, she pondered why the servants were German, not Irish. *Of course, each nationality forms an enclave. The German staff must find us Irish people perplexing.*

When Ulrike put clean linen into the big press on the landing, Brigid asked where the German immigrants lived.

'They live in the southern area of Boston, Ma'am. Many can't speak English and want to keep their Teutonic customs and religious practices.'

The scales fell from Brigid's eyes. *The free Americas also experience sectarianism. I could author an article on it.*

CHAPTER 31: CONSOLIDATION

By the spring of 1870, Brigid had amassed enough material to author several articles on her investigations. She wrote under a male pseudonym and set up a mailbox address for anonymity.

Her first article covered the plight of families in Boston tenements, and The Boston Publication Press and Post accepted it.

Readers' comments included: '...Oh, I did not know...' or '...The poor souls, I'll pray for them...'

However, one helpful reviewer suggested establishing a soup kitchen. Brigid followed it up, returning to the tenements, where she found Norah and requested her help. The woman's face brightened, and she agreed. She soon became indispensable to the project.

Brigid then canvassed the wives of fellow professors and other wealthy citizens for funding. Soon, she had enough funds to rent space in a warehouse where Brigid installed a paraffin stove for cooking and bought inexpensive crockery from scrap stores and penny bazaars. She raised funds to install a pump and a sink for washing up. Sympathetic wealthy Bostonians donated other items, like tables, tablecloths, and napkins.

Brigid's concern for the poor of the city impressed people. She had found her calling in helping others, not killing them like O'Brien and his ilk. Over supper one warm night in June, she and Finn argued about Brigid's growing notoriety. Finn's negative attitude surprised his wife because he had previously supported the concept of women working.

'It isn't your work that concerns me; it is how people

perceive it in Boston's society. My colleagues prefer wives who do not pursue unpopular causes that could affect their children's prospects.' Finn stomped outside to smoke a cigar on the terrace.

Brigid joined him, sat on a teak chair with her coffee, and gazed at the emerging stars, entranced by their brightness.

'This young country can't make progress without its immigrants pushing boundaries. Our deeds will be visible to everyone,' she said.

Finn puffed on his pipe and did not answer.

Tenement dwellers came to Brigid's soup kitchen with wariness at the start. Still, Norah spread the word, praising Brigid to the elderly and sick patrons. ''Tis your way, Missus, helping poor folk.'

Soon, grateful for a free hot meal, mothers and children joined the older folks. In time, Boston matrons joined in to provide help.

'You are doing so much for my Cormac. Let me help you, too,' said Mrs O'Connell. To Brigid's relief, the woman's colouring had improved, and the coughing lessened.

'Bringing Alice out of her accommodation and into a social setting has improved her self-confidence,' Norah said one morning as Mrs O'Connell served mutton broth. The task of helping others had helped someone overcome her troubles.

The venture exceeded Brigid's expectations when she wrote to all the wealthiest hosts in Boston, including her new society friends, requesting donations. Beatrice Stone organised luncheons with speakers, tea parties, and recitals. She invited Brigid to speak on the project at women's philanthropic meetings. After their first full year in Cambridge, Brigid became a minor celebrity, respected everywhere in Greater Boston.

Despite his initial misgiving, Finn became proud of his wife's efforts. 'I know you are a clever woman, Brigid. Your mind smote me, remember? But I had forgotten just how resourceful you are. Other professors have congratulated me on having such a self-motivated wife.'

Finn and Brigid seldom met until supper time. But Brigid made sure she returned home when the children returned from school. One day, after they had discussed the week's menu, Mrs Frankel asked about Brigid's work.

'Are there any non-Irish people attending your soup kitchen?'

'They are all Irish. Expanding into non-English-speaking areas is difficult. I need a German-speaking helper in the German enclaves and an Italian speaker in their enclaves, for example.'

'I know many German immigrants need support. If you agree, I'll find a helper and contribute some time to setting up a kitchen.'

Mrs Frankel spoke with a strange mix of German and Boston drawls, which fascinated Brigid, who granted her time off, and the housekeeper returned with a beaming smile the following Tuesday.

'I have found two helpers and an empty office that will serve as a kitchen, Ma'am.'

Thus, a second soup kitchen opened, to Brigid's delight. Mrs Frankel helped Brigid write letters in German to the wealthiest German ladies.

'They need language classes in a country where the national language is English. I shall ask my husband about that idea.'

Finn said he would make enquiries and had an answer two weeks later. 'I spoke with the current Professor of German, who advised me to contact Professor Schmidt. He sent a list of his wealthiest German friends whose wives speak little English. He suggests you contact them. He has news for us, too. The family does not plan to return to Boston as he has secured a permanent position in Toronto. Professor Schmidt will sell this house when our lease ends and has given us advanced notice to buy it.'

Brigid gasped. 'So soon? Could we afford to buy this house, Finn?'

'I'll make enquiries about a loan. I shall not mention my income from the Irish Comrades but say I have a private income from writing. I have contacted the leadership in New York about the matter. Instead of a salary, they will continue to fund the children's school fees and maintain the Boston office.'

Dumbfounded by this sudden change in their circumstances, Brigid examined their financial records. She calculated their monthly expenditure, excluding school fees, and subtracted it from all sources of income. She gave Finn the figure of the maximum loan they could afford. Finn took it to the bank owned by a retired Confederate army officer, Richard d'Estaing. Finn said there he had wrangled over interest on the loan and beat Richard to one and a half per cent annually.

'We can now afford to make the Schmidt's a fair offer. Let us see what their lawyer thinks.' Finn's face split in a wide grin.

Meanwhile, after Brigid closed the soup kitchen for the summer, the family enjoyed a holiday at a friend's home on Cape Cod. Aisne had many new scenes to paint. She loved catching atmospheres in the clouds on the horizon while Daniel built sandcastles with Finn. It thrilled Dermot to be offered a summer assistant position by a fisherman. Despite his prowess in the school's swimming lessons, Brigid worried about the value of such a job for a boy.

'If I fall overboard, Mammy, I can swim and return to the boat.' Dermot's froggy voice sounded pleading.

Brigid gazed at her son's eager face. 'How will your friends' parents view us allowing you to become a fisherman's assistant? Will they disapprove?'

'Didn't you comment on immigrants pushing boundaries?' Finn said, grinning.

Brigid met the fisherman and his wife at their weathered clapboard home beside the dock. Their warm and friendly manner reassured her. Thrilled, Dermot rushed off to share the news with a friend.

At Brigid's insistence, the fisherman kitted Dermot out for inclement weather, and the boy soon became a key crew member. Aisne learned to throw pots with a local potter and proved an adept student. Her creations were painted in bright colours, which were much admired,

On their return to Cambridge, Aisne spent hours in the playroom making more pots with the potter's wheel she brought home. Brigid coaxed her outside by promising her a kiln. Mrs Frankel and Brad offered Aisne supervision with such an activity.

Daniel helped Brad in the herb garden and Mrs Klocke with baking. 'Your son has talent. Daniel made the bread you ate Easter,' said Mrs Klocke, beaming at his receding back as the child ran off to play.

Brigid, who couldn't believe she had the free time to author a book, began writing. Finn heard from Professor Schmidt's solicitor when the maple and beech trees were dressed in russet and gold. He had accepted their offer on the house sale.

'Mrs Frankel will receive instructions on what to pack for shipping to Toronto. We can purchase the remaining items for $60.00. My book has sold well in America and made us a lot of money.'

'Oh, what a load off my mind. The worry affects my sleep.'

'I have other news. As my current book is selling so well, I have received an advance on my second. I have also produced six erudite papers on aspects of French literature. Harvard is prepared to give me tenure next year if I get the course in Gaelic up and running.'

Brigid's eyes nearly bulged out of her sockets. 'I can't believe it; tenure so soon?'

'In the past two years, I have published the most books and papers in the Language Faculty.' A grin of pure joy spread across Finn's face as he explained their life in Boston, which gave him much satisfaction.

Brigid contemplated how much time he allocated to his work with the Irish Comrades but deemed it unwise to enquire. But she knew from the long hours away from home he must put in some time, and a sense of unease gripped her, a foreboding of an unpleasant event to come.

With Brigid's help, Mrs Frankel supervised packing the Schmidt family's belongings. They chatted as they worked, and Mrs Frankel confessed to her name being a courtesy title agreed by Mrs Schmidt because it sounded more businesslike. 'I have never been married. My fiancée died on the boat from Hamburg. You are my employer now and may wish to give me notice.' Tears puddled in her eyes. 'But this is my home. I have held the housekeeper's position for a decade.'

Brigid felt tempted to hug the woman, a spinster without a family, but it would not be seemly. However, the conversation prompted her to speak to the staff about their futures. To her relief, nobody wanted to leave. Mrs Klocke said she had been married but widowed not long after arriving in America. While childless, she had a natural mothering instinct. Daniel often chatted with her after school over cocoa and a new recipe in the winter months. He learned how to make gingerbread people.

'I'll make some to eat at Christmas, Mammy. Mrs Klocke will help me make a gingerbread house.'

As the splendid display of red and gold leaves waned, Brigid took a subscription to the Boston Herald newspaper. She wanted the most up-to-date American feelings on the plight of immigrants. Brigid read an army general's letter, proclaiming Britain '*as a third-class power.*' Brigid smiled, amused by the writer's ignorance of British dominance in Ireland and his lack of awareness of its impact on the broader world. *His views are insular. I want the world to know what prejudice immigrants face, including a lack of compassion. I could author articles on the matter.*

They discussed Finn's work with the Irish Comrades in the parlour one evening in late October. Finn told Brigid about a breakaway Fenian group in Canada and how American Fenian cells, including the one in Boston, were fund-raised to support ex-Confederate army-led armed insurrections in Ireland and England.

'During the Civil War years, the Confederate army recruited single Irish men off the ships.

Brigid thought of some of her soup kitchen attendees. A few were from the South and were of African descent.

'Richard d'Estaing, our banker, used to be a wealthy Georgia plantation owner,' said Finn. 'Wounded at Gettysburg, Union soldiers captured him and sent him north as a prisoner of war. But the war destroyed his land, and marauding soldiers killed his wife and two daughters before setting fire to his home. After escaping prison, he returned to the South but found his old life had gone.'

He lit and puffed on his pipe, releasing clouds of smoke that Brigid, coughing, batted away,

'He is an astute businessperson who had moved his money north before joining the Confederacy because he guessed they would lose. He returned north having sold his land to a carpetbagger and opened our bank in Boston with it.' Finn piled coal on the fire. 'Let's invite him to supper. He has become a friend who understands what it means to escape tyranny.'

This conversation had Brigid think about her home in Ireland. It had been three years since Caitlin had last contacted her, and Brigid realised with a sinking heart that, in truth, preoccupation with her work and the children had led her to be neglectful. She must make amends and write to her old friend.

Caitlin wrote back that Ezra had sold the business and retired. *We purchased a cottage in the country with the money and intend to spend summers there. Ezra has scaled down his work with*

Saor-Éire, too. He functions as a consultant and isn't involved in insurrection or bomb-making.

A sense of gratification washed over Brigid as she read until she read about Stephen.

His physician weaned him off alcohol by putting him on cocaine. But Stephen developed a worse addiction and is now in an asylum. Diedre took to her bed for a week with shame. You would not recognise him, as he is thin to emaciation, his teeth rotten, and his skin grey. He shakes if he does not get the drug. Cecilia gained an annulment and went to Alexander's cousin's family in Scotland as a governess. She married a Scottish gamekeeper and now has a baby daughter. We understand from Amy, who is fond of her nephew that Alastair flourishes under the gamekeeper's care.

Caitlin continued by writing that Amy and Alexander had moved again to a bigger house in the exclusive neighbourhood of Merrion Square.

Robert has a grand force of police officers patrolling Dublin's streets. Alexander's practice has prospered, and he will become a judge soon. Amy is a Dublin socialite who gives extravagant dinner parties and engages in philanthropic work, such as distributing leaflets in English to people experiencing poverty.

Caitlin added it would be a pointless exercise: '*Since most poor people can't read Gaelic, never mind English.*'

Brigid, reading this comment with a wry smile, agreed.

In one letter, Brigid mentioned her articles on immigration. Caitlin requested copies to reprint in Dublin. They agreed she would publish under Edward Woodward's pseudonym to avoid any association with femininity. Caitlin wrote: *The articles are discussed extensively in Dublin society.*

Caitlin asked for news of the children. Brigid wrote the boys had attended a first-class school and had excellent grades: *Dermot has expressed his wish to become a priest, although I hope it is a passing phase.* But as she wrote the words, she knew in her heart he would take that path.

Daniel wants to study mathematics at Harvard or Yale. He

has Finn's brains and that intense stare. It catches me unawares sometimes, and I'm looking at the child in Finn.

Aisne's passion is art. She hopes to study fine arts at college. Her dream is to graduate and study sculpture. I'm worried about her future. Women can't take degrees, though they study as hard as men. She is so independent minded she does not see herself as a Boston matron. The idea of playing bridge or hosting tea parties bores her. Will she engage in philanthropy and use her artistic talent as a pastime? I doubt it.

Caitlin wrote back and told Brigid not to worry. *Aisne has always been a determined child. She will forge her path. Do nothing about it except to let her be free.*

Brigid and Caitlin continued to correspond until Brigid sent a letter in the summer of 1872 but did not receive a reply. A second letter went unanswered, and Brigid became concerned for the welfare of the now elderly couple. *Would it be worth my time to travel to Dublin and find out? Ezra may have passed* away. Tears filled her eyes at the thought.

Then, in October, Brigid received a letter from Caitlin, who wrote: W*e spent the summer at our cottage in the Wicklow mountains. You would adore it there. Do visit us.*

Brigid wrote to apologise for being too busy with her three children and philanthropic work to make the trip to Ireland at present. Still, she would make the trip when the children were older.

However, contemplating a journey to Ireland caused Brigid to consider her status in America. In 1868, the United States government added an amendment to the Constitution regarding citizenship. Brigid suggested to Finn that they all take American citizenship.

'It will make travel easier if we have proper documents,' she said.

Finn disagreed but would not say why. Brigid wanted to change his mind, but he remained implacable.

'It makes no sense to delay because we carry no papers claiming to be Irish or any other nationality, although I think we are British citizens at present.' Brigid implored her stubborn husband to agree, and after much pleading, he did. But he never explained his reluctance.

The family became citizens of the United States of America in 1873. Brigid felt proud of their new status and documents. Hidden in a drawer in her desk lay a yellowing folder containing other records, including her and her children's baptismal certificates and Niall's death certificate, and she added the new documents to the folder.

She closed the drawer and saw her now familiar room, decorated pale green with a matching rug. She liked the independence it gave her. *Times have changed, and so have I*, she thought prophetically.

The playroom had a makeover to become Aisne's art studio. She soon filled it with watercolours and oil paintings in swirls of colour, emphasising light's effect on the subject. She often painted outdoors, setting off with her artist's paraphernalia to join fellow art students by the shore or in an exciting street. Brigid studied her work and learned the style originated in Paris and was called Impressionism.

Dermot's face lit up with joy when Brigid agreed to convert his bedroom to a study bedroom with a desk and filing cabinet. Every morning, he woke up early to assist the local priest during Mass, showing a firm commitment to the Catholic faith.

'I want to help people find the Lord,' he said, his eyes shining fervently.

In 1875, Brigid became accredited as an accountant in Massachusetts. It had taken her longer than expected, but with children's college fees looming, she needed to make more money than by authoring articles, so Brigid set up a private accountant's business. She continued her work as a treasurer and with the soup kitchens, knowing they valued her there.

Brigid learned Cormac had now succeeded in school. His mother had given birth to another son, and his father had a steady job as the school janitor. The position came with a two-bedroom apartment. For them, life in America had improved so much that at Brigid's urging, they became American citizens.

With Cormac's time freed up in her schedule, Brigid considered sitting in on university courses of interest and took one in investment banking. Despite her studies lacking a degree, a transcript of her courses could enhance her employability, which pleased her. She also took a flower arrangement course, as Beatrice Stone advised.

'You have a beautiful garden with such a profusion of flowers. You must learn how to arrange them, and I know the person to teach you.'

You know everything and everyone in Boston, thought Brigid sagely. But to her surprise, Brigid found she had a talent for artistic decoration, and soon, summer living became filled with fresh flower displays. She helped Daniel improve the herb garden, planting herbs such as fennel and St John's wort. She even concocted some bottles of cough mixture in the scullery, causing Mrs Klocke to remark,

'Where did you learn so much about herbs, Ma'am?'

'Oh, in Ireland. I once thought of becoming an herbalist. I like to hear I know more than working in a soup kitchen.' Brigid smiled and waltzed from the kitchen to her office, as she liked to call it, to make a start on her day's correspondence and some new accounts.

CHAPTER 32: LOSS

Daniel became a student at the Latin School in the autumn of 1874. His teachers soon identified his mathematics genius and placed him in an accelerated programme, expecting him to graduate a year earlier than some of his peers.

The children had many friends, and the house would resound with giggles and laughter. The family spent summers in a rented property on Cape Cod. Dermot was in his element, helping the local fishermen every day. Aisne brought her sketchbook and watercolours and spent many happy hours sketching boating scenes and painting exotic flowers like bougainvillaea. Daniel joined the Latin School's swimming team and later its rowing squad.

Brigid felt a deep contentment as she read books under a parasol. Her reading material was eclectic, and she read about far-off lands, nature, and healthy eating, including Mrs Beaton's cookery book, where, to her amusement, she learned how to make 'toast and water.'

Mrs Klocke did not find it amusing when Brigid showed her the recipe. She flounced off in a huff, muttering, 'English ruling class cheek. I would not serve it to a dog.'

Dermot won a place at St. Mary's University and Seminary in Baltimore, beginning in the autumn of 1874. He explained his goal was to become a missionary in Africa or Central America.

Brigid said, 'I'm sure your father is proud of you, Dermot.'

She gulped back the lump forming in her throat and hugged her eldest son, whom she loved so much.

The archbishop ordained Dermot into the Diaconate in Boston's Catholic Cathedral in July 1878 after he graduated from the seminary. He sailed for Rome in late July, where he intended to study for a Doctorate in Theology before ordination in the Vatican, a privilege granted to few students. *I wish his father were alive to witness these events,* Brigid thought,

Finn began spending more time in the Boylston Street office that summer and seemed preoccupied at home. Brigid grew concerned he was planning something dangerous. She visited the office receptionist, Carmel, who had emigrated some years earlier and with whom Brigid felt an affinity.

'Your husband is involved in planning the rescue of prisoners in Australia,' Carmel said.

'I hope he isn't planning to go to Australia and rescue them himself.' Brigid's pulse thrummed in her ears, and she swallowed. 'Carmel, have you seen any sign that Finn owns a gun?'

Carmel blanched. 'I have heard your husband mention he has a small pistol. But he does not keep it here, so if it exists, he must keep it at your home. The Irish Comrades keep bullets in a filing cabinet drawer.'

Does he keep it in his office at Harvard? Thought a worried Brigid. She couldn't get Finn's comment in Dublin about a pistol out of her head. Her gut told her something was amiss.

In early February 1881, Ronan O'Brien visited and stayed briefly in the Boylston apartment. Carmel admitted over coffee and gingerbread biscuits, for which she had developed a taste that O'Brien's presence in Boston was supposed to be secret. Brigid knew Finn must have met with him, but Carmel did not hear their discussions.

'Their plans must be secret since they don't meet until I go home. The most I know is that some dangerous missions are under discussion. I got that from a cryptic telegraph to O'Brien from Texas. I heard no mention of your husband's name, and I have no further information.'

Brigid feared Finn intended to engage in violent action with O'Brien. 'Could they be planning something in Ireland or England?' she said. 'If so, could it involve guns or ammunition? I detect O'Brien's hand in these matters. He has always had a firm hold on Finn.'

Carmel did not know. 'They do not tell me any details,' she said.

At home for the Easter break, Aisne spotted her mother's anxiety and asked what was wrong. Brigid concealed the matter to avoid distressing the children. 'I wake up at night drenched with sweat. It affects my mood.' Brigid spoke the truth and recognised she was going through the female 'change' with hot flushes and erratic menstrual courses. Aisne accepted this explanation and told her mother to rest. Brigid knew she couldn't relax when her husband was involved with something dangerous.

After Easter dinner on Sunday, 28th March, Finn put down his dessert spoon and wiped his mouth and moustache. 'The new St. Louis University in Missouri invited me to lecture on French literature. St Louis is a staging post for fur trappers, many of whom are French. I'll be away for much of April and May.'

Brigid's heart skipped a beat, and she almost choked on a mouthful of Mrs Klocke's blancmange.

Daniel said, 'That is a long time to be absent. You know it is my birthday, and my high school graduation is in June. It would mean a lot if you were there, Da.' His voice wheedled like a child, which made Brigid cringe.

Finn leaned back in his chair to take out his pipe, a habit Brigid disliked at the table. 'I leave on 2nd April and plan to be back by the third week of May, which means I'll be back in time for your graduation, Daniel.' He damped some new tobacco into his pipe but did not light it, for he caught Brigid's disapproving eye. 'I'll travel by train, but I'm also willing to take a stagecoach if needed, and I look forward to the adventure.' He lit his pipe tobacco in a defiant gesture.

Brigid bit back her retort about *looking forward to it or enduring it for O'Brien?* Though her heart filled with dread, she pasted a winning smile on her face. Her palms dampened, and she wiped them on her napkin.

Finn stood up. 'Daniel, come to the library. We'll partake of our after-dinner brandy there,' he commanded.

Brigid got up, too, her face burning from being excluded. 'Come, Aisne, let's take our coffee to the parlour.' Her voice dripped acid.

Aisne rose and gave her mother a surprised look, but Brigid dismissed it by shaking her head. Sitting around the blazing fire, Brigid picked up a book that had arrived that morning.

'Here, Aisne, indulge me and read this contemporary novel by Mr Dickens, please.' She needed something to calm her nerves.

In her stubborn manner, Aisne did not open the book but queried, 'Why is Father going to St. Louis, Mammy?' Making it clear with sarcasm, she ensured Finn was not confused with her Da. 'Hmm. It is unlikely he is going such a distance just to give lectures. It is almost two thousand miles. Is there some Fenian activity involved?'

So, Aisne has suspicions. 'It's the first I have heard about the trip, honey, but I have no reason to doubt its veracity. I'll make enquiries, though.'

Brigid dropped by the Boston office on the following morning with some of Mrs Klocke's gingerbread biscuits for Carmel. The receptionist had alarming news. 'Your husband is engaged in a Fenian mission. It involves gold that belonged to an Irish Confederate army officer turned riverboat gambler.'

Brigid's gut twisted. The trip's danger made her desperate to know what Finn had told Daniel. She returned home ready to confront her son.

'I asked for more information, but he dismissed me with one of his ice-cold looks.' Daniel's face was unsmiling. He had found the conversation difficult.

Brigid confronted Finn in the privacy of their bedroom that night, and he looked at his wife with a frosty gaze. 'Carmel is correct. A riverboat gambler has died and left his money to the Irish Comrades in atonement for his gambling sins. It is some gold bullion. Someone must accompany it to Boston for O'Brien.'

Brigid chortled. 'For O'Brien? Is he going to purchase firearms with it? That isn't much of an atonement.'

'I have committed to undertake the mission. The invitation for the lecture arrived a few weeks ago, and it occurred to me I could integrate the two without Harvard becoming aware.'

Brigid's gut twisted. 'It sounds like a dangerous mission to me. Doesn't such a long journey require a younger man?'

Finn climbed into bed. 'O'Brien wants to avoid implicating New York. Nobody else in the Boston office has a suitable excuse, young or not.'

Brigid climbed into bed, too. 'I hope they will pay you.'

'Yes, a handsome sum. The Irish Comrades refuse to fund a woman's college fees. I have calculated the college fees for next semester, and they will deplete our savings, even with Daniel's scholarship. Dermot's fees and ordination have already burned a hole in them.'

Brigid lay back. 'Are our savings being under threat?'

'The fees for two students at top colleges are steep, and with Aisne's living costs, it will be a squeeze. Thank God the diocese is funding Dermot's time in Rome. We couldn't afford that, too.'

Brigid could hear her blood thumping in her ears, 'How will you transport the gold?'

'It will come upriver by paddle steamer from New Orleans to Laclede's Landing in St Louis. I shall meet the steamer and bring the gold back to Boston. O'Brien intends to transport it to Ireland by ship from Canada, but I declined, as I won't risk my professorship.'

Brigid thought, *your life is too valuable to risk.* Her nerves had not been in such shreds since the arson attack in Dublin. 'Will you travel alone?'

'I'll travel alone to St. Louis but have an armed escort on my return journey. O'Brien says the guard is a proven shot. We'll meet at Laclede's Landing on the banks of the river Missouri.'

Brigid's heart fluttered, and she spoke in Gaelic. 'Feck, Finn, someone could rob you or worse.'

Finn twisted a lock of his wife's hair. 'I admit O'Brien has grown more violent with age. But I must make the trip. Not doing so puts my position in the Comrades at risk, and we need the money.'

'You are so deep that you have become O'Brien's errand boy,' Brigid retorted. 'You must watch your back, dear.'

'I am nobody's errand boy. The faculty has arranged the St. Louis lectures. Some time ago, I organised the gold shipment to fit the schedule. Enough. Blow out your candle. I have a tutorial in the morning.' Finn's tone dripped with vinegar.

That is why O'Brien visited Boston. Brigid thought and felt so anxious that it took her two hours to fall asleep.

The next evening, after supper, she demanded a full itinerary. 'What if something happens to us? How and where do I contact you?' Brigid did not add what a twisted gut said to her about his fortunes.

Finn smiled under his new brush moustache. 'I'll ask the faculty secretary to outline my itinerary for you tomorrow. I have reserved a room at Planter's Hotel on Fourth Street in St. Louis for a week while lecturing, and you can contact me there by telegraph. I'll use the telegraph to reach the faculty secretary, who will relay any messages to you.'

Finn kindled his pipe, a practice Brigid continued to loathe at the supper table. He puffed a cloud of smoke, making Brigid's eyes water, and continued.

'On the afternoon of 27th April, a paddle steamer, the Robert E. Lee, will arrive carrying the gold under armed guard. I'll meet my escort at the Missouri River's levee that day, and we'll leave St. Louis on the next available train. I'll send a telegraph to the faculty secretary before the train departs. As it is a long journey and I know you'll be worried, I'll telegraph progress. So don't worry, honey, everything will be fine.'

Finn kissed his wife and fondled her breast in bed later, but Brigid pulled away. She was unwilling to indulge in lovemaking when Finn had agreed to such a dangerous mission. Visions of Niall's injuries came to her unbidden while Finn snored. Brigid finally fell into an uneasy sleep with the break of dawn and the melodious chirping of birds. When she awoke, the sweet-smelling odour of camellias drifted through the open window. Brigid, alone in their bed, wept.

Later that day, Finn packed his clothing. Brigid emphasised taking enough shirts and collars and packing a new suit for his lectures. She guessed he had not packed enough shirts when she examined his wardrobe. She discovered something bulky in the case as she folded two more. A little exploration made her heart leap to her mouth. *So, Finn does own a pistol. Is he expecting trouble?* Brigid hoped he knew how to use it because if her gut twisted anymore, it would rotate clean in half.

The following night, fear threatened to overwhelm her, and Brigid threw herself into passionate lovemaking, hoping to disguise it. However, Finn assured her everything would be fine and that he would return home in mid-May. Brigid lay stiff in the darkness, every fibre of her body singing that something would go wrong.

For the next three weeks, Brigid kept busy by authoring more articles, taking extra shifts at the soup kitchen, attending an undergraduate course on poetry, and preparing the accounts of two small businesses. As night fell, she lay with dreams of the walking dead, long forgotten, leading her to toss and turn.

As the warm evening of April 20th settled in, Brigid, Daniel, and Aisne gathered around the table for supper. The aroma of roasted chicken filled the air. The clinking of silverware against plates was the only sound as no conversation occurred.

The banging of the door knocker startled them. Mrs Frankel entered with a courier-delivered telegram announcing Finn's safe arrival at his hotel. Brigid's heart filled with blessed relief, and excusing herself, she went to bed before Mrs Klocke had served dessert.

Four ribboned gifts sat at her place on the breakfast table the following day. The children wished her a happy birthday. Finn had left his present with Aisne. It was a leather-bound book of poems by Samuel Taylor Coleridge. Brigid was deeply touched by Finn's considerate gift, knowing she had only started the course in March. He had written a private message of affection on the flyleaf, which moved Brigid to tears. His empty chair wrought more anguish, for Brigid's wounded heart believed it might never hold him again.

For the next week, she kept busy at the soup kitchen and spent time in the herb garden, as the weather had turned fine. Mrs Klocke permitted Brigid to cook colcannon and potato cakes, and the family sat around the parlour table, reminiscing about their journey to America.

Finn telegraphed from his hotel on the 27th of April to say he was checking out and looking forward to getting home. Brigid's heavy heart and weary body lightened, and she slept that night. But insomnia plagued her as the week progressed, an owl's hoot resonating with her lonely thoughts. The stars glimmered, and the benevolent moon looked down, yet a knot of fear gripped her stomach, causing her to shiver despite the warming weather.

One night, Brigid lay awake as the clock atop the steeple of the Lutheran church nearby struck three. She concluded she must visit Carmel later that day and try to glean more information about Finn's travelling companion.

Carmel greeted her with warmth, eagerly tucking into the gingerbread biscuits Daniel had baked.

'Stan Case is your husband's travelling companion,' she said. 'He is a known gunslinger from Texas. O'Brien sent me word a few days before your husband left St. Louis. I have some other information. The Archbishop of St Louis is a Fenian sympathiser, and he arranged the shipment and onward transport of the gold.'

Another feckin' priest is risking hell? Thought Brigid with acerbity. *What have you become involved with, Finn?* Her pulse rate rose with fear, and she left the office, her boot heels clicking in time with her fast-beating heart. She did not trust this Stan Case person. Brigid busied herself with some embroidery that afternoon. But she had no appetite and picked at her food, even Mrs Klocke's potato cakes.

At the start of the second week, Finn telegraphed to say they were headed east via Pittsburgh. But Brigid had no map to show her their 4exact route. She grew more anxious because she knew they were crossing the dangerous Native American country.

Brigid awoke on 5th May, hot and damp, with a body aching with fear. She spent the day in the soup kitchen while her gut remained in a tight knot.

Grasping Brigid's arm, Norah took her aside. 'What's up, Missus? You are having difficulties. I can see them in your face.'

Brigid's eyes were misted as Norah was the only person outside her family, and Carmel was the one she dared confide in regarding Finn's activities.

'Finn is engaged in Fenian work and. I don't know where he is beyond passing through the Ohio plains. He is returning to Boston from St. Louis.

'He isn't involved with that feckin' bastard O'Brien, is he?' Norah's eyes opened wide. 'I heard about his activities from my brother before we left Ireland. Did your husband come to Boston with O'Brien's group?'

Brigid nodded her head and sought her handkerchief.

'Oh my God, that man is a dangerous villain.' Norah crossed her breast. 'I never believed your story about why you came to Boston. When do you expect your husband to get home?'

'Not for another week or two. But I have learned that Stan Case, a gunslinger, is escorting him. Fear grips my heart at the mere mention of his name.'

Norah crossed her chest again. 'I'll ask about him fer you. I'm on shift on Friday. Come and speak with me then.'

Brigid felt less worried when Norah showed her support.

'Thank you, Norah. But finding who the escort is won't help. I must remain calm and wait for word from Finn.'

Brigid had trouble reading that evening because her thoughts kept wondering about her husband's journey, and she read the same section more than once. In bed, she tossed and turned with agitation. After lunch the following day, a meal that everyone pecked at like chickadees, Brigid put on old clothes. Gardening was the one task that distracted her troubled mind, and she set out to deadhead late daffodils in a secluded area of the grounds. Thus, Brigid did not hear Ulrike's tremulous footsteps approaching.

'Ma'am, Ma'am,' Ulrike called with urgency in her voice.

Brigid straightened her back, shielding her gaze from the sun.

'What is it, Ulrike?'

'Excuse me, Ma'am, but two police officers are at the door, seeking to speak with you immediately.' She fiddled with her apron. 'Shall I show them into your parlour?'

Ulrike's pale face looked like she had seen a ghost. Brigid's hand shook so much she dropped her secateurs. Her legs trembled, and with a frog-like croak, she said, 'Yes, Ulrike, show them in there.'

'Umm, shall I make some tea, Ma'am?'

Ulrike's voice wobbled, and she wrung her hands, something unfamiliar to Brigid, whose heart beat faster than a drum at taps. Brigid nodded as her throat had stuck shut, and her tongue turned to old leather. She removed her gardening gloves, adding them to the secateurs lying on the ground, and pushed tendrils of hair behind her ears to calm her nerves. In her heart, she knew why the police officers had come. Brigid walked up the path to the kitchen door where Mrs Frankel waited, her face pale and brow puckered.

Brigid grasped the doorjamb before entering the kitchen, feeling dizzy. Her body shook as Mrs. Klocke closed the door. Mrs Frankel made Brigid sit and gave her a glass of water. She helped her to her house shoes, her face full of concern.

Brigid stood up, unsure if her legs could move. Mrs Frankel took her arm and guided her to the parlour. Two burly police officers, caps in hand, greeted Brigid with a bow. Their solemn faces heightened her fears. *Oh, no, please, no.*

'Begging your pardon, Ma'am, but you should sit down,' a police officer with bushy white whiskers said.

Brigid lowered herself onto the back of her favourite sofa to avoid collapsing.

'We have unwelcome news, Ma'am,' the other police officer said. 'Your husband was a victim of an armed raid on a train travelling east from Pittsburgh four days ago. I regret to inform you he was killed in the incident. New York's Albany police informed us this morning that they are sending his body home today.'

Brigid felt faint, and her head dropped to her knees as Ulrike entered with the tea.

She touched Brigid's shoulder, 'Ma'am. Mrs Klocke has added some gingerbread biscuits.' The delicate china cups rattled in their saucers as Ulrike put the tray down, and one fell to the floor, shattering along with Brigid's heart.

Brigid raised her head. 'Ulrike, fetch another cup and pour brandy into it. Please sit, officers.' Brigid gestured to the sofa.

Ulrike, her eyes wide, did as bid, but the tea slopped into the saucer as she handed the cup to Brigid. *She knows. I'm sure all the staff know.*

'Ma'am, we need a family member to collect and identify the body at the police station. Then they can release it for burial,' the younger officer said.

Brigid felt like a January Nor'easter wind, and a suffocating fog had blown into the room, making breathing difficult. She sipped her tea to moisten her mouth and steady her nerves, tears puddling in her eyes. 'What time does the train arrive?' she said in a squeaky voice.

'Around four this afternoon. Ma'am, can someone accompany you, a family member, or a servant? I'll be there to help.'

'My son Daniel is in his last semester at the Latin School. Could you ask the Principal to send my son home?'

'I'll see to it, Ma'am,' the officer said. 'I express my condolences for your loss. I can take myself from the house.'

The older officer stayed with Brigid for a few more minutes; his kind face creased with concern, and his hand touched hers. 'Ma'am, it's not pleasant to ask, but we need you to tell us about your husband's journey. I'll take your statement at two o'clock tomorrow afternoon if that's convenient.'

Brigid nodded her head, barely taking in his words. Standing up, the officer bowed, put on his cap, and departed.

After ringing the servants' bell, Brigid mumbled, 'Ulrike, please ask Mrs Frankel to join me.'

She then dropped her head towards her knees, stifling her tears as Ulrike left the room. Soon, muscular arms surrounded her as Mrs Frankel sat down, and Brigid gave in to her sorrow. She wept bitter tears of anger and regret onto Mrs Frankel's shoulder.

An hour later, Daniel arrived. Brigid couldn't suppress her tears when she saw Daniel's face resembling a thundercloud. 'I will collect Father's body, Mother. No woman should have to do that.' He hugged his mother, who sobbed into his shoulder as overwhelming sorrow consumed her.

Dry-eyed, Daniel lifted her chin. 'Mother, we need to tell Aisne.'

Brigid sniffed and felt for her handkerchief. She knew

Aisne's grief would be short-lived.

'She is joining her friend Arthur and his sister after lectures today. They will have supper and attend a Beethoven concert. Let her enjoy this evening.'

Daniel left the house at three-thirty, accompanied by the younger police officer. Brigid rang the servant's bell, and Mrs Frankel came to sit with her again. Brigid was numb in body and mind when Ulrike brought more tea.

'How did it happen?' Mrs Frankel's cheeks looked pale.

With a shake of her aching head, Brigid covered her face with her hands and wept.

Daniel returned just after five. 'Father's body is with Flynn's Undertakers. They will arrange the funeral when you are ready.'

Daniel vanished to his room and only emerged during suppertime when they ate a meagre supper. The household became enveloped by a veil of dark and forbidding gloom. Brigid waited until the morning to tell Aisne. She held her mother in her arms as Brigid sobbed.

That afternoon, the older police officer returned. Mrs Frankel brought him into the parlour.

'Please take a seat, officer. I'll ask the housemaid to bring coffee,

They waited in awkward silence, the officer running his cap through his hands until Ulrike poured two cups and withdrew.

'Ma'am, we have added information about the incident. A single bullet killed your husband through his forehead. Powder burns at the entry wound suggest it might have been an execution.'

Brigid's stomach dropped to her knees as the officer sipped his coffee, and she longed for comforting arms to appear.

'We are unsure about the motive, but it appears to have been a calculated assault to steal valuable contraband, such as silver or gold, and murder your husband.' He took out a notepad. 'I'm sorry to ask at such a time, but can you provide the details about your husband's journey?'

Brigid's mind whirled as she sought the right words to protect the children's futures.

'St Louis University invited him to give a series of lectures. He journeyed by stagecoach and train. I'm sorry, but I don't have any further details.'

'I apologise for asking this question, but is anyone in your husband's life who might want to harm him?'

Throughout the sleepless night, Brigid's mind had grappled with this. *Had O'Brien executed Finn?* But she had no proof. Brigid wouldn't implicate the children's father in some Fenian conspiracy and ruin their lives in America. She shook her head.

'No, nobody, officer.'

The officer's brooding look suggested he did not believe her. He took another sip of coffee and then stood. 'Ma'am, I am so sorry for your loss but must leave now. Please let us know if you have any further information. I'll see myself out.'

Brigid lay back on the sofa. *Had Case double-crossed O'Brien, or was the outlaw a paid assassin?* Then she thought of a third possibility. *Had the British military killed Finn?* But on reflection, the transport of gold suggested a double cross. Brigid was determined to reveal the truth. She would go to extreme lengths, even scratching out the potential perpetrator's eyes to achieve her goal.

At the inquest, the Medical Examiner ruled a person or persons unknown had shot Finn. Brigid was relieved they did not question her, as secrecy was vital to guard her children.

CHAPTER 33: WIDOW'S TORMENT

Rain fell in stair-rods the day Brigid laid Finn to rest. Daniel said that friends, colleagues, students, and even some brotherhood members packed the cathedral, but Brigid was too distressed to notice. 'At least two hundred individuals came, Mother,' Daniel said in an awed voice.

Brigid had arranged for Finn's oak coffin to arrive in a glass-sided, japanned coach pulled by four plumed black horses. She placed a spray of lilies on top of the casket. Five of Finn's fellow professors functioned as pallbearers, along with Daniel, who they positioned at the front. Daniel maintained mature dignity throughout the service and gave the eulogy.

Brigid's and Aisne's faces remained composed, hidden beneath black mantillas. At the graveside, the three stood impassive. Brigid's mind flitted back to Niall's funeral, which had been less formal, and her heart overflowed. *Is God punishing me for leaving the Church?* Tears trickled down her cheeks, but nobody saw them behind the mantilla curtain except God. She clasped her children's hands and wished Dermot were present too. It began to rain as they threw clumps of dirt on the coffin. Then, the mourners turned away, and Daniel guided his mother to a waiting carriage.

Mrs Klocke set out an assortment of finger foods for the wake in the dining room. Brigid steeled herself to be polite to people, no matter what she felt inside. She requested donations to the soup kitchen in Finn's memory, and an anonymous donor gave $100.00. Aisne greeted people and, as

Brigid foresaw, was not in much distress.

Brigid found conversation with Finn's colleagues from Harvard difficult. She had to maintain a facade over the reason for his death. His colleagues had many compliments, and to her relief, Brigid guessed they had not known about Finn's Fenian activities.

Once everyone departed, Brigid enjoyed a relaxing, hot bath. She lay in the lavender-scented water, knowing the day had stretched her nerves like twine between two posts, and marvelled the cord had not snapped.

As the bath water cooled, Brigid got out, wrapped herself in a fluffy towel, entered the bedroom, and lay down, thinking, *I'll sleep alone forever,* and the cord broke. Brigid sobbed her sorrow into Finn's pillow but must have fallen asleep, for it was dark when she came to consciousness. Her clock said nine, so Brigid donned her nightgown and climbed into bed. After taking the sleeping draft left by the family doctor, blessed oblivion followed.

Brigid visited Carmel and asked if she knew the role played by the Archbishop of St Louis. She felt deep in her core that the cleric was an accessory to murder. Her anger was all-consuming when Carmel revealed the archbishop had sourced Case and provided his private carriage to the railway station. 'He planned the route to Boston, travelling via Pittsburgh across the Iroquois and Ohio plains.'

'O'Brien's hand in the killing is everywhere,' Brigid, her face burning with suppressed fury, said. 'When they returned his belongings, the pistol which I found when he packed was missing. I bet Case removed it somehow, then Finn couldn't fight back.' She quelled her burning pit of anger and hailed a cab home, where she donned old clothes and started digging in the vegetable garden.

During the last weeks of school, Daniel matured into a man. Dermot became the head of the household upon his return from Rome in June. Brigid felt overjoyed when her eldest son walked into the parlour wearing a priest's soutane and enfolded her in his arms. She wept into his shoulder, heaving sobs while Dermot smoothed his mother's hair.

An Italian bishop had ordained Dermot at Easter. He had almost finished his three years in Rome by authoring his thesis. His superiors gave him two months' leave. He joined his family when Daniel graduated First in Class. Brigid's eyes filled with joy as Daniel, looking like Finn in his stance and fierce gaze, walked up the steps to receive his diploma. Finn would have been so proud of his son, and her empty heart ached for him. Dermot held her hand, sensing his mother's longing for Finn's presence.

After the ceremony, the family returned home to a quiet lunch and drank a toast to Daniel. After the meal, Aisne made her mother go to bed. Brigid couldn't sleep without the aid of the sleeping draught and knew she had deep bags below her eyes. She lay in bed at night wondering which was worse, losing a husband to a dreaded disease or a murderous outlaw.

The doctor's sleeping draught silenced her musings.

The family's financial status emerged as Brigid's first concern after the funeral, and she turned to Richard for advice. Finn had taken out a comprehensive insurance policy to pay off the mortgage, and Richard revealed he had a second one.

'Harvard ensures all tenured professors for the care of the family if they die. It provides financial security for their widows.' Richard steepled his fingers. 'The income it provides and what you earn from your writing and accounting businesses will give you sufficient money for a comfortable life. But I advise you to reduce some of your outgoings.'

Richard gazed with soft eyes at Brigid. 'Are you getting any rest? You look exhausted. We can sort out the finances in a few weeks if you prefer. I'll make sure you have enough funds in your account.'

'No, I require immediate clarity on my status. If there are papers to sign, I want to sign them today.'

'Well, if you insist. Finn's will must go through probate, which I'll expedite as quickly as possible. I have prepared for you to meet with his lawyers at your convenience. But as a determined woman, I guessed you'd want to complete matters today.'

Brigid nodded, and Richard shook a tiny bell and handed a note to his junior assistant, who hurried off. Richard got up, opened a small cabinet, and poured Brigid and himself a whiskey while they waited. He was about to pour a second glass when a knock at the door announced Finn's lawyer, a tall, thin man with pale skin, fair hair, and eyes that Brigid, scrutinising, thought looked Scandinavian. *He isn't Irish; I couldn't bear that.*

Finn bequeathed everything to Brigid, who was unaware of the substantial revenue generated from his Fenian work. The realisation that much of it was built at the expense of others who risked their lives made Brigid queasy. 'Thank you for helping me, Richard. What would I do without you?' Brigid's eyes filled, and she felt a tear trickle down her face.

Richard got up, handed her his handkerchief, and put his arms around her, holding her close. 'You are the strongest, bravest woman I have ever known. You'll come through this.' Other words lay unspoken, but Brigid knew them. They had been present in his eyes from the day they met.

Brigid returned home with a lighter heart and called a family conference. She discussed the staff situation with the children, and they agreed she couldn't afford a housekeeper and housemaid. One had to be given notice.

Upon hearing this, Ulrike said, 'I'll be married in the fall. I intended to give notice, anyway, Ma'am.'

This was a surprise, for nobody, not even Mrs Frankel, knew Ulrike was courting. But the girl revealed she had been meeting the butcher's son, Dexter, on her Sundays off. They had kept their marriage plans to themselves because of Finn's death, but Dexter had proposed while Finn was in St. Louis.

'He has secured the lease on a butcher's shop in Medford, north of Boston. The current leaseholder wishes to retire, and an apartment comes with the shop. Ulrike's face was aglow. 'Please come to my wedding. You are like family to me, and I shall miss you.'

Brigid had to change the other staff duties, as there would soon be no housemaid. She asked Mrs Klocke if she would do the laundry in return for Brigid's cooking. Monday suppers.

'We can save some money by doing without the laundress.' Brigid said, guessing the subterfuge might work because removing the laundress would please Mrs Klocke.

'That arrangement fills me with joy. I don't want to leave this house, my home, for many years. But I'll be relieved when the laundress leaves.'

Mrs Klocke then exuded an air of ownership, stating her ability to do a better job with less mess.

Next, Brigid asked Mrs Frankel to hand over the household accounts to her.

'I will raise your salary in the autumn to compensate for your less pleasant duties like lighting fires in winter. I can manage my toilette with your help on special occasions. Do you think this arrangement is satisfactory?' She crossed her fingers.

The housekeeper nodded her head, her eyes too full to speak.

With these changes agreed upon, a sense of purpose developed. Brigid expected to lose old friends and seek new companions among other widows. *However, I'm determined not to lose my social standing and to continue my philanthropic work.*

The Massachusetts summer swept in hot, humid, and energy-sapping. The family attended the Independence Day Parade, where some Irish Comrades hid among the crowds. If O'Brien showed his fleshy, bearded, swarthy face, Brigid would cut out his heart. *Or I'll shoot him with Finn's gun, for he deserves to be shot.*

Brigid's anger did not dissipate with time. Instead, it consumed her. The soup kitchen and garden provided respite. Work had supported her in the past, and it helped again. She gave the older gardener notice, wrote a glowing reference, and took over his tasks. She did not close the soup kitchen until the end of July.

Brigid dedicated mornings to assisting Norah, who now had charge of the kitchen and received a wage. She spent the afternoons tending to the garden, weeding, and digging. Dressed in her oldest clothes with a hat and gloves, she revelled in the smell of damp earth, roses, lilies, and bougainvillaea surrounding her as she worked. The dogwoods, silver birches, and maples all soothed her tortured mind. Digging relieved her tense shoulders, driving away the whirling visions of death. She ceased work when the sun dipped behind the conifer trees.

Luxuriating in the bathtub later, she let the water wash off her sweat and remove the unfettered darkness in her soul. As the weeks passed, and with the aid of St John's wort, her mood lifted. *Once the mourning period ends, I'll entertain guests again, if only for the children's benefit.*

CHAPTER 34: COLLEGE

Dermot had almost finished his thesis and had not returned to Rome. The archbishop found him space in his grand house to complete it.

Daniel began his studies at Harvard, where he joined the rowing club at the start of the semester, and practice took up much of his time. His physique strengthened, and his resemblance to Finn in his walk and the fierceness of his gaze became more apparent. Sometimes, his looks undid his mother's composure, so she ate supper alone at a small table she had installed in her bedroom. The move prevented uncomfortable silences during family meals when even Dermot couldn't console his mother.

One evening, after Daniel had spent the entire weekend in his bedroom, Brigid said,

'You understand I can't afford to pay for lodgings, don't you? However, I'll turn the library over to you. You need your own space to study and meet with friends.'

Daniel's face lit up, his eyes shining. 'Thanks, Mother.'

He ran from the parlour into the library, and Brigid grinned. A boy still hid inside her sophisticated Harvard-educated son.

Aisne started her studies at Cornell in 1879, as planned. But despite economising, Brigid couldn't afford fees and living costs, so Aisne applied to Radcliffe for the third year of her studies and was accepted. Though the fees were high, Brigid could also manage them without the accommodation cost.

'It is time all university authorities realise women have brains and award degrees. I know some women at Radcliffe intend to protest,' said Aisne, pouting.

'Protest, in what way?' Brigid's mouth dried. She couldn't manage riot outcomes.

'They mean to prevent any men, including professors, from attending or giving our lectures, as they sometimes do. They will blockade the entrances.'

'Please don't become involved.' Tears filled Brigid's eyes. 'I can't manage such trouble at present.'

She turned away to hide her tumultuous emotions from Aisne. The girl assured her mother she would not take part in this protest. However, she did not promise never to be involved.

'Women should get degrees after studying as hard or harder than men.'

Brigid had to agree with that. *Why shouldn't women get the same rewards for their hard work? The system was not fair when women faced discrimination.* The issue became the subject of an article.

The Archbishop of Boston decided Dermot would take a curacy at a local Catholic church.

'He recommends parish work for four or five years to prepare me for the overseas missions where I may be the lone priest of a parish stretching hundreds of miles. I must also learn the basics of medical treatment, so I shall attend Boston College.'

This news gladdened his mother's heart since Dermot would be nearby. She needed his quiet strength and gentle manner as she negotiated a life without Finn. Brigid cooked traditional Irish dishes for her family every Monday, and after she had done the laundry, Mrs Klocke had the remainder of the day off. Brigid helped with ironing clothes, and the two women developed an enduring friendship.

The children's lives became Brigid's, and she composed articles about child development for women's magazines based on her journal records. The pieces received acclaim, and her income increased. More small businesses brought their accounts to her and added to her income. Despite the loss of Finn, she stayed afloat, and after a year of mourning, she announced it would cease. Brigid no longer needed sleeping draughts, and if depressed thoughts caught her, she went for a long walk or dug up weeds,

Aisne was overjoyed because she could wear summer dresses, not the hated dark colours of mourning. The splendid Independence Day festivities in 1882 featured fireworks and supper parties that preceded the Harvard Ball. Brigid took Aisne to Madame Solange, who made her a breathtaking gown in deep green silk trimmed with seed pearls. She threaded seed pearls through her hair for the event. The dress was expensive, but Brigid felt Aisne deserved it and used some of Finn's Fenian funds, which she had not touched. Aisne's old beau, Arthur, asked her on dates and escorted her to several concerts. Concerned for her daughter's marriage prospects, Brigid asked Aisne about Arthur's intentions.

'I'm not in love with him, if that is what you are asking. He is stimulating company, but it's where his father keeps his yacht. I stayed with Arthur's sister during the yachting season, and Mr Benton taught us to sail. We sailed the boat to Martha's Vineyard in a race. I even shortened a skirt so I would not trip up.' She blushed because she had said nothing to her mother.

Brigid had noticed Aisne's penchant for tying her hair in an American ponytail with an enormous bow but had not enquired why. Now she understood. Aisne had grown tall like Niall and dwarfed her mother.

Aisne laughed when Brigid pointed it out. 'Ach, to be sure, Mammy, you are shrinking with age, so you are.'

When the leaves changed to their glorious New England colours, Brigid took a brief holiday in Maine, where a friend had a house by the sea. She walked the coastal path daily, enjoying the salty sea air and the wind in her hair, letting it hang loose, held only by a clip, under her hat. Brushing it one day after her walk, she discovered some greying hairs and plucked them. *Fifty-four is too young to have such hair.* Then she spotted wrinkles in her skin. *After returning home, I must start caring for my health and buy zinc oxide to smooth my complexion.*

One afternoon, Brigid found a notice for a palmistry fortune teller while browsing for gifts. Drawn by an unseen force, she entered a dark room smelling of violets. Purple drapes hung over the windows, and scented candlelight lit the dim interior, reminiscent of the fortune teller in Ballyconstór.

'A deep breath, then let it out, Madame.' The palmist turned Brigid's palms over and smoothed them. 'You have long lifelines, my dear. Your heart lines show many trials, but you endure as you have a strong heart. I see your future involves a man. Ah, you have been married twice, my dear. Is that right?'

Brigid nodded as tears pricked her eyes.

'You'll remarry and go on a long journey. You have fortune ahead.' She released her grasp on Brigid's hand and held her gaze. 'I read you have had recent troubles. Let them go, my dear, for fortune smiles upon you.'

Brigid paid her ten cents, which she thought was expensive for ten minutes, but she was on holiday, and fortune-telling was fun. Lost in thought over the woman's prediction, she questioned who she would wed, as none of the men in her social circle attracted her.

Brigid walked down the street, browsing in small shops, feeling her energy and enthusiasm returning. She stopped outside a shop selling home-baked cookies and treated herself to butterscotch-flavoured ones plus a cup of hot chocolate. As she sipped the hot drink.

When I get home, I'll author more articles for a women's journal, beginning with a travelogue of this trip. My life experiences will provide the background for writing an 'agony aunt' column for a magazine.

Brigid reflected that in her internal thinking, she had reverted to Gaelic. Niall's face often appeared unbidden before her eyes, and she wondered why. Brigid nibbled a butterscotch biscuit and recalled that Aisne had refused a celebration for her twenty-first birthday, preferring a quiet family picnic by the sea at Boston's Singing Beach. She had wanted to save the money for Cornell. Now that the mourning was over, Brigid held a ball in Aisne's honour. She hired Harvard Hall, an orchestra, and friends to help with catering.

Beatrice took charge and forbade her from worrying about the cost.

'I'm not a charity case,' Brigid said, bewildered.

Beatrice did not know she made a tidy income from her writing and accounts businesses. Nobody but Richard knew her actual income.

Beatrice said, 'We need help sometimes. God did not bless me with a daughter, so please let me indulge my fancy.'

She was such a fine friend, ensuring Brigid had invitations to her famous suppers (and provided her with escorts from the most dashing of eligible men, even if none interested her beyond friendship) that Brigid let her organise the event. The most suitable man among her escorts was Richard. He was a convivial host and a charming and attentive escort at supper parties. But Brigid made it clear she had no romantic feelings for him. They enjoyed each other's company as close friends without complications, and he agreed to escort Brigid to Aisne's ball.

The evening was a resounding success. Beatrice and her helpers arranged a dazzling event with music by a harpist, a sumptuous banquet, a magician, and a juggler, followed by dancing to an orchestra and fireworks at midnight. Aisne's dance card was complete for the entire night, and she shone with luminous beauty. However, she had discarded poor Arthur and did not have a permanent beau. Brigid worried about what her daughter would do with her life.

'I told you long ago I wished to be a famous artist. That is still my intention. After I graduate, I'll decide on my next goal.'

Brigid spotted a gleam in her daughter's eye and guessed she already had a plan. Brigid wondered what it was, but neither of her sons knew. Indeed, Daniel appeared indifferent.

'She will do what she wants, Mother. She always has,' he said.

One morning in November, Brigid spotted a young tabby cat wandering into the soup kitchen. Brigid was tempted to take it to the animal rescue place she had briefly worked with. It sat by the door and washed its paws. She asked one helper if she had seen it before. 'Yes. Hector belonged to a widow who passed from a fever last month. We 'ave fed 'im scraps, but he keeps returning for more. I dunno where he sleeps or what will happen to him come to the snow. He is thin for a cat ain't he?'

Recalling Scamp, Brigid said she preferred dogs, but she bent to stroke him, and he purred and licked her hand. As winter crept in, she rescued the cat and took it to live with her family.

Otherwise, he will starve. He is a mouser and will rid the scullery of the field mice who torment Mrs Klocke.

But Mrs Klocke raised her flour-covered hands and said, 'How did the mangy cat get into my kitchen?'

'I brought him, Mrs Klocke,' said Brigid with a wry smile. 'I found him in my soup kitchen. Since the poor mite is homeless, I thought he could provide us with some company. If you let him sleep in the scullery, he will keep down the invading mice.'

Mrs Klocke harrumphed. 'He will. But with all due respect, Ma'am, I refuse to clean up after him.'

'I'll do that. As a child, I had pets.' Brigid did not refer to Scamp; the memory was raw.

Mrs Frankel examined the cat and said, 'Please excuse me, but you must clean him with the delousing powder in the stable before he can enter the living quarters. He may have fleas.'

Brigid agreed and took him to the stable, where she deloused him. The cat sneezed.

'You must learn manners, Hector. Mr Frankel takes immense pride in a clean house.'

Hector took no notice, sneezed again, and then purred. Brigid brought him to the parlour, where he slept on an old cushion by the fire. The children adored him.

'Mrs Klocke gives him titbits when she thinks no one is looking,' Mrs Frankel commented as she helped Brigid dress for a supper party. 'Aisne sneaks him into her bedroom, too.'

You don't know he sneaks into mine when Aisne is out?

Brigid felt surprised, but since she cleaned her bedroom now, Mrs Frankel had not noticed. In short, the household spoiled the animal rotten.

As Hector grew, he became a sleek cat who crept around the house and garden as if he owned it, caught mice, and dropped them at Brigid's feet. Hector made her smile, and she talked to him about important matters. He was clever and did not challenge any decisions she made. Instead, the cat might look at her with narrowed, disapproving eyes. Then he purred and washed his paws. After being shooed from the kitchen, he sought refuge on his parlour cushion. Hector soon ruled the house, which resumed a cheery atmosphere, and Brigid felt a pleasant rhythm return to her life.

At Aisne's ball, Daniel met a girl from Radcliffe. Candace was an English major who minored in fine arts and met Aisne while studying the same course module. She hailed from an old Boston family with many connections. By the following spring, Daniel, now in love, told his mother he wanted to propose.

'Daniel, you are far too young to get married. It will be best if you experience life first. Go out and meet lots of girls before you settle down.'

But with his father's fierce will, he resisted his mother's

entreaties. 'I have found the love of my life and don't need to meet other girls.'

So, he visited Candace's father, George Garland, a wealthy man who had invested in shipping and the new railroads traversing America. Candace was his only child, her mother having died giving birth to the girl, and her father adored her. She stood to inherit an enormous fortune that her husband would control according to the law.

Daniel was still under twenty-one, and Brigid was his legal guardian since his father was deceased. Brigid believed she had a right to know Candace's father's opinion. Daniel explained George had been cordial but had questioned his motives.

'I told him I was in love with Candace and wished to spend the rest of my life with her.' Daniel paused, examining his forefinger nail.

'Before he spoke, Mr Garland steepled his fingers on his desk. Then, staring at my face, he said, "I'll not give my daughter permission to marry anyone until she reaches the age of twenty-one. Whoever marries Candace must have an impeccable background and judgment, as he will someday control her fortune." He gazed at me like I was worthless and continued, "Son, you need to prove yourself worthy of my daughter's hand in marriage".'

Brigid watched her son's face show Finn's determination in the set of his jaw and ice-cold eyes. Even if Candace's father considered Daniel worthless, it would have made him ponder unless he had some knowledge about Finn's Fenian activities. Beads of sweat formed on her brow.

'Mr Garland asked me if it was correct that I'm a mathematics major and what I intended as a career. I told him I intended to enter the banking profession. He had done his research and was aware of Father's status as a professor. He studied me for several seconds, making me uncomfortable. Then his gaze softened, and he said Candace had told him of her feelings for me and agreed to my courting her with a view to marriage if we are still together when Candace turns twenty-one. He is determined to avoid any scandal. I'm uncertain about his definition of scandalous, but I'll do nothing that could be detrimental to the girl I love.'

'I suspect Mr Garland meant no premarital relations, Daniel. My advice is to continue your studies with renewed vigour and let me soften him by taking an interest in his daughter since she has no mother.'

Brigid began by inviting Candace to coffee and gingerbread biscuits with Aisne. Aisne took on the role of an older sister for two girls with a shared experience of losing a parent. Brigid saw the girl needed female support to enhance her development and that George Garland had done an excellent job as a single parent. *But a woman's hand will help ease her way into adulthood.*

Daniel and Candace led busy lives, with Candace playing croquet with serious intent. Sometimes, she joined the family's Monday suppers. The young couple's love became evident in Daniel's attentive and gentlemanly care, and Candace blossomed into a confident young woman. George Garland mellowed, and it became tacit for close friends to become one family. Dermot even agreed to marry them.

Brigid invited Richard, a Democrat, to Monday suppers. He and George, a Republican, engaged in political debates. The conversation could become heated, and Aisne would join in. She relished the discussion when it turned to emancipation for women and their right to education and degrees. Brigid often had to frown or nudge Aisne's foot to stop her from dominating the conversation.

Dermot would bring up the topic of Christianity. Since his time as a theology student in Rome, he had grown in confidence. He had a liberal viewpoint on America's place in the world. As a priest, he contributed to Catholic George's mellowing. It heartened Brigid to see Dermot thrive on parish work. He was much sought after for his wise and kind advice.

A bittersweet feeling filled Brigid's heart because Niall could witness his son's accomplishments. He would have been so proud. For his part, Daniel avoided any form of confrontation lest he incurred his future father-in-law's displeasure.

When Aisne was at home for supper, she and her mother took coffee in the parlour after supper. On one such evening, Aisne had a surprise for Brigid.

'I have received a letter from my old tutor at Cornell. He suggested I go to Europe to study sculpture. He says I have a rare talent and encourages me to develop it.'

'I did not know that you had maintained contact with Cornell.' Brigid tried to smile.

'My tutor there is fond of me and has kept a fatherly eye on my studies ever since.'

Brigid found this a most generous association, but she was filled with unease as she contemplated the financial implications of the venture. Her brow wrinkled.

'I need to determine if I can get a loan for your expenses. Please ask your tutor to give us an estimate of costs.'

Meanwhile, Brigid visited Richard to enquire about a loan. But when he heard the reason, he insisted on paying Aisne's expenses.

'I have no children, so seeing her talent put to use will please me.'

Brigid's heart was overflowing at his generosity, and she accepted, knowing he aimed his gesture at her. 'You must understand, I'll never marry you. I love you like a brother, not as a lover.'

Richard nodded, his eyes soft. 'I know, Brigid, but let me indulge you.'

Brigid then spoke about Daniel and Candace. Richard commented on what a fine young man Daniel had become.

'I'll offer your son a position in my bank when the boy graduates. If he progresses well, I'll recommend him to the board as my replacement as the bank president when I retire. That should satisfy George's concern about Daniels's prospects.'

Brigid's eyes filled with tears at the man's generosity, and she wished she could love him as he deserved.

Aisne was overjoyed. "I have had a letter from Professor Coppola, who enclosed an estimate of costs. He is setting up my two-year study programme at the University of Florence, where a colleague will mentor me. He will find accommodation and give me fatherly advice. Being over twenty-one, I don't require a guardian.'

Although Aisne's absence would leave a big hole in her life, Brigid knew better than to argue with her headstrong daughter and let her make the arrangements.

Aisne enrolled in a Boston language school to learn Italian. She was a diligent student with a surprising knack for languages. Professor Coppola arranged her passage to Italy for the spring of 1884, sailing from New York to Genoa. Dermot found his sister chaperones for the voyage through his clerical connections.

Letters arranging details flew between Boston and Florence on speedy ships. Brigid agreed to accompany Aisne to New York and hand her to her chaperones. Richard wanted to come too, but she forbade it.

'I know how to care for myself, Richard, and disagree with restrictive conventions on women's behaviour. I have taken care of myself since I was a young girl.'

Richard did not know Brigid's history, and she felt better that he did not.

Brigid and Aisne took the train to New York and stayed in the Park Avenue Hotel. Although Aisne had an enormous trunk of belongings, Brigid took her daughter to Bloomingdale's and treated her to two new dresses. Aisne chose one in dark green velvet with a low neckline and another frothy lace concoction over a deep red taffeta skirt and fitted bodice. She also bought a straw hat to shade her face from the

Italian sun.

'Is it a different sun than Boston's, then?'

Brigid grinned as her daughter blushed. Yet her heart swelled with pride to see her daughter so confident and animated.

'Your father would be so proud of you, as I am.'

Aisne blushed, and over supper, Brigid asked her daughter about any marital plans.

'Have you considered marriage on your return to Boston? You'll be well past the usual age for marriage these days. Girls snap up the most eligible young men. I know you are no longer with Arthur. Yet he adores you, and I'm sure he will wait.'

'I don't adore Arthur, Mammy. He asked me to wait for him to finish his training at the Juilliard, but I turned him down. That is why our relationship ended. I have not forgotten your advice to marry only a man you love, like Catherine loved Heathcliff in *Wuthering Heights.* However, I want to become a famous sculptor and sell my work worldwide. My commitment lies in my art, and I wish to establish a reputation without relying on a man.'

'I hope you meet a good, kind man like your father one day. When you are in love, you may change your mind.'

Aisne shook her head. 'I wish to be free, not controlled.'

With nothing more to add, Brigid retired early after their busy day. They met Aisne's chaperones for lunch the following morning with their son, a seminary friend of Dermot. Aisne chatted to them in fluent Italian and translated for Brigid.

'Friends and relatives can board the ship for an hour before she sails. The captain will blow a whistle when it is time to leave. You'll come and wave goodbye, won't you, Mammy?'

The following day, Brigid said a tearful farewell in her daughter's cabin, hugging Aisne tight because some of her did not want her daughter to leave. She feared she would lose her forever. So, with a heavy heart, she descended the ramp to the dockside, and when Aisne's tall figure appeared at the ship's stanchions, she waved to her mother. Brigid waved back among a sea of friends and relatives, who all waved with vigour as the vessel slipped her moorings and sailed from the harbour.

Brigid stood watching and contemplating the grey hairs and persistent lines on her face she had seen in the mirror that morning. Her arm ached from waving goodbye, and she was about to leave when another ship slipped her moorings to dock in the vacated place. The ship made her way forward amid much rope hauling and dock hands shouting. There was something familiar about her shape, so Brigid stayed to watch. A tug came alongside and guided her in. Brigid saw the ship's name as the vessel drew close, and her stomach lurched; it was the Apollo.

Brigid gazed at the captain on the bridge. He had a grey beard and lined face, but there was no mistaking him: John Lansdowne. But John did not get off his ship while Brigid was on the dock, and many passengers disembarked. Feeling disturbed by old memories, she walked on, trying to distance herself. But it was of no help. Her feet felt drawn back to the boat like iron to a magnet. She watched John descend the gangplank, his long legs striding down, a kit bag slung over his shoulder. Her mouth dried, but her feet moved, and Brigid almost collided with the man. She dropped her purse. Apologising, John stooped to pick it up. As he straightened, his eyes met hers. They locked, and John looked stunned.

Brigid found her voice. 'Hello John, do you remember me? My family travelled on the Apollo in 1867.'

John's deep-set blue eyes opened wider, and he swallowed. 'How could I forget your gorgeous red hair and green eyes?'

Brigid's cheeks burned as they used to do when she met Niall. The same tumultuous emotions filled her senses. She knew it would undo her if the lovebird called.

'Do you live in New York? I recall Boston was your destination.' His gaze devoured her like an animal on its prey.

'I still live in Boston but am visiting New York to see my daughter depart on a ship bound for Genoa. She is spending two years in Florence to study sculpture.'

John's eyes held Brigid's for several seconds, making her cheeks burn, and she lowered her eyes.

Then John gulped. 'Would you care for a coffee? I know a quiet, friendly place near Central Park.'

Brigid nodded and walked by his side to pick up a cab. John's male scent, tinged with salt, heightened her senses. Brigid found she couldn't look at him, for if she did, their eyes locked, so she kept them lowered, her hands in her lap, while her nerves jangled like dockside chains in a gale. It was reminiscent of Dublin, and the young girl who lived in Brigid's head felt giddy with forgotten emotions.

John helped her get out of the cab and took her arm to enter the coffee house. Seated opposite each other in an empty booth, he reached out his hand to hold Brigid's, a gesture against etiquette, stroking her fingers. Brigid knew what he was thinking.

'I am a widow.' She paused, seeking his eyes. 'Did you ever marry again?'

He shook his head while holding her hands. 'Your face stuck in my mind. It is still there.'

Ah, that strange accent that had once fascinated her did so again. 'My children have grown up. My elder son is a clergyman, and my younger one will soon be married. I saw my daughter Aisne leave for Italy this morning. I'm alone in New York.'

The waiter arrived with two coffees. 'Anything else, sir?'

Brigid felt ravenous because she had eaten only a little of her breakfast. 'A piece of chocolate cake, please?' She looked at John.

'Make it two.'

John held onto her hands, staring at them as if he had not seen them before. He seemed utterly lost for words, so Brigid broke the spell.

'You have not changed. I recognised you on the ship's bridge. But it surprised me to see you as an active captain.' The cake arrived, and although she pulled her hands from his, unmoving, she stared at her slice.

John gulped his coffee. 'This is my last trip. I handed over the Apollo to a new captain today. I plan to retire to my home in Barbados and take passage on the next available boat.'

Brigid, drawn by that unseen force, knew she had to act fast. 'Come to Boston with me instead. You'll like the city.'

John's eyes searched hers. 'Brigid, I have loved you from the first moment I saw you. You transfixed me with your beauty and courage. But it was an impossible situation; you were married.'

'I'm not married now. A gunslinger shot Finn dead on a train.'

The words flew out of her mouth before she could stop them.

John's face paled. 'What, murdered, did you say?'

He watched her face, and Brigid lowered her eyes, unable to speak as she did not wish to be interrogated.

'Oh, then let me take care of you. Marry me, please.'

Without knowing she spoke, Brigid said, 'Yes, I'll marry you,' and revealed that she had a room booked at the Park Royal for two nights. 'I planned to do some sightseeing tomorrow.' Her voice trailed off.

John continued to gaze at her, and his right hand stretched across the table to touch her face.

'Is it you, Brigid, or am I dreaming?'

'You're not dreaming.' Her thoughts drifted to the palm reader. She kissed his hand.

John's face flushed, and his voice dropped to a whisper. 'We could get a special licence and get married tomorrow.'

'We could, John.'

They drank their coffees, finished the cake, and walked to Brigid's hotel together. She collected her key from the concierge, and John joined her as she climbed the stairs to her room. He locked the door, and his fingers traced Brigid's face. She undressed and folded her clothes. Then she stood naked before him. Gulping, John discarded his clothes, too. Soon, they were lost to the world. Exquisite sensations filled Brigid's loins as he entered her, stroking her breasts and kissing every part of her body. They came together in a kaleidoscope of colours.

Brigid had forgotten what love meant. Sexual intercourse was often cerebral with Finn, but she felt lost with John, as she had been with Niall. When evening shadows stretched across the park, they surfaced. John admitted to loving no other woman except his wife.

'Despite having been with many women…' His voice trailed off.

Brigid traced his body with her fingers. 'John, I am reborn. I feel like the virgin I was on my wedding night with my first husband.' Brigid twisted her wedding ring with discomfort at such unexpected and intense feelings.

'Forget the past. We'll have a future together. Come to Barbados with me when you have settled your affairs in Boston. I promise an interesting and relaxed life there.'

Brigid smiled. 'I have many responsibilities, John, but I'll come to Barbados. Is it possible to divide the time between our homes?'

John nodded, gazing into her eyes, and they were lost in love and desire.

The next day, John sought a special licence. Brigid telegraphed Mrs Frankel via Carmel, with whom she had maintained friendly relations, to say she was staying for a few more days to enjoy the sights.

John bought her a ring with a cluster of diamonds and a matching plain gold band from a jeweller on a side street off Fifth Avenue. They went to Bloomingdale's, where Brigid bought a pale green silk dress, and John purchased a new white shirt, a blue spotted neckerchief, and some polished shoes.

The next day, he had his captain's uniform sponged and pressed by the hotel's services and a haircut and beard trim in a Turkish barber's shop. Brigid visited a ladies' hairdresser and showed how to pile her hair on top of her head in the latest fashion. The concierge organised a wedding bouquet and wished them luck.

They married two days later at eleven at the Office of the Civil Clerk and emerged in the bright spring sunshine. The cherry trees and magnolias in Central Park bloomed around the area, their aroma scenting the air. Arm in arm, the newlyweds walked back to the hotel, the joyous chirping of birds in their ears and new life springing up everywhere. On impulse, Brigid threw her wedding bouquet into the air. A passing girl caught it with a look of surprise, her mouth shaped in an 'O,' and Brigid said,

'Your turn next, sweetheart.'

At the hotel, John stopped Brigid from collecting her key.

'No, you don't, Mrs Lansdowne,' His voice was firm, and his hand guided her elbow.

A concierge attendant took them to the bridal suite. All Brigid's things were in her case, and the four-poster strewn with petals. A new pale green negligee lay in a box. A bottle of champagne stood in a bucket, with two crystal glasses beside it and caviar on blinis sitting on a plate.

Brigid called the attendant back. 'Please bring me another glass and an extra towel.'

The attendant looked at her with surprise in his eyes. 'May I ask why, Ma'am? The manager will wish to know.'

'Because I want to perform a Jewish custom meant to bring luck. A lovely Polish man was there for me when I needed a friend. He taught me the tradition.'

The attendant returned with two glasses and a towel. He

snickered.

'I thought you would want an extra glass, Ma'am. Bah. Goyim, who knows Jewish customs.'

'Thank you. Please ask a housemaid to clean up any glass later.'

The attendant smiled and held out his hand for a tip. He placed his hand on the doorknob.

'Would six o'clock be convenient for the maid, Ma'am?' He whistled as he closed the door, throwing Brigid a last sniggering glance.

With quizzical eyebrows disappearing somewhere near his hairline, John turned the key. He poured the champagne, and then they linked arms to drink. Giddy with love and champagne, they stamped on both glasses. After that, they ripped off their clothes and, limbs entwined, made passionate love. They drank champagne, giggling like a callow youth and a young maiden.

Over supper in the hotel restaurant, Brigid explained she had agreed to arrange Daniel's and Candace's wedding.

'I can't abandon that task. Candace has no mother.'

She watched John's expression. But to her surprise, he smiled.

'Of course, you must honour such an obligation, Brigid. It will be fun getting to know the family I have joined.'

How Brigid loved her new husband for those words. She found she couldn't leave his side for a second. 'I have a fine house and beautiful grounds you'll enjoy. With its coastal location, Boston provides many opportunities for fishing.

'Dermot, a priest in North Boston, is a keen fisherman, so you could fish together,' she said over breakfast.

'Dermot is a priest?' John's voice sounded guarded. 'How will he take our civil wedding?'

'He knows that I have been uninvolved with religion since I turned sixteen, only attending church for family weddings and funerals.' Brigid gazed into her husband's eyes, seeking his acceptance.

John lowered both his eyes and his voice. 'I would like a church blessing on our union. I'm not much of a church attendee, but it will please me.'

Brigid was silent for a few seconds. 'If it is a service with no fuss, I'll accept it because I love you.'

John raised his eyes and held tight to Brigid's hand. Love so fierce passed between them it could have lit the table. Brigid sent Mrs Frankel another cable the next day, saying she would return with a house guest in two days. The newlyweds then shopped for new clothes as John's kit bag held a pitiful range of ragged shirts and trousers. He traipsed with reluctance around the stores.

'I don't need many clothes,' he said, bewildered by the choices.

'You'll live a different life now. I have society friends to introduce to you, not to mention my son's prospective father-in-law. You must dress fashionably,' said Brigid.

While Brigid found much joy in taking charge of John's clothes, he took charge in bed.

'Whoa, John, I'm fifty-five, not twenty-five.' John poured champagne and tickled her.

Their train was on time in Boston, but they needed a porter's help with the extra boxes of garments. Brigid knew the porter, who had used her soup kitchen.

'Hello, Mrs Hayes. I see you have been on a shopping spree. Let me get you and your friend a cab.'

His narrowed eyes surveyed John's tall frame, and Brigid smiled. *News of John will soon be the week's gossip.* She imagined Boston's matrons clucking their teeth over Colombian coffee and a game of bridge.

In Cambridge, cherry trees and magnolias bloomed on the streets as she briefed John on the staff as they strolled around the neighbourhood.

John referred to himself as 'A lamb to the slaughter.

Controlled by women.'

Brigid introduced John to Mrs Frankel as an old friend and requested tea to refresh them after their journey. But Brigid had a tough time keeping her voice level. She wanted to burst into giggles.

Mrs Frankel raised one well-plucked eyebrow. 'Yes, Ma'am. Mr Daniel is staying overnight with Mr Garland.'

She bustled off to see Mrs Klocke, her skirts flapping more than usual. Brigid smiled; Mrs Frankel was rattled.

'Some of our servants are German. Mrs Klocke is an excellent cook, and I'll ask her to prepare a fish supper.'

Mrs Frankel reappeared with a tea tray bearing some of the cook's delicious, iced cupcakes. Brigid spotted John eyeing them, and Mrs Frankel looked him up and down.

This will be fun. Oh, to be a fly on the kitchen wall.

Mrs Frankel poured two cups. 'Sir, do you take milk or lemon?'

To Brigid's surprise, John took the lemon. Then Brigid remembered he came from the Caribbean. It surprised the housekeeper, too, who glanced at Brigid, her lips pursed.

'If Mrs Klocke has fish on ice, please ask her to cook it for supper.'

Brigid kept the staff guessing all afternoon. John wanted to explore the garden and smoke his pipe. She felt like a young bride.

'If you meet the gardener, don't tell him you are my husband. I'm enjoying the staff's curiosity. Let them gossip longer.'

Brigid discovered Mrs Frankel had taken John's possessions to the blue guest suite. She studied her new wedding ring. It gave her such joy that when she looked at her reflection in her bedroom mirror, her eyes sparkled, and her skin glowed. Brigid couldn't stop admiring her rings and wondered if Mrs Frankel had noticed. Not much missed her eagle eyes. They sat together by the parlour fire, lost in wonder as the evening shadows danced on the walls.

Mrs Frankel knocked at the door. 'Shall I draw the drapes, Ma'am?'

Brigid nodded. 'Thank you, Mrs Frankel.'

'Mrs Klocke says supper will be ready in thirty minutes. Dermot left some sea bass yesterday.' Mrs Frankel bobbed a curtsy and, lips pursed, shut the door.

The supper was superb, for Dermot had caught the delicate fish the cook had placed on ice to keep fresh. John's tone displayed satisfaction as he stated, 'It tastes perfect, like the sea.'

They took their coffee and John's brandy to the parlour sofa before the fire, and Brigid snuggled into John's arms.

'Let's go to bed,' John whispered in a husky voice, and they disappeared until the next day.

In the morning, the housekeeper, her lips pursed, brought John a hearty New England breakfast. Brigid spoke to her, putting her out of suspense,

'Mrs Frankel, I have an important message. John is more than a friend. He is my husband. We married four days ago in New York.'

Mrs Frankel's eyes almost popped from her head, and she opened and closed her mouth like a gasping fish.

'Your husband, Ma'am? Donner wetter. I wondered why your face looked so smiley for a mother whose daughter sailed for Italy.'

Later, in the privacy of her study, Brigid explained how she and John had met and watched the housekeeper's eyes fill.

'You may tell Mrs Klocke and the gardener but no one else. I want to tell Daniel.'

John was in the garden, smoking his pipe, when Daniel arrived home in his rowing clothes, face flushed and sweaty.

'I had an early morning practice and stayed at Candace's home last night, Mother.'

'You don't need to explain, Daniel, but please don't rush off; I have something important to say. Do you remember the ship's captain when we emigrated?'

Daniel thought for a few moments. 'Yes, he had a bushy beard, and he let me sit on his knee and look through his spyglass. Why?'

'I met him by chance in New York. He is now your stepfather.' Holding out her left hand, Brigid wiggled her fingers.

The cogs of Daniel's considerable brain turned as he looked his mother over.

'Have you married him? Is that what you mean, Mother?'

His eyes opened wide, and with Finn's fierceness in them, his gaze pricked Brigid's conscience.

She swallowed, nodded, and wiggled her hand again. Daniel, otherwise an excellent conversationalist, was mute with shock. He stared at the rings as if he saw a large wart. Then Daniel looked at his mother's beaming face.

'Well, I'm jiggered,' he said in Gaelic, looking every inch like his father.

John came in and shook Daniel's hand. The boy looked his stepfather in the eye.

'Take care of my mother, sir. She is the best mother in the entire world. Wait until I tell Candace. She will be stunned.' He released John's hand, 'Excuse me, sir, but I must bathe and change. I have a tutorial at eleven.'

Brigid knew her son aimed to graduate with honours, being at the top of the Dean's List. With his intense work schedule, John and Brigid usually had the house to themselves. But Brigid introduced Candace and George to John at a Monday night supper.

George took to John and wanted to hear about his seafaring life.

To Brigid's surprise, George said, 'I considered joining the US Navy when I was a boy, but my father forbade it, insisting I get a college degree. Then, I met Candace's mother and settled down. But she died giving birth to Candace.'

Tears filled his eyes. Brigid touched his hand in sympathy.

John regaled them with seafaring tales from near shipwrecks in Atlantic storms to the beauty of the Caribbean Sea and its islands. He explained how changes in navigation and sturdier ships had transformed sailings. George's eyes gleamed with fascination, and John was soon a friend.

Daniel graduated with top honours and began work in Richard's bank. Candace travelled to Europe with her aunt from Pittsburgh to visit galleries in London and Paris. Daniel gave Candace her mother's engagement ring, a delicate heart-shaped mix of sapphires and diamonds. They set the wedding date for the following May. George held a ball in honour of their engagement. Despite his craggy features from years at sea, John was a handsome man. His thick white hair and beard, trimmed to perfection, set off those features. He made women feel important; many wanted his name on their dance cards.

So, it was after midnight before Brigid got him to herself. They sat outside on the terrace, looking at the stars. John puffed on a Meerschaum pipe, bought for his recent birthday, enveloping them in smoke.

'Brigid, I can't take you from your family and friends.'

He puffed hard, muffling his deep voice, a sign of discomfort.

'You can, my darling. We can settle in Barbados during New England's winter. As one gets older, the cold can cause rheumatics.'

Brigid took his hand and held it to her lips.

He smiled. 'I couldn't live long in a cold, damp climate, although the gardener said winters are crisp and snowy here.'

John and Dermot sea-fished most of that summer until the weather turned, and John attended Sunday Mass in Dermot's church. In October, Dermot agreed to marry them again in a religious ceremony. Daniel, Candace, and George witnessed the union. Brigid basked in the warmth of family, and her heart filled with joy. John beamed with glee, and Richard gave him investment advice over a celebratory lunch.

One frosty evening, Brigid asked John about Barbados, thinking she should have asked sooner.

'Didn't I speak of it on the Apollo? I can't remember.'

Brigid recalled discussing her past was dangerous then, so it was unlikely. But she'd needed to explain her name was Hayes for the wedding licence. John had listened awed to her story.

John settled into the cushions. 'I was born in Barbados, where my father owned a large sugar cane plantation. After the Act of Emancipation in 1833 ended the diabolical slavery issue, the business became uneconomic with so many wages to pay, so Father sold most of the plantation.'

John paused, gazing into the flickering flames, his face clouded. 'My mother died when I was twelve, so my older brother James inherited the remaining plantation. He sold it and set up a merchant business in Bridgetown. Father left me a small legacy and house in Speightstown with the provision that my unmarried sister Gertrude live out her life there, too. James offered me a share of the business, but I declined. I made a living as a fisherman, using my legacy to buy a boat. A friend told me about the new British Merchant Marine, so I joined as a midshipman and met my wife in Bristol.'

Brigid kissed the top of his beloved head. 'Please come to bed, honey. Tell me the rest there.'

In the afterglow of lovemaking, John continued his tale. 'Jenny and I had two children, Annie, born not long after we arrived in Barbados, and George, three years later. Jenny succumbed to a fever while I was at sea, so I had to leave the children in my sister Gertrude's care. But she, too, perished from a fever, and I returned to find the children in James's household. I took them to England, away from tropical diseases, on my next voyage. Emma, Jenny's sister, took them in. After that, the sea became my life.'

'Honey, do you have any grandchildren?'

'I have two, Florence by George and Frederick by Annie. I have never seen Frederick. I heard the news in a letter I received last Christmas. He must be over a year old by now.'

'You must see your grandchildren. We can make a trip to England together.' Brigid kissed her husband goodnight, thinking the palm reader was correct. Hector's lack of purring showed he felt put out to find his customary place on Brigid's bed, usurped by John. After a one-sided conversation in which Hector gazed at John with narrowed eyes, they agreed to share her. Soon, Hector lay between their feet, purring. A happy cat.

CHAPTER 35: WEDDING OF THE YEAR

John decided not to go to Barbados that winter. Their diary held too many parties and too much preparation for Daniel's wedding. Instead, the family adopted the European custom of decorating a conifer tree for Christmas. John chose one growing in a remote section of the garden and cut it down. He brought it into the house in a sturdy container.

Brigid encouraged Daniel and Candace to decorate it. They hung candy canes and sweets tied with colourful red, silver, and gold bows on the boughs. They added tiny candles in holders, which they clipped to branches. The tree had a magnificence it lacked when hidden in the garden's corner.

'I shall have a tree like this in our home next Christmas.'

Candace stood back to check her handiwork. She had a rare talent for artistic decoration. Brigid invited Candace and her father to join them for two nights over the holiday. They arrived on Christmas Eve, and Dermot said he hoped to join them by midmorning on Christmas Day.

Mrs Frankel prepared a German Christmas Eve supper, which only Daniel and Brigid had experienced before. She served a mix of salmon and hake as centrepiece dishes accompanied by potato salad, sauerkraut, wiener sausages, and fried potatoes, followed by a stollen cake made of dried fruits, nuts, and spices. George supplied some excellent German wine. Mrs Frankel also made little marzipan cakes for guests with their coffee.

Afterwards, everyone stood around a piano bought by

John, who could play the instrument. But Candace took over to play popular music, including Wagner, reminding Brigid of the far-off night of the fire in Heytesbury Street. It made her sad, yet joyful, too. At least the fire hurt nobody. She wondered about Liam, and tears pricked her eyes.

At eleven-thirty, the guests and John left for Midnight Mass, which Dermot would celebrate with the bishop. John did his best to persuade Brigid to join them.

'No, John, I'll not be a hypocrite.'

'But you'll love the music and singing. Please come.' He held out his hand,

Brigid, stubborn, shook her head. 'I'll enjoy the music but also be a hypocrite.'

Visions of Father Byrne filled her mind, and she shuddered.

'Put your warmest coats and boots on, everybody. It is snowing, and it will become a blizzard later. Horses become fearful in blizzards,' Mrs Frankel said, her brow puckered.

The guests bundled in blankets in George's cab, and the horse clopped off, leaving Brigid feeling bereft on the parlour sofa in front of a coal fire. But wily, Hector slunk in, jumped on her lap, and purred. He had Brigid to himself, and she felt comforted by stroking his fur. He purred louder, a lucky cat.

Mrs Frankel asked if Brigid needed anything after the guests had left. Her disapproving look suggested she thought Brigid should have accompanied them.

'Please bank the drawing-room fire and place warming pans in each bed for the guests' return,' said Brigid.

Brigid put a purring Hector on his cushion and went to help Mrs Klocke prepare glühwein. Afterwards, she sat dozing next to the fire in the parlour. Niall's face appeared in her dream-like state.

You should have gone with them. Next year, do it for me.

Brigid blushed at this request, even though she knew it was her imagination playing tricks, and yet...

Voices filled the hall when the front door banged, and Brigid hurried to greet the returning guests. They enjoyed glühwein and stollen while chatting about the service, outfits, choir members, and other unimportant gossip. Brigid felt she might join the worshippers next year. *Have Father Joyce's prayers been answered?*

Standing before the fire, John laughed and stamped his feet in his new slippers.

'We shall go to Barbados after New Year. The cold church made my old bones ache. They are creaking, so they are.'

The Irish brogue in which he spoke had everyone laughing, and he stood, legs spread, basking in the attention.

Brigid smelt her husband basked in something else.

'John, move from the fire before your breeches catch alight.' Her voice held a note of urgency that alarmed everyone.

'Yes, I'm getting toasted,' he grinned. But as he moved away, a curl of smoke left with him.

Brigid sighed. *His best breeches, which we bought at Bloomingdale's.*

It was gone two o'clock in the morning before people retired.

A sense of unease gnawed at Brigid. *I have not received a word from Aisne for Christmas. Has a storm delayed the boat?*

She said nothing to anyone, but her heart ached at the emptiness no contact brought. Mrs Frankel handed her a letter from Aisne at breakfast on Christmas morning.

Brigid glanced at it and spotted the words: *If you get this letter, a storm has delayed our ship.*

Our ship? 'Mrs Frankel, is Aisne bringing a guest?'

'She did not say, but as she requested, I prepared the blue guest suite.'

Brigid gave Mrs Frankel a pointed gaze. 'Who is she bringing?'

'I'm not sure, Ma'am. Aisne sent me a letter and requested

that I give you the enclosed letter today if she had not arrived. Those are the only details I have.'

Brigid felt Mrs Frankel had withheld something, and her heart pounded as she attempted to discern who Aisne was bringing from Italy. The housekeeper dropped a curtsy and left.

After breakfast, when she had some privacy, Brigid re-read Aisne's letter. But it did not answer her questions.

The morning passed in friendly conversation. Daniel and Candace built a snowman and threw snowballs at each other. They laughed, their faces flushed with exertion and youthful eyes sparkling with fun. The older generation read the newspapers as they drank their morning coffee. Delicious smells arose from the kitchen: spiced apples and brandy butter.

At noon, everyone gathered to open presents. John gave Brigid a beautiful pearl necklace, and she gave him a gold tiepin with a diamond centrepiece. George picked up a large box tied with a red and green ribbon.

'Open it with care.' George gave a mocking smile.

Twenty stunning Waterford crystal glasses and a matching crystal bowl nestled inside the mountains of tissue paper.

'It's a joint wedding and Christmas present.'

Brigid, overwhelmed, kissed his cheek. 'Thank you, George. It is a thoughtful gift.'

She wondered if he had once hoped for a deeper relationship. Her cheeks burned at the thought.

John handed George a supply of his favourite tobacco and twenty Havana cigars he had shipped in by a friend in Cuba. Daniel gave Candace a glittering broach shaped like a peacock, and he received a gold watch on a chain from her. They embraced, giggling. Then, people chatted as they drank the most refined French Champagne George's cellar could provide.

A loud knock startled everyone, and Mrs Frankel hurried

upstairs to open the door. Brigid stood frozen in place, her mind unable to comprehend the sight of Aisne on the porch with a tall, slim, dark-haired young man. Aisne removed her boots and stepped into the house, her dark eyes sparkling.

Embracing her speechless mother, she said, 'Mammy, I have something to tell you.' She turned to the young man standing shoeless behind her and stretched out her hand. 'This is my husband, Viscount Vincenzo Da Lucca.'

Brigid stepped back, found the nearest chair, and sat before her legs gave way.

'You're what? Are you married?'

'Yes, Mammy, and that isn't all. I'm with a child. It will be born in April.'

Brigid gasped, speechless, and John brought her a small brandy.

'You need this, Brigid. Your face has turned ashen.'

She took the glass, and A flash of heat traversed her body as she drank the alcohol, leaving behind a light sheen of moisture on her skin.

'We should have docked yesterday, but a storm blew up and slowed our ship's passage,' Aisne said.

Brigid spoke. 'When did you marry?'

'Last October.' Aisne lowered her head.

The full import of her words hit Brigid like one of Da's fists. Then her eyes almost popped out of her head as Aisne removed her gloves. Her left hand bore the most enormous emerald Brigid had ever seen. Overwhelmed, her mind refused to take it in. Mrs Frankel, wide-eyed, took Aisne's mink fur coat as if handling something that could shatter. Candace was the first to speak with her usual no-nonsense approach to life.

'Welcome, future brother-in-law. I'm Daniel's fiancée, Candace.' She curtsied to him.

Daniel, like his mother, was in shock. He walked forward, his sea-green eyes so like Finn's, and extended a shaky hand to his brother-in-law.

'Welcome, Vincenzo.' His voice quivered, and Candace took his arm.

John was the next person to react. He stepped forward, kissed Aisne on both cheeks and shook the young man's hand.

'I'm your stepfather, and your mother is overcome with surprise.' Aisne's mouth gaped in surprise. Then, in a flash, she was in her mother's arms, and Brigid wrapped her in a cloak of love. Aisne was home for Christmas. Nothing else mattered.

Vincenzo spoke accented but fluent English. Over Christmas dinner, he explained how he had met Aisne.

'My papa is an Italian wine producer with several vineyards in Tuscany. He gave a banquet and ball last summer. I fell in love with Aisne when she walked into the ballroom with her regal, red-haired head. She had a different bearing from any other girl I knew. We danced, and I claimed the last three dances by signing my name on her card.'

He sighed and clasped his wife's hand. Aisne took over the tale.

'I, too, fell in love and wished for the night to last forever. The next day, we met at a small café in Florence to enjoy wine and each other's company. After that, we met every day. We took walks together in the evening's cooler air, and Vincenzo proposed in his father's vineyard. We intended to keep it quiet for a while, but our love was so strong that he came to my studio.' She lowered her eyes and blushed.

'In late September,' said Vincenzo, 'I told my mother. She is Italian and understands these things. Her brother is a priest, and he married us in October at the little chapel on our castle's grounds. I bought Aisne the emerald betrothal ring because she told me she is from the Emerald Isle.'

A castle, vineyards? I ran from a falling-down Irish tenant farmer's cottage with nothing but the clothes I stood up in. Brigid's body shook.

'We have leased a house and will stay there until spring so Aisne can have her baby here and attend her brother's wedding. But I'm my parent's heir and play an active role in the business, so we shall make our home in Italy.'

He paused, watching his mother-in-law's face.

'Aisne will continue her sculpture work, as she is so talented. My father is building a studio on our grounds, where the light is most beneficial. Her sculptures are awe-inspiring.'

Brigid was in awe of the divine Viscount, now her son-in-law. *I can't believe it.*

Christmas that year was the most joyous Brigid could remember. *Having my family around me gives me such happiness,* she thought.

After Christmas, Brigid returned to work in the soup kitchen. John accompanied her twice but found the building too cold. However, he said the venture was admirable, especially after visiting the tenement, which shocked him.

'I knew my steerage passengers were poor, but I never imagined such poverty in America.'

Norah congratulated Brigid on her marriage to John.

'Nobody deserves happiness more than you, Missus.'

She remained the only person who knew about O'Brien, and Norah vowed to keep the secret. It had emerged in conversation while stirring soup that the two women had grown up near one another. Norah's father had been a tenant farmer, too, and they starved in those awful winters. However, Norah was a Fenian sympathiser, a secret that bonded them.

The winter that year was brutal, with much snow, and Daniel took Vincenzo to ice hockey games. At first, Vincenzo was unsure of the rules, but Daniel guided him onto the ice, and they raced after the puck. Aisne's bump grew too big to allow her to skate, so she and Candace spent much time with their heads in ladies' magazines, studying the latest trends in Paris fashion and home decoration.

George had purchased a dilapidated brownstone house near the city's Central Park house for Candace's twenty-first birthday. It underwent a complete renovation to be completed in time for the wedding. Daniel planned to move in a month before and give the house his snagging check before Candace moved her belongings.

One of Brigid's friends recommended Vincenzo engage the best obstetrician and midwife in Boston. Throughout the birth, Brigid remained by her daughter's side as she dealt with the challenge of the baby needing to be turned. However, Aisne did not have the complications that ended Brigid's childbearing. After over fifteen hours of labour, a lusty cry exploded from the child. Alessandro Da Lucca was born on the 6th of April.

After putting his tiny lips on his mother's breast, the midwife bade Brigid take the baby.

'Let the new mother sleep, Ma'am and give him the bottle to suck if he cries.'

She gave Brigid a small bottle with a teat and some sugared water.

'I know how to feed a baby. I have done it before, nurse,' said Brigid, annoyed.

r Ma's face appeared as she held her grandson, who had Aisne's red hair, and she seemed to whisper, *the child is grand.* Brigid wondered if the menstrual change brought about such strange imaginings.

Vincenzo held his son in his hands like a china doll.

'He won't break, Cara Mio. Give him to me, please,' said Aisne.

Brigid saw she was like Mammy in her calm manner and that motherhood had given her maturity.

After the birth, Brigid arrived home happy but with an aching head. Mrs Klocke made a vinegar cloth, and John commanded her to retire for the night.

'Your considerable brain may know what to do, Brigid, but your body isn't so young and needs to rest.'

Influenza, scarlet fever, and dysentery raged through the tenements. Brigid knew, but her obsessive desire to help in her soup kitchen overcame any wish to stay healthy. Brigid had experienced many diseases and continued working regardless of the dangers to her health.

She came home one afternoon with another raging headache, and John ordered her to rest. Her limbs and head ached, and her stomach revolted at the sight of food. She lay in a fever as sweat creased her brow and leprechauns danced at the foot of the bed with John at her bedside in lucid moments, ready with the laudanum.

After four days, the fever broke, and Brigid awoke without hallucinations.

John smoothed her hair. 'We feared typhoid or even smallpox and, on advice from your friend Beatrice, sent for a doctor from the Massachusetts General Hospital. After examining you, he concluded it was influenza, also a dreadful disease. I was worried you would not survive the crisis. But you did because you are strong, my darling.' He gazed with fierce love into Brigid's eyes. 'When the doctor heard of your soup kitchen activity, he opined you had caught the infection there. He recommended complete rest when the fever broke.' John's voice caught in his throat.

Mrs Klocke made Brigid many kinds of tempting sweets, broths, and simple dishes like coddled eggs. John had been sleeping in a guest room when not beside his wife's sick bed, and the staff had relieved him in turns to ensure he got some rest. Their kindness humbled Brigid.

After a few days, Brigid got up, her legs wobbling, but her strength did not return for another two weeks, so the end of April came before she could walk the ten minutes to the cab rank. The magnolias and cherry trees made a magnificent sight of cream and white flowers, and she sat on the terrace reading, wrapped up in Aisne's Christmas present of a thick green lambswool shawl. But she had difficulty seeing the small print.

John needed spectacles to read. 'You need to see a spectacle maker when you have recovered your strength.'

Brigid raised her eyebrows.

'It is called age, my dear. It is the better alternative, which we feared had caught you.'

But Brigid knew. *Dr Death has knocked at my door before.*

An exclusive Boston dressmaker made Candace's wedding dress using a French pattern. Candace sent Brigid a note asking her to attend the last fitting. The dressmaker lived in a small, terraced house in Back Bay near Brigid's dressmaker. Candace had a tiny twenty-inch waist. Her dress in the palest ivory silk had a fashionable bustle and a low neckline. The girl consulted a hairdresser who would pile her hair on her head. 'Then my long veil will fan out behind me. What do you think, Brigid?'

'You look exquisite, my dear,' Brigid said, her eyes glistening. Her heart wished it had been at Aisne's wedding, whose bride's attendant gown the dressmaker stitched too, though Aisne did not get her figure back as fast as she wished.

'It takes at least six weeks, honey.' Her mother grinned. 'But you look slim to me.'

'Mammy, please pull these corsets as tight as you can. What do I measure now?'

The dressmaker measured her. 'Twenty-four inches. But Madame, you can't breathe.'

Aisne shook her head. 'It will be twenty-three inches in another week. She sighed. 'I'll not have more children if I lose my waist.'

'Vincenzo will have something to say about that,' said Brigid, and Aisne pulled a face,

Candace arrived at the cathedral in a glittering coach pulled by grey horses with white plumes. Daniel looked resplendent in dove-grey morning clothes, his best friend from the Latin School as his groomsman. He beamed as his bride took her place at his side. Brigid saw George's eyes mist as he gave his daughter in marriage.

As Niall's son married them, Brigid's mind wandered back to her first wedding day, her stomach fluttering with the memories.

Niall is a grandfather now. So many years have passed without him.

Tears trickled down her face as the images flashed across her mind until a hand slipped into hers. John held it tight. He understood because Brigid had told him about Niall's and Finn's Fenian associations. Nobody had ever caught Stan Case. John had made inquiries and learned that the outlaw ran a bandit operation in Mexico. But no one had seen him for several years, and rumours suggested someone shot the outlaw.

Daniel and Candace left for a European honeymoon, and Vincenzo invited them to stay at his parents' castle. They intended to visit Ireland first and left Boston bound for Dublin. Their itinerary would take them to Paris, Zurich, and Rome, and they altered their Italian leg to fit in a few days in Tuscany.

Richard gave Daniel a leave of absence for the honeymoon, and although Brigid protested, George financed the trip. Brigid thought how fortunate the newlyweds were, remembering Amy's expensive honeymoon trip to Switzerland. It had been years since Brigid had heard from Amy, and she wondered how she fared. She pondered about Angela, too, but she had lost her address.

As she waved her son and his bride off to catch their train, her eyes misted with the memories.

Alessandro's baptism took place in June. John felt honoured to become the child's godfather. George lent Vincenzo and Aisne his cottage on Cape Cod for two months to escape the summer humidity in Boston. John and Brigid joined them, and the sea air improved her health. Brigid enjoyed time with her grandson while John taught Vincenzo to sail.

'Aisne has not forgotten her skills. She is a mean sailor. She could outstrip Trinidadian authorities single-handedly,' John said with a rueful smile, having explained about his near arrest for fishing in the Trinidadian sea.

Brigid laughed. 'Can you see Vincenzo letting her do that?'

'He couldn't stop her. She is your daughter, isn't she?'

Daniel and Candace came home from their honeymoon in late July. Candace had been seasick en route from Naples, and nausea did not abate on dry land. So, Brigid, guessing, asked her why.

Candace blushed, 'I have consulted Aisne's obstetrician. He confirmed my pregnancy. The child is due next February.'

Brigid hugged her. 'Another grandchild? How wonderful.'

But she worried about what John would say. He planned to go to Barbados in November after the hurricane season and stay for several months.

John smiled on hearing the news. 'A grandchild's birth is more important than my trip to Barbados. 'He hugged his wife's shoulders. 'Do not fret over everyone and everything, Brigid. It makes you too depressed. Things will work out fine.'

Brigid, mollified by his words, consulted a physician about the depression. Except for Angela during the famine, no one had remarked on it so clearly before.

The doctor was unsurprised when he heard about her life events, age, and recent illness. 'You are still grieving, Mrs Lansdowne. Delayed grief for all your losses. They are not here to share in your joy. Give yourself time to heal.' He prescribed a bottle of St John's wort, which brought tears to Brigid's eyes with memories.

But she felt brighter when she left the physician's office. John was the grandfather in all but name and deserved the happiness it gave him. Brigid was determined he would see his own family after they visited Barbados. 'John, we'll leave for Barbados after the new child's baptism. You need to go home.'

The child, a daughter, was born on 24th February 1885 and baptised four weeks later. She favoured Candace in looks but with Daniel's eyes. She besotted Daniel and John, and when one of them held the child, she would scream at the top of her tiny lungs.

'Maeve has a fine pair of Irish lungs, which is for sure. She cries louder than her grandmother and aunt.'

Brigid caught Vincenzo's eye, and he smiled. Brigid would bet a dollar, but they had had spectacular arguments when Aisne wanted her way. She suspected Vincenzo gave in, for if ever she saw a man smitten with his wife, it was him. The thought pleased her. Aisne had found the right husband.

CHAPTER 36: BARBADOS

When they arrived in Barbados in early March, Brigid's eyes feasted on the sight of the white sand and swaying green palm trees. The Caribbean Sea was a brighter blue than any she had seen before, including the sound of Martha's Vineyard. The sun glittered on the surface, and the surf at the water's edge roiled with a white splash. According to John, sailors must avoid reefs at sea and be cautious of treacherous undercurrents along the north coast. 'But I'll take you to see it one day because it is beautiful. Miles of white sand and rolling waves.'

After disembarking and collecting their luggage, a dusky servant greeted them and escorted them to James's home. The house was a sprawling two-story colonial design with a wraparound porch, shutters at the windows, and a garden with a profusion of colourful subtropical plants like oleanders and bougainvillaea. Birds such as finches, warblers, and hummingbirds fluttered between the bushes and trees.

James made profuse introductions. Brigid thought he looked overfed and full of self-importance. In a blustering manner, he said, 'I had a delivery of Indian tea this week, so I have instructed the cook to prepare refreshments. My servant will bring them to the garden shelter I had constructed to protect visitors from the fierce sun and occasional rainstorms.'

He likes to boast, thought Brigid, watching him perform like a peacock.

The shelter was a wooden structure with open sides and a shingled roof. As Brigid stared at it, James said, 'Rainstorms lasting around thirty minutes happen most days, but we stay dry under this canopy until the storm passes. It shades fair-skinned ladies from the sun, protecting their skin from turning red. I have parasols should you wish to tour my grounds.' James leered at Brigid as Seamus had done, and she shuddered.

A fair-skinned housemaid brought the tea on a silver tray. 'Your tea, sir.' The young woman had a Cork accent.

The girl's auburn hair caught Brigid's attention, but her demeanour intrigued her as she observed her movements.

'Will there be anything else, sir?' Her eyes were penetrating in their intensity.

James did not reply; he waved his hand. The woman bobbed a respectful curtsy and withdrew.

The tea was delicious. James had gone to some trouble to make them welcome, and Brigid complimented him.

'I make a fine living, and we enjoy a comfortable lifestyle, don't we, Catherine?'

Catherine, a woman younger than Brigid, lowered her eyes and whispered, 'Yes, James,' while blushing. Her skin was alabaster white, and her shoulder blades protruded above her muslin dress. Brigid could count the bones in her spine.

James must have seen Brigid's eyes widen. 'Please forgive my wife. She has been ill with malaria.'

But Brigid thought it looked more than sickness, recalling the stories of Seamus's wife.

'Because of the prolonged closure of his house, John only has a cook and gardener as servants. I have asked Erin to be your maidservant. Since you are both Irish, I expect you'll have much in common.' James smirked at Brigid.

Brigid bristled at the implied slur, and a negative opinion of James's character took shape. But she forgot the remark as the sun dropped low in the sky, becoming a fiery red glow brighter than any Brigid had seen. It was a magical sight, and Brigid loved the island. They left for John's house in Speightstown the following morning. Busy with little fishing crafts, the sea was like a millpond beyond the port's shore.

'All going out to their lobster pots.' John's eyes shone with delight.

A lovely, dark-skinned lady welcomed them. 'Hello Wilhelmina,' said John, 'It is wonderful to see you again. Ambrose has done a superb job of keeping the garden tidy. Let me introduce my wife, Brigid.'

Wilhelmina bobbed a curtsy, eyes lowered. 'Yes, Massa. The joy of making her acquaintance has lifted our spirits.'

She curtsied, and her dark eyes sparkled. Brigid's face brightened as she greeted the lovely buxom Wilhelmina. John, gazing out to sea, turned to his wife.

'Ambrose and Wilhelmina are my caretakers. Their home is that pink and blue chattel house at the side of my garden. Despite their advancing age, they have been part of the family since my father's era, and I have a strong affection for them.'

Wilhelmina said, 'Massa John, I sent Ambrose to catch fish for your supper. Marlin tastes good this season.' She faced Brigid, bobbed another curtsy, and said, 'Missus, come in. I'll show the house to you.'

She lifted her ample skirts and led up wooden steps to a beautiful interior with open shutters that let in a light but refreshing sea breeze. The gossamer curtains billowed, and Wilhelmina hurried to tie them in the middle with some blue ribbon, so they hung still. Brigid liked them billowing but thought it wise not to say so.

John's bedroom was smaller than Brigid's in Boston. Yet, it held a four-poster bed covered with a white crocheted counterpane strewn with colourful cushions. Two colourful rag rugs on the floor brought back memories of Brigid's childhood. Seascapes and other sea-related artefacts hung on the whitewashed walls, including shells in intricate patterns. Brigid considered it to be exquisite. She counted three more bedrooms but found no bathroom and wondered if sea bathing sufficed for John. Brigid would ask Wilhelmina if she could locate a tin bath. She noticed the living room, dining room, and kitchen interconnected downstairs.

The kitchen held a sink with a pump, cupboards, shelving, and a table. Brigid also spotted a small range. The ocean's salty aroma covered everything, and Brigid soaked it into her core. She loved the house's simplicity and proximity to the sea.

'I cook much food outside, Missus,' said Wilhelmina, pointing to a large, well-used brazier.

That afternoon, Erin arrived. 'She will sleep in one of the smaller bedrooms during their stay,' John said. 'Erin is an indentured servant, and I believe she has two or three more years to serve until she completes her allotted ten.'

While his tone was non-committal, Brigid found the notion of servitude an unpleasant reminder of her time with Seamus, and a chill crept over her body. She vowed to treat Erin as a valued helpmate, not an indentured servant.

I must exercise caution until I understand the relationship between landowners and their servants on the island.

John was up early the following day, waking Brigid as he left the room.

'I'm off to catch fish for our supper,' he said, his face beaming like the early morning sun. 'I hope I don't get caught too far out and chased by fishers from Trinidad.'

'That joke is wearing thin. You used it about Aisne, too.'

Brigid grinned at her husband. She rose and threw a shawl over her bare shoulders to watch John sail a small fishing boat out to sea. The cloudless day was sunny, and the sun glistened on the waves, reminding Brigid of Dún Laoghaire. She thought of Dermot and his love of fishing. *He will be in his element here if he visits.*

Brigid's eyes misted. But a gentle knock at the bedroom door disturbed her reverie. Brigid opened it, and Erin stood there with a cup of tea.

'Thank you. Your thoughtfulness is kind.'

The girl blushed and curtsied after she gave the cup to Brigid and, turning to close the bedroom door, said, in Gaelic,

'Wilhelmina will have some breakfast ready for you in

thirty minutes. Do you need my help to dress, Ma'am?'

Brigid did not need help to dress, but she did to bathe.

'I would like to have a bath tomorrow. Can you show me how I get one, please?'

'I'll prepare one for you.' Erin curtsied and closed the door.

Breakfast was composed of cornmeal porridge with bananas and coconut mixed with it, accompanied by watermelon and Bajan bakes, a kind of cornbread. Wilhelmina also made Brigid's favourite coffee, which she had brought from Boston. She ate at a small table under the porch, watching the dancing waves and hearing the cries of seabirds. Brigid's heart was at peace in the delightful setting.

That afternoon, wearing loose clothing and a wide-brimmed hat, she took a stroll along the beach with John. Brigid asked him about Erin and the other Caribbean-Irish people.

'What happens to them when their indentured time is complete?'

'Many men buy a small acreage and grow their sugar cane. The kilns are not exclusive; a community owns some. The women marry and have children, or they stay as paid servants. Some go to other islands; Montserrat is a favourite. They call it Ireland in the Caribbean. Some go to Nevis, St Kitts, or Jamaica.'

'What do you know about Erin?' Brigid said in a conversational tone.

'I know little. The girl arrived on a boat from Dublin bound for New York, having run from a convent in Ireland when she was sixteen. Rogue sailors hope to make a few extra dollars if they tell immigrants they earn high wages in the Caribbean. Immigrants then persuade a ship's Captain to divert. However, the sailors don't tell them about their potential indentured status. James bought Erin in a dock sale. I understand she worked in a mill in Ireland and is about twenty-seven years old.'

'Where did she learn to call ladies, Ma'am?'

'Knowing James, he taught her because he entertains rich American merchants from time to time.'

'Something about her disturbs me. It's her eyes. They remind me of someone.'

As she spoke, a vision of Finn appeared. Brigid knew Erin's eyes matched his, with the same sea-green colour. They showed the same penetrating, mesmerising stare when assessing someone, too. Erin could be Finn's daughter, and although Brigid had no proof, her heartbeat faster and her gut tightened.

Finn had said something about his children after he had the mumps. *What was it?* Brigid had a flicker of remembrance. *I have enough children already.*

That was it. *Is the girl his child?* Brigid's mouth dried as she contemplated the possibility. *If my gut instinct is correct, the girl is my putative stepdaughter.*

Brigid said nothing to anyone but decided she would discern the facts. *Erin deserves to know her family. I'm sure Daniel is her half-brother. The likeness is unmistakable.*

Brigid vowed to question the girl with care if the opportunity arose. Like herself and Cecilia, Finn could have bewitched Erin's mother. But Brigid's blood boiled as she thought about the girl's abandonment into the care of nuns. Brigid knew how the clergy treated girls in Ireland – as if they had sinned, not their parents. So, she felt righteous anger towards Finn for abandoning the girl's mother. However, it was typical of his behaviour in those far-off days. The opportunity to question Erin came when she prepared Brigid's bath one day.

'Please soap my back. I get so salty in this climate,' said Brigid.

Erin bobbed a curtsy, blushing, 'Yes, if you wish.'

'I surmise you are from Cork by your accent. Is that correct?'

'I'm unsure, Ma'am.' Someone rumoured my mother to be

from Cork.'

'What happened to your parents? Did they die on the passage here?'

'I never knew my father, and my mother died in the poor house in Skibbereen. I can't recall her features. Some man took me to a convent where the nuns took me. That is all I know.'

Brigid looked up and saw Erin's pupils widen, and tears glisten on her lashes.

'How did the nuns treat you? Did they teach you to read and write?'

Erin's composure faltered. 'The nuns were cruel, so they were. We worked hard for no wages, scrubbing and cleaning twelve hours daily with little food. They taught us to read and write, and we had to recite the catechism for the priest. If we got a word wrong, we got beaten and banished to the dormitory without food. When I was fifteen, I ran away, so I did. The Reverend Mother had some money that I stole while cleaning her office. I hid it in my lodgings while I worked in a mill and used it to pay for my passage to the Americas. I reckoned she owed me that money and more for all my unpaid work.'

'You did?' Brigid smiled at the coincidence. 'Was the man your father?'

'I don't know, Ma'am. He had wild black hair and visited me in the convent once or twice a year. We sat in Mother Superior's room with another nun watching us. He asked if I was well and how my schooling had progressed. I told him it had ceased when I was twelve. He disappeared when I was about thirteen, and I never saw him again.'

Brigid deliberated on her choice of words. 'Can you remember the man's name?'

Erin's eyes looked guarded. 'I know my mother went by the name Roche. Her first name was Maura or Maureen.'

Horrified at the potential name match with Da's woman friend, Brigid asked the girl to wash her hair. When Erin rubbed the hair dry, Brigid asked,

'Does the name Finnbar Hayes mean anything to you?'

Erin's eyes became guarded when Brigid met her gaze.

'While lighting the fire for the man's last visit, I spotted a receipt on Mother Superior's desk. I remember thinking it must be the man's because Mother Superior addressed him as Mr Hayes when she gave it to him.'

Brigid gasped inwardly. 'Erin, please pass me the other towel; I have some news for you.'

Erin's sea-green eyes turned wild, as if she wanted to escape a beast of prey.

Brigid wrapped herself in the towel and said, 'Don't be fearful. I believe I know who your father was.'

'What are you trying to tell me?' Erin's face turned ashen.

'Erin, I married Finnbar Hayes, and we were blessed with a son, Daniel, who looks like his father. You have Finn's eyes and his penetrating gaze. You even walk like him, too, more so than my son.' Finn's face appeared in Brigid's mind.

'Then...' Erin couldn't speak.

'I'm sure Finnbar Hayes was your father. If so, I'm your stepmother.'

Brigid caught the girl as she fainted. She dragged Erin up onto the bed and applied some smelling salts.

After a few seconds, the girl's eyes opened, unfocused. 'Where am I?' She sat up but quickly sunk back to the pillow.

Brigid poured a glass of water from the carafe beside the bed and held the girl's head as she drank. Some colour returned to her cheeks, but her eyes remained wild.

'You know my father?'

'Yes, honey. I think your father was my second husband. He came from Waterford.' Brigid recalled the occasions he disappeared to visit his sister, and her mind raced with possibilities.

Did he go to Skibbereen, see Erin, and visit his sister? Was that his cover?

Erin twisted her hands together. 'Your second husband. Was he Irish?'

'Yes, and we had a son. You both resemble Finn, so you do.'

Irish colloquial speech slipped out amongst the Boston drawl John teased her about.

'Are you saying I have a brother?' Erin's soft voice betrayed disbelief.

'A half-brother, yes. You have a sister-in-law, Candace, and a baby niece. You have a stepbrother and a stepsister, too.'

Erin's eyelids blinked, her eyes staring at Brigid with Finn's unmistakable gaze.

'I have a family?' Her tone was filled with incredulous disbelief. 'Where is my brother?'

'Daniel and his family live in Boston, America, where I have my home.'

Sweat broke out on Erin's brow as she struggled to take in this news. 'Are you sure?'

Erin swung her long legs over the bed, a gesture so reminiscent of Finn that Brigid gasped.

Swallowing, she said, 'Honey, it is impossible to prove. But I do believe I'm your stepmother. I want you to come to my home in Boston with John and me.' Brigid choked on her own words.

Erin's eyes grew wild again. 'But, Mister James, he won't let me leave. I'm an indentured servant. I have two years left to serve.'

Brigid had recovered her composure. 'Leave James to me. We'll say nothing of this to anyone except John. You must continue to be my maidservant until I have spoken with my brother-in-law.'

Brigid hugged her and thought conversing with James would be fun.

I'll outwit him because I dislike the man.

Brigid's pulse rose again at the thought of Finn abandoning his daughter, and while Erin's eyes still looked in turmoil, she stood erect and tall, just like Finn.

'None of my children are servants. You are my daughter now, and once I have spoken to James, the servant's role will cease.'

Brigid considered paying off the man, expecting it to be costly, as she doubted he would negotiate.

'Perform your duties here in the meantime, honey.'

Once Erin recovered her composure and continued her duties, Brigid saw more of Finn in her. The girl had his mannerisms and smile. She told John about her conversation with Erin over the fresh marlin supper, which he caught that day.

'We must release her from servitude,' he stroked his beard. 'James is a tough person to manage. Some of his business dealings are unscrupulous.'

Brigid did not doubt him. 'Catherine looks like she fears him.'

'She does. I believe James has beaten her in the past and put her down in public. She was a lovely girl once, but James destroyed her spirit. The story about malaria isn't true. He uses it to cover himself.'

'John, I'll have to pay him off. How much money will he want?'

'I don't know, but I'll make discreet inquiries. A friend had another woman released from indentured servitude so they could marry.'

Pale, Erin came to clear their plates and serve fresh pineapple and cream from the Jersey cow "Bougie," John owned. He smiled at her.

'I have heard your story, Erin, and I'm sorry for any mistreatment you may have endured at the hand of my brother. However, now I am your stepfather, so please join us on the front porch. I'll ask Wilhelmina to serve us all coffee.'

Erin's face crumpled, and she wept. Brigid put her arms around her, and the girl cried against her shoulder, heaving great sobs. The noise brought Wilhelmina to the door, her face creased with concern. Brigid smiled and asked her to bring out coffee for three. She suspected Wilhelmina had heard their conversation but knew she would be discrete.

The next day, John visited his friend, Percy Arbuthnot.

'Percy paid ten pounds for each outstanding year. His wife had known Erin and confided she knew James was not averse to whipping his servants and raping them.'

Brigid had little doubt that he whipped Catherine. *Had he raped her too?* It did not bear thinking about

John said, 'We'll see James's tomorrow. The sooner Erin is free, the better, and you'll tell him you want her as your maidservant rather than discuss her background. But I'll clarify that she is to leave his service.'

Brigid thought this an excellent plan. *It will avoid the unpleasant outcome of James's curiosity about my background.*

She knew James would start digging, given half a chance, and she would not give him that opportunity.

John, Brigid, and Erin left for Bridgetown the following day. After a heated exchange of words between the brothers, John agreed to pay thirty US dollars. Brigid wrote a check for that amount and requested a receipt. She also demanded a letter releasing Erin into their keeping.

James obliged when John threatened to expose his tasteless behaviour to valued friends. 'Why do you think I took my children to England, you evil man? They would have had a dreadful childhood with you. Annie would...' John couldn't finish his words, a look of hatred in his blazing eyes.

After collecting her belongings, they took Erin back to Speightstown, where Wilhelmina greeted her with a hug.

'James, he is a nasty man. He beats his servants and wife. You are a clever chile. I remember you singing when you came to Massa James's house. Now, Massa John is a kind man. He will take care of you.' Wilhelmina wiped her eyes on a handkerchief.

Brigid asked Erin to confirm whether James had whipped her.

She caught a Finn-like guarded look as Erin nodded, and Brigid feared there was more. 'Did he do anything else to you?'

Erin's cheeks turned red. 'Yes ... um...what do husbands do with their wives?' Her voice broke.

'Oh my God, you poor girl.' Brigid experienced a sudden epiphany, and it horrified her. 'When did he beat you?'

'Sometimes, before sex, he beat me. It pleased him. I had a child, but she vanished. I don't know what happened to her after James took her from me. I never saw her again. Did she die? I wanted to call her Frances.' Erin's eyes glistened. 'James has other children. He keeps an African woman in a shack on the island. I heard he fathered a son with her.' Erin broke down, weeping.

What a brute, Brigid thought, holding Erin's sob-wracked body.

'No man will hurt you again, Erin; you have my word.' She would protect the girl with her own life. Under John and Brigid's care, Erin flourished. She took Brigid to a local field to see sugar cane cut and boiled. Brigid found the procedure fascinating, just as John's ancestor had described.

Erin had a friend from the same immigration boat whose master treated her kindly.

'She works near here. I would like you to meet her.'

The girl, who had fiery red hair and striking green eyes, said she came from Kilkenny, where she had heard about Saor-Éire.

'So, you belonged to the movement?' she said, her face animated.

'Yes, I got involved through my first husband.' A memory of Sweeney surfaced. 'But it happened many years ago.'

They chatted about fishing next. Brigid shared information about Finn's murder with Erin's friend when Erin was out of earshot visiting the privy.

'My sister wrote about it in a letter. Upon hearing, she stated that Ronan O'Brien was furious and ordered men to go after the gunslinger for the money.' The girl paused, chewing her thumbnail. 'My sister wrote in another letter that someone killed Case in a shoot-out in Texas near the Mexican border. I think the man who killed him was an ex-Confederate army officer. The bandit escaping and O'Brien not finding his money became the top gossip of Kilkenny.'

Brigid had a sudden insight. Then she heard Erin's footsteps in the distance.

'Please keep what you know about O'Brien to yourself; don't tell Erin. To save her pain, I have not told Erin the truth about how her father died.'

The girl nodded, and her eyes flicked sideways. The three women continued their conversation about life in the Caribbean. The girls informed Brigid about the island's illnesses and the small hospital in the north. Although they had not visited, the girls knew the hospital treated people with malaria and yellow fever.

'They call the village nearby "Isolation," and the inhabitants are dark-skinned people from Africa. The women are excellent nurses, and the men clean the hospital and move patients between the wards,' said Erin. 'I wanted to help, but James said I would get dreadful sick. He ordered me to stay as far away as possible.'

Brigid thought, *to save his skin, the fecker*. Instead, she said, 'I would like to visit.'

Erin, her pupils wide, said, 'Don't go, Ma'am, please.'

So, Brigid told both girls about her mother, brothers, and Niall. 'Disease does not scare me. I have survived so far.'

'Who were your grandparents?' said Erin's friend.

'I don't know. They died before I was born.

The girl laughed. 'I bet that's a fishy story waiting to be told.'

Brigid ventured to Isolation alone, wearing gloves and a scarf around her face. Despite the apparent disease cases, the staff impressed her with the standard of care, but none of the patients were servants. *Who cares for them when they get sick?* Wondered Brigid.

While Brigid and John took a stroll along the beach after supper, the vibrant sun painted the horizon with fiery red and gold hues. Brigid opined she could organise the island's wealthy ladies to generate funds for the hospital—a philanthropic undertaking.

'Whom should I speak with about fundraising?' Brigid said they lay in bed, basking in lovemaking's afterglow.

'James will be a start. I hear he wants to run for office in the island's government. He may think that is a worthwhile cause to promote.'

Brigid grimaced. 'Maybe Catherine will be interested. It will give her a focus outside Bridgetown. I'll visit tomorrow.'

Brigid announced her plans to Catherine over tea in James's absence. He was out supervising the unloading of cargo unloading. Colour entered Catherine's cheeks as she said,

'James will like anything that helps him with his political ambitions, so I'm certain he will be interested.'

In Speightstown, Brigid heard of a woman who made hot spicy sauce and considered selling it for fundraising.

'She lives somewhere in the rainforest, but I'm unfamiliar with her name,' said Brigid's informant.

Wilhelmina knew her. 'She lives deep in the rainforest. She is Ambrose's cousin.'

Ambrose took Brigid to see his cousin, who agreed to Brigid's proposition, provided they paid her a fair price. The woman's initial project involved making ten bottles. As Brigid hoped, the sauce sale to affluent island ladies soon made a profit.

Then James muscled in. He wanted to export them to neighbouring islands. 'It may advance my political ambitions,' he said in his self-important voice.

'Catherine can help you. I hope to be appointed Governor one day.'

Away from James, Catherine's health improved, and Brigid encouraged her to eat luncheon. Soon, Catherine's hazel eyes had lost their haunted look, and her flesh filled out. Curious, Brigid asked her how she met James.

Catherine said, 'James wanted my dowry, not me. I was eighteen when I married him. But my parents are dead, and I have lost touch with my brother and sister. James and I lost our one-year-old son to yellow fever. I couldn't bear to lose another child, so I locked the bedroom door and refused to let James come near me.

We have lived like that for eighteen years. I know James has liaisons with maidservants and women of colour. He keeps one in a chattel house, and I have heard rumours of a love child somewhere on the island.'

She looked Brigid in the eye. 'I was an innocent bride, but I soon learned what sex meant to James. I felt degraded.'

She buried her head in her hands and wept, and Brigid held her while she cried. Brigid now knew why John removed his children and sent them to England.

The weeks passed by at the gentle pace that was the island's hallmark. Three months into their stay on the island. John said, 'We must depart for Boston soon to evade the hurricane season,'

'How can I leave my work now? Catherine isn't ready for the responsibility.'

Brigid did not have the confidence to entrust her project to Catherine. She reconsidered when she saw her sister-in-law again. A confident woman now inhabited the body of the inhibited, sad woman Brigid had first met. It was a relief to her frazzled nerves.

Catherine smiled when Brigid commented on her improved health.

'I entertain ladies in my home, and James has ceased belittling me.'

'Ah, he needs your support for political office.'

James joined them, easing himself into a chair and wearing a brooding look. He had a careworn appearance, and Brigid wondered why.

Erin's absence has left a void. I suspect the lack of attention has affected his mind. I expect he will purchase a replacement from the next boat.

Brigid discussed the project with John, who devised a plan for running it in Brigid's absence.

'Let's designate the Speightstown house as the fundraising headquarters. I'll inform James there must be someone living here to take care of the business. Catherine can do that. He may like not having her in his house so he can dally with whom he chooses.'

When she heard James had agreed, Catherine's smile was as wide as Barbados's Turtle Bay.

'James wants you to entertain ladies at his political dinners and the wives of his associates for tea parties, but otherwise, you can live here. I have instructed Ambrose and Wilhelmina to look after you.'

Catherine's voice trembled as she looked at John and Brigid with gratitude.

'I love you like a sister, Brigid. You have saved me from certain death, for I was withering.'

Brigid did not reply, for she knew it was true, but gave Catherine a warm hug.

Arthur Cunliffe, a friend of John's from childhood, was a wealthy man whose wife had died of malaria in the Isolation hospital a few years earlier. He told Brigid he knew all about James's servant girls and knew where a love child would be so that he would make discrete enquiries. His hazel eyes lit up when Brigid told him Catherine would move.

'Catherine will write to me if you get any news. She knows about James's indiscretions.'

The Lansdownes and Erin sailed on the steamship

Bridgetown for New York in early September. It was close to the hurricane season, but they couldn't get an earlier passage with two empty cabins. Luckily, they did not encounter a hurricane, though they encountered a storm, and Brigid and Erin felt seasick. When they reached New York, the summer had finished, and the humidity-driving clouds had vanished to be replaced by clear blue skies. The leaves had changed to their autumn rusty colours, with maple trees dominating the vistas. Brigid felt a warm glow suffuse her body upon returning home.

'How pleasing to see you look so healthy, Mrs Lansdowne. I declare you have freckles on your nose,' Mrs Frankel said.

Then, knowing she had overstepped the mark, she added,

'My apologies, Ma'am, but you look so well I couldn't stop the words from escaping.'

'Don't worry; we are family here. It is gratifying to hear you think my features look healthy, even with freckles.'

Brigid introduced Erin as her stepdaughter.

Mrs Frankel said. 'What a pleasant surprise to learn you have a daughter, Herr John. Her room is ready.'

She turned to Brigid and said, 'I'll fetch the tea and cupcakes, Ma'am.'

Mrs Frankel curtsied and bustled off to the kitchen. Brigid felt the woman's skirts could talk and wondered if the housekeeper would guess Erin's true parentage.

Erin's face showed bewilderment in her wide, staring eyes and pale cheeks as she looked around, and her new home smelled of beeswax polish. The mirrors sparkled, and the tables shone, dust-free. Lilies adorned the central table in Brigid's best Waterford crystal vase in the drawing room. *Oh, how I'll enjoy soaking in my indoor bathtub tonight.* Brigid hoped Mrs Frankel had put out her favourite lavender bath crystals.

Brigid later relaxed in the drawing room, the drapes and French doors open to the afternoon breeze. The air felt fresh, not salty, and the bushy freesia planters drooped with flame-coloured flowers. The lawns looked neat, trimmed by the new lawnmower, with no weeds in the gravel pathways. The gardener had kept her flower beds weed-free, petunias, zinnias, and begonias all blooming. Brigid's heart felt light.

Tea was delicious, not spicy Bajan food, but the cook's iced cupcakes and the Darjeeling tea she knew Brigid favoured. She savoured every bite of the cake. When they had finished, Brigid suggested John smoke his pipe in the garden while she took Erin to her room.

The opulence overwhelmed Erin, for Brigid's home was grander than James's. Brigid gave her Aisne's former room. Erin sat on the bed, her eyes almost popping from her head.

'Please, is this my sleeping room?'

She gazed, awed around at Aisne's artwork covering the walls, her early sculptured figurines on the dresser, and her needlepoint cushions on the bed.

'I can't sleep in such a fine room.'

'Yes, you can, honey. It was my daughter's room, but she is married and lives in Italy, and now it is yours. You may redecorate it.' Brigid smiled at her wide-eyed wonderment.

'We have indoor bathrooms here, not tin tubs. Yours is across the hall. I'll show you how to use it later. Oh, and don't call me Ma'am. Call me Brigid, please.'

Brigid left Erin to unpack. Erin had so few garments that a shopping spree lay ahead to fit her with an entire wardrobe, and Brigid hoped Erin would enjoy it.

She found Mrs Frankel had drawn her bath. Lavender-perfumed bath salts stood on the windowsill, and the housekeeper had dropped some into the water, as Brigid liked. She luxuriated for half an hour, washing the grime and salt from her body. She spotted Mrs Frankel had left a bottle of Guinness for her use. Brigid poured it over her hair, touched by how well the woman understood her needs.

An hour later, refreshed, her damp hair tied back with a ribbon, Brigid sifted through the mail, piled high in her absence. Many items were letters of introduction or advertising material, so she selected those that looked personal to read first. *A secretary would be helpful. I wonder if Erin might enjoy the role.*

The thickest letter was from Aisne, with the news she was expecting again in the spring. Even though Aisne complained about her waist size and stodgy spaghetti, Brigid was ecstatic. Aisne had included more sketches of her son and wrote she had sent a sculpture. Brigid found the box, and within, nestling among cotton balls, was an exquisite statuette, capturing Alessandro's smile. Brigid put it on her desk, glowing with a grandmother's pride.

The next letter puzzled her; it bore a mark from England and looked official.

With trepidation, she slit the manilla envelope with Finn's silver letter opener. She took out a single sheet of headed notepaper written in an educated hand. Brigid noted the heading was embossed and the paper manila thick.

Who had written to me from England? Brigid turned the paper over, pushing her spectacles up her nose.

Spendlove and Bell, Solicitors

Deanebourne

July 10th, 1885

Dear Mrs Lansdowne,

For the past ten years, we have sought the whereabouts of Miss Brigid Power from Ballyconstór in County Wicklow, Ireland, who was born on 16th April 1829. Our research confirmed the incumbent Catholic priest baptised an infant named Brigid Power in April 1829. Further enquiries determined that Miss.

Power emigrated to America in 1867 under the name of Mrs Brigid McGrath. Our enquiries lead us to conclude that the lady has been married three times. As our business with the former Miss Power is to her considerable advantage, we request verification before proceeding further.

Your obedient servant,

Thomas E. Spendlove, LLB

Brigid, puzzled by the location, called. John to her side, handing him the letter. 'Is it a hoax? What does this Spendlove person mean by: "*To Miss Power's considerable advantage*"?'

'It suggests they are dealing with an inheritance. Do you know anyone in that town?'

Brigid shook her head.

'I'll write to Jenny's sister. She will find out if the firm is genuine,'

John re-read the letter. 'Do you have a birth or baptismal certificate?'

'Ireland did not record births in those days. But I have a baptismal certificate.'

Brigid opened the lowest drawer of her desk, took out a file yellowed with age, and pulled out the contents. The certificate, also yellowed with age, was among the papers. While examining it, Brigid recalled how she had changed the name. She handed John the certificate, her head spinning.

John perused it, too. 'It looks like someone changed the name. Are you sure it is yours?'

Brigid blushed. 'When I ran from Seamus, I took it from the pile in Da's press. I did not read it until I needed it for my wedding to Niall. It was easy to fix the error, though I wondered why it happened.'

'Hmm ... Can you recall what name you changed?'

'Pore or something. Letters being alike made it easy to change. How could you tell?'

'When you are a ship's captain, you must keep a proper manifest and records of your crew. I became skilful at spotting changes in identification documents. Escaped convicts will alter documents to sign on as hands.' John studied it further. 'It meets most needs, but not a solicitor. Do you have any idea why it had the wrong name?'

'I suspected the priest was drunk. Da couldn't read, so he would not spot the error. The church must have an accurate record.'

'If Emma confirms they are a genuine firm. In that case, we'll write to Mr Spendlove saying you have lost your baptismal certificate and ask how he wishes to proceed. You must be the heiress to a vast fortune.' John's eyes twinkled, and he stroked his beard.

'Nonsense, John. Here, take my seat and write to Emma.'

Brigid retired to the parlour, sitting in Finn's old leather armchair, thinking about her childhood. Then, as the shadows lengthened and with a lurch of her stomach, she remembered Erin. She hurried to her room, where Brigid found her fast asleep. Brigid touched her shoulder, and the girl awoke, rubbing her eyes and looking confused. Brigid led her to the bathroom, filled the tub, and left Erin to bathe.

She rifled through dresses Aisne had left behind, found one that should fit, and left it on the bed. When Erin came downstairs, the wild look had gone. She gazed around the house with wide-eyed wonder. 'I thought James's house impressive, but yours is overwhelming. Where do your servants live?'

'They have rooms at the top of this house. I'll take you on a tour tomorrow. But let us go outside before supper. Boston is a city beside the sea, and we can buy fresh fish daily. Mrs Klocke will prepare sea bass tonight. Come, my dear, let me show you the fishpond before the light fades.'

Brigid took her arm, and they strolled across the patio to the lawned area with the pond. Erin's smile grew wide as she watched the carp swim, lighting up her face.

'I have never seen that variety of fish before,' she said as they glided and turned in the water, hiding under the lily leaves.

'They are beautiful.' Erin's animated face transformed her, and Brigid thought her striking.

Mrs Klocke served the sea bass, accompanied by sweet potatoes and a mixture of vegetables from the kitchen garden. She served ice cream for dessert. Brigid watched Erin's expression as the woman ate, and her wide-eyed delight reminded Brigid of her first taste of the confection.

'Did you enjoy the ice cream?'

'Oh yes, I did. How do you keep it so cold?'

'I'll show you tomorrow.' Brigid expected her to be interested in the icehouse. She doubted Erin had ever seen one.

After supper, John disappeared outside to smoke his pipe. Erin and Brigid sat in the parlour to drink coffee. 'The room adjoining this parlour was once my children's playroom. Then, it became my daughter Aisne's art studio. Aisne's art is unconventional. Look.'

Erin gazed at the room, her forehead furrowed by the flamboyant colour-filled artwork on the walls.

'Aisne will want to meet you when she returns to Boston. She can explain her work. It is called Impressionism. But we can remodel the room to your taste, and it will become your private space.'

Erin nodded and lowered her eyes. Brigid saw a tear trickle down her cheek.

'You are too kind, Ma'am, er Brigid,' she said, her voice quivering.

They returned to the parlour, where Brigid picked up her most recent photograph of Finn from among those displayed on a side table.

'Is this the man who visited you?'

Erin stared at the photo with a frown, her brow creasing and her lips pursed.

'Yes, it looks like him, though he was less well-groomed.' Erin hesitated, turning the photo's silver frame in her hands. 'So, this man was my father?'

She choked on the words, awe glistening on her lashes.

'Yes, honey. You should have the same name as your brother, "Hayes." My other children's last name is McGrath. Their father was my first husband. Your father died on a long train journey when his heart gave out.'

Brigid had forgotten how to lie and thought Erin would see through her deception if she spoke more about Finn's death. Still, she felt lies would be less disturbing than learning the truth. The woman had suffered enough instances of death and degradation. Brigid would introduce her to society as a member of Finn's extended family.

Brigid suddenly had a flash of insight about James and his sexual proclivities. *Erin's sexual health will need examination,* she thought.

Brigid engaged an eminent gynaecologist from Massachusetts General Hospital. After an intimate examination, the doctor pronounced Erin healthy.

However, Erin looked unhappy afterwards. 'Being examined by a man is degrading,' she said, her eyes glistening. 'It reminded me of...' Erin left the words unsaid.

Brigid understood and thought the girl needed time to adjust to her new life before she entered society. *But I'll introduce her to Daniel.*

Brigid sent a note inviting her daughter-in-law to tea with Maeve, saying they had a house guest.

When Candace arrived, she gazed at Erin's features and stopped in her tracks. Her eyebrow shot up her pleated forehead, and she mouthed *Daniel?* to Brigid, who nodded as she took Maeve into her arms.

'Who is she?' Candace said in a whisper, staring at the girl.

Erin paled and said, 'Begging your pardon, Ma'am, I must go to my room. I have a headache coming on.'

Brigid did not stop her; Erin's wide-eyed, pale-cheeked expression told her she felt overwhelmed. But as it was a glorious day, Brigid took Candace to the terrace, where the sun shone from a cloudless sky. They had settled in the teak chairs with a cup of Darjeeling tea. Brigid said,

'We believe Erin is Daniel's half-sister. We found her in John's brother's household, where she was an indentured servant. Her accent tells you she is Irish, and the resemblance to Daniel and his father is unmistakable. Candace, how will Daniel react?'

'How old is she?' said Candace, her brow pleating again.

'Older than Daniel. About twenty-seven or eight, we think. She has no birth or baptism certificate, so it is guesswork. She was born long before my marriage to Finn. He had family in Waterford and spent many years travelling across Ireland before submitting his doctoral thesis to Trinity College.'

Candace's eyebrows rose, and Brigid could see she guessed the truth.

'Do you know who her mother is?'

Brigid decided not to say and shook her head, hoping Candace would not question further.

She did not. 'Let me break the news to Daniel,' she said in her no-nonsense voice.

Brigid agreed, and the two women chatted about the summer and Brigid's adventures in Barbados. She commented upon how much Maeve had grown. The child could now crawl, and Maeve set off towards the pond. Brigid ran after her, picked her up, kissed her plump, rosy cheeks, and she gurgled.

After an hour, John, who had gone sea-fishing, arrived home with haddock he had caught, and Mrs Klocke put the fish on ice. John took Maeve from his wife's lap, and the child tugged his beard. She favoured Candace in her delicate features but with Daniel's sea-green eyes and dark hair.

Brigid asked Daniel and Candace to come to supper about a week later. Daniel looked unsettled when they arrived, a blood vessel beating in his temple. He and Erin gazed at each other for several seconds until an invisible force drew them together. Daniel stepped forward to embrace her, and both were overcome with emotion.

Then they parted, staring at each other.

'Hello, little brother,' said Erin with a nervous giggle, breaking the awkward silence.

Everyone laughed, as Daniel was not "little." He was tall

like his father and had filled out since marriage.

Brigid wondered whether the girl's intelligence was as sharp as Daniel's. The nuns had taught her to read and write, but her intellect could be such that an education far beyond that provided by the nuns beckoned.

When Brigid broached the matter, the girl's face lit up.

'I wish to become a doctor. I could return to Barbados when I qualify. The island lacks female doctors.'

Her faraway look showed she missed the island.

Brigid said, 'I'll seek a tutor for you to sit the entrance examinations to Boston University. You'll need top grades because they don't prefer women as entrants.' She paused. 'I think we must stop speaking in Gaelic, too, because your studies will be in English.'

A new chapter in Erin's troubled life opened because of Brigid's generosity of spirit. Erin's beaming face was all the thanks Brigid needed.

CHAPTER 37: BRIGID'S SURPRISE

In October 1885, John heard from his sister-in-law that Spendlove's firm was genuine. It had been a successful business in Deanebourne for a hundred years.

John arranged for Brigid to swear under oath to a judge that she was the former Miss Brigid Power of Ballyconstór. The judge then wrote a copy of the oath to Thomas Spendlove.

Brigid pondered, *Is it all a waste of time? I know nobody in England.* She dismissed the thought and focused on preparing for the coming holiday season. Candace had offered to host Christmas in her beautiful brownstone home, and Brigid looked forward to the occasion.

Candace's home showed her impeccable taste. The walls were decorated in pastel colours and hung with tapestries and expensive works of art. She sent many paintings from Europe on her tour. The furniture was rosewood and mahogany, and deep pile Wilton carpets, imported by George, graced the floors. The extensive grounds boasted fruit trees and a kitchen garden. Daniel bought a horse and buggy kept at a nearby livery. Before Christmas, he found a conifer, which he cut down for Candace to decorate. She and Erin had fun hanging it with candy canes, crimson and white bows, and candles in clip-on holders on the boughs.

The winter that year was bitter, and during dinner one evening, Erin discussed the freezing temperatures of winter in Ireland.

'The nuns demanded that a window remain open throughout the entire year. They would beat any girl they encountered sleeping with another for warmth, but we all joined in. Our thinning blankets offered no protection, and the biting air seemed to thicken around you beneath them. I felt such relief in Barbados when I escaped the pain of chilblains.' She examined her fingertips. 'They used to crack and bleed.'

'I know what you mean. Mine also cracked,' said Brigid, pondering on her past.

You unfortunate girl, like me, cleaning a bloodstained handkerchief and cuddling with Angela. We have much in common, but you don't know it yet. I will tell you one day.

Christmas was a joyous occasion, and Candace's Italian cook prepared some exhilarating dishes that delighted Brigid's taste buds. One of them, spaghetti, which she served on Christmas Eve, had everyone laughing as they ate the wiggling strands. However, John had no trouble.

'I often docked in Naples, where I learned to eat spaghetti.'

In January, Brigid received a reply from Mr Spendlove. The oath allowed him to declare her as the exclusive beneficiary of a will. He urged Brigid to visit at her convenience.

Dumbfounded, she showed the letter to John.

'I can't believe this. I have no connections to anyone who would leave a will unless it is Ma's Aunt Bessie. Who could it be if not her?'

'Brigid, you must sail to England in the spring and find out. I'll go with you.'

'But what about Barbados? You must spend time at your house while I check the sauce project.'

'Don't worry, dear. Barbados will be there on our return.'

John booked passages from New York to the port of Southampton in England on a Cunard Line steamship. They left in May 1886, and with fine weather, the ship crossed in less than three weeks. Brigid read books for much of the journey, sitting on the deck, covered by a thick rug, while John joined the captain, a friend from John's seafaring days, and enjoyed taking a turn at the helm.

After staying at a hotel in Southampton, the Lansdownes travelled on the Castleman's Trail train to Dorset. On the route, they passed through beautiful countryside. The New Forest in the county of Hampshire had ponies and quaint thatched cottages. In contrast, the green fields of Dorset had piggeries and sheep, reminding Brigid of Ireland. New leaves had budded on trees everywhere, and Brigid's eyes filled with tears with the memories they evoked.

'You are getting maudlin' in your old age,' said a laughing John, holding his wife's hand when they disembarked the train in the market town of Deanebourne.

The place had muddy streets, small shops, and thatched properties. However, quaint from the outside, the hotel appeared seedy inside, with their bedroom up a rickety staircase. About the town, Brigid discerned people spoke with the strangest accent, a kind of burr. *A bit like a Barbados accent,* she thought, holding up her skirts to cross the muddy streets. She noted the town boasted no sidewalks or cobbles, and the smell of uncleared horse manure overpowered everything, reminding Brigid of Dublin.

Mr Spendlove's office in the town centre had a brass plate on the door. *It needs a proper polish,* thought a critical Brigid, recalling another grubby door knocker.

Mr Spendlove looked to be getting on in years, bent with white hair and whiskers, and he spoke with that strange, burred accent. He welcomed them into his cramped office, where books and papers lay on every surface.

Two worn chairs stood before his desk, and he gestured for them to sit. A young boy hovered nearby. 'Frederick, bring us some coffee and biscuits, please,' said Mr Spendlove in a gruff voice that made Brigid wince.

'Mr and Mrs Lansdowne, how good to meet you at last. Did you have a pleasant journey from Southampton?'

'Yes, sir,' said John. 'A most pleasant journey, thank you.'

'Good, good show.'

As the boy set down the coffee and biscuits, Mr Spendlove coughed, shuffled a few papers on his desk, and seized Brigid's sworn statement to examine.

'Mrs Lansdowne, I have both pleasing and displeasing news.' He steepled his fingers under his wobbling chin. 'I'm sorry to inform you that your brother Padraig died from a heart condition several years ago. Your sister Angela has died, too.'

Brigid's heart fluttered, and her breath came in gasps.

'My sister and brother are dead?' Her mind couldn't comprehend the news. 'How did my sister die?'

Mr Spendlove harrumphed. 'It was tuberculosis. I gathered from Angela there is a history of the disease in your family. She left a letter for you in my keeping, which explains things.'

He opened a drawer and took out a sealed letter. 'Your Aunt Bessie left the entire estate to Angela because she knew the terms of her brother's will.'

Brigid took the letter from him with trembling fingers.

'Aunt Bessie? I was unsure of her relationship with me. Are you saying she had a brother? Who was he?'

'Why your grandfather, of course. Did you not know? Angela did not.'

'No. I knew neither of my grandfathers. I knew everyone in the village except our landlord.'

Brigid's heart began to thump in her chest. Their landlord had been her grandfather. She felt nauseated.

John took out his hip flask and poured a dram into the cap. 'Please drink this, honey. You have gone pale.'

Brigid did, and the fiery brandy warmed her insides.

Mr Spendlove slurped his coffee and sat back in his chair, placing his laced hands over his ample stomach.

'Your mother was Lord Pope's daughter, Lady Susannah Pope. I understand she ran away to marry your Catholic father, whom I regret to say has passed.' Spendlove's lip curled. 'Since all other legatees are deceased, including his son, who died without issue in the Crimea, you are the sole heir. In short, you inherit Lord Pope's entire estate and title. The inheritance is not entailed to a male relative.'

Mr Spendlove paused, his gimlet eyes nauseating Brigid.

Brigid's thoughts whirled, and she recalled the original name on her baptismal certificate. *Why did the priest write Pope? The church records must hold the correct name; otherwise, Spendlove would not have found me.* Tears filled her eyes as more memories surfaced

Mr Spendlove emphasised he had made strenuous efforts to find Miss Power.

'Our searches exposed a mysterious Fenian organisation with which she had associations. The search resulted in excessive costs for my firm.'

Mr Spendlove showed his disgust with a sneer that lacked sincerity.

Brigid felt a flush of heat. John, glancing at Brigid's expression, spoke in a firm voice.

'What is the estate worth, sir?'

'We estimate it amounts to over four million pounds. The inheritance includes the Lordship's estate here in Dorset, his estate in County Wicklow, and other substantial investments. These include tenants' cottages and their rents, fishing rights, a hunting lodge on a large estate in Scotland, and stocks and shares. So, you are a wealthy woman, Lady Pope.' He took off his spectacles and gave her an obsequious smile.

Brigid's mouth gaped, but no sound escaped, so John clasped her hand.

'Please forgive my wife. She is awestruck by the immensity of her inheritance.

And the man's disdainful impertinence towards me, as a woman

Mr Spendlove nodded. 'The size is why my firm has gone to such lengths to find your wife and insisted on confirmation that she is the genuine legatee.' He displayed crooked, yellowed teeth while wringing his wrinkled hands.

Like Uriah Heep in Dicken's recent novel David Copperfield, thought Brigid, still unable to speak.

Mr Spendlove leaned forward towards Brigid as if she were deaf or an *eejit*.

'I'm required by law to read you the will, then you may take a copy to read at your leisure.'

He licked his moustache-dripping lips, an action Brigid found distasteful. She nodded her assent. As Mr Spendlove read the document out loud, Brigid fanned herself with her hand.

'I have asked our local bank manager, Mr Jepson, to advise you this afternoon at three o'clock. His bank is in the square.'

Mr Spendlove gave Brigid a penetrating stare and coughed.

'Er, the legatee must pay certain duties from the estate, including taxes, our fees, and the private investigators' fees.'

Brigid had heard enough. She rose to her feet, wobbling before her temper shattered.

You are a greedy, chauvinistic, insolent little man.

'Thank you, Mr Spendlove,' John said, steadying his wife. 'You have discharged your duties with indubitable efficiency. Good day.'

He ushered Brigid out of the building before she exploded. She breathed in the Dorset air tainted with cow dung, not irritating solicitors, and her hunched shoulders relaxed.

'I know why you are angry, and I think you need to drink. Let's return to the hotel.' John held her hand tight and led her across the street.

Brigid found her voice. 'I'm incensed at the mention of the solicitor's fees when I have just learned of the death of my siblings. The liberty of arranging for a bank manager to see me without my consent angers me, too.' She stepped over the muddy road to their hotel,

I don't need the money. But since I have it, I want Richard to

take charge, not some obnoxious Dorset bank used by my arrogant, heartless grandfather.

John made Brigid sit beside the hotel's fireplace and requested two whiskies, handing one to her.

'I'm married to a wealthy lady, so I am,' he said, using his best Irish accent. 'We'll visit the old country and the family estate. Should I bow to you?'

But Brigid did not laugh. 'I'm doubtful about the idea of visiting Ireland. There are too many ghosts. I think I'll sell the estate.'

Sad memories of the famine years surfaced through the haze in Brigid's brain.

'It's time you confronted those old ghosts. You could also visit your old friends, Ezra and Caitlin. After touring your estate, we can investigate Erin's provenance in Cork.'

'But what about your family? You need to see them.'

'We could cut out our sightseeing tour of London. That would give us time,' John said, thinking with clarity.

'I guess you are right as usual, darling.' Brigid felt comforted by a husband who put her needs above his own.

The Lansdownes had a tense encounter with the bank manager when Brigid refused his advice by saying,

'Sir, I am a qualified accountant in Massachusetts. I have managed my finances since I was sixteen. My son is my banker in Boston, and the bank president is a dear and trusted friend. I shall engage a London firm of solicitors to oversee legal work and a firm of accountants to manage taxes and fees. I do not need your services.'

The manager's thundercloud-dark, glowering look told all as Brigid stood and pulled on her gloves. *He is after my custom so that he can take his percentage. He reminds me of obsequious rent collectors.*

She drew her body to all its five feet four inches in height.

'Good afternoon to you, sir.'

Brigid spun around and walked off, angry, just as she had

done with Peggy Devlin. She returned to the hotel and treated herself to tea and crumpets. John chased after her, arriving with a smirk on his face. Brigid cast him a glaring look.

'I'm not a vulnerable woman seeking guidance from a narrow-minded lackey for them to charge me a significant fee. The audacity is astounding. Women are treated like brainless cattle.'

John laughed.' It brings me joy when you show your feistiness, Brigid.'

She offered a mock grin, with her teeth bared, and he burst into laughter again.

'Aren't you curious about seeing your Dorset property?'

Brigid shook her head. 'Why would I want to see where my grandfather lived while we starved? Not fecking likely.'

The couple set off for Liverpool to catch the boat to Dublin a few days later. The sea crossing was rough, and Brigid, feeling nauseated, lay on the bed in their cabin. As the ship yawed and rolled, memories of her childhood invaded her mind. As the waves settled, she absorbed the contents of Angela's letter:

C/O Spendlove and Bell, Solicitors
Deanebourne,
May 1881

My dearest Brigid.

If you receive this letter, God has answered my prayers, and you'll know that I have left this world for the next. But I must provide you with some explanations about my situation. I moved in with Aunt Bessie after Cahill died because I contracted tuberculosis. This made living with my daughters impossible. Aunt Bessie, being elderly, had a nursemaid and so agreed to take me in. We became fond of each other, and Bessie told me the story about our parents.

They fell in love when Ma visited one summer, and Da was the Manor House gardener. When Ma became pregnant with Padraig, she and Da wanted to marry. But Ma needed Grandfather's permission, and he refused. His intense fury caused him to disown Ma and almost gave Da the sack, but Bessie dissuaded him so Da could at least provide for Ma and the child. When she turned twenty-one, Ma married Da in the Catholic church.

I was the first legitimate child born a month after the wedding. Brigid, I understand our grandfather stipulated that his inheritance must be passed to someone directly in his lineage. His son died intestate in the Crimea, and Padraig and his sickly son passed away from heart disease years ago. I have little time left to live, and neither does Aunt Bessie, so you'll inherit grandfather's entire estate.

It saddens me we shall not meet again. I should have written to say I had moved. But I was extremely sick and lost your address. I hope you will forgive me.

I wish you joy and love forever.

Your devoted sister,

Angela.

Tears streamed down Brigid's face as she read the letter. *If only I had written to Angela before her passing. I had one letter returned and no forwarding address. I lost sight of the close connection we had as children. Oh, how I miss her now.*

Regrettably, Angela provided no contact details for her daughters, and it was apparent from her unstable handwriting that she was most unwell. Mr Spendlove might know their contact details, but Brigid did not enquire. He brought back too many memories of another greedy man from her past. Spendlove would expect her to compensate for his valuable time.

'He should be called Mr Spendalot for the clients willing to pay him fat fees,' she said to John with a wry smile. 'I can't stand the man.'

The |Lansdownes departed the following day, taking a cab to a hotel in Dublin's city centre. John encouraged his wife to visit Heytesbury Street and bought candy for Caitlin and tobacco for Ezra.

Caitlin answered the door to Brigid's knock.

'We don't deal with hawkers here, so we don't.' Caitlin tried to close the door.

'It's Brigid, Caitlin.' She held the door open with her booted foot.

Caitlin's paling face showed her sudden shock. 'Brigid, is it you?' She drew a sharp breath and blinked in the intense light.

'It can't be. I have weak eyesight.' She peered at Brigid. 'Ezra has just woken up from his afternoon nap.'

The woman's gnarled hands shook on her walking stick as Brigid followed her to the parlour. She stared at the house she had not seen for over twenty years. The worn appearance caused Brigid to regret never visiting before.

'Ezra, we have visitors,' Caitlin exclaimed.

With rheumy, clouded eyes and bent fingers, the wizened man looked up from his chair. A large grey cat jumped off the man's lap and arched his back, hissing.

'Ezra, it is Brigid. She is here with her chaperone.'

'Hello, Ezra. My chaperone is my husband. Captain John Lansdowne.'

Ezra stood up with a groan, clutching at an ebony stick. His clothes hung from his slight frame.

'Who are you?' he said, his face pale from surprise and shock.

'My friend, I'll buy back some old ring for nine guineas plus the ten-percentage fee, so I will,' said Brigid.

Ezra's face lit up. 'It is Brigid. Only she would say those words.'

Brigid bent to kiss his cheek. His memory had not deserted him.

'It is lovely to see you, Ezra. I came to see how you are doing, as I promised Caitlin some years ago. I have some news to share which I think will astonish you.'

'News, what news?'

'I learned two days ago that I have inherited my

grandfather's estate.'

Ezra sat down and stared at Brigid.

'Your grandfather? I thought your grandfathers were deceased.' He tweaked his thumb and forefinger with a grin on his toothless, wrinkled face. 'How much money?'

'Enough to buy that ring for a thousand pounds.'

'I presented it to Caitlin on our twentieth wedding anniversary.' Ezra grinned again. 'Buy me a crystal vase or a brass clock instead.'

'I can't believe it is you, my dear Brigid, after all these years,' Caitlin mouthed in Brigid's ear. 'Ezra can die happy. The doctors predict he has but a few months to live. His heart, you see.'

Her eyes glistened, and she touched Brigid's face.

'You are like a daughter to him, you know.'

'You have got a rare one there, Captain. Take care of her for me. 'I doubt I'll be around much longer,' said Ezra sanguinely.

'I will, sir; she is a precious commodity.'

Ezra grinned. 'I learned that a long time ago, son.'

Brigid thought *I should have visited years ago. I have neglected my duties.'* Guilt caused her heart to constrict as tears filled her eyes.

After sharing a cup of tea that Brigid helped Caitlin prepare, they hugged each other before parting. Tears ran down Caitlin's face, but Brigid kept her composure until the cab left. Then, so many memories came flooding back that she sobbed on John's shoulder as they travelled on to visit Niall's grave. Brigid had brought flowers to place on it. Memories of her first love consumed her mind, and John left her alone with her thoughts.

The next day, they proceeded to Ballyconstór, a village surrounded by so many memories that neither Brigid's heart nor head could process them all at once. The odours of mown grass, cow dung, and peat fire smoke intermingled to assail her nostrils. She drank it like some Boston society hostess's strange cocktail, and it shook her foundations.

The sound of children's laughter on the boreen brought back memories of her childhood when she and Angela used to play with Scamp. She swallowed the tight knot in her throat as they walked through the village, where she saw few changes except a school built on rough grazing land. After a few minutes, the Manor House appeared, perched on the promontory, its views commanding.

Tears clouded Brigid's eyes as they arrived at the ornate wrought iron gates with flowers threaded into the design. The gates had not appeared to hide dark secrets when she was a child. But now Brigid understood why her mother never spoke of her childhood. *The breach must have been total.*

The fire pit of anger sent flames into her brain, awakening dormant thistles.

'John, the means to save my brothers, lives lay less than half a mile from the cottage where they died in agony. My grandfather's cruelty defies belief.'

Brigid tried the gate's handle, and to her surprise, it opened. With John holding her hand and her heart hammering, they walked up the path, and a large man ran, puffing, to meet them.

'Good morning to you. I'm the caretaker, but I'm sorry the house is closed to the public.'

Brigid assessed the man. 'How long have you been the caretaker?' she said, though her heart still hammered.

'For fifteen years, I have shouldered the responsibilities of ghillie and caretaker.'

He gazed at Brigid with narrowed eyes. 'I never met my employer. Did you know him?

Brigid glared back. 'No, I did not. But I'm your landlord now and would value your help to take us on a property tour.'

The caretaker paled like he'd seen a ghost. In a shaky voice, he said,

'Excuse me, Madam, but who are you?'

'I'm Lady Pope. Your [SG1]new employer. I inherited my grandfather's estate.'

The man gulped. 'His Lordship's granddaughter? Forgive me, but I thought you were a local by your accent, m'Lady.'

Suspicion flashed in his narrowed eyes, mingled with a touch of curiosity.

'I grew up in Ballyconstór, but I live in America now. I never met my grandfather.' Brigid paused, her gaze taking in the splendid proportions of the Manor. 'May I ask your name?'

The caretaker removed his cap and gave a slight bow. 'Eamon Doyle, m'Lady, at your service. Please follow me.'

Doyle took them on a house tour, whose faded grandeur sent shivers down Brigid's spine. He commented a peacock must once have roamed the grounds because someone had him stuffed, and he graced the entrance hall. Doyle removed a white sheet.

Brigid gasped, her eyes misting, and she clutched John's hand. 'It's the peacock we watched through the fence knothole. We got a beating from Da when he found out. Oh God, what horrors my poor mother endured.' Tears blinded her eyes as she sought her handkerchief.

Putting his cap back on to tour the grounds, Doyle commented about a breach in the wall he had found in a distant area. He had mended it and installed a swing for his children on a large apple tree branch nearby. 'His Lordship housed chickens in a small coop nearby. I pulled it down as the wood was rotten,'

Doyle looked at Brigid with a pointed gaze. 'Do you wish to occupy the house? My wife has kept the place clean.'

'I'm not sure. I may choose to sell it.'

The thought of living in this house of horrid memories filled Brigid with dread.

'If I sell, I'll recommend you to the new owner as an excellent caretaker and ghillie. I'll ensure you have suitable accommodation if you retire.'

Doyle doffed his cap. 'Thank you, m'Lady. I appreciate your kindness.'

As the caretaker closed the entrance gates behind them, Brigid, her voice quivering, said,

'How could my grandfather be so cruel as to disown my mother for marrying a Catholic?'

Tears fell unchecked down her cheeks, and John held her as she wept. Brigid hated her grandfather for what disowning her mother had done to her family.

'At least he did not write his legal grandchildren out of his will. But he must have been a lonely man,' John said, patting his wife's back. 'I wonder when his wife died?'

Brigid neither knew nor cared, and the Lansdownes continued their journey to search for Erin's relatives, beginning with a visit to the convent in Cork.

Brigid requested an urgent audience meeting with the convent's Mother Superior. The nun they spoke to asked them to wait, speaking through a narrow sliding grille in the door. Fifteen minutes later, she returned.

'I'm sorry I kept you waiting. Mother Superior was in the chapel praying her daily office. She will see you at eleven-thirty tomorrow.' The portress nun closed the grille's cover, and John's eyebrows rose.

'Nuns may not mix with the public unless they are teachers or nurses.' Brigid opined. 'They practise custody of the eyes, so the portress nun will keep them lowered in case the sight of us disturbs her.'

The next day, the Lansdownes arrived at the appointed time, and the portress nun opened the door, her eyes lowered as Brigid predicted. She glided across the polished hallway and opened the door to an elegant room dominated by a large mahogany desk. Behind it sat a diminutive nun with piercing blue eyes and a beak-like nose on which perched round spectacles.

'Please take a seat, captain.'

The Mother Superior gestured to two chairs by her desk, her eyes averted from Brigid as if she was poison.

'I understand you seek information on a girl who may have run away from our school. One girl fits your description. I was a young nun then. We received the child out of charity. A man who resembled her, a relative, brought her to the convent. He told us the mother was unmarried and had died a pauper.'

The nun's eyes swivelled to glare at Brigid.

Brigid did her best to keep anger from entering her voice. 'Do you have a record of the man's name, please?'

Mother Superior's eyebrows rose. 'Sister Madeline, please fetch me the record book for 1856.'

The nun glided off, returned with a heavy ledger,

'Ah, here we are.'

The Mother Superior, whose title Brigid thought should be Mother Arrogance, ran her finger along an entry in the ledger.

'The child arrived with Mr Finnbar Hayes. The record states she was about six years old and an orphan.' Her mouth set in a grim line. 'Mr Hayes visited her once or twice a year and sent our quarterly payment until the girl left us.'

The nun pushed her glasses up her nose. 'I recall she was a trial. Refused to obey rules and caused other girls to misbehave.'

Brigid glanced at John and then watched the nun's face, but no frown or pursed lip altered her expression. 'We are seeking her mother's relatives by the name of Roche.'

The nun lowered her head, removed her spectacles, wiped them on a handkerchief pulled from her habit's folds, and replaced them.

'I doubt you'll find any living relatives. The veracity of her surname, Roche, is unknown.' The nun sneered at Brigid; her face puckered.

'There is nothing more I can do for you, Mrs Lansdowne.'

She turned to the other nun. 'Escort these people out. I must say the Angelus.'

She departed to the sound of a chiming bell from within the convent.

Outside the convent, Brigid fumed. 'What rudeness. I'm glad Erin escaped this evil place. The Catholic church and Irish men rule women with a rod of iron. Erin's plight makes me feel like someone gutted my innards like a filleted fish because her only sin was to be born. Do you now understand why I turned against religion?'

'Ah,' John said with his usual optimistic attitude, taking his wife's hand and patting it. 'Prejudice exists everywhere. One can't elude it. Only change it. Let us enquire in the village shop.'

The proprietor provided information on two Roche families. At the first house, a woman kneeled before a well-kept terraced cottage to clean her doorstep and shook her head.

'Nobody has died a pauper in this family.'

She resumed scrubbing, a disgusted look on her face.

The second family lived in a run-down thatched cottage with about an acre of rough land extending behind it. The plot reminded Brigid of her childhood home. Outside, a middle-aged man cut up large chunks of peat. The scruffy man and the tumbledown cottage exuded poverty. The thatch was ing, and the man was bare-chested and shoeless. He put down his shears and glared at them as if they were felons.

'What do ye want here?'

'I seek the relatives of Erin Roche. Her mother's name was Maureen Roche. Erin, my stepdaughter, might have been born somewhere in this area.'

The man's face paled. 'Maureen's child is your stepdaughter. How many feckers did he give you afore he made you an honest woman?'

He scowled at Brigid and gave a hollow laugh, burning hatred blazing from his dark eyes.

'You've grown wealthy on your immoral earnings by the look of yer grand clothes.'

Brigid shivered, her temper rising faster than water in a boiling kettle, and she stepped forward, her hand raised, ready to strike him for the slurs, but John stayed it with his own.

He spoke in English, 'My wife married Finnbar Hayes, but I can assure you of no impropriety, as the man has died. They had a legitimate son and emigrated to America many years ago.'

The man leaned back on his elbows against the cottage wall, staring at John.

'I don't think he speaks English,' Brigid said and translated as the man glowered.

'How did you find this child, then?' His eyes raked Brigid's body, and her hand still itched to slap him.

'We found Erin working as an indentured servant in the West Indies.'

'Where's that?'

'It is a chain of islands off the coast of South America. Erin was working as a servant on the island of Barbados.

'How the devil did she get there?' The man's eyebrows arched.

'She emigrated destitute after growing up in an appalling convent and then working in a mill for a pittance for four years. My husband's brother gained her as a bonded labourer in Barbados.'

The man's evil eyes became hooded as he stared at Brigid.

'My parents threw Maureen out when they learned she expected a child. I don't know what happened to it after my sister died. I thought the child died of starvation. Tell her she has six cousins, and I'll pray for her.'

He straightened his back, coughed, and spat out the phlegm. Then, he picked up his shears and resumed cutting peat. He did not look up, and his action dismissed them.

Brigid felt incensed. 'What is the matter with these people? Have they no manners?'

John shook his head. 'My love, you have changed. Travel

does that you and you have travelled far. You are no longer an Irish peasant, and it scares them.'

Brigid remembered something. 'My parents once had a furious argument over Ma teaching Angela and me to be literate and have polite manners. I couldn't understand why Da opposed it. Nor did I know where my mother had learned the skills, but I do now. She told me Da was handsome in his youth. She must have loved him very much to defy her father.'

Before they left Ireland, they paid Amy a brief visit. In her elegant drawing room, Amy told Brigid that Isabella had married a doctor and lived in Galway. Douglas was a lecturer in physical science at Edinburgh University, and a third child, Andrew, was studying law at Trinity College. Alexander had the largest law firm in Dublin and many high-profile clients. Brigid noticed Amy's once youthful face had grown coarse and her figure thickened.

Amy said life as a Dublin socialite fulfilled all her needs. Brigid watched her friend's demeanour and asked about Stephen.

Amy's eyes clouded. 'He blew out his brains in his apartment where our father found his body, a suicide note clutched in his hand.' Amy took out a lacy handkerchief and dabbed her eyes. 'He was a confirmed drug addict.'

Brigid felt sadness at such an outcome. As she had feared, addiction ruined Stephen's life.

'I'm so sorry, Amy. I know how much you loved him.'

She hugged her friend, promising to write, and wished her well. They both had tears in their eyes when they said goodbye. They might never meet again.

The Lansdownes left for England to visit John's children and grandchildren. Annie, John's daughter, married a potter and was skilled in art, throwing exquisite pots she painted by hand. Annie was interested to hear that Aisne was a sculptor. She discussed her work with Brigid and showed her how to throw a clay pot, which she found fascinating, but Brigid failed to produce the desired effect. 'I'm not good with my hands except for making bread or pastry,' she said.

'It takes practice,' Annie said, grinning at Brigid's clay-covered fingers.

Brigid bought one of the beautiful flower-painted creations, which Annie promised to ship to Boston, and Brigid beamed.

'It will enhance the drawing room's beauty, John.'

John's son was a carpenter in a town called Amesbury in Wiltshire. He made exquisite mahogany and rosewood furniture and had a thriving business. John bought a small rosewood table, which his son agreed to inscribe and ship to Boston.

John basked in his children's presence. Brigid felt so pleased for him when he had fun with his three grandchildren. Their developing relationship made her heart sing. John took his young grandson to walk by the river and admired his granddaughter's needlework. She embroidered his initials on a handkerchief and gave it to him with a shy smile.

Brigid drew sketches of the grandchildren for John's Barbados house. While drawing her tense muscles from her encounters with Mr Spendlove, Mother Arrogance, and Erin's uncle relaxed. But before many days had passed, the pull of Boston Air and Mrs Klocke's marzipan cakes told Brigid it was time to go home.

CHAPTER 38: THE LEGACY

The couple arrived in Boston towards the end of July. By then, Brigid had arranged to donate substantially to the Isolation Hospital in Barbados. She posted a letter to Catherine about her inheritance at the dockside post office.

Before Brigid left for England, she enrolled Erin in some Boston University summer courses. The woman then moved into Daniel's home to be closer to the university and help Candace, who was expecting another child, care for Maeve.

When they met next, Brigid saw a changed woman. Erin's confidence had soared, and she was not afraid to speak her mind.

'You look well, Brigid. The trip must be good for your health.'

Brigid's eyebrows rose in astonishment.

'Someone is courting her,' Candace said. 'They have gone for rides in Daniel's buggy, picnics by the beach with Maeve, and long walks without a chaperone. He has taken her to the theatre and opera, followed by dinners at expensive restaurants.'

'Who is he?' The lack of knowledge mystified Brigid.

Candace rolled her eyes. 'I promised not to reveal his identity.'

Candace's tight lips were uncharacteristic, and Brigid wondered what kind of man Erin could have met.

Among the letters accumulated in her absence was one from Catherine. The island's doctor had diagnosed James with syphilis. The infection was now in his brain, and the doctor had moved him to the isolation hospital. Brigid wondered if

James had passed away since the letter was over a month old. She showed John the letter, and he shuddered.

'My poor brother, I adored him as a child. His drastic change is a mystery to me.'

Her husband's distress saddened Brigid.

How did two siblings raised by the same parents develop such contrasting personalities as adults?

Brigid remembered the lectures on Darwin's theory. When she arrived in America, she thought it wise to get Erin checked for the disease.

When Erin returned to Cambridge, Brigid explained James was dying.

'He may have already died,' she said.

'Serves him right. The cur slept with many enslaved Africans and his servants.' Erin paused, her eyes misting. 'I received a letter stating that I have found my daughter living in a red-leg commune, so I plan to go back to Barbados and establish a life with her once I become a qualified doctor.'

'That is grand news. Who told you?'

Erin ignored the question. 'I hope to visit next year and meet my daughter. I may bring her to Boston so I can educate her.'

Brigid thought that was an excellent plan, though she wondered where Erin had planned to live in Boston with a child.

Who is the man she is courting? Desperation consumed Brigid's desire to know. *He must be very wealthy*.

Brigid kept the news of her inheritance from her family until Thanksgiving. By then, probate would be settled. She visited Richard as soon as possible to inform him of her new financial circumstances.

His thick brows disappeared from his forehead, and he set his Meerschaum pipe down with a clang.

'How much did you say?'

'Over four million pounds.'

Richard gazed at her face in astonishment before calling for his assistant.

'Bruno, bring me the finest Veuve Clicquot, nothing cheaper, please.'

'Please don't tell Daniel. I want to tell him myself.'

When the employee returned, Richard opened a cabinet and extracted two crystal glasses. He poured the champagne.

'To your future. May it be ever fruitful.'

Brigid took a sip of the champagne and noticed Richard's eyes focused on the middle distance as if his heart were elsewhere.

'This is quality, Richard, thank you.'

Richard smiled. 'Only the best for you, my dear Brigid, and of course, I won't tell Daniel.'

'I have several ideas for using my inheritance. First, I want to endow an isolation hospital on the island of Barbados with an extra wing for treating African and Irish workers.'

'That is a commendable ambition, Brigid. I'll help you find the right people to draw up plans.'

Grateful for Richard's friendship, Brigid raised her glass to toast him.

'Richard, I have a question. Did you track down a gunslinger in Texas?'

Richard's face and neck grew red. He coughed to cover his embarrassment. 'Ask no questions, and you'll be told no lies, Brigid.'

Brigid's face now burned; her informant was correct. Her next question concerned the estates with tenant farmers. 'I want to review the rents for each tenant and conduct repairs. Few farmers have spare funds. I may sell the Manor House but build the caretaker a cottage on a piece of my land to which he has the title.' She took another sip of champagne. 'I wish to sell the Dorset and Scottish estates.'

'I think you'll need to appoint an agent. I have a contact in London,' Richard said as he sipped more champagne.

'Thank you, Richard. I have one other plan. I intend to gift my Dublin house to Erin so she has an income of her own. She plans to study medicine and will need money for fees. However, I want the property properly renovated and a clause in the contract for the house to remain my elderly friends' home until they die. Erin is free to do whatever she wishes with it afterwards.'

Richard nodded. 'I'll deal with all the financial and legal matters. Don't worry about anything.'

Feeling less burdened, Brigid departed and hailed a cab home. On her way, she thought about her Cambridge property.

Should I buy somewhere more opulent? But she loved her home, and the children had grown up there. It was the staff's home, too. *I will purchase a house in Cape Cod for Daniel and a boat for John and remodel the Cambridge property. I can now afford to employ a housemaid and convert the spacious attic into a staff parlour. The staff could get a salary rise, and I could afford to hire an ostler and buy a horse and carriage.*

The thoughts pleased her, and as the cab swayed along, Brigid must have dozed, for the cabby woke her with a jolt that sent shock waves down her spine as he pulled the carriage to a halt by her front door. She dismounted and paid him, noting the ordure left by the steaming horse.

I'll instruct my ostler to pull up more gently and to clean up after his horse.

Brigid discussed her ostler idea with John.

'It is your money, Brigid; do what you want. Let us invite Richard to supper. He told me his family owned several horses before the war.'

Richard came alive during the meal, conversing with vigour. 'My family owned and bred horses in Georgia. My late wife was an excellent equestrian who rode to hunt. It was how we met. I'll enjoy going to a horse fair again.'

Richard kept his word and negotiated a deal with a family that owned a small Lexington farm northwest of Cambridge.

'They intend to move to California, taking two sturdy horses to pull their wagon. But they have a carriage and a three-year-old filly they wish to sell. Their ostler needs a position to complete the deal as he isn't going to California. He is getting married next year and will need a job with accommodation. I have negotiated a price of $300.00 for everything. The ostler's current wage is $25.00, plus accommodation and food. Do you wish to visit?'

Brigid's face broke into a wreath of smiles. The following Tuesday was a chilly November day. Brigid and John travelled by train to Lexington, and Brigid wore a mink coat she had bought at Jordan-Marsh's new store in downtown Boston.

The filly was a beautiful, deep chestnut bay with large, sensitive eyes and strong teeth. She was well-shod, and her coat gleamed. Named Honey, she munched an apple from Brigid's open hand.

John examined the condition of the carriage. It was in excellent shape; the brass gleamed, and the leather was well-oiled. Brigid interviewed the ostler, a young man named Sean Boland, who had emigrated from Galway. He had trained as a jockey and had hoped to race in America. However, the American racing style did not suit him. So, he became an ostler. Brigid asked about his fiancée.

'Orlagh is an orphan. Her parents and sisters died of diphtheria. Afterwards, she emigrated, and we met on the emigration ship. She found a job as a lady's maid to be near me. But she must leave when we marry.'

Brigid liked Sean and empathised with Orlagh. She employed an architect to remodel the rooms above the stable into a family home so Sean and Orlagh could move in right after their nuptials.

In the past, Brigid had given the staff the day off to celebrate Thanksgiving with their families or friends. In contrast, her family dined in a hotel, and Brigid preferred celebrating Christmas at home. But she made Thanksgiving

1886 memorable by celebrating it at home as well. Brigid's beating heart told her there was much for which to be thankful.

Mrs Klocke's face lit up when she heard.

'When you went to Europe, my sister died. I never warmed to her spouse, and he courts someone else. I would not be welcome.'

'Thank you, Mrs Klocke.' Brigid squeezed her hand. They understood each other.

'The plan will be welcome to Mrs Frankel, too. She has joined a widowed friend in the past, but the woman died of pneumonia earlier this year.'

Brigid hired a cab to visit Dermot. His latest parish was in an African American area, and Brigid alighted with a cheerful demeanour. But Dermot had unwelcome news.

'The archbishop has posted me to a mission in Africa, and I leave in three weeks. I shall miss you and all my family, but it is what I want to do with my life.'

His mother enveloped him in a warm embrace.

'I'm thrilled for you if you have set your heart on the foreign missions.'

He looked like Niall, possessing the same cleft in his chin, height, and mannerisms. Brigid suppressed the lump in her throat. She would miss his gentle presence in her life very much.

Brigid invited George and Richard to complete the table. Mrs Klocke had the menu drawn up within the week.

'I suggest we get a big turkey from Faneuil Market, Ma'am,' she said, her eyes sparkling. 'I'll make three pumpkin pies and add sweet potatoes and red cabbage to the principal dish.' She paused. 'What is your choice of first course?'

'I'm not sure,' Brigid said, creasing her brow. 'Could you prepare blinis with caviar to accompany the champagne I'll serve guests before the meal? Then we could sit down to your delicious mushroom soup.'

This idea pleased Mrs Klocke, who bustled back to her kitchen, grinning. Meanwhile, Brigid had a wonderful time supervising the builders and decorators who put up scaffolding and began external renovations before winter. The Irish workers spoke in Gaelic, and Brigid recognised one worker, her soup kitchen helper's husband. She said,

'If you go down the fecking poteen bar today instead of working, I'll tell your wife, so I will.' She wagged her finger at him.

Blushing, he almost fell off his ladder, and a grin appeared. 'You are that crazy woman who came to my street and stopped me on the boreen. I did not know about your wealth, nor would I have paid you more attention.' He gave a deep belly laugh, and Brigid warmed to the man.

But John took Brigid's arm and led her away, saying such behaviour was neither ladylike nor professional. However, Erin, seated on the terrace with her tutor, a mathematics professor from Cologne University, had to suppress giggles.

'Oh, begorra, 'tis the season for cutting the turf, so it is. Get the shovel, Mammy,' she said in Gaelic.

Her tutor couldn't understand either their language or their sense of humour. His brow puckered, and he turned to John, saying in accented English, 'Zee, Irish speak in a strange tongue, Herr John.' He glared at Erin and Brigid. John nodded, but Brigid watched the touch of a mischievous grin appear. John went indoors and brought two glasses, and a bottle of whisky bought in Ireland. He poured two drams and passed one glass to the professor. 'To your health, Herr Professor Meyer.'

Meyer swirled the amber liquid in his glass and gulped as the fiery alcohol hit his gullet. Then, spluttering, he said, 'Grus Got. Velly good Amerikan visky, sir.'

Brigid smirked, and Erin covered her mouth. Both women felt pleased that Mrs Frankel was shopping. She might not have understood John's whisky-dry sense of humour.

Brigid requested her guests arrive at noon for Thanksgiving and hired a waiter to help Mrs Frankel. She served champagne cocktails, and Mrs Klocke prepared a suitable range of blinis and other 'hors d'oeuvres' to accompany them. When everyone was busy chatting, Brigid called them together.

'Quiet, please, everyone. I have an announcement.' Brigid cleared her throat. When John and I were in Europe, we saw a solicitor in Dorset, England. I have inherited extensive estates in Ireland and England, Scotland, and other investments from my maternal grandfather.' She coughed. 'I'm now Lady Pope of Deanebourne in England.'

You could have heard the proverbial pin drop as the room fell silent.

Daniel, his face suffusing with red, said, 'Your grandfather? I thought your grandfathers died years ago. For feck's sake, Ma, how much is this inheritance?'

Brigid swallowed and cleared her throat again. 'Over four million pounds.'

Several mouths, including Daniel's, dropped open as the staggering amount sank in.

After a couple of seconds of silence, Daniel said. 'Feckin' hell, Mom, are you serious?'

He had turned Irish American. Brigid nodded, too choked to speak.

'It explains the house remodelling. I wondered how you could afford it.' He paused and clutched Candace's hand. 'Oh God, might I inherit the title one day?'

Brigid nodded again, thinking *Dermot would have to pass it up, being a priest.*

Erin, in contrast, took the news in her stride and clasped Brigid's hand.

'I, too, have an announcement. My dearest Richard has asked me to marry him, and I have accepted. We shall be married in the spring.' The room erupted in joy at this delightful news.

Brigid's mouth fell open in shock. *Richard has been courting her. No wonder Candace would not reveal his name.*

Richard stepped forward and placed a diamond ring on Erin's finger to symbolise their engagement. 'We want a quiet wedding, and then we'll go to Barbados for our honeymoon,' Richard beamed a smile broader than Brigid had ever seen before. 'When we return, Erin will begin her studies to become a doctor, and I shall fund her.'

The men patted Richard on the back or shook his hand, and the women kissed Brigid's and Erin's cheeks. Brigid remained poised while waiting for the clamour to cease, then invited everyone to raise their glasses to pay homage to the absent family members.

When the new front doorbell sounded, she almost dropped her glass as she rushed to see who was calling at this hour. As the door swung open, she let out a breathless gasp. Aisne, Vincenzo, and their offspring stood on the porch in a bone-chilling wind that blew the squeaky swing.

'Sure, 'tis cold in this country, so it is.' Aisne put an elegant foot over the doorstep and clasped Brigid to her bosom. 'Ma, are you still shrinking? Or have I grown taller with Italiano food?'

Brigid was amazed. *My Aisne had arrived. In thanks, I could dance the polka barefoot with the devil on my icy, windswept porch.* Happy tears filled her eyes.

With everyone seated at the dining table, Candace admitted knowing about Aisne's visit and Richard's proposal. Vincenzo had written to say the family intended to stay until the spring. Brigid's heart was overwhelmed with love. But then sadness gripped it because Dermot was not present. But he was doing what he loved, and that was all that mattered. The family and guests had started on Mrs Klocke's soup when the doorbell clanged again.

Brigid put down her spoon with a clatter. 'Who in the world is that?'

She got up, excusing the intrusion, and hurried to the front door. There, she found Mrs Frankel taking a snow-covered coat from Dermot, his face flushed, and his breathing laboured. 'I'm not late, am I, Mrs Frankel?' Dermot turned to face his mother, who stood by the lintel, her mouth open but speechless. 'I am here as penance for telling lies by omission. Fortunately, the severe weather has delayed my passage. My superior is sick, and I had to say High Mass today...' While catching his breath, he couldn't finish.

Brigid hugged her dear son to her breast, her eyes welling with happy tears. She led him to the table, and cheers erupted. Dermot's calm demeanour as a priest deserted him, and he blushed.

Aisne poked out her tongue at her brother.

'I thought you would be in Africa hearing confessions. Offer the blessing for us instead.'

Vincenzo frowned at Aisne, whom Brigid thought had not changed. Her daughter's rebellious side still dominated.

Upon finishing the meal, John, and Vincenzo, who had never tried the delicious dish before, lauded her for the pumpkin pie. Then, before the ladies left so the men could smoke cigars, John excused himself and returned with a colourful bow-decorated box.

He presented it to his wife. 'Open it, Brigid, it's yours by right.'

Mystified, Brigid unwrapped the box. She gasped with surprise; inside sat the stuffed peacock from Ballyconstór with his feathers restored. She lifted the bird from the package and placed it before her. The peacock reminded her of her heritage and its link to the family's future. Brigid smiled, thinking that having her family together on Thanksgiving was the best gift.

'I shall use my legacy to help those less fortunate than me. Everyone I love and everything I need is here today,' said Lady

Brigid Pope with a wide grin.

The assembled company burst into cheers and claps, drowning out any further announcements. Brigid smiled, the grin lighting up her face.

ABOUT THE AUTHOR

Sasha is a British wife, mother, and grandmother with family on both sides of the Atlantic. A retired teacher and lecturer of biology and psychology, she came late to the art of creative writing, achieving a master's degree during the Covid-19 lockdown. Her studies turned a novice's writing into a passion, and she authored this novel.

Sasha lived abroad for seven years and knows first-hand what it feels like to be an immigrant, leaving behind all that is loved and familiar. She has visited exciting and exotic places, but her favourite destination is the Caribbean. Genealogy research revealed that her paternal great-grandfather and great-great-grandfather were born of British descent in the Caribbean.

Other research revealed that her maternal great-grandmother emigrated from Ireland to England in the 19th century. She met and married Sasha's maternal great-grandfather while working in a cotton mill in Lancashire.

A strong-willed, independent streak runs through Sasha's heritage, and the novel's protagonist, Brigid, exemplifies this trait.

Contact:

A website is under construction.

Sasha can be contacted at wordsbyarial@gmail com.

Printed in Great Britain
by Amazon

56368965R00225